THROWING SPARKS

THROWING SPARKS

Abdo Khal

Translated by Maïa Tabet and Michael K. Scott

دار بلومزبري-مؤسسة قطر للنشر
BLOOMSBURY
QATAR FOUNDATION
PUBLISHING

مؤسسة قطر
Qatar Foundation

English edition first published in 2014 by

Bloomsbury Qatar Foundation Publishing
Qatar Foundation
Villa 3, Education City
PO Box 5825
Doha, Qatar
www.bqfp.com.qa

First published in Arabic in 2009
as *Tarmi bi Sharar,* Al-Jamal Publications, Baghdad/Beirut

Qur'anic verses from *The Qur'an:*
A New Translation, Tarif Khalidi, Viking Penguin, 2008

The moral right of the author has been asserted.

ISBN 9789992179093

Typeset by Hewer Text UK Ltd, Edinburgh
Printed and bound in Great Britain by CPI Group (UK) Ltd,
Croydon CR0 4YY

'Go forth to [...] the flames, which scatter sparks, as from massive logs, coloured like tawny camels.'

Unleashed, 77:30–33, The Qur'an

'As the apple tree among the trees of the wood, so is my beloved among the sons. I sat down under his shadow with great delight, and his fruit was sweet to my taste.'

The Song of Solomon, 2:3, The Holy Bible

A wave is a marker of distance, of absence.
And Tahani never raised her hand …
How I betrayed her when she did not wave from afar!
This confession, in all its sordidness, is for her and for all the
others I ruined along the way.

Tariq Fadel

OUTCAST AND DISPIRITED, I embraced a life of crime.
Standing in the punishment chamber, I would contemplate my naked body, bruised and degraded by the cruel and brutal acts it had performed. There had been hundreds of torture assignments, some more successful than others, and I approached each with steadfast purpose, unmoved by the victims' agonised cries and pleas for mercy. I carried out my duties down to the most minute detail as required by the Master, ensuring that nothing would mar his enjoyment while he watched me sodomise his rivals.

I would dismount from my victims only after I had pounded them to a pulp and all that remained was a heap of moaning and gasping bones.

At the end of these sessions the Master had taken to handing me photos or video recordings of the victims. As a result, I knew all my victims, at least by sight. I kept a complete archive of the recordings and images, which could have been valuable had I been inclined to use them. I could have blackmailed the victims, exploiting those compromising pictures for the right sum. But I never dared to, knowing that the Master would instantly make mincemeat of me if he ever found out.

Even though I had spent many years punishing his rivals, I received no appreciation from the Master, other than when he was watching me at it. I served no other purpose; only when he had a victim in tow would everyone scurry around the Palace looking for me as if in search of a lost key.

There was no escaping him, even after I eventually moved out of the Palace and into my own place, ostensibly to look after my aunt. He watched my every move, my every start and stop. I was at his beck and call around the clock, expected to show up on demand. He held me tightly as if flying a kite – all he had to do was tug on the fine thread and I would tumble down and wait, covered in dust, to be lifted up to the wind.

'Tariq! Get over here!' His voice over the cell phone was irate.

I thought the game was up and that I might have to plan an escape. I called Maram for any news she might have, but she said it was unlikely he knew anything. There had been none of the usual early warning signs of his rages, no 'alerts' had been issued, and I should just get over there, as he demanded. I headed north over King Abdullah Street to get to his new palace in Sharm Abhar within the half-hour. But just as I was arriving, he called again to instruct me to meet him at his old residence instead. It was so typical of him to change his mind all of a sudden, without rhyme or reason – and God help you if you commented on or questioned a new command.

I wondered what he needed. I spun the car around and headed south, my mind racing.

A small fish caught in a net behind a fishing boat yearns to escape the trap. But the boat needs to stop long enough for the fish to break free. Ever since falling into *his* trap, I nurtured the hope that the Master would stop calling me every minute of the day, that he would slow down long enough for me to wriggle out of the snare. Sometimes we need to be still to determine the best way ahead, to decide whether to advance or to retreat. But that viper never had a day of rest. Distracted by his incessant motion, his prey could neither gauge the speed of the attack nor figure out the best escape.

I dreamed of breaking free from the instant I became trapped, believing that, with time, the Master would slacken the pace. I came to the realisation that nothing short of death would slow him down, and judging by his good health, that eventuality was a long way off.

I stepped into the marble foyer of the Palace where he usually held court. Some poor wretch lay across the floor surrounded by guards with their boots shoved into him. He was in such a pitiful state that it took me a while to recognise his features. I stood rooted to the spot and shuddered as I looked down on his crumpled body. All the years we had shared trickled back in tiny drops of brine. The excitement and adventures of our now distant adolescence coalesced into the memory of that night when he had come to my rescue and shielded me from my pursuers.

Who would shield us from one another now?

The Master ordered two guards to pick up the victim and take him to the punishment chamber. 'Now to your final assignment,' he commanded.

Though I knew it well, I looked around this den of cruelty as if for the first time. I felt a dizzying revulsion. I was completely shattered. It had never crossed my mind that one day he and I would be face to face in this very chamber. We looked each other in the eye, taking in our defeat and our torment.

The sole instrument of torture in this room was the method I had developed and perfected since my first assignment, and whose mastery had been demonstrated on countless occasions. My job was to loosen the hardened bond like a key bearing down on a rusty, seized-up lock. After which, the key was hung up for safe-keeping until the next time it was needed.

In all such instances, torturer and victim were inexorably drawn to the edge of the abyss. Their individualities dissolved and they became one, united in torment.

This time, though, everything was wrong – the place, the person, the timing. No sooner had I begun working on him than the evening call to prayer rang out, its melody and reson-ant words penetrating our very core as our bodies shuddered and convulsed. We begged each other for mercy and choked back agonised cries for our mutual suffering to end. Relieved and spent, torturer and victim buried their faces into the mattress, finally freed from each other.

I had been in the punishment chamber many times, feeling heavier and fouler each time. Whenever I had tried to extri-cate myself from the snare, the Master had tossed me back in, keeping me submerged to rust and corrode like a piece of metal abandoned in a dank and murky pit. I had grown accus-tomed to living exposed and raw.

I pulled up my loose-fitting shorts as soon as I had finished. Covering my shame and privates was easy enough; shoring up my frayed and tattered spirits was not so easy, given the filth in which I was steeped. I felt drained, battered and exhausted.

The evening call to prayer seemed endless. It felt as if the muezzin's injunction to the faithful went unheeded long into the night. The words of the sacred call reverberated through-out my being but offered no respite from the unrelenting

xii

darkness trapped within. The doors to my heart had been slammed shut by sin a long time ago, and the pools of darkness had grown and widened, enabling my wounded soul to engage in ever more cruel acts of torture. The process did not stop just because the time was up.

There was no safe harbour for our wayward souls. Our wounded spirits carried on with their outpouring of pent-up grief until all our days and nights in Jeddah seemed like a journey through a vale of tears. We were like boats racing towards some nearby harbour only to be blown back out to sea, the shoreline obliterated by a sprawling mass of walls and buildings.

Time passed, the call to prayer continued uninterrupted and night fell, gathering up its cloak, not to cover us but rather to expose us, bound together in our shameful act.

Picking up my clothes, I left my victim to collect himself. I was now resolved that I could no longer carry on with such terrible acts, but said nothing for fear that my turn would be next.

The Master looked me in the eye and congratulated me on successfully completing the assignment. 'You're as good as you always were,' he exclaimed. 'Maybe I should reconsider that decision to retire you.'

I spat on the ground without the Master seeing, while he directed a thick wad of spittle at the victim. He brimmed with contempt for him.

This was the most difficult assignment I had carried out since working at the Palace. It was supposed to be my 'grand finale', as the Master had put it, and he had invited his closest associates, his inner circle, to witness it. I had no choice in the matter – refusing would have meant either becoming a victim myself or being jailed on charges of conspiracy to murder. The specifics would be irrelevant; the Master could fabricate whatever charge would lead to my sentence, complete with irrefutable evidence and maybe even a personal confession.

I now doubted this would be my final act. Make a deal with the devil, and life is certain to set up a vicious and inescapable trap.

Dear God, help me. Please help me.

My decision to kill the Master had fully ripened. I had been carrying around images of his dead body in my mind for a very long time, summoning up visions of murder while lying in bed, killing him a different way before falling asleep every night.

First threshold

How many women have been violated or forced into prostitution without anyone coming to their assistance – no court, no defender of human rights, no self-proclaimed reformer? Mayhem is upon us. No good can arise in a nation that punishes the weak and turns a blind eye to the deeds of the rich and powerful.

From a Friday sermon by
Sheikh Ibrahim Fadel,
Imam of the Salvation Mosque

I

his uncle worked for Master's father

50 yrs old

→ since 19 yrs old

IHAVE NOW BEEN CARRYING around this old carcass of mine for half a century. The Master had snatched thirty-one out of those fifty years, without realising that he was sinking his teeth into carrion. It was on that darkest of nights – obscured now by the mists of time – that the barely tender nineteen-year-old had for ever hardened.

I no longer remembered the exact sequence of events: they flashed helter-skelter through my memory and I mixed up where and when they occurred. What I did know was that when I crossed the threshold of the Palace gates I stepped into an infernal life and became enslaved.

No one knew the Master as well as his entourage.

He had as many moods as he had outfits and could adapt his facial expression to suit any circumstance – and God help you if you had the audacity to suggest he might have picked the wrong thing to wear.

'He's just like a kid who throws tantrums,' Uncle Muhammad Rikabi told me once, but I was not convinced. Uncle Muhammad had been employed by the Master's father, and as the most senior employee at the Palace, everyone called him 'uncle' out of respect.

The Master's craggy face featured prominently in the

3

mass-market newspapers. The depictions were invariably angelic, portraying him as someone who relieved the suffering of the huddled masses in the swoop of his wings. His smile could warm the stoniest of hearts, giving the lie to any suspicion one might have that it was fake. Newspaper and magazine photographs suggested an amiable and gentle-hearted man who was virtuous and righteous to a fault.

A headline above one of the shots lauded his donation of ten million riyals to a special-needs charity. In another photo, he looked straight into the camera and flashed his most charismatic smile as he handed a cheque to the president of the Association for the Disabled. In the accompanying statement, he chastised the wealthy for their stinginess and expressed his hope that they would redouble their efforts, calling for new initiatives and bolder philanthropic endeavours. He exhorted his well-heeled peers to focus on assisting the less fortunate and to lend a hand in launching voluntary support and relief projects.

I watched one of the gardeners dragging his lame leg as he crossed the grounds to prune the trees at the back of the Palace; their thick, intertwining limbs had begun wrapping themselves around the lamp posts and were obstructing the Palace lights.

Always mindful of the possibility of further impairment, the gardener was not one to postpone a chore. All those who served at the Palace had some kind of handicap. A casual visitor might think well of the Master for taking on so many disabled people and providing them with dignified if humble employment.

But those on the inside knew only too well that such disabilities were the inevitable fate of anyone who remained

4

long enough at the Palace. Every able-bodied person who
started work there expected to acquire some kind of impairment and could only pray that it would not prove fatal. Even I
could be counted among them. After I entered 'Paradise' – as
those on the outside called the Palace – the Master toyed with
me and abused me at will, although I remained able-bodied.

He spent a lifetime tossing me back and forth, this way and
that, like a cat delighting in its prey's surrender, watching and
waiting intently with claws primed, killing time before satis-
fying its instincts. My complete submission made him appear
indifferent but I could tell his eyes were always on me, even
if from a distance. Any move or gesture on my part and he
would lash out, drawing me in with his claws. Wrenching me
back forcefully only served to excite him.

The Master sought every pleasure, and with each new
pleasure came the pursuit of the next; his drive to hedonism
was as unrelenting as it was insatiable. As one adept at mutila-
tion, he filled his Palace with a variety of human puppets and
his incessant abuse left no one whole: eyes were gouged,
limbs broken, hair and nails pulled out. Some were burned,
others castrated and still others were emotionally maimed or
made chronically sick. For those lucky enough to escape
bodily injury, inner demons and untold nervous disorders
would soon appear. In his perpetual search for new diver-
sions, all of us were disfigured in some way or another. That
is what puppets and dolls are made for; which child could
resist playing with his toys?

One – merciless – day, long ago, I became his new plaything and I learned to ignore the scratches along the way.

I yielded to him without reservation because of a great
piece of wisdom I stumbled upon when I was very young.

5

While many years have passed since the incident, it taught me a valuable lesson without which I would long have despaired over all the strife I have caused in my life and in the lives of others.

Many decades ago, when loudspeakers broadcast Eid prayers through our hot and humid neighbourhood, we were filled with joyful anticipation and a sense of wonder at the prospect of the coming celebrations. People trickled on to the streets in their bright white clothing, faces shining as they happily exchanged greetings, blessings and congratulations. Boys and girls chirped as they raced from door to door in their new outfits, hoping to receive their *eidi* – a gift of cash – rather than more of the sweets that were already spilling from their pockets.

I too paraded in my new clothes, dreaming of the treasure trove of cash that would be mine if I obeyed my mother and wished all our relatives and friends a happy Eid.

It was dawn and I surrendered to a scrubbing by my Aunt Khayriyyah, whose hands unearthed a store of dirt in all the hidden nooks and crannies of my body. But her cleaning was not as thorough as it could have been; her hands moved at lightning speed, never quite ridding me of all the accumulated dirt. I later understood that this was to spite my mother by inciting my father against her – not that he ever noticed my less-than-spotless appearance.

All my friends were subjected to the same periodic cleansing. Eid was an occasion for the entire community to remember the Creator: home furnishings were changed and walls and doors were repainted so that everything would gleam to usher in the holiday.

We all attended to this day with care, decorating our homes

6

and replacing old and tattered clothes with brand-new ones. But the public spaces were disregarded and remained as filthy and littered with rubbish as they always were, like a feast left out for the flies that had been shooed from people's houses.

I was on my way to visit my relatives and had to be careful not to trail the hem of my new thobe through the dirt in the alleyways. A muddy puddle blocked my path and only seemed to grow larger as I considered jumping over it. I tried tiptoeing around it but the puddle just kept growing, so I stepped back to find the narrowest point to leap over without splattering my clothes and spoiling the holiday.

Since I knew I would be punished if I dirtied my clothes, which was likely to happen if I attempted to jump over the puddle, I took my time and collected rocks and pieces of wood to build a makeshift bridge. I was determined to get to the other side of the neighbourhood unsullied.

As I teetered across the improvised bridge, a hand poked out from a rooftop above me and dumped rubbish right on my head.

I saw no point in trying to avoid the squalor of the streets any further and hurried back home, considerably filthier than I had been at the start of the day. This led to a thrashing – Aunt Khayriyyah obliged even on Eid – and I swore to remain in my dirty clothes for the rest of the day.

Neither my aunt nor my mother attended to the customary duty of receiving Eid well-wishers. Instead, they spent the entire day bickering. I sobbed my heart out not because I had dirtied my holiday clothes, but because the holiday had passed and I had missed out on my *eidi*.

I learned a valuable lesson that day. By the evening, I had realised that it was not important which rooftop the rubbish had been thrown from, simply that it had come from above. There was little point in caring about what was underfoot when worse was sure to rain down from the heavens.

That was the great wisdom that stayed with me throughout my life.

After that incident, I no longer cared whether I was defiled or not. On the contrary, I would pursue every wicked path before me and scale every mount of malice. It was the height of sin that would lead me into service at the Palace. Once inside, where there was no escape from depravity, I came upon another piece of wisdom: being human means hiding behind our own sinfulness while always pointing out the sins of others.

During the wild parties at the Palace, when luxury cars filled the interior parking lots, servants in brocaded suits glided all but invisibly among the guests, bearing trays of beverages and fruit and all manner of desserts. No one cast so much as a glance at their movements, and they remained to all intents and purposes as unseen as the houses of our neighbourhood across the way. From the Palace, our houses looked like prostrated servants forbidden to straighten up.

These parties were the scenes of undulating bodies as women set the nights on fire with their ostentatious flirting, of heads growing heavy with hackneyed phrases and pent-up desire, and, finally, of lust unleashed as the first drop of blood spilled on to the earth, perpetually seeking fresh blood to fuel its blaze.

Lust, blood, victims: the unholy trinity that contravenes the teachings of every religion and sacred tradition. It is this alternative trinity that delineates the parameters of human endeavour. This is how history is made.

8

One of the Palace regulars, Joseph Essam, was christened at the Church of the Virgin Mary in Beirut. Despite such immaculate credentials, he was not above doing missionary work under the cover of selling religious trinkets and semi-precious stones to would-be pilgrims.

'If you seek purity,' he once said, 'acknowledge your sins and forgive your enemies, for our Father in Heaven has borne your suffering through eternity and to this day.'

'So who is this father of ours?' I retorted.

The way Joseph Essam stood during dawn prayers led by the Master was comical. It was clear to me that his religious zeal was contrived. He would recall that he had not set foot in a church since coming to this country. After every fracas he was involved in, an exit visa would be stamped into his passport so that he could go and perform a belated pilgrimage to some church or other, as though he were duty-bound to perform his version of the Hajj. I thought that if he had genuinely sought salvation and purification, he should have travelled to Rome.

Religion is a long, dark tunnel: we pick and choose our way through it to justify our goals, both honourable and immoral. We follow the passage all the way into the subterranean workshop that stitches and cuts cloth to suit every mood, whether bright or downcast. To every design, there is a fitting demeanour and comportment. For those who stray from their personal faith, every thought is a snare, a bottomless pit of iniquity. As the pit fills, they are either buried alive or left to stagnate like standing water.

I have been struggling with my beliefs day after day for fifty years. I have come to realise that history is made up of deviants, grafters, thieves, opportunists, panderers, fornicators, pederasts, megalomaniacs and connivers. Low-lifes advance the story of mankind as much as saviours.

At the Palace, the partisans of decadence and immorality congregated nightly to re-enact the unholy trinity: victims were devoured, blood was spilt and lust was stoked. Lust thirsts for new blood like malignant cells multiplying, immune from destruction. It is lust that propels us to endure until the very end, to strive against and cleave to one another like magnets in an endless cycle of reproduction. No one is impervious to some form of vice, but we are all very careful to cover up and hide our shame. Only the lowest of the low parade themselves in open view. And I count myself among them.

My eyes would roam over the women of the Palace looking for Tahani, perhaps the only person to invalidate my theory about the inherently foul nature of human beings.

One evening, back in the neighbourhood, after I had crept into her room and planted a kiss on her exquisite long neck, Tahani had whispered in my ear, 'I'll never leave you. Wherever you go, I'll be there.'

In a sense she kept her promise since she lived in me during my time in the Palace. I could believe she was watching me covertly, her eyes following me everywhere, looking for the woman I might have selected in her place.

Women are like the fruit of the earth, each with a unique provenance and a particular flavour to entice us. They are gone one season and back the next and we eagerly anticipate their return. Summer and winter: seasons change on earth as in our souls and our desires.

I could not free myself of Tahani's memory. It would come

back to remind me of that first delectable taste of a fruit in season that lodges itself deep inside.

Most often it was my childhood friend, Osama al-Bushri, and his outbursts that brought Tahani to mind. But on those occasions, the memory was laced with bitterness and I began to look at every new woman who came to the Palace and wonder fearfully whether it might be Tahani. The Palace was full of women with tragic lives and I became convinced that she was among them, hiding in some corner or other. There were times I could have sworn she had been there and had left after seeing that I was as much of a pariah in the Palace as I had been in the old neighbourhood.

Whenever I thought of her, I imagined her entering the marble foyer, taking off her abaya and – right before the Master's eyes – inviting me to kiss her. She would hold me tearfully for a while and then jump out of my embrace to offer her body to whichever man happened to be in the vicinity. She would surrender every last drop of her womanliness, then spit in my face and leave, gathering up the sadness. This was how a woman would lose a beloved who had been so unworthy of her true heart.

Tahani was one of my victims.

I fled thirty-one years ago, severing our relationship so brutally that there would be no chance of mending it.

What had become of her? If she had really ended up in the Palace, into which of its many crevices had she fallen?

Whenever I felt a longing to recapture our lost innocence, I would recall her story. It was Osama who reminded me of how I had shattered her life. We had agreed not to talk about Tahani so as to avoid bitter rows and all-out hatred. For each of us to be able to sleep at night in our cocoons of regret, we lay down the bone of contention between us and refrained from digging it up.

But whenever news of Tahani reached him, Osama would forget the agreement and our lives would turn into a battleground again. On those occasions, we could not stand the sight of each other as hatred resurfaced to course through our veins.

As friends, each of us felt forsaken and we lay in wait for the right moment to throw the other down in the dirt and relieve the aching wound in our hearts. It was like needing a mirror to see a disfiguring outbreak of acne; each needed the other's gaze to grasp how bad the condition had become.

I needed time to recover, but whichever way I turned, there, before me, was the implacable servitude demanded by the Master. He wanted us around every waking and sleeping moment. Osama and I attended the wild parties at the Palace, avoiding the Master's eyes. But in any case, the Master was invariably busy checking out the women who swayed to the musicians' beat, and scrutinising the dancers to decide which of the bodies he would most like to ride. He was always the centre of any gathering, with his inner circle fawning over his every word and marvelling at his every discovery. He would raise a finger as soon as his glass was empty and a servant would magically appear to refuel his intoxication.

During one such meaningless party, Osama leaned in close and hissed into my ear, 'How much more of this until we can get out?'

He had always had a sense of urgency about him, even when we were younger and lived outside the confines of the Palace, life still pumping through us. At that time, the Palace was at the periphery of our neighbourhood and entire families would sit mesmerised by its brilliant lights and dream of entering its walls.

I believe that even to this day, some on the outside are still haunted by these old dreams and continue to ask themselves how they can enter the Palace.

Whereas those of us on the inside count the days to our escape.

2

T HE PALACE WAS VISIBLE from every direction and anyone
entering Jeddah would see it. But while the Palace was
there for everyone to behold, few were granted the privilege
of seeing the man who built it – the first Master.

Were it not for Crazy Jamal, the residents of our neighbourhood would never have even glimpsed his features.

The Palace stood right across from our dilapidated neighbourhood, but its massive walls and gates were well fortified
against our avid curiosity. We became so eager to catch sight
of the man of the Palace that whenever we thought we might
see his white Rolls-Royce, we gathered in a vacant lot
between our houses and the road that led to the main gates.
We poured out of every nook and cranny of our neighbourhood and on to the main road for a chance to see him, causing
a hubbub. Determined to prevent the din from spoiling the
occasion, we shushed each other loudly as we tried to catch a
glimpse of him.

Day after day the white car sped past, denying us even a
fleeting peek. We could just make out the curtains – which
we assumed were made of silk – that hung on the windows to
conceal the face of the man reclining in the back seat. Only
the Sudanese chauffeur stood out clearly with his spiralling

14

white turban like an uneven mound of snow. His body leaned away from the crowd as he sped away as though protecting a sugar cube from a swarm of flies.

The car soon receded into the distance, slipping into the Palace like a knife slicing through butter, finally disappearing as the massive gates closed behind it. The towering Palace walls stood their ground against our gawking eyes.

But our curiosity was satisfied the day the car's front bumper hit Crazy Jamal, throwing him to the ground. The white Rolls-Royce was forced to stop and we were finally able to take a good look at the man from the Palace. He was elegant and his features were immaculate despite the scowl and cheeks flushed with indignation at the crowd that had mobbed his car and was gaping at him. He was a man of advanced years; the bluish arteries that bulged around his ears and Adam's apple bore witness to the many decades they had strained to pump life through his body.

All of us would later revel in recounting some aspect of this sighting. Our listeners hung on our every word and they too went on to enhance and embellish the story with additional details. The sighting set off such a flurry of gossip in the alleys of our neighbourhood that, with countless retellings to friends, neighbours and even casual passers-by, the event became all but unrecognisable.

Issa Radini had been dismissive of our daily attempts to see the Master of the Palace. During one of our neighbourhood gatherings, he had even offered to put our curiosity to rest by describing the man's features. But no one had believed him and even his closest friends made fun of his description. He had stormed off, vowing that they would live to regret their mockery.

We were all too fascinated by the Palace and its owner to listen. Never before had we seen such imposing walls. We lived in the shadow of dying dreams, fantasies that withered and perished inside us before that impenetrable barrier. All that our feeble gaze could accomplish was to imagine what went on behind those mighty walls.

In the first bloom of youth, when we still entertained ourselves by counting the number of lights illuminating those walls, we imagined that the din of excitement that drifted from the Palace was caused by the descent of *houris* – virgin companions from heaven. This seemed to be confirmed by the barely audible love songs that accompanied the excited voices until dawn.

The high walls fuelled our desires; they were impenetrable barriers that blocked our vision only to unleash our imagination.

Construction of the Palace had dried up the sea before our very eyes and hundreds of tonnes of cement had walled in our tears, which seeped into our souls and collected there in pools of sadness and regret.

There were aspects of our dilapidated neighbourhood that people were glad to forget: the fetid alleyways swollen with rubbish and the crumbling houses propped up by makeshift metal girders and trusses. After the neighbourhood was made to relinquish its original name and consented to being improved with broad, well-lit streets that were paved and lined with trees, the Palace became our new address.

It became the landmark reference for anyone coming into the city.

Strategically located on a large expanse of coastline, its exquisitely crafted white marble shimmered all night long in a sequence of rainbow colours. These were projected from lights that had been subtly concealed by a state-of-the-art lighting design.

The Palace was built concentrically, with its back to our neighbourhood, in an arc that enveloped the north of the city and extended all the way out to the sea, effectively denying us access to the shore.

References to the Palace became so dominant that the name of our neighbourhood was soon forgotten. We knew it as 'Hell' or the 'Firepit', but newcomers to the area just referred to it as the 'Palace District'.

The Palace was at its most magnificent after dark when all the lights came on; boys from the neighbourhood competed to count them all and then argued heatedly over the tally.

But it was also resplendent during the day. The Palace seemed like a gift from heaven, as enchanting as a droplet of water turning into a snowflake as it floats to the ground. It was suspended between the great blue of sea and sky, at once mesmerising and redeeming. Gazing at it, all one wanted was to enter and see it from the inside.

Going in was like entering a world of underwater glass chambers where one shared the space with all the creatures of the sea. They floated so close one could almost reach out and touch them. Ascending the marble staircases, the sight was breathtaking: the city unfolded like a man in a gesture of supplication. The towering outer walls were dotted with golden domes, the bases of which were embossed with dark green calligraphy inside double-helix crowns. Above these, precious stones glinted, set in the veins of polished pink marble imported from Spain.

The Palace had been furnished from the outer reaches of

the world; its grounds were a succession of lush gardens, luxuriant with flowers and fruit trees, and also with birds, horses and other animals. Whenever the space grew too confined, the sea was there to be reclaimed, making way for the arrival of the latest models in luxury cars, yachts and motor boats, as well as ornamental statues.

Despite their lofty stature, the towering walls could not block from view all the branches of the trees that hung heavy with fruit. Those young or reckless enough tried to shimmy up the walls to snatch a mango or orange from a low-hanging limb; others pelted the branches with stones until they broke, bringing the fruit down with them.

Loitering around the Palace to steal fruit was a risky business, but we carried on until the day one of the boys from the neighbourhood was caught in the act and sent to jail for an entire year. Not only had the boy climbed the wall and stolen fruit, but he had inadvertently seen white bodies splashing and frolicking in the sea between the rocky breakwaters. This was before the Palace courtyards were enclosed by additional walls that swallowed up more of the adjoining land.

In the beginning, there was all manner of speculation regarding the owner of the Palace. No one knew his exact name, where he was from or why he had chosen this spot on which to erect his imposing structure.

Rumour and speculation abounded. Since we could never quite agree on who he was, we felt ambiguity was the safest course when discussing the anonymous owner. In that way, the mystery remained whole, full of potential and promise. We settled on calling him simply the *Sayyid* – the Master.

When he began living at the Palace, an aura of mystery came to surround his person and we would venture out to catch a glimpse of him coming or going at various times. We would see him in the distance as his white Rolls-Royce took the road between the western flank of the neighbourhood and the main gates. He was always seated in the back seat, seemingly indifferent to the faces gawking at him. We watched the car as it crossed the unpaved section of road that was still within the boundaries of our humble neighbourhood, before that piece of land was also expropriated for the Palace. The car sent a thick cloud of dust into the air like a miniature cyclone unleashed from the sleeve of a skilled sorcerer.

We barely caught sight of the man's handsome features as he reclined against the back seat of the car. We were only able to confirm our impressions after Crazy Jamal blocked his way and we came in for a closer look. Rumours spread that Jamal had been deliberately pushed in front of the speeding car by someone who was tired of the daily disturbance caused by our gatherings. Whatever the truth in the matter, Jamal was struck by the car and fell, groaning and bleeding on to the unpaved road.

The chauffeur hopped out of the Rolls-Royce and began to curse us. He dragged Jamal by the sleeve and flung him to the side of the road, seemingly unperturbed. By contrast, the Master was visibly fidgety but remained seated in the car. Only his darkening brow betrayed his impatience.

We were probably little more than parasites to him, creatures who had surfaced from the primeval mud to annoy him with our childish stunts. But we stood transfixed by his noble complexion, amazed that a man with such shiny and fair skin could roam the face of the earth. We forgot all about Crazy Jamal lying in a pool of blood and crowded around the car to stare at this person whose patience had, by now, been exhausted. His right hand flew up to wipe his brow and cheeks as if to remove dirt that had stained his face.

Finally, at a short, sharp movement of the Master's lips, the chauffeur returned to the driver's seat and took off, delivering his passenger from our gawking. The car sped away in a whorl of dust, leaving us behind to shout and gesticulate madly.

Just as we ventured out during the day to catch a glimpse of the Master, we came out at night to watch the illuminated Palace shimmering with lights. We would bet on the number, colour and even shape of the lights. But our enthusiasm for that game soon receded before the impossibility of the task.

One evening we noticed the bright lights had gone dark. It was so dark that we imagined the sea, raging with fury at the inroads made by the reclaimed land, had consumed the entire Palace. We considered the absence of light more seriously the following day when the Palace remained shrouded in darkness.

The blackout lasted three nights and news spread that the Master had died, leaving all his wealth to two sons, who went on to bring unprecedented levels of rowdiness to the Palace. One of the sons ascended the throne to become the new lord of the manor – the second Master – and the news reignited the hopes of everyone in our neighbourhood who dreamed of entering the Palace.

The death of the old Master coincided with the disappearance of Issa from the neighbourhood. Rumour had it that Issa had been hired by the new *Sayyid* to work for him, which only fuelled our longing to be inside those walls. Though the rumour of Issa's employment was hotly disputed

20

for some time, it was eventually confirmed by one of our local Palace snoops.

One of the boys greeted the news with the ominous words: 'From that Palace, life will flow.'

In hindsight, the statement was oddly prophetic. It could be interpreted in two, contradictory ways: a soul gaining more out of life from the experience of being in the Palace or, conversely, of the Palace squeezing life out of every living soul. All those who eventually entered the Palace, including me, found out for themselves that before life left their bodies, their spirits had been utterly crushed.

Maymoun Abdel-Hadi was the very first victim of the new order. He broke through the main gates one day in a state of uncontrollable rage to demand payment for land he owned that bordered the Palace grounds and that had been expropriated by the Master. His ranting culminated in barely veiled insults and he was dragged off by the collar to languish in the Palace jail. When his family tried to obtain news of him through intermediaries, the local notables who interceded on their behalf became marked men. They came back from the Palace chastened and never again made any reference to him or his story, leaving the family to cling to hope of his return for many years.

Hamdan Bagheeni would scurry through the narrow, twisting alleyways of our neighbourhood with a polka-dot shawl covering his mouth and a hand holding his nose shut. He hurried to reach the other side of the neighbourhood in the old heart of the city, propelled by dreams of entering Paradise and desperate for a breath of air that did not carry the putrid stench of Khalil Masawi's decomposing chickens and pigeons.

21

The birds had met their end in a bout of avian flu that struck an isolated chicken coop. Poor Masawi never found out how it had happened and was so distraught that he left the carcasses untouched, and the pervasive smell of rotting flesh was carried by the wind. He vented his rage on whoever happened to be within earshot, cursing and swearing and blaming the untimely death of his poultry on the Ministry of Agriculture. Following the death of a first batch of chickens, the ministry had failed to supply him with vaccines to save the rest.

'Now, you wouldn't happen to be the reason those poor chickens died, would you?' Aunt Khayriyyah asked, winking at me knowingly. I only understood the insinuation later, when she began to tell me that all my actions were evil and to hold me responsible for every misfortune and mishap that befell anyone in the neighbourhood.

A very long time has passed since Aunt Khayriyyah's insinuating question and Hamdan's desperate bid to find a way into the Palace. Like every other boy from the neighbourhood, Hamdan spent much of his leisure time looking for a breach in the road whose course had been diverted to prevent access to the main gates.

Dr Khalid Bannan, who was in the Master's inner circle, loved to hold forth and pontificate on the rags-to-riches dream. 'Dreams are the drug we inject to induce an instant of oblivion in which all of our wishes, both fair and foul, can be fulfilled,' he would say. 'But dreams are like sleep, and the dreamer is in a trance when the body slows down.'

Referencing his wealth of scientific knowledge as a professor of psychology, he dispensed advice liberally to whoever was present at Palace events, regardless of whether or not his advice was pertinent to his listener.

On the brink of old age, I look back on the 'dream-drug' that made us all so high – magic stuff so pure that most of the neighbourhood boys became instantly hooked. Life passed us by while we remained in this state of protracted stupor.

Once on the inside, I remembered the Firepit – the old neighbourhood – and dreamed of going back. I yearned for it with the same longing that once propelled me so obsessively to enter Paradise.

That realisation came as a crushing blow. I have no doubt that every single one of us who entered the Palace has had such moments of nail-biting regret, unequalled by any others.

Back in the days when the neighbourhood's inhabitants swirled around the Palace full of hopes and dreams, boys stood and pointed at its towering walls and heads were filled with lush dreams of fertile ground behind the massive gates. Few of us could imagine that we would be inside the Palace in our old age pointing to our dilapidated neighbourhood and longing with every fibre of our being to return to those Elysian Fields of our youth. We sit and rake through our memories in the hope of collecting some scraps from a long-buried past. Decades have passed since the pigeons took flight from the rooftops of our ramshackle houses, fluttering in unruly formations towards the Palace and its gardens. Even the birds were enticed by the bright vision bordering the shore – a pillow offering rest to the weary bones of dreamers.

Every day, Hamdan would run through the stately avenue that bisected the city and our universe: Paradise here, the Firepit there.

It was Hamdan who first coined the name the 'Firepit'.

Every day after the sunset prayer – *adhan al-maghrib* – he set

23

off with his tattered school satchel to attend a literacy class at night school. He wanted to obtain his primary school certificate in order to improve on his rank of private in the army; after ten compliant years in the service, he had not gained a single stripe. He was spurred to do this after his father-in-law referred to him as 'an ass' and said that 'iron wouldn't turn to gold even in a million years'. These words were uttered when the father came to retrieve his daughter, Hamdan's wife, and take her away.

Hamdan had dropped out of school early and, as a young adult, no one would give him a job besides the army. So while the other boys of the neighbourhood started better jobs and progressed within their chosen careers, Hamdan laboured away as a private in the army for ten years.

He thought literacy classes would help him to advance and so he persevered with night school in order to gain the respect of his father-in-law and his superior officers. As soon as he completed the sunset prayer at the local mosque, before the imam had even intoned the closing of prayer and with his tattered school satchel and prayer mat vying for space, Hamdan would leap to his feet and bound into the twisting, rubbish-strewn alleys, holding his nose against the putrid stench and muttering to himself.

When he reached Masawi's dead poultry, he had to cover his mouth to quell his surging nausea. Simultaneously he would take in short breaths of air to keep him going as he hurtled towards the west side of the city, with its gardens, street lights, neon signs, villas and luxury cars, as well as a plethora of construction sites, opulent shopping malls, entertainment centres, hospitals and banks. Once there, he would take a long, cleansing breath to fill his lungs to their maximum capacity, and then invariably exclaim, 'At last, I've made it to Paradise!'

The letters of the alphabet exhausted him, in the way they were so similar and yet so different from one another. He sought help from a neighbour who attempted to make the Arabic alphabet accessible to a mind that knew only the configurations of domino pieces and playing cards. Hamdan could never get through this daily rote without being struck by the difference between the letters *noon* and *jeem*, and was completely mystified by the notion that some words that began with one of those letters could have a synonym that began with the other.

He voiced this observation one day at the neighbourhood hang-out, where some men and boys had gathered to discuss what could be done to stop raw sewage from spilling into the alleyways and to put a decisive end to the stench. Hamdan jumped right into the discussion with an idea he believed was unique and that would solve all their problems.

'Our situation might improve,' he said, 'if we changed the name of our neighbourhood.'

This caused an immediate outburst by the assembled men who mocked his suggestion and harangued him.

Hamdan held his ground. 'Just listen first,' he insisted, 'and then decide.'

The men quietened down and grudgingly gave him a chance to speak.

'There is a paradise of riches a stone's throw from our neighbourhood,' he began, pointing in the direction of the Palace. 'Why is that?' he asked them. 'Can you tell me why?'

There was a moment's silence.

Hamdan answered his own question. 'Because there is

25

Paradise,' he said triumphantly, stressing the Arabic word *Jannah*. His finger still stretching westward, he continued, 'There, it is *Jannah*, a word that begins with the letter *jeem*. And as everyone knows, *jeem* occurs early in the alphabet – and Allah always starts at the beginning of the alphabet when bestowing His blessings.'

Upon hearing God's name used this way, some of the men started to shout, warning him that this was close to blasphemy.

Hamdan was undeterred. 'But we are in the *Firepit*, don't you see?' Again he stressed the Arabic word *Naar* and his finger shot down to indicate the ground under their feet. 'And as everyone knows, *noon*, which is the first letter in *Naar*, is near the end of the alphabet. So we get nothing from Him but hardship.'

This time most of the men shouted, some in loud prot-estations of their virtue and others, louder still, admon-ished Hamdan for his blasphemy. A few, however, nodded and liked the contrast he had drawn between the two sides of the road.

They brought up the suggestion in subsequent get-togethers, albeit sarcastically at first. But gradually Hamdan's names were adopted by the residents of the neighbourhood. From then on, they referred to the western flank as 'Paradise' and the eastern one as the 'Firepit'.

But Hamdan did not know that the word 'firepit' had a synonym beginning with the letter *jeem* – *jehannam,* or hell – nor, for that matter, that the synonym for 'paradise' was *na'eem*, which began with the letter *noon* that was closer to the end of the alphabet. Residents of the neighbourhood had no need for knowledge beyond what they already knew in their

26

bones: that they were burning up inside a raging inferno and that this was reason enough to escape the blazing flames at the first opportunity.

The Palace extended as far as the eye could see on the west side of the neighbourhood. Its huge gates were operated by remote control and were quickly shut after they were opened as if fearful a flame might escape from the Firepit to lick at the vast and magnificent grounds. The massive gate across the way was a constant reminder for the miserable wretches, tormented by physical privation and poverty, of their desperation for a place in Paradise.

Almost overnight, the poverty-stricken Firepit wedged itself to the flanks of the Palace like a clinging mass of barnacles. Those wishing to jump ship needed only to lay down the burden of life – that is, the heavy weight of conscience and morality – if indeed they carried it at all.

Issa convinced me that we should go through life together. 'We've been friends since we were kids,' he said. 'So let's just carry on.'

We were all so ready to leave our pit of privation that the mere idea of leaping across to the other side spread like a contagion. But the idea died on everyone's lips as soon as it was expressed because we did not have what it took to reach Paradise.

Abu Yunes the plumber worked day and night at an indoor metalwork shop but never made enough money to buy a house for his ever-growing number of offspring. One day when he was bone-weary he asked the question that had seeped into everyone's mind: 'Who dares enter the Palace?'

It was a provocative question since each of us was scheming to find a way into the Palace or, at the very least, to stand and behold its huge gates from close up. Even those who had done neither claimed to have been there. People who boasted they had been inside the Palace and swore they had met the Master became the laughing stock of the neighbourhood.

Egged on by Issa and this contagious desire, all I wanted was to find a way in, and my ambition had little to do with high walls or resplendent lights.

When we were young teenagers, Issa would not join our light-counting contests. He just looked towards the shimmering bulbs and repeated confidently, 'I'll count them when I'm on the inside.'

Everyone jeered and mocked him so that, like a small fish making room for itself in a school of sharks, he had to raise his voice to make himself heard. Even though he was interrupted repeatedly, that did not deter him from recounting his exploits and what he had seen when he had hidden on the island of Umm al-Qumari. The islet was just offshore from the Palace's reclaimed land and the deeper Issa got in retelling his story the more he succeeded in silencing his sceptics.

This was in the days before Crazy Jamal was run over by the Rolls-Royce. So what was indeed strange was that Issa was able to describe the features of the first Master long before we had ever laid eyes on him in the back seat of his car. And when his son, the next in line to the throne, became the new lord of the manor, we called him the Master while his father became known as *Sayyid al-kabeer* – the old Master.

Until Issa's whole story came out, I remained puzzled by his detailed description of the older man's features.

At the Palace, I belonged to a group known as the 'punishers', a label reserved for people whose despicable deeds were considered beyond the pale.

28

Its members were collected from the dregs of the city's poor neighbourhoods and their sole mission was to destroy their victims' sense of manhood through sodomy. If they overexerted themselves in the course of their work, they would be confined to their quarters to recuperate or assigned to other, equally distasteful tasks.

I had been recruited for one particular purpose, but soon found myself taking on all sorts of foul assignments, and always in the dead of night. I knew that I was lost and that not a prayer could save me.

Very few people knew my true role inside the Palace and I was sometimes alarmed when I overheard some of the staff talking about me. 'He's the one who alters the Master's mood,' they would say and my blood would run cold at the thought that anything that might be said about me, or him, should get back to the Master.

Many people avoided my company, fearing they would be tainted. Men who Issa brought into the Palace greeted me from a distance, almost grudgingly, and at times they ignored me altogether.

The punishers were housed in a remote section of the Palace. Given our reputation, only those who had lost their way ever wandered there. Whenever one of us emerged from our quarters, rumours would spread like fire that a new victim was now in the Palace, and screams and pleas for mercy could be heard even before we reached the punishment chamber.

Many of the servants and staff at the Palace went about their business like ants, performing their duties with painstaking diligence and with fixed smiles on their faces. They never looked behind them nor met anyone's gaze; their uniforms served to indicate their function at the Palace.

No common history bound them and none of them knew each other's personal history. With the exception of a group of employees from our neighbourhood who were assigned different jobs, all of us discharged our duties anonymously, whether in the open or behind closed doors. Our given names were unnecessary to our roles and we were known by the jobs we performed. No one asked about anyone's past.

Dr Bannan was one of the few exceptions. He had fallen into the Palace through some sort of trapdoor and would talk about his past and pontificate on fate. 'Our destiny,' he would say, 'is the only true darkness through which we can navigate unhesitatingly and recklessly.' His endless quest for a way out of the snare consisted of making presentations at various low-level conferences and of publishing mediocre political articles in second-rate newspapers that nobody read. Not that it stopped him from reading out loud those articles to anyone who happened to be within earshot.

His attendance at these conferences had nothing to do with his intelligence or the depth of his knowledge; rather, it owed entirely to an exchange of mutually beneficial favours with the organisers. This helped him to pad his curriculum vitae with a long list of professional memberships and dozens of lectures and papers.

Whenever he heard the most senior employee at the Palace, Uncle Muhammad, bemoaning the 'good old days', he would offer what became his infamous dictum: 'In our yearning to recover our true selves, we continually fall into the deep well of the past.'

Despite his pompousness, once in a blue moon a nugget of wisdom would actually tumble from his mouth, though often he would merely be repeating or adapting someone else's theories. He no longer had work to occupy himself beyond, that is, keeping the Master company, hanging on his every utterance and grovelling at his feet.

While absolutely everyone grovelled in the Palace, Dr Bannan was like a moon bending in its orbit around its planet. He was the Master's constant companion, whether in motion or at rest, and became his partner at the card game *balut*. Playing *balut* was complete drudgery since everyone made sure the Master always won; during those sessions, the good doctor would click his tongue to warn the other players whenever the Master had a winning hand.

We were as lifeless as the cards in that dreary game. Our role was to be flicked and tossed indifferently by the Master. Neither he nor his so-called opponents ever cared whether the cards landed face up or face down.

Stepping through the Palace gates for the very first time, I was hit by a blast of cold air the likes of which I had never before felt. At the sight of the Palace and its gardens, as well as all the yachts, cars and stables, I really thought I had set foot in paradise.

The first money I earned was for performing a foul act that I thought would be over as soon as my panting stopped. But after a succession of repeat performances, vice became the signal marker of my life. A darkness I had never previously known descended on me, and I became desperate to hide from everything and everyone, including myself.

Whenever I felt the need to hide I would bring to mind the rubbish landing on my head that distant Eid. Sometimes that memory alone was enough to dispel my sorrow at having left the old neighbourhood.

31

When asked about their place of work, many of the staff declared with pride that they were employees of the Palace. I was the only one who kept my reason for being there a secret. I had chosen an immoral line of work, and performing my job had ruined my life and deadened my soul.

Uncle Muhammad liked to say we were abandoned ponds that had been left to breed gnats and grow slime, and whose stagnant contents belied all the life-giving properties of clean water. That is how I came to feel.

I had not felt that way during my early and reckless adolescence. Back then, I felt full of myself and elated by my actions and I paraded before my friends like a puffed-up rooster, vaunting my stuff and flaunting my colours. I would hunt down 'prey' to ensure my elevated reputation among my circle of friends, violating my victims not so much to relieve my lust as to show off my virility. In doing so, I was also able to fend off the predators in our neighbourhood who would have made me their victim.

Life yields its secrets too late, after we can no longer turn back and erase or rectify our mistakes. When we are finally ready to pass on the baton, it is rejected because the next generation, the young people, are naïve and believe their lives will be different.

Uncle Muhammad tried his best to explain this to me on my first day at the Palace, but I was too young to listen. How I wish I had stayed in the Firepit! That wish can never be granted because I have fallen to the very bottom of the abyss.

Gravity is an immutable law. Even though we are all governed by it, we have trouble understanding the precise way it affects our lives. The process of falling is gradual; it does not happen all at once, but in stages. The consequences of the fall are apparent only once the process is complete.

I fell gradually, stage by stage, and now I am at the bottom of the fall.

I fell, and from there I fell further.

3

PEOPLE WERE LODGED INTO every nook and cranny of our dilapidated neighbourhood like grains of sand blown in by the wind. Whether it was called the 'Pit', the 'Saltmine', the 'Depths of Hell' or simply the 'Firepit', all the designations rhymed with suffering and described our miserable lives inside the neighbourhood.

It had not always been so.

Lying against the bloated and belching sea, it was once a place that stirred even before the first rays of the sun could cast their beams on the windows of the houses. The neighbourhood would wake up to the clamour of children wending their way to school down the narrow lanes, to the din of boisterous fishermen returning with their catch from a night at sea, and to songs blaring from radios that were as dewy as the dawn of the day they celebrated. Like the fine mist from a summer rain, the songs refreshed our spirits and pierced our hearts, and our lungs filled deeply with energising breaths.

The early morning commotion would include the clatter of shopkeepers as they pulled on the whining shutters of their shops and the shouts of street pedlars selling sweetmeats and cheap tinny toys to schoolchildren. Others sold street food that caused a sudden rush of diarrhoea in all but those with the constitution of an ox.

Day after day, the cycle was repeated without interruption, with the sun circling in the sky to reach its zenith and the merciless rays beating down to bleach the last trace of colour off people's faces, off the neighbourhood's walls and doors and off the washing hung out to dry on rooftops. Everything dried in the blink of an eye.

At the end of every day, its blaze exhausted, the scorching sun undertook its final journey and descended peacefully in the direction of the Palace foundations.

Life is a filthy journey that starts out pristine, and we are driven on that voyage of discovery by words of encouragement and censure. In reality, it is only by committing sins that we become fully human. Like millions of people everywhere, it was only after I had left that I realised where I was from.

I had emerged from a humble home buried at the end of the neighbourhood, a gathering-point for the Huroob, Jahnaan and Rawaabigh tribes, who considered city life a stain on the purity of their stock. When Jeddah's city walls burst, so to speak, people from all manner of descent mixed together, making the neighbourhood appear as if it had been deliberately designed for chaos. In this respect, it was no different from many other neighbourhoods that proliferated outside the old city walls.

My maternal grandfather had arrived from Hadhramaut in Yemen, bringing with him his merchandise of Indian textiles and Javanese incense and sarongs. He built a spacious house, which he had planned to fill with human pups. A man of considerable sexual appetites, he set up four women, one in each corner of the large inner courtyard, consorting with them in turn. His pleasure peaked with my grandmother, Saniyya.

She was of Turkish extraction and had a stunningly beautiful face and a body to match. They say his desire for Saniyya burned undiminished and that, to be fair to his other wives, he always started with the other three first. After his passage through the first three doorways, he would bathe, groom himself carefully and come to Saniyya as fresh and energised as if he had not spilled a drop of his sap earlier.

During his morning sessions with his friends, my grandfather would boast of his prowess with the four women, unaided by the prescriptions of Abu Rasheed. The apothecary of Indian descent had a vast knowledge of herbs and claimed to possess a secret elixir that would give any man the strength of a crocodile and the ability to take on ten women without flagging. Indeed, Abu Rasheed was venerated by men whose vital forces were spent and who had become desperate for his remedies to keep their honour in the bedroom upright.

In a bid to grow his business, Abu Rasheed approached my grandfather with a proposal and, for a while, they became partners in marketing traditional remedies. But the project was short-lived, coming to an abrupt end with the invasion of cheap products to treat the same woes.

Years later, my mother convinced my father to dabble in the trade. However, her recollection of the recipes and concoctions was incomplete and my father's success in the profession was therefore mixed. But she did remember Abu Rasheed's most secret concoction and my father used it to boost his own prowess.

While my father's virility was enhanced by the apothecary's potions, mine flowed directly into my veins from my grandfather without the need for any treatment. I have been governed by ravenous lust all my life, and in the absence of decent outlets for release, I have channelled it in twisted ways.

Sexual prowess was a badge of honour worn by all men and it was doubtless a desire to prove constantly their competence in the bedroom that caused the population explosion in our neighbourhood.

Small markets sprang up across the length of the main road to cater to ever-growing demand; the burgeoning population also brought on a proliferation of telephone, electricity and sewage networks. Once the roads were paved, the neighbourhood attracted all sorts of people from every imaginable race and language group. Secreted into its winding lanes and tired of hatching in crowded and modest homes, this pullulating life spilled over into secondary streets and sinuous byways.

We arrived late in the game. Our fathers, already past their fifties, were still raising the banner of their prowess on the undulating hills of women, outdoing past sins with more wicked ones. Most of the neighbourhood children were fatherless and clung to mothers worn down by the daily grind of their lives and the battle to keep their frail children alive.

The neighbourhood choked with people and all means of livelihood had dried up. After the fishermen had to give up fishing and the old artisanal trades died out, all that was left for people were jobs that emaciated their bodies and brought in meagre incomes.

Our generation was raised on fantasies and nursed on envy. Our sole inheritance was the jealousy that showed in our eyes

37

as we leered at the mounds of savoury food, designer clothing and luxury cars, at the rivers of cash in shops and at the women who wandered through the souk wedged in between our houses and the winding alleys of the neighbourhood. The dreams nurtured on covetousness came true only in our imaginations. We pictured ourselves sitting in expensive restaurants, ordering endless courses of refined food. We wanted to own this or that fancy store. We fantasised that any woman could be ours for a wild evening. We clothed ourselves in those dreams until they were so soiled that we tossed them in the laundry pile and picked out fresh ones to dirty. That is what is meant by a life of hardship: a life of constantly changing dream clothes that are all, in any case, illusory.

Several of the neighbourhood boys longed to leave this desert of dreams behind and went in search of the reality outside. They scattered to the four winds, like so many paper scraps floating in the air.

Our nights were like a sultry tunnel that we stole through in the incessant pursuit of furtive pleasures. As evening fell, we were overcome with suppressed longing, the flaming embers of our desire stoked by our fantasies, and we throbbed with lust against each other until we crested the wave and climaxed.

Tahani was the only bright spot in a life otherwise cloaked in darkness and gloom. She would wait for me every night like a bright guiding star shining the way for an errant wanderer.

At night her face was even more enchanting, framed by long flowing hair that nestled coyly between her twin domes whose fullness I had ascertained. Seeing her in the alleys of our neighbourhood, clutching her abaya tightly to reveal the

38

ripeness of fruit ready for plucking and weary of waiting, I was stung by jealousy. I could no longer stand the mere exchange of letters and glances.

One day, I fell into step with her, handed her a note and hurried off. The note read: 'If you don't let me spend some time with you, you'll never see me again.'

Tahani relented after I disappeared from view for two weeks, and started to let me into her bedroom at night. She would make sure everyone in her household was asleep before opening the door; it was so late that even the narrow lane deep inside the neighbourhood where we lived was fast asleep.

I would slip in and spend what was left of the night going back and forth tirelessly over the peaks of her two mounds, not daring to approach her virtue but inhaling the scent of her body sprinkled with aromatic oils and the mists of her desire.

One night, I almost reached the point of no return. But Tahani snapped out of the mood and dug her nails into whatever part of my body was within reach. She drew blood and I instinctively pulled away even though I was still wildly desperate for release. Shocked by what she had done, she sat me up to dab the scratch marks dry, licking the drops of blood with her tongue.

She started to cry as a stream of apologies rushed out of her. 'I love you, Tariq, more than my soul,' she said. 'I don't want your love to die in my heart.'

She looked away for a second.

'I'll be yours as long as I live.' She added after a moment's silence, 'Just don't spoil our love.'

Once the Palace was completed, it cast its shadow over the entire front of the neighbourhood, blocking the sea breeze.

Between houses that were practically joined at the hip, the air hung so thick and heavy that it caused our chests to tighten.

A body submerged in water is full of ease; we, however, ended up feeling like sea monsters for whom dry land was a burial ground. Had we remained immersed any longer, we would have been swallowed whole. After the Palace was built and its massive walls obscured the blue waters, the sea no longer held the appeal it once had and going to the beach became an arduous task.

In the late afternoons, those of us who were swimming enthusiasts used to meet up with Waleed Khanbashi to be driven to the now distant shore. We would drag ourselves away from the waves only when night fell and our fear of lurking sea creatures outweighed our desire to remain in the cool water.

We emerged dripping and shivering, our teeth chattering wildly since we had nothing to dry off with until we returned to Waleed's car. Being resourceful, he always brought along tatty old sarongs – two or three people having to share one – and charging each user half a riyal for that privilege. By the third person's turn, the makeshift towel was hopelessly wet and useless.

Before the Palace was built, there were two places where we liked to submerge our bodies in the sea: the Plage, a stretch of shoreline to the south of Jeddah that fell into disuse after its access became unsafe, and Al-Hamra, which the city's mayor turned into a promenade adorned with sculptures by international artists and kept gleaming by an army of labourers. For many of us from remote neighbourhoods, just being on the promenade was something to boast about and gave us bragging rights over kids from even more remote neighbourhoods. But it also deepened our sense of grievance when we remembered what this length of asphalt did to us.

More than just screening off the azure sea, the concrete walls lining the shore served to split the population, driving a deep wedge between people that was based on inequity and class.

Jeddah woke to hundreds of workers walling off its shore-line. The sea was parcelled off and no one batted an eyelid as city councillors and their retinue of bureaucrats, lawyers, brokers and developers all got their share. Nothing was left for the rest of the population.

The fishermen were the first to suffer from this de facto exclusion from their time-honoured fishing grounds. They never gave voice to their complaints and one after the other collected his fishing tackle and bid a heart-broken farewell to the sea. Their traditional way of life was gone for ever, buried as surely as the surf that once lapped at their feet.

When they first brought in the tonnes of earth from nearby wadis to reclaim the sea, Hamed Abu Gulumbo looked around for his favourite place on the shorefront and found it gone. He was a fisherman with a gift for poetic improvisation and from that moment, he began to hold impromptu poetry sessions with his fishing companions, warning them of the coming drought.

At first his friends mocked his verses and interpreted Hamed's many references to the impending loss of their way of life as a lament for a deceased lover. His friends were amused by his poetry, all the more since he responded to their ridicule with even more verses. They were not yet overly concerned. Whenever they saw him, they teased, 'So when are they going to steal the last wave from us?'

They changed their tune the day Uthman Kabashi got up and left, turning his back on all of them.

Uthman had inherited his trade from his shipbuilding father. Like him, Uthman was mild-mannered, tolerant and respectful. He was a man of his word who inspired trust. His trade was confined to selling affordable boats that he brought in from Port Sudan, giving the always cash-strapped fishermen plenty of time to pay for their new vessels. But one fine day without warning, the man whose word was gold reneged on all the contracts. This decision, which so undermined his standing, was made the instant he saw all the heavy earth-moving equipment on the shoreline, preparing to start work on the Palace foundations.

Uthman had close ties to the head fisherman, Sheikh Omar al-Qirsh, who knew his friend's unimpeachable character in matters of business. Sheikh Omar had had no reservations in awarding Uthman contracts to supply the fishermen with waterproof boats that could withstand many years at sea.

'What is going on, Sheikh Omar?' asked Uthman as they took in the swarm of busy machines and labourers on the shore.

'Well, you can see for yourself,' replied Sheikh Omar. 'They say the whole seafront will be reclaimed.'

That night, Uthman met the fishermen and told them he was cancelling all contracts. Faced with an eruption of accusations that he was breaking his word and reneging on his commitments, he tried to reason with them that he was only acting in their best interest. Clearly, he argued, business in this particular trade was about to founder and he did not want to see their meagre resources squandered on buying boats that would never set sail.

42

But his reasoning failed to convince the stubborn fisher-men and so Uthman arranged for a private meeting with his friend Sheikh Omar.

'I'm very sorry,' he told him as he handed him all the advance money he had received for the new boats. 'Please tell everyone how sorry I am.'

The fishermen had planned to lure Uthman to another meeting to pelt him with their turbans and force him to go back on his decision. But their plan was foiled when they caught sight of his huddled figure on a dinghy heading out to rendezvous with a freighter sailing to Port Sudan. Their deeply cherished dreams had evaporated and all that was left for them was to shower Uthman with their curses.

Uthman's fall from grace did not last long, however. The men soon found out for themselves that they were being evicted from their fishing grounds. Long after the land grab, they finally acknowledged the new reality they had to contend with and realised that their beloved fishing spots had as little substance as the bleeding colours of brightly hued turbans floating in the water.

Issa's father, Youssef Radini – or Abu Issa as he was better known – never forgave Uthman for cancelling the contracts, even though he knew Uthman was not to blame for the fishermen's predicament. Abu Issa cursed Uthman to the end of his days, likening the man to a wide-eyed owl – a creature that never sees the light and that jinxes the day when it does.

But after most of the fishermen restored Uthman's good name, they also started to pay attention to Hamed's impro-vised poetry. Their change of heart brought no joy to Hamed.

'We all failed to protect the sea,' he said dismissively as he picked up his nets and tossed them into his skiff. 'Now go find yourselves a new sea if you can.'

A deep slumber descended on the fishermen and a chill blew over the Firepit, leaving residents who lived on the water's edge sedated and numb to the depredation of their land and fishing grounds. They were confident the sea could not be purloined since they thought their multitude of land titles and deeds of sale, duly stamped with thumbprints and tucked away in cupboards, would protect their interests. Their land, whether on the shore or adjacent to it, had been passed down from father to son for generations. But when they showed up with their documents in the halls of justice, they discovered the decree for expropriation had already been issued; flying in every direction, they lodged complaints. All their protests fell on deaf ears. The seafront was parcelled off to the highest bidders and the high and mighty succeeded in hiding the seafront from view.

That long stretch of shore was where neighbourhood folk used to head out at dusk to freshen up and to wash their sheep and cooking utensils. By the time residents awoke from their stupor, their patch of the sea was already buried under hundreds of thousands of tonnes of earth and divided up into valuable plots of real estate and housing developments. None of the carefully preserved deeds confirming their ownership could help them recover the lands of their ancestors. However many complaints and appeals they lodged, their skiffs were once more battered by the high waves on the open sea and all the heavy construction equipment just went on shifting earth, turning water into new land.

The fisherman-poet, Hamed, watched this vast carpeting of the sea with tears in his eyes and redoubled his output of

44

free-flowing verses. But his voice could not compete with the roar of the engines and he watched helplessly as the new concrete jungle was poured over the sea that had given him life and cradled him. When the driver of a bulldozer reached his skiff's mooring spot, Hamed could not bear the sight any longer and he threw himself in front of it. By the time his body could be pulled free, his family had already dug a grave for him at the cemetery.

Hamed died and his death accomplished nothing; no one did anything and the earthworks continued.

Sheikh Omar, the head fisherman, did his best to look for the silver lining on the horizon, beyond the bulldozers, and failed. Sighing heavily, he told his men, 'Our mayor has turned Jeddah into a giant sugar cube and the swarm of flies feasting on it has dried up the sea.'

From there, it was all downhill: the fishermen's moorings, our playgrounds, our swimming spots, all our favourite places, plunged down into the memory hole. We were being eaten alive. Drawn by the bloodletting of our mangled flesh, the sharks came in for the kill. Our playgrounds and swimming spots were stolen, and with them our childhood.

Day after day, the sea was walled in as we lay slumbering. Walls engendered more walls, followed by pavilions and palaces, beach bungalows and amusement parks. Now if we wanted to go swimming, we had to travel a good distance north.

The Palace had taken over our stomping grounds and become the object of everyone's fantasy. It had a hold on our imaginations. Searching for some sliver of shore wide enough to swim in, our patience would be completely exhausted as we circumvented the gargantuan spread of the Palace grounds. Once the towering walls were in place and there were watchful eyes everywhere, we could not walk anywhere near the perimeter of the Palace, nor could we approach the inviting piers beyond.

When we were children, the shoreline was wide open. The sea's endless expanse welcomed our mischievous play and the water buoyed our little bodies as we frolicked until sunset.

But now we had to go further north, and northwards from there, in pursuit of the sea that receded from us every day. Every sunset the sea would release our teenage bodies further up the coast. We would pile into Waleed's car, taking turns drying off with his soggy sarongs. This was how Waleed came by his livelihood. He was able to save up all the money he made transporting us in his decrepit car to the few remaining beaches on the coast that had not been buried under the earthworks.

Waleed was five years older than me and the son of a blind widow who, having lost her husband early, was completely dependent on him. He was resourceful at making money despite leaving school at fifteen.

Transporting us from the neighbourhood to the now remote beaches became a growing source of income since he charged a fee for driving us and for his shabby towels, and also sold water, flavoured drinks and all kinds of food that he had cooked up at noon. Not one to miss a chance, he could always extract another piastre, plying us with a variety of nuts and dried fruit. No sooner did we come upon a good swimming spot than he would be standing before the car peddling his wares and repeating, 'Everything has its price.'

Waleed's mission to part us from the little hard-earned

money we had meant that we could buy on credit so long as we paid him back the following day.

Issa was the only member of our swimming group who was allowed to buy whatever he wanted, paying back whenever he wished. At the time, we did not understand why Issa had such credit privileges and whenever we asked him, he only responded with a throaty chuckle.

This act of favouritism would become clear two years later, when Waleed married Issa's maternal aunt and suckling sister, Salwa.

Salwa proved even shrewder than her husband when it came to generating income. She encouraged him to apply for a bank loan to buy four minivans to transport female teachers to their schools. In time, Waleed's business grew to the extent that we became small fry – a distant memory for him that was as tattered as his towels.

During our childhood we were never absent from the shore for long. Our access was blocked only after the city began drowning in a flood of money, and everyone – individuals and companies alike – scrambled to suck on the udder of pumped-up riches. When plain sucking was no longer enough, those with a good eye scooped up everything in their path, guzzling, mauling and burying along the way.

While all this daylight robbery was taking place, the people of our neighbourhood turned a blind eye and used their pent-up dreams as new ornaments on a shrine. Only a small minority transformed their dreams into reality: one of our schoolmates started a real-estate business, and from there went into leasing and contracting, leaving us far behind.

Even those who made good did, for the most part, what their fathers had done before them, staying put and shuffling around the walls of the old neighbourhood. Blinded by pay increases, they used their spare cash on such petty pleasures as travelling abroad and acquiring what had been beyond their means previously.

In those days, developers were grabbing up vacant lots and abandoned properties everywhere. The more devious ones among them managed to reclaim the sea, thereby acquiring vast tracts of untitled land in what was tantamount to theft.

We were too young to understand what was happening. What infuriated *us* were those walls that blocked our access to the sea and prevented us from floating on the vast expanse of water.

The towering walls sprang up and caught us napping, and when we went looking for that vast expanse we found that not one bit of it remained ours. In its place, palatial villas vied with each other for yet more of the seawater, jostling to be closest to the Palace itself.

This was how, seemingly overnight, as if emerging from a collective sleep, everyone in the neighbourhood was infected with a single, overarching dream: to enter the Palace or, at the very least, to stand before its majestic gateway.

This desire naturally peaked when news started to spread that Issa had found a way into the Palace and that, moreover, he could usher in all of us who wanted, myself included.

To this day, people squat outside the Palace, dreaming of gaining entry; here I am, body and soul submerged in the sea's embrace yet again, longing for a way out of Paradise!

The alarm went off in the east wing of the Palace, warning of the presence of intruders. I immediately thought that news about the impending New Year's celebration had leaked, tempting uninvited guests to risk gate-crashing the party.

The extravaganza was planned in the external gardens directly overlooking the waterfront. The spot was chosen because it was cooler and less humid there and also to accommodate the large number of guests and provide sufficient space for the many performers hired for the evening's entertainment. While male and female celebrities from all across the Arab world had been sent invitations, few were actually aware of the real reason for the party.

New Year's Eve happened to coincide with Maram's birthday, and the Master of the Palace had moved heaven and earth to ensure a fabulous event for that occasion. Maram was the Master's new lover and he was so besotted with her that he had even named his yacht *The Dazzling Beauty* after his endearment for her.

News had spread of the arrival of female performers and dancers, which encouraged uninvited guests to try their luck at the gates. They were further tempted by the fact that the main gates were undergoing renovations. In the wake of a terrorist attack on the US embassy, the whole design was being changed to increase security; the gates would open by retracting below ground and shut by drawing up mechanically to form an impregnable wall. Eventually, the new gates would have the added advantage of being electrified.

The blaring alarm alerted three Filipino guards, who came running with their dogs. They combed the area just across from the front of the Palace, but were having to goad their dogs constantly. Despite being a particularly vicious European breed, the dogs were altogether rather passive – a fact not lost on Hassan Darbeel, who was in charge of the Palace kennels.

As their supervisor, he berated the trainers harshly, blaming them for the dogs' diminished hounding instincts.

'Haven't I told you to stop fattening up the dogs?' Hassan shouted. 'Look at them – giving up on the job they were brought here for!' He barked for one of his assistants to fetch the Saluki dogs he himself had trained. 'No one knows the smell of the locals as well as the local dogs!'

Hassan started to laugh, and then coughed and sputtered since he had just inhaled a lungful of cigarette smoke. He recovered his composure by the time his Salukis came into view, yapping and snarling as they made their way towards the east wing, leaping sprily and gracefully over a railing.

Hassan was no longer coughing and could therefore chime in with his howling dogs as they sniffed the air for intruders.

The snarling Salukis alerted the would-be gate-crashers, who took to their heels before being caught. No one wished to share the fate of the boy from the neighbourhood who was imprisoned for an entire year for climbing the Palace wall.

'*Akh*,' Hassan said to himself. 'A new crop of dreamers.'

His love for the local breed stemmed from childhood. People who knew Hassan had trouble believing his position at the Palace. Before, he had literally been in the rubbish dump, ragged and quarrelsome. Cast there by the vicissitudes of life, he had reached the point of going through refuse and discarded junk for something he could salvage and sell, and to retrieve the rotting remnants of a meal to feed his dogs.

At that time, labourers were beginning work on building the embankments that would surround the Palace, and a corrugated tin fence had been erected that hid the sea from view. Driven from their waters, the fishermen had hauled their boats in and beached them against their houses, waiting for the moment they would be allowed to set sail again. In the meantime, they entertained themselves by spinning yarns and dredging up memories of their seafaring lives.

Saleem Baygheeni was both a fisherman and a maker of fishing nets. His life had turned topsy-turvy and there was nothing he could do about it. He sat in his single room, examining his fishing nets and knotting the ones that needed tightening, even though there were no takers for them any more. He was not interested in trying his hand at another trade, so he remained the maker of nets he had always been and waited for the fishermen to set sail again.

When he realised that the old fishing days were truly dead, he began to pine for the sea with the same anguish as Hamed. But unlike the dead fisherman-poet, who had to be dug up from under a pile of earth, Saleem chose to die in his old fishing grounds at sea.

On his first attempt to set sail, he was forcibly prevented by the guards stationed on the shore since he was contravening a regulation that banned all boats on that stretch. After several unsuccessful attempts, he finally found a way to outwit the guards by making himself invisible. He painted his skiff black, put on black clothes and set out in the dead of night, returning before daybreak. This went on night after night, until one fine morning he was found floating like a piece of regurgitated cork, tossed by the waves against the concrete of the embankments. His bloated corpse was spotted by labourers working on the construction site after it got snared on the metal girders protruding from the concrete. They raised the alarm, fished his remains out and swiftly disposed of him in a grave that was large enough to accommodate the horrific bloating.

Death is not always noteworthy. The death of a dog, a cat or an anonymous person does not cry out for the attention of the living.

The day following Saleem's death dawned much like the day before it. Busy and exhausted labourers raced against the clock to meet the Master's deadline for completing the construction project, while neighbourhood residents watched as sand mixes were poured and support columns were raised across from the corrugated tin fence. The din of heavy construction equipment permeated the days, which dragged at a snail's pace.

At night the drab darkness was infused with a dash of colour: people became familiar and convivial, and laughter rang out among the fishermen, drunks and other revellers. Some people were glued to their televisions while others played dominoes or backgammon, slamming the pieces against wooden boards. Everyone had their own problems and though they were uninterested in predicting the future, they kept their ears open for any morsel of news from which to weave a new yarn and pass the time.

They felt mildly concerned about Saleem's death, but pushed out of mind its ominous circumstances. They did take note, however, when Hassan remarked that the nightly clamour of the neighbourhood was oddly devoid of barking.

Ordinarily, the nights were filled with dogs roaming in packs through the alleyways and rubbish heaps, yowling and barking at each other or at anyone who came out to drive them away or chase them for sport.

Hassan was the only person who cared about the strays and

52

he tried to train them with compassion. Some people claimed that one of the bitches had nursed him with her pups after his mother gave up on him, exhausted from having nursed ten boys before him. This, they said, explained both his bluntness and his speech peppered with barking and yelping sounds. He only ever liked playing with the strays and, back in those days, it was common to find him wandering the alleyways with a pack of dogs in tow, following his every command.

He would start his days with these dogs. Rounding them up from all over the neighbourhood in the early morning, he would set out with them to the meat and vegetable market where he begged the butchers for scraps or offal that no customer could possibly want, packing whatever they gave him into a large cardboard box. Then, with his suckling brothers taken care of, he would head off to work in a carpentry workshop. He also ended his days with the dogs, devoting every evening to them as he accompanied them on their nightly rounds of the neighbourhood. Moreover, every week, he set aside two days to take them to the beach, where he bathed them with unstinting care and devotion.

No one dared to harm Hassan or make fun of him. He only had to give the signal and a pack of half-starved Salukis would pounce on the offender.

Hassan immediately noticed that there were fewer dogs in the neighbourhood and that their nightly barking had diminished. The loss of his companions dealt him a succession of blows and he was the only one concerned enough to get to the bottom of the mysterious disappearance.

At that time, Issa had not yet left and was still tearing around the neighbourhood frightening the more timid among us. He was accused of using the dogs to break into abandoned houses and old people's homes. He was even arrested one night and taken to the police station to be charged with stealing an old woman's jewellery, after she reported the theft and claimed to hear barking dogs. Seconds before the lashes from a policeman's cane could begin to extract a confession, news came from the old woman that she remembered she had stashed her gold at her niece's house, precisely to guard against theft.

With that, Issa picked up the undershirt that had just been yanked off him, put it back on and stormed out of the police station fuming and vowing to get even. There were actually two charges: robbery as well as dog-snatching, with intent of larceny. Until the case of the missing Salukis was solved, Issa and Hassan had a series of altercations. They remained sworn enemies until the identity of the dog-snatchers became known and Hassan offered Issa a sweeping apology.

Hundreds of tonnes of cement, steel, wood and breeze blocks, as well as heavy construction equipment lined the shore in readiness for the embankments that would block off the seafront, and an army of workers prepared to start work on construction of the Palace.

The boys of the neighbourhood began to sneak into the construction site to play hide-and-seek, much to the annoyance of the labourers who constantly grumbled in an incomprehensible language. The workers had narrow eyes, broad faces and flat noses, and their spiky black hair stood straight up on their heads like sharp, shiny pins. Their deep-sunk eyes did not light up even when they smiled.

As he went out to wash his dogs and clean whatever bits of refuse had stuck to their coats, Hassan befriended a few of the workers and came back from a grooming session one night howling with dismay.

'The Koreans are eating the dogs!' he moaned.

No one believed him and, in any case, people in the neighbourhood were not overly upset by the declining number of dogs; on the contrary, they were glad for the more tranquil nights.

'The Korean workers catch them and then slaughter them and eat them,' exclaimed Hassan. 'I saw them with my own eyes!' He was filled with mixed emotions since, despite the horrible truth about the dogs, it did at least exonerate his neighbourhood friend from the dog-snatching accusations. 'We were so wrong about Issa Radini,' he said.

'Dogs disappear and other dogs appear,' one man shrugged. Issa had acquired a bad reputation well before the first Saluki ended up on someone's plate.

With the dog numbers in decline and the labourers buried in the embankment work, rumours began spreading that they were building a corral for taming wild horses. Many of the people of the neighbourhood fell prey to this rumour and took up new, equestrian-related occupations. All of a sudden there were coachmen and harness-makers, fodder merchants and saddlers. Some people even went off to Sudan or Egypt to learn how to become groomers and trainers, and with the departure of the equestrian hopefuls and their trades, an economic slump struck the neighbourhood.

On their return, the equestrian migrants set up behind the corrugated tin fence that stretched as far as the eye could see and hid everything on the other side, and simply waited for the arrival of the horses to start on their new occupations.

Finally, after three years of continuous construction work,

the fence was peeled away and discarded to reveal the magnificent Palace.

Anticipating the imminent arrival of the horses, groups of men took turns waiting along the road leading up to the Palace gates. Every day that passed whittled away a little more of their patience.

The horses finally appeared one day and were installed in custom-built stables. But along with the horses came professional groomers and handlers, and the hopefuls of the neighbourhood were expelled from the approaches of the Palace, moaning and complaining.

Downcast, they resumed their former trades but still lived in their fantasies. Whenever they heard a horse neigh, they rushed over to the Palace, believing their services would now be needed. They returned even more downcast and dispirited.

With the corrugated tin fence gone, Firepit residents would stand in wide-eyed amazement at the dazzling splendour of the Palace. However, that moment of awe was fleeting as a new batch of Palace guards was always there to push them roughly away.

This was how the Palace became the main topic of every conversation in the neighbourhood, fuelling every dream – even though not one of these men had set foot inside it. The closest they ever got was to the wide plaza in front of the Palace, and on the basis of that experience alone they would return with fantastical tales of the strange and the miraculous. They told of prancing horses whose sheer number impeded access to the gates and of gardens lush with trees and fruits never before seen. They described brooks that fed into a stream as wide as a river, which in turn ran through orchards divided into sections with all the varieties of fruit trees planted in neat rows.

This last description was too much for some people. 'Rivers in the middle of the sea?' someone cried with disbelief. 'Are you crazy?'

But they swore to God that the Palace had a river flowing through its grounds and that money worked wonders.

The descriptions of the Palace would have ended there had it not been for a group of boys from the neighbourhood who wormed their way in, determined to bask in its radiance. Some of them were given short-term jobs that ended once they had completed the assigned task.

Then, one day, even that trickle of eyewitnesses dried up when residents of the neighbourhood awoke to discover they were expressly banned from ever setting foot in the Palace plaza. This decree was issued shortly after the Master learned that supervisors had been recruiting local men to do some cleaning jobs, water the gardens and prune the trees. He forbade them to employ anyone who had a national identity card — that is, a local — without his express and personal permission.

The Palace staff and servants were brought in from all corners of the world, while the locals looking for work were stopped from even reaching the main gates. This did not deter Issa. He vowed not only to get into the Palace, but also to take with him whomever he pleased from the neighbourhood.

His words were invariably met with ridicule, which only made him more determined and belligerent. 'Mock me now,' he countered, 'and the only way you'll enter Paradise is by grovelling on your knees.'

Those were the days before they walled off the shore – before, that is, our yearning to enter the Palace had permeated every fibre of our being. Back then, we had not yet lost our greatest pleasure: simply throwing off our clothes and plunging into the deep.

4

SHEIKH OMAR STEPPED ON to the deck of *The Dazzling Beauty* and was assaulted with questions about when the yacht would set sail.

'Just as soon as I get my instructions,' he replied curtly, straining to hold himself in check.

He was not accustomed to taking orders. His venerated position as head fisherman had not prepared him for this state of indecision, which was like a slap in the face. Where was his booming voice now? Where was the unquestioned authority of his word among his fellow fisherman after he succeeded his father as their leader?

His father had groomed him for the succession, providing him with advice and a breadth of experience that far exceeded his years, which served him well when he staked his claim to become the leader of the group. Even though his peers thought him too young for the position, he had followed his father's directives so well that he quickly won everyone's respect.

But now, instead of giving orders he was following them, reduced to a mere link in a chain of petty managers under the Master's thumb. Disgusted with his situation, Sheikh Omar did not feel he had a shred of self-respect left. On any given day, he found himself tolerating things he would never have dreamed of putting up with even hours earlier. He blamed Issa Radini for the humiliation he now endured and no words were vulgar enough to curse that man.

Another guest asked him when they would set sail.

'Just as soon as I get my instructions,' he repeated, sighing with exasperation.

'And when do you get your instructions?' persisted the guest.

Sheikh Omar detected a hint of insolence. 'If the Master heard you talk like that, he'd soon make sure you never asked another question.'

He left the deck and returned to the captain's cabin, closing the door behind him and shutting out the sound of the tinkling laughter and bubbling conversations of men and women mingling together as light music played in the background.

It was hard to believe that the scene on the boat was taking place. Women without abayas or modesty revealed their alabaster endowments with such nonchalance. Servants scurried with bottles of every shape and colour to fill glasses with liquor, while dancers swayed provocatively to lessen the boredom of the long wait. The dancers stopped only after being told to conserve their energy for the long night ahead.

This display of flesh and decadence upset Sheikh Omar intensely. He muttered under his breath as he moved among the mingling guests with his head down and his eyes averted. At times he even stopped up his ears with his fingers and barricaded himself inside the captain's cabin. His demeanour was openly disapproving except when the Master was on board. Sheikh Omar would then feign enjoyment and sway to the tunes of old favourites played by the musical ensembles that animated Palace parties.

He had recently been promoted to captain of *The Dazzling Beauty* and also supervised game-fishing expeditions. This was as a result of the successful hunting trip in the Guinean jungle that he had organised the previous summer and for which he could thank his old friend, Uthman Kabashi. After cancelling the contracts to supply the fishermen with boats and before setting sail for Port Sudan, Uthman had commended him highly to the Master, planting the idea that Sheikh Omar should be given the responsibility of organising hunting expeditions in and around Sudan.

The submissive life he now led daily had all but destroyed the man of his youth. Sheikh Omar found solace only in people who, like him, had deep roots in a purer and simpler past and with whom he could share the shame of being sullied, at the end of their lives, with such dishonourable tasks.

Given the security hiccup with the would-be gate-crashers at the previous New Year's Eve party, this year's venue had shifted from dry land to the open sea aboard *The Dazzling Beauty*. Guests, screened in the Palace lobby to avoid letting on board anyone deemed undesirable by the Master, gathered on the yacht early to secure the best spots.

The yacht was anchored across from the recently built golf course that covered an entire islet.

Before the Palace was ever built, there were many such islets. In our teens, we would head to them to catch our breath after a long swim or to fish from their rocky reefs. Every evening as the last rays of the dying sun cast their shadowy beams on the islets, we hurried to end our games and head back to shore, guided by the feeble light from our homes. We stashed freshwater and tinned food on the islets so that there was always something to eat and drink for whoever

swam there next. We did this in a spontaneous and uncoordin-
ated way; it was like an unspoken agreement among us.
Unwittingly, we were perpetuating the ancient mariners'
practice of providing succour to anyone stranded at sea.

Generally speaking, the islets were visited only by strong
swimmers and fishermen. For the small group of us who were
able to swim to them, the islets became the markers by which
we measured our long-distance ability, the sites for many of
our games and our fishing grounds. The narrow passages
between the dense coral reefs became denser the deeper one
went, and by laying out our nets close together along those
passages we would easily trap entire schools of fish.

We also swam out to the islets whenever we needed to hide
or take refuge after a fight. The islets had been there since time
immemorial, and their deep crevices had lain undisturbed by
the crashing of the waves and the comings and goings of humans
through the ages. According to the old fishermen's tales, which
still filled us with wonder in those days, anyone who fell into
one of the crevices would never again be seen.

Issa claimed he had spent two days and three nights inside
one of the crevices, hiding from his father. Whether he did or
not was debatable, but he certainly emerged more scurrilous
than ever. And something did happen out there that would
change all our destinies.

Issa had stolen all of his grandmother's savings, which she
had set aside for the Hajj pilgrimage that year, and used the
money to buy himself a donkey to go rabbit-hunting in the
wadis east of Jeddah. His younger sister discovered the theft
and told on him to their father, Abu Issa, who swore that
Satan himself had not conceived the kind of punishment he
would inflict on his son.

When Issa realised he had been found out, he abandoned the donkey and made himself scarce.

Abu Issa retrieved the donkey, sold it for piastres at the souk and, returning home, became determined to teach his son a lesson he would never forget, a punishment that would for ever impress on the boy the fate reserved for thieves. He settled on the idea of sending his mother on the Hajj riding his son's back. This thought appealed to him so much that he laughed all the way home, tickled merely by the picture of his mother sitting astride Issa's shoulders, her legs dangling off his back.

However, by the time he reached the house, the idea had lost some of its appeal and he wondered whether, rather than carrying her on the Hajj, Issa should just be made to bend over and walk back and forth between the house and the municipal parking lot with his grandmother on his back.

In the end, he thought better of that too, and decided Issa should simply carry his grandmother one trip the length of their street. Issa's father settled contentedly on this punishment.

When Issa came home, his mother warned him his father was furious, especially since the money for the donkey had not even come close to the original amount Issa had pinched. His mother, known as Umm Issa, suggested that it might be better to wait for his father out in the street rather than confront him in the house so that a neighbour might take pity on him and come to protect him from his father's wrath.

Issa decided there and then to run off and hide on the islet called Umm al-Qumari.

He was hurrying down the street when he heard his father roar, 'Don't you dare run away!'

Issa spun around and stepped back instinctively. 'You're going to hit me,' he said with alarm.

'No, I am not going to hit you,' replied Abu Issa sternly. 'But I am going to punish you.'

'Punish me?'

'That's right. I've sworn that your grandmother will be going on the Hajj riding on your back.'

'And you think I'm crazy enough to let your fat mother go to the Hajj on my back?'

'Shame on you,' his father shouted. 'Don't you dare talk like that about your grandmother.'

'Yes, she's my grandmother. So I'm supposed to carry her and break my back?' Issa stood a safe distance away even though he knew he could easily outrun his father. 'If you're so concerned about your mother going on the Hajj,' he added, 'why don't you carry her on *your* back?' His legs were ready for flight and he glanced around quickly to stake out the best escape route.

'Where's the money you stole?'

'You already know I bought a donkey with it.'

'Why bother when you're already such an ass?'

'Yeah, and another ass sold the donkey for less than it was worth, huh!'

At this brazen rejoinder, Abu Issa could no longer contain himself and he lunged at his son, who dodged and jumped up on to a wall by a neighbour's house. From his perch, Issa decided to change tactic and apologise.

But his father was too angry to listen to Issa's pleas. 'By God,' he fumed, 'I'll see your grandmother make the Hajj on that back of yours if it kills me!'

At this point, Issa was also playing to an audience, pleading for mercy in the hope of drumming up sympathy from the crowd that had gathered. '*Ya Sheikh*,' he begged, choosing the term of respect like a dutiful son. 'Have some pity. It would kill *me*. My grandmother is heavy enough to break a camel's back!'

Abu Issa was not amused. He ordered his son to come down off the wall and when he failed to comply, he reached down to pick up some stones which he threw at his boy.

Issa hopped down to the other side of the wall and disappeared.

Abu Issa returned home, his blood boiling, swearing that he would show the boy what was what as soon as he could lay his hands on him.

Umm Issa was annoyed with her husband. 'You won't be satisfied until we lose him, will you?' she asked accusingly.

Issa was gone for two days and three nights, hiding out – he claimed – in one of the islet's crevices and setting in motion a chain of events that would determine all our destinies.

Finally, driven by thirst and hunger, he swam ashore and, standing dripping wet before his family, he said to his father, 'I'll carry your mother to the Hajj for the next two years.'

'Son of a gun!' exclaimed Abu Issa, desperately relieved to see his son. But he had to show his displeasure, so he added, 'Where've you been hiding?'

'I was waiting,' replied Issa. 'I waited for Grandma, but she never showed up.'

At this, the grandmother burst out laughing and Issa bent over and told her to climb on. 'Hurry up now, Grandma, your donkey is waiting.'

She pounded her hands on his back, overcome with mirth. She was as amused by the thought of riding her grandson to the holy sites as by the idea of going on the Hajj in the wrong month. 'Do you honestly expect me to go on the Hajj in *Sha'aban*, you dolt?'

'Who cares about the month?' Abu Issa said seriously. 'What's important is that I keep my word.'

The grandmother said nothing and Issa stayed bent in half.

'Just hop on his back and he'll take you to the end of the street and back.'

Since she hesitated, Issa took the initiative, darting in between her legs and hoisting her up on to his shoulders, which almost caused her to fall flat on her face.

Abu Issa rushed to steady her and then, grabbing a thick cane, he set about thrashing his son.

The boy screamed and hollered.

Salwa, Issa's aunt and suckling sister, burst into tears and added her voice to his, crying for someone to come and save Issa from the caning that had already lacerated his back.

No one in the neighbourhood could believe that Issa had spent three days hiding in the crevices of the islets slumbering on the surface of the sea. But from then on, the crevices became our refuge, a secret place of solace and comfort. We would sneak into them, too old now to be scared by fishermen's tales or to listen to our mothers' dire warnings. Our mothers held that the crevices sheltered only wayward and rebellious spirits, the unfortunate souls destined to endure the miseries and agonies of both this world and the next. With every passing day, we – the neighbourhood ruffians – sneaked into those crevices in growing numbers.

The largest of the islets, Umm al-Qumari, was the first to fall victim to the Palace's need for ever more space to expand its dominion. After it was reclaimed as a marina, it became the anchorage of *The Dazzling Beauty,* the most luxurious of the yachts anchored there by Jeddah's business elite. From the marina, yacht owners ran regattas, threw raucous parties and set off fireworks. To the oldest residents of the Firepit, Umm al-Qumari remained a landmark, the springboard from which their most rebellious children had learned to jump.

Piloted by Sheikh Omar, *The Dazzling Beauty* set out on its excursion two hours later than scheduled. The guests were unable to disembark or even change places during that time for fear of provoking the organisers, and everyone now knew better than to ask the ship's captain the reason for the delay.

The Master had appeared at the appointed departure time, only to retreat to his cabin where he could unleash his fury, unobserved.

I was at the receiving end of his profanities over the interphone.

'Where is Maram?' he barked irately.

The fact that I did not know did not stem the tidal wave of obscenities.

'I'll fix you later, and *then* you'll be sure to know how to do your job.'

A good many phone calls had to be made before Maram finally emerged from the Palace and, as soon as she stepped on board, the Master dashed over, grabbed her hand and led her directly to his cabin. Despite speaking in hushed tones, his features clearly revealed the extent of his exasperation at the wait he had endured.

Only Maram could still ignite such passion in his otherwise cold and lifeless body.

She was his dazzling beauty.

Until her arrival at the Palace, the Master would spend every night in the company of a different girl.

All that changed with Maram. After just one night in her company at the last New Year's Eve party, he could no longer bear to carouse if Maram was not there with him, at the centre of the gathering.

Before her, he had spent New Year's Eve in Geneva or Madrid or on the French Riviera, but after meeting Maram he lost all interest in travelling to distant places. Now, wherever he went, she had to go, too.

Until Maram stepped into the Master's life, he had needed a steady supply of new girls, deploying teams of scouts across the city to pimp for him. At the head of each team there was always an achingly handsome young man who sweet-talked nubile girls with amorous banter.

The love games were practised with an old whore who had been the Master's lover when he was young. Having grown bored of her, both in body and spirit, she was nonetheless able to strike a deal whereby he promised not to discard her if she, in return, kept him supplied with young women to invigorate his jaded appetites. She spent her last years catering to his whims and dedicated herself untiringly to procuring all kinds of girls, whether she knew them personally or not.

The Palace staff never used her real name and only referred to her as 'Madame'. When it became my job to hand out payments to the young women who were in charge of the entertainment at the parties, I'd try and spot Madame among the women parading themselves before the revellers.

Before the teams of young pimps were deployed through the souks of the city, it had been her job to scout for girls. She would go out every night accompanied by two black women who walked behind her and referred to her as the *Sheikha*, implying noble lineage.

She spoke little and with a mere gesture could convey to her assistants when her observation should be interpreted as a command. Her bearing was such that people did her bidding unquestioningly. At every stop they made through the souks, people whispered with excitement, 'The *Sheikha* is coming' or 'The *Sheikha* is leaving.'

She made the rounds in places known to throng with young women such as weddings and malls, and enticed them with descriptions of fairytale nights at the Palace where they would be safe from scrutiny or detention by the ubiquitous religious police – the roving squads from the Commission for the Promotion of Virtue and Prevention of Vice.

For a while I even entertained the thought that Madame might be none other than Tahani. I was haunted by Tahani's words to me those years ago: 'I'll never leave you. Wherever you go, I'll be there.' I became obsessed with meeting Madame.

In all, there were three women who were involved with procuring a steady supply of nubile young women to Palace parties; they also trained the young men in the best approaches to lure girls and ensnare the more difficult ones.

Osama was trained by a woman who had worked Beirut's nightclub scene until the Israeli siege of the city in 1982, when the Master extended her indefinite hospitality at the Palace. Cosseted in luxury and accolades, she groomed Osama in the arcane art of luring women. He became very successful and always came back from his forays with freshly caught game still rosy with life.

Osama had reeled Maram, the dazzling beauty, into the Palace, like countless women before her and since. He had set his sights on her but had not imagined the Master would be so captivated by her good looks that he would be unable to let go. It was not the first time a woman had entranced the Master, and those who knew him well had believed Maram would go the way of all the others – seduced one day, discarded the next. They were totally confounded when Maram breathed new life into him.

From the minute I first laid eyes on her, I too was bewitched.

5

ISSA ESCAPED FROM THE Firepit and only returned to smuggle the rest of us into Paradise. I was among the first victims of this human trafficking.

Bound together by a miserable childhood, Issa, Osama and I were foul-mouthed children. For those we regarded as opponents, no obscenity or profanity was too vile or hurtful, no sarcasm too biting. The neighbourhood folk avoided us and then shunned us altogether. Although we came from decent families, we were regarded as deviants who had strayed so far from the norms of decency that we had become unredeemable.

Osama's father, Muhammad al-Bushri, periodically left his family to pursue his livelihood as a pilgrimage guide – a *mutawwaf* – in Mecca. Whether for the Hajj or the lesser pilgrimage, the Umrah, he welcomed the pilgrims at Bab Ismail, accompanied them on their seven circumambulations of the Kaaba, and was grateful for whatever munificence they bestowed on him. In the evenings, he repaired to a café inside a small souk and quickly went to sleep so as to be up bright and early to welcome the pilgrims after dawn prayers and get a head start on earning his living.

Muhammad had grown accustomed to being away from

71

his family, disappearing for a week and sometimes two weeks at a time. When he came home, he would soak his swollen feet in warm saltwater and his wife would massage his feet and relieve him of the discomfort from the long hours he spent on them. He would fall asleep groaning with relief. In fact, when Osama's father was home, he spent most of his time lying in bed to rest and recuperate.

It was on one such trip to Mecca that Muhammad lost his life to a random bullet in the courtyard of the Kaaba. A self-proclaimed Mahdi and his band of heavily armed men chose the dawn of a new century in the Islamic calendar – 1 *Muharram* 1400 AH – to take control of the entire site, and Muhammad al-Bushri was one of the many victims to fall that day. His was killed trying to escape from the holy sanctuary after refusing to pledge allegiance to the Mahdi, who would meet his own death three days later.

Muhammad's family received no compensation or blood money for his death, so Osama's only inheritance was the *ihram* clothing his father had worn to perform the circumam-bulations and a few religious books. Among these was a book of prayers that Muhammad had known by heart and that his son could not even begin to decipher.

Osama's mother had wanted her son to inherit the mantle of pilgrimage guide. But her wish was never realised because the senior *mutawwafs* ranged themselves against Osama on the grounds that he was too young, wayward and unruly. While his forehead bore the black mark from frequent prostration, they felt his conduct had not exhibited the requisite reverence for such a holy place.

The first day Osama donned his father's *ihram* clothing and performed the seven circumambulations of the Kaaba, he had not even bothered to tame his head of hair. He actually welcomed the pilgrims with words that were too abominable to repeat. His transgressions were reported to the head guide, who grabbed Osama and dragged him away from the Yemeni corner of the Kaaba, warning that he never wanted to lay eyes on him again. Osama had scuttled his mother's plans for his future. He left Mecca and returned to the neighbourhood and to a life of vice. He did so surreptitiously, in order to maintain a reputation for piety that he had attempted to cultivate to appease his mother after being expelled from school over a porn magazine scandal. At the time his mother had promised that if he mended his ways, she would betroth him to her niece, the beautiful Tahani.

Osama had a proclivity for fair-skinned boys. In pursuing them, he was imitating the neighbourhood's old pederasts and also joining their ranks. The wizened old wolves still stalked him in the dark alleyways and he was so dashingly handsome that after his father's death even the head fisherman, Sheikh Omar, made a pass at him. But Osama knew the old men and their tricks, and he refused their gifts.

Sheikh Omar was undeterred and he persisted until one day, after the sunset prayers, Osama grabbed the microphone in the mosque and, in front of the entire congregation, warned the man to keep his hands off him. Sheikh Omar was stunned and, despite repeated attempts to clear his name, his reputation was for ever ruined.

Later, Sheikh Omar approached Osama and tried to explain that his overtures had been misinterpreted – they were purely honourable, sanctioned even, given the heavenly reward promised to those who provided succour to orphans. But Osama's allegation and public warning caused a lasting rift

73

between the head fisherman and the rest of the community.

Just as Sheikh Omar had pursued him furtively, so too did Osama resort to subterfuge in his pursuit of boys younger than he. He had taken to shaving long before the incident with the fisherman in order to appear older and fend off the pederasts. By the time he was twelve, his moustache and beard were already growing out.

Osama was expelled from his first school for being what school officials called a 'depraved member of society'. He was caught distributing porn magazines to his classmates by the school janitor, Gebreel Musa, who had been asked to keep an eye on the boy. Gebreel offered Osama the use of his quarters in the school as a safe hiding place for the magazines in case of a surprise search. Later that week, at the first signs a search was in progress, Osama dashed over to Gebreel and, extracting sixteen full-colour porn magazines from his schoolbag, he handed them over to the janitor for safekeeping. Gebreel proceeded to take them straight to the headmaster.

Osama would probably have stayed in school were it not for the worst caning he received in his young life and for the fact that the disgrace was made public. The students were made to line up in the courtyard while the headmaster gave a scathing speech about him over the public address system, thereby broadcasting the scandal to every house in the neighbourhood. Before the froth on his lips had dried, the headmaster got Gebreel and a teacher to hold Osama in place, and reached for his cane.

Three whipping canes were broken on the soles of Osama's feet that day, and Osama vowed he would get back at Gebreel at the first opportunity.

As a child, Osama was stuck to Tahani and she led him on, even though she was four years younger. However, when she was not around, he clung to her older brother instead. With his father habitually absent in Mecca, Osama learned all the secret ways to crush a man's virility in the alleyways of the neighbourhood and decided early on to join the ranks of the predators rather than the prey.

The three of us – Osama, Issa and I – broke all the rules and violated all the taboos in the crevices of that islet. It was the launching pad to the slippery paths that all three of us followed, in lives dedicated to the single-minded pursuit of pleasure and sensual gratification.

Despite our delinquency, the three of us managed to get through school. It was generally accepted that the school examiners had been lenient in passing us, year after year, even though our marks were the lowest possible in nearly every subject.

Osama's marks actually improved after he was expelled from his first school. As he started in his new school, he did not try to deny the porn magazine scandal that had preceded him there. On the contrary, he went to great lengths to appear contrite and remorseful, going so far as to rub his forehead in the sand for hours in order to acquire the tell-tale black mark on the brow and dupe people into thinking he spent his spare time prostrated in assiduous prayer.

As further signs of his newfound fervour, he let his beard grow out, shortened his thobe to reach the middle of his calf and, from his first day at the new school, took on the responsibility of reciting the noon prayer, intoning the call to prayer himself. This show of zeal won him the mentorship of the assistant headmaster, who put him in charge of the school's religious education club. This also impressed his teachers, who gave him extra credit for his participation in the club and who, subsequently, over-looked what should have been a complete failure in the final oral examination. Utterly stumped, Osama had been unable to answer a single question.

When the results were announced, we sat together under the loudspeaker as the names of the graduating students were reeled off to the sound of loud cheering everywhere. We could not believe it when we heard the amplified voice – hesitant and straining as if to swallow a mouthful of mud – call out our three names.

That night, Osama and I became mortal rivals. Puffed up with pride, we sowed the seeds of hatred for one other.

The successful graduates spilled out on to the streets, passing out fizzy drinks to everyone, friends and strangers alike. Cheers rang out across the neighbourhood. From their windows, the mothers of graduating students showered the streets below with sweets and nuts to the sound of *zaghroutas*.

My own successful graduation was a rare opportunity for me to see my mother happy. She hugged me and babbled phrases I could not quite understand. My father was away with his third wife, and Aunt Khayriyyah, who was washing some underwear, cocked her face to one side and exclaimed, 'Even muddy balls will roll.'

Aunt Khayriyyah still believed that all my actions were evil and even on my graduation day, she had nothing kind to say about my success. While I did not expect any ululations from my aunt, I had hoped for a *zaghrouta* from my mother – but our home was tight-fisted in matters of celebration.

76

So I left them and went looking for Tahani, hoping she at least could provide some cheer. I stood in front of her house and looked up at her open window, squinting to see a shape behind the lattice screen. But she was not there.

I could see her mother and her aunt leaning out of another window, busy throwing sweets and nuts and ululating above Osama's head. As my attention turned to the children who had gathered on the street and were rushing to catch the sweets, I spotted her.

Tahani darted out the front door and, right under the noses of her female relatives, came to stand next to Osama. He turned, leaned in towards her and whispered something in her ear which caused her to burst out laughing.

That day I realised how much I hated Osama.

When the three of us met up later in the day, we teased each other about graduating and even mocked former class-mates who came to congratulate us. But I was not really with them; my mind kept re-enacting a succession of images – the empty window and Tahani laughing with another boy.

Osama had become my rival. He, too, wanted her and now, as the images were seared in my mind, I could no longer be sure which of us was the intended recipient of her coy smiles and surreptitious gestures.

Gnawed with doubt, I avoided Tahani in the days follow-ing our graduation. But one night she tossed a cassette in my path, a compilation of songs by the popular Egyptian diva, Najat al-Saghira. Attached to the tape was a brief note that read:

Darling Tariq,
Life without you is without taste and without flavour.

Don't deprive me of you.
I am so happy at your success – a million congratulations!
You've graduated and you're going to start university.
Our dreams will come true.
I love you maaaaaaaaaaadly.
Don't deprive me of you.
Here's hoping ………..……….. (fill in the blank!)
Your sweetheart for ever,
Tahani
Love of my life, I will always love you, Tahani.

Before the country became awash with money, and residents of the old neighbourhood broke with their old ways, evenings in the Firepit had been lively.

The Palace was the watershed in our lives. It marked a point in time, the transition of an era – from 'before' to 'after' – as surely as any calendar. Whenever the older generation recounted our history, they would make clear the period by appending 'before the Palace was built' or 'after the Palace was built'.

Before the Palace was built, people would roam through the neighbourhood in search of any available distraction. The women devised celebrations and other occasions to get together; the men congregated at local hang-outs and told the same old stories, alternating between laughing and crying as they reminisced about their youth; the children ran around the alleyways looking for open spaces in which to play.

As for us, the teenagers, we kept watch on street corners for glimpses of feminine charm. The young girls of the neighbourhood were coming of age and their womanly attributes were becoming ripe for plucking, if only with our eyes.

However insignificant the occasion, our evenings were festive. Always ready for the next adventure, I would slip away from view of Aunt Khayriyyah's lattice-screen window, escaping both her spiteful tongue and her beady eyes.

It was as if she had a sixth sense about me.

She seemed to know what I was up to from the time I was knee-high to a grasshopper. The very first time I sneaked into my father's room to rummage through his pockets, she caught me before I could savour the triumph of my first larceny. She pinched my ear, dragging me as she shouted, 'You little thief! Practising to be the next Ali Baba are you?'

Her shrill, piercing voice woke my father and he proceeded to discipline me in the manner he favoured throughout my upbringing. My body was not sufficiently grown to withstand the brunt of his wrath. He raged with shame at having produced a son who was a thief, which elicited another biting remark from Aunt Khayriyyah.

Referring to my mother, the sister-in-law she detested, she said, 'What did you expect? Saniyya only ever laid rotten eggs.'

Those were her choice words, the ones she invariably repeated whenever she had a row with my mother, or when she wanted to needle my father about marrying my mother in the first place.

I had always hated her. Right from the start, Aunt Khayriyyah subjected me to relentless vigilance, as if I were nothing more than a device for her to sharpen her own surveillance abilities.

Our home was very small and she could always catch me

when I misbehaved. Confident I would fall into her trap, she would set me up and watch with glee for my inevitable stumble. Her greatest delight – yes, delight – was derived from being able to thwart my plans before I had even embarked on them.

My mother entrusted Aunt Khayriyyah with my care. She saw her own role as being limited to disciplining me or lending a hand in my punishment when my aunt found me doing something wrong.

I was the eldest of my father's children, sprung from a womb that could not bear to swell after me. Suffering from a sense of inferiority at having only one offspring, my father sought out more fertile women, but they, like my mother, proved unable to bless him with the gaggle of children he hoped for.

I was the only child from his first wife; his second wife provided him with two additional sons, one of whom died young, leaving Ibrahim, the apple of my father's eye. His third wife gave birth to one child, a girl so beautiful she broke the mould – at least that was what I had heard, since I had never actually met her. My father also sought out his pleasure between the thighs of a variety of other women, all of whom were discarded, one after the other.

I inherited my virility from my most immediate forebears. My father and both my grandfathers had irrigated a good many women in their day, although with me signs of that vigour were particularly precocious.

Even as a very young child, I discovered the nature of the ogre that we are born with. All it took was a little friction and I would become aroused and hurtle to the verge of that blissful abyss. I remembered the story of Aladdin rubbing his lamp to make the genie appear in a plume of smoke, and realised that bodily fires could also be ignited, and quelled, by rubbing.

On cold nights, my maternal cousins and I would snuggle up in two beds that had been pushed close together. We would spend the night tugging the blankets from each other to warm our bodies against the biting cold. One night I discovered that the familiar warming flames could be generated using the friction of two bodies. I cleaved to one of my younger cousins and as our supple limbs rubbed against each other, I began thrusting rhythmically.

I thought the covers would conceal my frenzied movements, but Aunt Khayriyyah saw me, as though she had been lying in wait for just such an act to provoke her anger. It was my first sexual encounter and, at first blush, a foretaste of my unbridled physical appetites.

Before I could finish, Aunt Khayriyyah barged in and burst into a screaming fit that went on the better part of three days. Even much later, whenever she recalled that event, she would grab me with one hand and pinch whatever part of my body her other hand could reach. If that did not quell her fury, she would get hold of a length of cord and use it to vent her wrath, screaming the foulest obscenities her tongue could muster as she whipped me.

Aunt Khayriyyah humiliated me with all manner of punishment and I harboured untold bitterness towards this odious woman no man would ever look at.

'Come on, boy,' she would later say viciously. 'Pump it up like a jack-hammer.' My aunt was using the nickname the young men in the neighbourhood originally gave me, although the moniker was later shortened to 'Hammer'.

81

We used to say those on the receiving end had been 'hammered'.

The hanky-panky under the covers with my cousin was disastrous at first in that I became the object of everyone's scrutiny. Gradually, however, people looked elsewhere, except for Aunt Khayriyyah, who continued to watch my every move.

To this day and after all of these years, I still do not understand what impelled her to lead me astray, or what her motives were for crippling me. It was enough to drive anyone to assist Azrael, the Angel of Death, to set her hateful soul free.

6

NOTHING FALLS UPWARDS, FOR the heavens are beyond our reach. The act of falling is what brings us down.

When I was on the verge of the precipice, absolutely no one extended a hand to prevent my fall. Everyone just stood by and watched. My fall was not the type that ends with blood splattering everywhere.

My father died when he fell from scaffolding. His work-mates climbed down and carried him carefully to the hospital where he was hooked up to a respirator. But his lungs collapsed from the pressure of the oxygen and he had to be taken off the respirator after his internal organs were satur-ated with blood.

It was my half-brother Ibrahim who took charge of the burial and hosted the condolence gathering with the help of some of our relatives. It may not have been deliberate, but even though I was the eldest of our father's children, I stood behind Ibrahim in the condolence line.

We were hardly old enough for such a line, and a host of close relatives jostled to the front. I found myself almost at the end of the line; at any rate, I felt I had little connection with the recently departed.

Even some of Ibrahim's friends were further up the line

than I was and did not even bother to offer me their condolences. To them, I was just a failure – a heretic even – and had been written off as the lowest of the low.

Aunt Khayriyyah mourned her brother a long time. She blamed his fall on my mother and me, and secretly vowed to make our lives a living hell.

There is no helping hand for those who have gone astray.

Due to gravitational pull, falling is actually a gradual process. It occurs as a succession of moments, each taking us a little further down, closer to the bottom. We do not hit rock bottom in one fell swoop.

Aunt Khayriyyah knocked me off balance, brought me to the edge of the precipice and then proceeded to push me into its gravitational embrace.

She did not watch me like a hawk out of any genuine desire to set me straight. Rather, she used my deviant behaviour to vent her own, deep-seated rancour towards my mother, a woman she detested because she felt my father had married below his station. Aunt Khayriyyah did little to conceal her hostility; her every breath exuded bitterness.

She was bent on demonstrating my mother's womb carried only rotten seed, and blamed her for my bad behaviour in every imaginable way. Sometimes, she would claim that she feared I might land in jail; other times, she would point out that my debauchery was at odds with our lineage. Once, she even went so far as to say that she feared I would be struck blind and tossed into a shallow grave.

I likened my aunt to a bush of prickly pears, its limbs sharp with spikes and its fruit covered in a down of thistles.

She never found a way out of her bitter wasteland. She was ten years older than my father, but no one had ever asked for her hand in marriage: no one could covet that fruit or coax any femininity from that harsh and desolate bush.

Aunt Khayriyyah was a thin, hard woman, inflexible as a tempered steel rod; even her smell was vaguely metallic. She never talked when she could bellow, and her tongue dripped with the same venom that coursed through her veins. There was simply never a moment when she was not mean.

Even when she was supposedly offering well-intentioned advice, she was in fact leading me astray. She made sure that once I had set out, there was no turning back. She goaded and taunted me as I climbed the neighbourhood blacklist until I came in second only to Issa.

Aunt Khayriyyah was the first person to train me in the ways of evil. Any misdeed on my part and she was there, first as the facilitator and then as the prosecutor. She was the first to find out about my misdemeanours because it was invariably she who had set me up.

We stumble on pleasure by chance and become hooked. Draining the cup to the last drop, we do not realise that it is leading to our downfall. Sensual gratification provides exquisite moments of abandon, but every time we experience the bliss of dissolution, the pool of darkness widens. Still we persist until we go into freefall. Sensuality is the chasm set in our path to snatch our lives from us and to alienate us from life.

I had been given the job of looking after Aunt Khayriyyah's sheep and making sure they were all in by evening, tied up in the pen right behind our house. She had a prized ram that earned its keep by propagating her own modest flock as well as by servicing the neighbours' ewes for a fee.

The ram was tethered separately from the rest of the sheep

and whenever my aunt selected the ewes she wanted serviced, she watched them in the act. She would watch with bated breath and enraptured as the ram leapt up tirelessly on to the ewes.

'I want you to be virile, like this ram,' she told me. 'You need to make up for your father who planted his seed in polluted soil.'

I was too young to understand the exact meaning of virility or to comprehend her implacable contempt for my mother. All I wanted was her approval and I longed to be worthy of her pride, like the ram. So I began doing what I had seen the ram do, jumping on top of the ewes and slithering off their backs.

Just as a spark lit by friction grows into fire, so too the precocious kindling of physical excitement leads to an insatiable desire for consummation.

In my mind, I was doing something truly great that would gain me Aunt Khayriyyah's unquestioning approval. I excelled in the role of the noble ram, cleaving, rubbing, cresting and, finally, experiencing the delectable languor that spread through my joints. I had no understanding of the nature of this precocious pleasure: all I wanted was for my aunt to be pleased with me. I went at the ewes hoping to demonstrate my prowess.

My aunt began to notice that I was gone a long time when she sent me to the sheep pen, and she came to realise that I was trying to follow the example of her prized ram. She was convinced the ram and I were of the same ilk, but before savouring her vindictiveness and punishing me, she would enjoy the sight a few more times.

She grabbed hold of my ear, her nails digging into the soft

flesh. 'May God curse you, boy!' she cried. 'Only the damned do it with sheep!'

I froze.

'Son of a bitch, now you've ruined their meat. And their milk!'

I was upset and confused partly because I had genuinely believed she would have approved. But instead of praise, I had been given the usual tongue-lashing.

But I was hooked and rubbed against anything that came my way to pleasure myself.

Aunt Khayriyyah began to take a different approach, goading me to forms of deviancy she carefully selected. Dangling me like a bucket, she flung me down into the well of debauchery.

One of the neighbour's young daughters, Souad, came to our house carrying a tray of stew that her mother had prepared. It was a gift to my mother who had been unwell. Aunt Khayriyyah went to the door.

'Looks like you're going to be well-endowed, girl. Just like your mother,' said Aunt Khayriyyah as she ran her hand over the girl's little breasts, already beginning to bud with the approach of puberty. She turned and, winking at me, added, 'Now *that's* what I call meat on the bone.'

I gave up chasing Aunt Khayriyyah's ewes and pursued Souad instead. She was not only accessible but she welcomed my trailing behind her as we searched the neighbourhood for a safe place to play. She turned down all of my suggestions, and in the end she chose where and when we should go to avoid getting caught.

Souad wanted one riyal since, she insisted, grooms had to pay their brides a dowry. I disagreed and we started to argue,

87

our voices carrying in the stillness of nightfall. I offered her half the sum, but she flatly refused, so I promised her the remainder just as soon as I got hold of some money. I proceeded to fish around for some change I kept tucked in my undergarments.

I had thought we would be on a secret mission somewhere without leaving a trace. She had chosen Jalal Mukbir's house, wedged between two sharp bends in the alleyway, because it was her favourite place to go and play bride and groom. It was also suitably dark since she had broken the light in the stairwell.

The night we chose for this children's wedding was ill-starred, however. We did not know that Jalal Mukbir's wife had invited a group of women to come and celebrate the circumcision of her second child or that the stairwell light had recently been fixed.

We stood in a corner of the stairwell, with only a faint glimmer of light from the roof, arguing about whether or not I could touch her buttocks. I got annoyed with her and cursed and, pulling her towards me, yanked her hair.

At first she fought back but then she gave in so that when, a minute later, the stairs were flooded with light from the landing above, we were caught clinging to each other half naked and grunting like two puppies learning to pant. We were just getting to the part where I had to push into her.

After a moment of stunned silence, all hell broke loose as the women on the landing above erupted into a frenzy of shouting and screaming. I pulled up my underwear and bolted out of the building, running for my life.

After that, the women warned their daughters – and their sons too – never to go near me or play with me again. The older girls, especially, were on notice.

The following day I could tell that all the boys from my circle of friends were avoiding me. Tahani tried to invite me to join her set of friends, but her older brother would not hear of it. Her eyes followed me as I went in search of a group of children who would let me play with them.

Souad was a child-sized whore.

Little girls learn very young that their smile is marketable, and that is the first step to perdition. They become harlots while still young and attractive and later, in their waning years, they become go-betweens. This opinion was proven when I ran into Souad at the Palace gates thirty years later. (I also used that chance encounter to pay off my long-standing debt of half a riyal.)

Souad was a child whose mother encouraged her to dally with the boys of the neighbourhood and wrest whatever she could from them by fooling around. Souad was born of a woman with a loose tongue and a demeanour to match. She was the offspring of a reluctant marriage which the groom disavowed immediately after the wedding ceremony. As the fruit of that unhappy union, Souad became the neighbourhood's plaything – boys toyed with her according to the extent of their bargaining skills.

Her mother had led the way. Women are like wooden planks, she told Souad, ever ready for a nail, be it crooked or straight. It did not matter whether the plank was thick or thin, whether it was hard or soft, long or short, as long as the owner of the nail could pay the price for hammering it into the wood.

Souad was nicknamed the 'Bride' because she loved to play bride and groom and especially loved to pocket the loose change that the boys handed her for a chance to hammer their nails in.

When she had suggested going to Jalal Mukbir's house, I never imagined that *I* would end up being a feast for the eyes of the women glaring down at us from the landing, their eyes practically popping out of their sockets. The incident inflamed the lust of the women, three of whom started to stalk me. There were countless retellings of what had been observed, and a good deal of exaggeration inevitably crept into the many versions, including the rumour that I had a third leg.

The first to try to verify the claim was Souad's mother herself. She repeatedly tried to entice me to come to her house when everyone was asleep. After that, there was Mona, whose husband worked for the health directorate, and then Iman. All three devised ways to be alone with me and see for themselves what all the tongues were wagging about after the scandal with Souad.

Transgressing became a way of life.

I was young and hot-headed and I left a broken heart here and there. The three of us – Osama, Issa and I – hurtled into young adulthood reckless and hardened.

Even when we are accustomed to promiscuity from a young age, we occasionally yearn for the warm and comforting embrace of tenderness. We enjoy recollecting moments of unsullied intimacy and feeling released from the squalor of our aberrant behaviour.

Tahani was tender-hearted and always stood by me. Even after my name was dirt and none of the other children wanted to play with me, she found ways to include me; she managed to find some justification for us to be together.

We walked the first stretch of the way to school together, down a long winding street that came to a fork. Then she would go on her way to the girls' school and I would catch the bus to mine.

Many girls walked to school, either alone or in groups. The boys walked behind, ogling them brazenly even though they wore abayas. Boys and girls from our neighbourhood woke up looking forward to this early morning interlude when furtive love messages could be exchanged – a word here, a glance there – before we filed into our different schools.

Tahani chose to walk to school by herself and never strayed far from my footsteps.

We walked in silence, our hearts aflutter, after listening to pop songs we thought were written just for us. We walked to school closer and closer together until, one morning, our hands brushed against each other. After school that day, whenever I looked up at her window, she would be there, her face behind the lattice, watching me smile or wave.

I was caught between two window screens: Tahani's amorous glances from one and Aunt Khayriyyah's unrelenting surveillance from the other. I would escape into the alleyways where I could hope that no one would be tracking me.

I already had an atrocious reputation in the neighbourhood which, with every new scandal, was further tarnished. Despite her attempts, Tahani could not convince those around her that I was not in fact a complete scoundrel. She confided that she wished I would stop misbehaving, which provided every-one with an excuse to shun me. She also warned me to stay away from her first cousin, Osama, as well as from Issa.

Vowing to put the past behind me, I did as she wished. I stopped chasing other girls and gave up the company of Issa and Osama.

I even started going to the mosque. I noted the looks of

utter disbelief from the worshippers as I prostrated myself, remorseful and teary-eyed. My half-brother Ibrahim was the happiest to see me there, plying me with books and urging me to attend recitation practice.

But a bitter plant will not turn sweet regardless of how much it is watered. A leopard does not change its spots.

Ibrahim and I came from the same wellspring, although we were born of two different women. While we were sown in radically different soils, we mirrored one another. From earliest childhood, the mosque had captured Ibrahim's heart. He spent most of his time there, diligently engrossed in prayer or memorising the Qur'an, which of course won him favour in our father's eyes. The disparity in our conduct was so great that not only was it immediately visible but it also became proverbial. One of the older men in the neighbourhood coined his own phrase to express the dramatic difference between us: 'Tariq and Ibrahim come from the same water – one is a stinking lech and the other a paragon of virtue.'

After Ibrahim suggested I should attend a religious study group at the mosque, I readily agreed because I really did want to cleanse myself and come closer to God. We gathered in a circle around the sheikh who led the study group and who, fixing his disapproving gaze on me, preached about how homosexuality and fornication were unanimously condemned by all religious traditions. He stared into my face, enunciating his words slowly, keeping his jaws tightly clenched.

'Only those who abandon the way of sin are truly repentant for the days they have squandered.' He looked straight into my eyes as he added, 'I believe some of you truly regret the grave offences you have committed and that have angered the Merciful.' He paused for effect. 'But not all sins are created equal. The sins of some among us today are enough to shake the very throne of the Creator. And I submit to you that a dog's crooked tail can never be straightened.' He paused again and then added for good measure, '*Never* – even if he enters the mosque and sits among us.'

At that point, he broke from his formal sermonising tone into a vulgar vernacular as he recounted the rumours about the three of us – Issa, Osama and me – without naming any names.

That was the proverbial straw that broke the camel's back. I started to heckle him and jeered at his vulgarity until, after several interruptions, he threw me out.

First impressions are indelible. A sinner who tries to redeem himself faces a bar that is always set that much higher, always just out of reach. I went from one study group to another and listened to a succession of speakers expounding on the nature of sin, ruminating on the subject like some pre-digested and regurgitated fodder. Like cardamom whose seeds are ground to a powder while the pod resists pulverisation, our transgressions were excoriated but we emerged unscathed.

Eager to support my search for guidance, Ibrahim accompanied me to religious lectures at various mosques. On one such occasion, the officiating imam gave a sermon after the evening prayer on the life of the Islamic scholar, Sufyan al-Thawri, a deeply flawed man who had also needed guidance. The imam focused on the error of al-Thawri's ways but made almost no reference to his legacy.

Time and again, preachers would cite the Hadith to demonstrate that man was able to overcome sinfulness through rectitude. However, they only ever emphasised the wrong-doing and not the good deeds. Human beings, including prophets, do not appreciate being singled out only for their errors and weaknesses.

During another deadening study group, and maybe by way of providing material for gossip, the sheikh enumerated all the errors and sins of the prophets. He had found enough material for an entire series of sermons and he developed the theme at various sessions after evening prayers. I went along with this until he got to the sinfulness of the venerable prophet Jonah, at which point I decided I could not stand another minute of this stupid, bullying nonsense. I got up to leave, convinced that my struggle to turn over a new leaf was in vain; I had already started to believe that I would never be able to put my own sinfulness behind me, just as an apple could never fall upwards.

Whenever she saw me getting ready to go and attend prayers or the study groups at the mosque, Aunt Khayriyyah would mutter, 'You won't be doing this for long. There is a streak of wickedness in you.'

The mosque circuit did not last more than a few months, after which I was back to my old tricks. Only Ibrahim and Tahani were sorry to see me give up on the mosque.

The downturn began with a nocturnal adventure with Mona, one of the three women who had stalked me after the scandal with Souad. I was on my way to the mosque when she burst out of her house, her cleavage openly showing, and asked me to come in and repair a faulty fuse in her bedroom. Her husband was away on a mission for the health directorate to vaccinate residents of coastal villages against meningitis.

I had many subsequent opportunities to sneak in to repair

94

her bedroom light, though the lamp remained broken long after her husband's return.

All these decades later, I have come to feel sorry about my lapse, now that my strength has been sapped and I stagger behind Ibrahim like a stone rolling down a precipice.

My work at the Palace did not brook a moral conscience. Regardless of the job, the mere fact of working there required the suspension of any kind of moral standard. The only way to get a return on one's investment from working inside the Palace was to disregard the values that existed on the outside. That is why I embraced every forbidden pleasure, convinced that my destiny lay in only one direction, that of hell.

I occasionally managed to shake off this despondency by bringing to mind conversations with Ibrahim.

'What happens when you trip up?' he once asked me. 'Do you stay on the ground or do you get up?' I did not feel like talking, so he answered for me. 'You get up, dust yourself off and keep going.' He added earnestly, 'That's what living is all about – you fall, you get back on your feet, you clean up and you get on with your life.'

He reminded me that God loves the return of sinners to his side, and quoted the Qur'anic verse: 'Oh my servants who have transgressed against themselves, do not despair of God's mercy. God forgives all sins: He is All-Forgiving, Compassionate to each.'

Even though I often went to Mecca on work-related business, it took me thirty-one years to summon up the courage to set foot inside the Mosque of the Holy Sanctuary.

On my way into and out of the city, I would drive by the gates of the Sanctuary and pause to watch the pilgrims as they picked their way among all the cars. I envied their serene faces, subdued voices and their general air of contentment. I would look up at the lofty minarets that broadcast the call to prayer, a balm to the worshippers' hearts that dislodged any build-up of sediment and decay corroding their spirits. The faithful responded to the call feeling as secure as the pigeons who had made the Kaaba their home.

There have been many times when I decided to return to the fold – and equally many when I recoiled from the very thought. Nothing could pull me away from the darkness that had descended on my soul so long ago.

Left to my own devices on the streets, my day would really only start at around ten o'clock in the evening. I would roam the narrow alleyways to hang out with the drunks and listen to them rant about their woes, to look for someone to play *balut*, and to ogle the neighbours' daughters. (This particularly angered Tahani who got wind of what I was up to from those girls who knew about our relationship.)

I also chased the boys we all lusted after. I undertook many a crowing exploit and Lu'ayy was the exception that proved the rule. He was the little creep who nearly landed me in jail. His father showed up at the police station charging that I had molested his son. My life could have taken a dramatically different course had it not been for the apathetic officer who registered the complaint.

Seeing that the process was going nowhere, Lu'ayy's father moved his family out of town before I could hammer his son. It was a valuable lesson for me: from that day, I realised that the children of the well-to-do were a real nuisance to those of us bent on the pursuit of cheap pleasures.

96

After I was done cruising, I would stop by a grocery store in one of the dodgier parts of the neighbourhood, where a solitary lamp cast a ghostly light on a deserted and narrow alley.

Mustafa Qannas would emerge from the alleyway under the cover of darkness, trudging heavily, mumbling incoherently and humming a little ditty that seemed directed at me:

'Pretty boy's gone away, gone, gone pretty boy.
Kith and kin drool over him, but he's afraid of strangers.
In her lap his mama holds him, and her heart I swear
    will break.
'Cos I will hold him like lovers do, like lovers do.'

Mustafa would offer me some of his revolting moonshine and I would oblige by pretending to take a few sips. He was about ten years older than me and, in his mid-twenties, was already thinking of settling down. But his wretched state and notorious reputation barred him from every door. Consequently, he spent all his time chasing after boys whom he wooed with this kind of banter.

He took the departure of Lu'ayy very badly and channelled his longing for the boy by reciting snatches of poetry. Sometimes he accompanied the words by plucking on an Arabian lyre – a *simsimiyya* – whose slack strings he was forever tightening. He had made the *simsimiyya* himself and it simply would not stay in tune.

He held me responsible for his misery after Lu'ayy was gone from the neighbourhood. When, at the height of his intoxication, Mustafa would start to slap his head with both hands and begin to wail, I would hurry away. I knew better than to stay around after he warned me once, dead sober, 'If

I find you anywhere near me when I start crying, I'm going to kill you.'

My father criticised me endlessly for keeping the company of drunks and often came looking for me in the middle of the night. If he happened to find me, he would grab me by the hair and drag me behind him like a rag doll without uttering a word – his iron grip conveying all I needed to know about the feelings roiling inside him.

As he dragged me through the alleyways, I had visions of knives being honed and waiting to spill my blood. Every time he found me in the middle of the night, I could swear he was going to kill me. But as soon as we got home, he would fling me in my aunt's face, muttering, 'Tie him up somewhere near you. I'll take care of him in the morning.'

Having been roused against his will, he would go straight back to bed and fall asleep. Since he was always out of the door at dawn, he would leave the house before making good on his threat.

The geography of our house changed radically with the sudden decline in our numbers. Soon, no one was left but the desiccated and vitriolic Aunt Khayriyyah.

To her, I was like mould encrusted in her drinking cup that she could not dislodge. She despised me and would say I was a 'stinking egg destined for a heap of rotting rubbish'.

She would hurl insults at me whenever she ran out of patience, and justified her outbursts by claiming she was only trying to mend my wicked ways. She loudly lamented that my father's lineage had not ended before I came on the scene.

Aunt Khayriyyah would rack her brain to find some defective strain that had entered her lineage, adamant that it was impossible I issued from the noble line of men in her family. She kept on with her insinuations until she got to my maternal grandmother's questionable chastity. This doubt was based on a murky rumour, whispered by the women of the family, each iteration of which added a lurid detail. In the final version of the tale, my grandmother was alleged to have brought a lover into her bed during one of her husband's absences and, by his return, her belly was already swollen from the infidelity.

Aunt Khayriyyah had no evidence for any of this, apart from the stories spread by family members. She was nevertheless convinced that my maternal grandmother Saniyya had desecrated her own, once pristine lineage. Since Saniyya's womb was polluted by some impure sap, my parents' marriage meant my aunt's lineage was now tainted.

As a result, our family had split into two rival and hostile branches. According to Aunt Khayriyyah, the first, of pure lineage, was dedicated to the mercantile trades, while the other was defiled by whatever parasitic seed had stuck to and then spewed out of Saniyya's womb.

Aunt Khayriyyah could not help yearning for her origins despite being cut off from them for all those years; she could not get over the circumstances that had compelled her to live with her only brother and his sullied wife. She claimed my father had been lured in by my mother's scheming ways and, in marrying her, had violated the purity of stock so prized by the family.

Their union was an historic mistake and she was unable to forgive my father on two counts: first, for having forced her to leave the family, which prized purity of lineage above all else, and second, for recklessly associating with the filth that was my mother, thereby tainting his own lineage. As far as Aunt Khayriyyah was concerned, my mother followed in her own mother's footsteps in her indiscriminate and insatiable appetite for semen.

Her suspicion that I was evidence of that rotten seed clinging to her brother was confirmed once she and I were the only two people left in the house. After my father's death, my mother remarried, taking for a new husband her first cousin on Saniyya's side.

As talk of family history was on everyone's lips, I came to learn that my mother had twice stood in the way of Aunt Khayriyyah getting married, condemning her to spinsterhood for the rest of her life. Her first potential suitor had been my mother's own brother. She managed to put him off from the start with descriptions of her sister-in-law's fulminating mouth and rank armpits.

The second budding suitor was a man of no fixed abode who was looking for a woman to take him in. In this case and perhaps overplaying her hand, my mother had accused my father of being so insensitive as to throw his sister into the jaws of a passing stranger. So my father ended up showing him the door.

That was how Aunt Khayriyyah came to harbour the well of venom and vitriol towards my mother.

7

M Y FATHER WAS CONSIDERED one of Jeddah's master builders. Even though he used traditional methods to calculate measurements, he rarely made mistakes. He was meticulous to a fault and would not tolerate assistants who strayed, however modestly, from his designs. He had a knack for erecting houses that were in perfect alignment and was adept at designing architectural plans that were still unknown when he was growing up in Jeddah.

He was inspired by the Hajj and Umrah pilgrims who came from foreign lands. He would ask the visitors what they did for a living and, whenever he came across fellow builders, he would sit them down and enquire about the sorts of buildings they had in their country, providing pen and paper for their architectural sketches.

Before long, he distinguished himself as a builder and his reputation grew. He had wanted me to succeed him in the trade, but I would just run off on the pretext that I had to study. When, instead, he found me wandering the alleys aimlessly, he wasted no time in telling me what I should be doing.

He had three permanent wives, in addition to several fleeting consorts, and the responsibility of generating enough income to feed all those mouths weighed heavily on him.

On the nights he was scheduled to spend with my mother, he would arrive at sunset and fall asleep at the dinner table, right in the middle of the meal. He refused to get out of his seat and go and lie down for fear that he would no longer be drowsy. So he remained wherever sleep overcame him, which meant that my mother also had to sleep wherever he happened to have drifted off. To avoid being in full view of the rest of the household while sleeping and scantily clad, my mother hit upon the strategy of ushering him into their bedroom as soon as he came home. This, of course, further fuelled Aunt Khayriyyah's resentment and she began to accuse my mother of deliberately keeping her brother away from her and of monopolising him, body and soul.

As I grew older, I began to suspect that my father had reached the point where he could not bear to stay with us because of my aunt's relentless screeching. She complained to him about my waywardness, about my mother's laxity with me and about her need for more housekeeping money. She hectored him about doing more for his relatives and lectured him on ways to increase his income and take better care of her interests, which she accused him of neglecting. Perhaps it was this constant nagging that precipitated his drowsiness and that gave rise to his unusual sleeping habits. By daybreak, he would be gone, leaving at the crack of dawn, as might be expected of a master builder who oversaw every last detail on his work site.

However, with the advent of modern construction, my father went from being a master builder to a mere foreman. Occasionally, when the project engineer was absent, he had the audacity to alter designs as he saw fit. He lost a good deal of standing among the workers as a result because whenever the engineer returned to the site and ordered the removal of the innovations – naturally, at my father's expense – the work had to be done all over again.

He felt diminished in this subordinate capacity and resented having to comply with engineers' instructions.

One fateful afternoon, he thought he had discovered an error in the pillar and beam supports of a roof structure he was working on. He wanted to verify his hunch before the engineer in charge discovered the mistake and became angry with him. Using his foot as a measure, he extended his leg beyond the ledge.

At that moment he lost his balance and, before he could pull his leg back to the solid surface of the roof, he fell off the scaffolding and ended up in a pool of blood.

He would never climb another scaffolding again or have to face the consequences of tweaking engineers' plans. For that matter, he would also never have to hear his sister's squawking. After a month on an artificial respirator, his lungs finally collapsed and the machine released him from this life.

I did not love him, nor did I hate him. As far as I was concerned, he was a low-maintenance guest – he came home in the evening, went to sleep and left quietly at dawn.

The sum total of his worldly legacy added up to two sons and one daughter. The daughter was born to his last wife, a week before his demise, and I had never met her. The three of us were left with nothing that might remind us of our father. We had little in common with each other, did not live together and each kept to their own.

The year before my father's accident had been the year of Egyptian soaps. Summer was upon us with its sticky heat and people everywhere were climbing up on to rooftops to adjust their television antennas or to wire satellite dishes. Soap operas from Egyptian channels were all the rage, and the installation of powerful receivers guaranteed improved reception. Egyptian programming was of particular interest to the neighbourhood women, who at social gatherings vied with one another to relay the latest twists and turns in the dramatic serials and to mimic the dance moves of the Egyptian celebrity, Sherihan.

My aunt and mother were no different and decided our antenna needed adjusting. I had told them I could not do it because I was on my way to a *shakshaka,* where Hijazi men gathered to sing and dance. I was not inclined to waste my time on something as trivial as Egyptian television.

On my way to the bathroom, wrapped in a towel, I heard the two of them draw straws. They both agreed that the loser would fetch the ladder, prop it up against the inner wall of the courtyard and climb up on to the roof, while the winner would stand below holding the ladder in place. Aunt Khayriyyah lost and then proceeded to contest the draw, saying that there had to be three consecutive draws and that only the third one was decisive. By the third draw, the result was reversed and all my aunt had to do now was hold the ladder.

As I washed in the bathroom, I could hear my mother shouting down from the roof, 'Is the picture coming in clearly now?'

'No, not quite,' Aunt Khayriyyah shouted back. 'A little more to the left. No, no. Wait. Move it to the right.'

'OK.'

'Yes, yes, hold it there. That's it. OK, done!'

I stepped out of the bathroom as my mother grabbed hold of the ladder to come down from the roof. Just as her hands reached the top rung, I could swear I saw my aunt pull the ladder away from the wall. For a moment, my mother remained suspended in mid-air but by the time she fell to the ground, blood was gushing from her mouth.

My mother had bitten her tongue so badly that a large portion of it had been sliced off.

Until his own fall, a year later, my father only ever came to the house to fulfil the moral and religious obligation of treating his wives equally. He typically spent his time holding forth as my mother responded with a nod or a shake of the head. I suspected that she waited until he was out of sight to open the floodgates and let flow the tears that had dammed up within.

As soon as my father would come in, barbed words began flying out of my aunt's mouth.

'So who is going to look after the mule now?' she asked him shortly after my mother's accident.

He asked whether she meant my mother or me. 'Haven't you done enough to her?' he went on, his voice dropping.

'*Me?*' Aunt Khayriyyah was beside herself with rage at the insinuation. '*I* have done nothing to her! She fell all by herself!'

Hoping somehow to reattach her tongue fragment, my mother stored it in the freezer. Without her knowing, I would watch her bring the mirror up close to her face and try to fasten the severed portion she held between her thumb and index finger. It invariably slithered out of her grasp. When it fell on the floor, she would snatch it up and, cradling it as if it were a nursing infant, run crying to rinse it off in the sink. She would do this over and over again, but it fell every time.

One day, the fragment was not in its usual place: she searched for it frantically, emptying the freezer, to no avail.

I knew it was lost for ever. Earlier in the day, I had seen Aunt Khayriyyah reaching into the freezer and tossing something at a famished cat that had wandered into the house meowing for something to eat. I had watched, transfixed, as the cat set to licking the tasty morsel and batting it between its paws.

Having just fed it something, my aunt half-heartedly attempted to part it from its quarry. 'Beess, beess, beess,' she called out to it softly and the animal bolted out of the house with the morsel between its jaws.

The cat had got her tongue.

From then on, whenever my father was staying with one of his other wives, my mother would sit alone and practise enunciating clearly since everything she said had become mangled and unintelligible. She made valiant attempts to say my father's name, but failed after repeated efforts. She buried her head in her pillow and sobbed with frustration.

She avoided going out of the house and stopped calling on her neighbours. She resigned herself to doing housework – cooking, cleaning and spinning wool. Since my mother was unable to entertain her neighbours, Aunt Khayriyyah had ample opportunity to bad-mouth her; she would describe my mother as a cripple who did nothing all day but lie in bed and stammer like an imbecile.

My aunt spent her evenings glued to the television, chuckling at her own imitation of the announcers' Egyptian accents.

Tahani would stand behind the latticed window, with the lights off, waiting for me. We exchanged glances and softly

106

whispered words throughout the evening until she would let me in after her family had gone to bed. I would spend the entire time pressed up against her. If we heard a noise or the sound of footsteps in the street that we thought might awaken someone in the house, I would dash out the door as she pretended to be tossing rubbish out of her window on to the alleyway below.

Although it is now buried in the furthest recesses of my memory, I remember that last, terrible night as if it were yesterday. It had started out quietly enough but the ogre was tired of lying in the shadows and it bolted into the light and set the universe ablaze.

Those with a particularly sensitive disposition suffer a lifetime of torment because a star continues to burn brightly despite the ashes and smoke of its dying embers. Stars are like that: they continue to burn even after they collapse.

Tahani would be my eternal star.

The night I stole her virginity, the ogre stole my life. It wrenched her life away, and mine with hers.

The rich and powerful men who milled around the Palace were afflicted with a sickness of their own. Their clothes were spotlessly white but their blood roiled with greed and excess, and their tongues became vicious if anything got in the way of their instant gratification. Moody and capricious, they were forever seeking new thrills, which quickly bored them. They were jaded and dissolute since nothing could make them happy. They had no purpose in life and were as impulsive as they were aimless. Whenever they spoke, such jumbled nonsense would spew out of their mouths that they sounded like madmen.

Some had grown effeminate in their search for ever more pleasure, especially if they happened to have been on the receiving end of the abuse I meted out to satisfy the Master. Instead of resenting me, they sought me out, and I could not get away from them. These were men whose virility was on the wane and who were willing to indulge in perversion to satisfy their thirst for carnal pleasure.

During the early years at the Palace, I was like the tethered ram in Aunt Khayriyyah's pen. But rather than slithering on ewes, my job was to service the other rams before they had a chance to wander out of the pen. My role at the Palace was to be the prized stud on call.

Many acts of debauchery were committed on the backs of men who, outside the Palace walls, were highly regarded members of society. Some of them begged for deliverance from my rearing over their backs, but the afflicted ones sought me out afterwards so that I could minister to their shameful disease.

Dr Bannan did not set much store by what he called 'primary feelings'. He held that they were akin to the infantile phase of 'discovering the world' – when the first stirrings of desire are cloaked in the garments of the woman in our life and to whom we ascribe feelings of love.

'People don't know this,' he declared monotonously, 'but underneath the blazing embers, there is nothing but darkness.' He nodded as he brought to mind a whole list of hackneyed aphorisms. 'Life is like that – today's brightness is yesterday's darkness. The past is the only darkness we can traverse unguarded and unescorted.'

His pronouncement was made in the course of one of the rambling monologues he launched into whenever the Master was bored with him and he had nothing better to do than coin pithy sayings that no one listened to. Whenever the Master's attention was turned away, Dr Bannan was like a dog, lying prostrate at his owner's feet, panting eagerly and awaiting his next command.

But then we were all begging and panting dogs at the Palace. As soon as we had completed our respective duties, we rushed back to lie at the Master's feet and looked up into his face adoringly, in anticipation of the next command.

From the time he first set foot in the Palace, Issa's role was to take care of the Master's family affairs, while Osama and I were engaged in that other line of work, that is punishing his rivals.

Osama and I were bound together not only by a shared youth and job at the Palace, but also by our feelings for Tahani. The hostility between us remained constant; however much our paths diverged, we were inexorably drawn back to each other by our rivalry over Tahani.

One night, Osama was particularly disaffected with life inside the Palace and wanted to talk about our youth: the first – and less antagonistic – of the ties that bound us together. Leaning towards me, he whispered, 'Who will give us back our innocence?'

I lent Osama my ear but kept my eyes open for any sign or gesture from the Master.

He kept whispering to me. 'Aren't *you* tired of all this depravity?'

It was like a barb aimed at my heart.

In life, the further we go, the dirtier we get. With every breach we cross, our spirit is sullied incrementally by the inherent squalor of existence. Driven by our basest instincts, we inevitably turn into a fetid pile of rubbish.

Only the spirits of our nearest and dearest, embedded in us like a seed in soil, keep us vaguely human.

Tahani was a seed that had divided into two: half was sown in me and, after I tended her with unholy water, she became pure spirit while I was left to wallow in her wake. The other half was sown in Osama's soul and withered there, laying bare his venomous nature.

8

THE PLAY OF LIGHT and shadow is life's adroit game. There are two competing and contrasting aspects to everything, the two faces of a coin. Life goes back and forth between them, and the choices we make determine the rules of the game. The hand of fate conceals the coin and we pick either heads or tails. When the hand reveals the result of our choice, our attention is always on the coin, never on the hand that put us before the quandary in the first place.

In that instant, our senses can feel the sweet thrill of victory or the disappointment of defeat. That is the illusion of freedom of choice: choosing, like falling, is just a momentary feeling to which we are captive. It erases nothing – on the contrary, it is part and parcel of a preordained destiny. No one journeys through life choosing his fate.

On my first night at the Palace, the Master organised an evening worthy of an obscene wedding night. Like a butcher bleeding the animal he slaughters to safeguard his professional reputation, I had to consume vast quantities of alcohol to get through it.

During the rainy season, the sky glinted with every shade of grey, a sure and unmistakable sign that the earth would soon receive a downpour. On that night, it never crossed my mind that I would be raining into rank and stagnant crevices for many seasons to come.

That night, I had blood on my hands twice, and was entreated to show mercy twice. But it was the first voice that would always haunt me. Wherever I went, I heard Tahani begging, 'Spare me, because I love you.'

A woman never forgets the first man who treads her virgin pastures and stains her purity with the blood of her maidenhead. Men, on the other hand, are marauders who cannot even remember where they have planted their stakes. They only care to discharge their sap on to any soil that comes their way – fertile or barren – unrelentingly, persistently and incessantly.

Samira and Tahani were two of the neighbourhood's loveliest young roses and they had a bevy of suitors competing for their attention. The rivalries to win their hearts sometimes led to fights and although our friends and relatives tried to find out what was fuelling our animosity, they never succeeded. Eventually Kamal Abu Aydah and I emerged the victors, as the neighbourhood would attest even to this day.

But our victories proved pyrrhic.

The young Samira was married off to the wretched petty thief, Abu Musharrat, even though she loved Kamal. The 'Slasher', as he was called, had spent a lifetime planting his manhood between the thighs of African women who were grateful for any amount of money that might relieve the daily grind of their lives.

He was nicknamed the Slasher on account of the unsheathed blade he carried everywhere. Abu Musharrat would plunge the blade into any hapless stranger who happened to be wandering about the neighbourhood. After stripping his victims clean, he would vanish into the narrow and winding lanes.

Abu Musharrat had spent sixty years pilfering and drifting about, and now that he was not far from the grave, he was desperate for someone to shed a few tears over his deathbed. Although Samira had always called him 'uncle' out of respect, her reserve and circumspection could not shield her from being shamelessly undressed by his beady old eyes. Before giving up the ghost, he wanted to feast one last time on ripe and ever so appetising fruit.

He approached the family with an engagement proposal tailored to Samira's father's grasping heart and, after his offer was accepted, the news quickly spread across the neighbourhood.

There was no one to stand in the way of Samira's fate, especially not Kamal, who certainly could never have proposed a dowry to rival the small fortune Abu Musharrat had paid for the girl. In order to savour the pleasure of divesting Samira of her maidenhead, the Slasher had handed a lifetime of loot to her father, who then enjoined his daughter to seal the deal.

Samira's wedding was held at daybreak. The girl made her way to the bridal chamber, her footsteps stumbling to the beat of the drummer-women, followed raptly by the female witnesses tasked with verifying the breaking of her hymen.

Limp as he was, the obligatory ululations of joy were far from guaranteed. One of the witnesses came to his rescue and, whispering furtively in Abu Musharrat's ear, was presently rewarded with the child-bride's shrieking cries for help.

The Slasher had plunged his thumb inside her and extracted a few rosy drops of blood. In possession of the requisite blood-stained white handkerchief, the witness stepped outside holding Samira's honour aloft and broke the silence of the gathered women with a *zaghrouta*.

The women soon dispersed, satisfied. Samira's parents celebrated their daughter's chastity as well as their good fortune. In addition to the dowry and all the gifts for the bride's relatives, they had received a sizeable pot of trust money. However, little could anyone suspect that the young girl's fate had been sealed by that marauding thumb.

Within a couple of nights, her body was racked with fever from a lingering case of leprosy that Abu Musharrat had picked up in Ethiopia. After being dutifully infected by her husband, the young bride ended her days at King Fahd General Hospital after less than a fortnight at the old man's home.

Since Abu Musharrat had not disclosed his infection, the attending doctor cited the cause of death as septicaemia. But the Slasher knew the truth and, shortly after Samira's demise, he revealed the secret from his deathbed when his turn came to face his Maker. Following the disclosure, however, people could not decide whether to believe him or the doctor.

Samira's death provoked all sorts of talk around the neighbourhood. Some women claimed that she had never had the chance to make good on her oath to kill herself rather than be married off to Abu Musharrat; others felt that, on the contrary, she had in fact kept her word, albeit after the fact.

Despite Abu Musharrat's dying confession about his leprosy and infecting Samira, most of the men of the neighbourhood still chose to believe that she had died from blood poisoning, overruling the women.

However, everyone could agree on one thing at least: not a soul shed a single tear over Abu Musharrat's deathbed.

I was almost nineteen and it was not clear what my future held, if even I had a future. While I had been accepted to university, I had no idea what to study. I was uncertain and felt nothing but confusion.

In the event, the hand of fate would show me the way, would reveal the result of the tossed coin, in the shape of Issa Radini. He obliged happily when, later, I would need someone to gather up my remains, carry them to the nearest dump and dispose of them without another thought.

Issa was visiting the Firepit as news of Samira's death spread through the neighbourhood. His new luxury German car attracted swarms of boys who gathered in the litter-strewn, narrow lanes to admire the vehicle and marvel at the plush interior. Issa gave a boy five riyals to go and fetch me but when I arrived he held me at arm's distance instead of reciprocating my embrace.

His appearance had changed radically since I had last seen him. At wedding banquets when guests dress up for the occasion, Issa used to arrive wearing a garish, synthetic sarong and a sweat-soaked tank top. His scruffy appearance would be completed by a speckled shawl thrown over his shoulders, ostensibly to hide the sweat marks and dark stains around the armpits, neck and back. The shawl somehow matched the striped *keffiyeh* which on Issa's head would gather into a cone lying askew. He would wear traditional Hijazi shoes, whose thick straps caused him to trip often as he waded, almost ankle-deep, through the rubbish on the streets. In those days, that was the extent of his sartorial sense.

His appearance did not cramp his style in the least. In fact, his modest attire had endeared him to the local gangs of boys. He was like a ragged rooster flapping its wings nonchalantly as it pecked about the coop.

After he started working at the Palace, however, he acquired a polished attire and an elegance that extended even to the way he spoke. Issa had taken on the high diction of the central region of the country, the Najd.

'I am inviting you to take up a new life, which means you need to give up your old ways,' Issa said, his fingers clicking prayer beads.

'What do you mean?' I frowned at him; Issa was so full of himself that he was almost condescending.

'You can't come to the Palace with me looking like that,' he explained, waving dismissively at my clothes. 'Brother, clean up, put on your best outfit, and then you'll be ready for Paradise.' He paused and then added, 'We'll meet here at the same time tomorrow night.'

'Why tomorrow night?' I asked quickly since he was about to leave. 'I'll see you in the morning if you're spending the night in the neighbourhood. I'll come to your house.'

He shook his head emphatically. 'There's no one in this wretched place who means anything to me.' He added, 'Meet me here tomorrow – and come prepared.'

Without another word, Issa climbed into his car and drove away from the Firepit, leaving me speechless.

Our meeting had been postponed to the following evening because Issa thought I looked too scruffy. Were it not for that delay, I would not have gone to Tahani's house the following night and violated her so brutally.

It was the darkest night – so remote and yet so close.

The night after Samira died, the neighbourhood was shrouded in a black veil of gloom. Streams of dignitaries and well-wishers headed to a pavilion, set up by the bereaved family, to offer their condolences on the premature death of one of their loveliest young roses.

That night, I sneaked into Tahani's house.

She was shattered, her body shook as she buried her head into my chest sobbing. 'Samira is dead, Tariq,' she moaned.

Samira was a friend and had often served as go-between for Tahani and me, even standing guard for us sometimes so that we could finish a conversation peacefully.

Until that night, Tahani had always slipped out of my embrace when I tried to hold her too close. But now, drowning with grief, she was in my arms. Her hair cascaded to her waist, her breasts melted into my ribs, and I was seized by a demonic desire to take her.

That night, pressed into a corner of her room, I held Tahani tightly against me. At first, she tried to cool my excitement. But as I nuzzled against her throat and neck, her passion was also ignited. Languid with desire, her body went slack while mine tautened with urgent tension.

Cleaving to each other, we moved slowly and gradually became incandescent, liquefied, and then frenzied. The last traces of resistance faded and she offered herself to the torrents of my passion. Her deepest vale flooding, she cried for deliverance.

I subjugated Tahani that fateful night. I was running my

hands all over her splendour when a sudden power outage plunged us into pitch darkness. Friction generates fire: at first, the sparks of passion only dispelled our inner gloom but soon the blaze was lit and we cleaved to one another, longing for release. Tahani seemed bent on self-annihilation, as if she wanted to follow in Samira's footsteps.

Where had the enveloping darkness come from? Everything died in that black night.

'Spare me, because I love you,' she cried in one last gasp of resistance.

I penetrated her forcefully.

She screamed, her voice carrying in the dead night.

Her cries alerted her parents and brothers and I was prevented from enjoying her fully. I could hear rushing footsteps, swiftly followed by a relentless pounding on the door.

Tahani was glued to me, crying, moaning, our breaths commingled as the voices outside thundered, 'Open the door!'

I shook her off and scrambled in the dark to the window, jumping down to the street below. As my feet hit the ground, I heard her father, Salih Khaybari, from inside her bedroom bellowing, 'Thief!'

Salih was now shouting from his daughter's window, 'Grab that thief!'

Her brothers ran out into the alleyway to chase the intruder, and as the father's yell reverberated throughout the neighbourhood people rushed to help. The call was picked up and repeated to anyone passing by in the dark.

The sound of running footsteps and the cries on everyone's lips echoed through that dark, cold night. Everything was engulfed in tumult and agitation that night – animals that had been left untethered, the odd vagrant, even the vacant streets. No one could remember a night like it.

The shroud of darkness hanging over the neighbourhood had muted everything; gone was the usual noise of men playing a late-night round of dominoes or cards and calling out boisterously when they were on the brink of victory or defeat. The dominoes lay scattered and the playing cards blew in the wind. The mourners at the condolence pavilion for Samira had also dispersed, scattering every which way in response to the call.

In the inky blackness of that night, people ran helter-skelter between the uneven walls, hurrying through the narrow, twisting lanes, their features indistinguishable, colours blacked-out and disembodied cries piercing the gloom. A single battery-operated radio provided the only counterpoint to the surrounding din of chaos, and the Saudi singer, Talal Maddah, added his plaintive voice to the night: 'And when you leave, my cry is silent as an echoless valley.'

My breath still carried Tahani's scent, but remorse gripped my heart like a vice. Candles and lanterns were lit and I passed a number of men clutching woefully inadequate torches against the pitch-black alleys. I greeted them tersely and added my voice to the insults they were heaping on the utility company for cutting the power at that inopportune moment.

'Grab that thief!'

Every time Salih's voice rang out across the neighbourhood, we let out a stream of invective.

Everything was engulfed in darkness, and I was desperate for someone or something to deliver me from the pall of gloom that enveloped me. Escaping with Tahani's blood on my conscience, my mind replaying the whole episode, I could no longer tell which had been louder: Tahani's languid moans or her cries begging me to stop.

I was in that confused and desperate state of mind when I went to meet Issa.

I found him at the prearranged rendezvous point. He had parked his flashy car between adjacent grocery stores and he switched on the engine and the headlights when he spotted me. I slipped into the vehicle and we drove out of the neighbourhood. I was grateful to put the night behind me.

But, much as I tried, I could not obliterate the sound of Tahani's cries. Her plaintive voice was seared into my heart and became mingled with the distant strains of Talal Maddah's song: 'And when you leave, my cry is silent as an echoless valley.'

9

NEWS OF ISSA'S UNEXPECTED appearance in the neighbourhood had swept through the alleyways and reached his
father, Abu Issa. No sooner did Abu Issa hear the news than
he began to prepare to welcome his son home. He was going
to let bygones be bygones and forgive Issa for his belligerence;
all he wanted after this long absence was to inhale the boy's
smell again.

Abu Issa set about rearranging the furniture in the house,
thinking of where his son would want to sit. He ran through
his mind the most important things he would say to his son in
the course of apologising to him, playing a series of scenarios,
until he settled on the simplest and most heartfelt: he would
clasp Issa's hands, kiss them and then implore him to return
home with his mother and reunite the family under one roof.

But his enthusiasm faded as midnight drew near.

Abu Issa showed up on our doorstep at one in the morning
saying that whoever had put out the news that his son was in
the neighbourhood had to be an abject liar. He refused to
believe Issa could have been in the neighbourhood without
so much as knocking on the door of his family home.

I had seen Issa barely an hour earlier – our first meeting –
when he had sniffed at my attire and told me to return the

following night better prepared for the Palace. 'Issa was here,' I confirmed.

'And you didn't bring him to see me, Tariq?' he asked reproachfully. 'Didn't you tell him that his father is no longer the man he once was?'

'He has also changed,' I offered by way of a reply as I brought to mind his fancy car, his new clothes and his affected speech.

'Didn't you tell him that I've become incontinent, that I'm going crazy thinking about him and his mother?' Abu Issa asked. 'All right, leave me out of it. Didn't you tell him that his brothers miss their mother?'

I could not tell him that Issa had refused to come inside the neighbourhood and had said there was no one there who meant a thing to him any more.

Long before this, when her son had disappeared for an entire week, Umm Issa had become convinced that he would never return home. She set about trying to glean snippets of information about his whereabouts from his closest friends, but none of us had any idea how to reach him and our guesses failed to satisfy her.

Umm Issa wanted to know for sure that her son was all right and since no one in her family would accompany her to search for him, she started asking the neighbours for help. Whenever her husband left the house, Umm Issa would go out and rope some young man into driving her around the places she thought she might find her son.

Eventually it got back to Abu Issa that his wife was going out unaccompanied by a family member. Livid with rage, he ambushed her when she returned from one of her excursions in the car of the neighbourhood's money changer. He flung the car door open and set upon her right in the alleyway, hurling insults at her and accusing her of carrying on with the young men of the neighbourhood using the pretext of looking for her son. He swore that if she went out one more time he would break her bones and she would never walk again.

Umm Issa became a prisoner of her own home and of her tears. Nothing could console her or provide relief; when one of her aunts tried to intercede on her behalf, Abu Issa became even more enraged and intensified his cruel and humiliating treatment by strapping his wife to the foot of his mother's sofa.

Issa stole back into their home one morning, after he had made sure that his father was gone for the day, and he took his mother away. He disowned his father and told his grandmother to convey the message to her son that he would never again set eyes on his wife.

Abu Issa would die without either of his two most fervent wishes being granted: to be reunited, by the grace of God, with his wife and eldest son, and to sail out to the open sea one last time.

Issa did not express himself obliquely or cryptically. Life in the streets had divested him of any notion of shame and he was quite blunt about the reason for his reappearance in the neighbourhood. During our second meeting, when I slipped into his car, he told me, 'Those vital juices of yours have a price and from now on, they will bring in their weight in gold.'

I sealed the deal with a nod. He probably thought it was debauchery and greed that motivated me. What he did not realise was that only moments earlier I had ruined Tahani and was now a fugitive. I had her blood on my hands and her disgraced honour on my conscience. As his car bumped along the narrow twisting lanes, the men of the neighbourhood were out scouting the alleyways for the thief who had broken into Salih Khaybari's house.

I went to work at the Palace with Issa's warning ringing in my ears. 'Don't even think about objecting to anything,' he said several times as he steered me into the Master's presence.

The *Sayyid* looked me up and down, his eyes travelling over every inch of my body and general appearance. He told me to take a few steps, then to turn, and then to stride from one corner of the room to the other.

'I hear from Issa that your life is tied up in your loins,' he said.

The Master had me come towards him and as I stood facing him he ordered me to get closer and then closer again, until I was less than a metre away.

Without further ado, he commanded, 'Take off your trousers.'

Just like that! The man's coarseness far exceeded anything which we, so-called street kids, were capable of. For someone immersed in a life of opulent luxury, his vulgarity was unbelievable – and it was like that throughout my employment at the Palace. I was the object of insults and profanity unheard of even among the lowest riff-raff. He was compulsively profane and not a day went by when he did not hurl obscenities at me.

By the end of my time at the Palace I knew why he had such a filthy vocabulary. But standing in front of him at our very first meeting, it never occurred to me that his depravity could so far exceed that of pimps and whores with a hallowed history in the business.

Standing before him with my trousers around my ankles and frozen with embarrassment, I had no idea what I was supposed to do or what he expected of me.

'Take off your underwear,' he ordered gruffly.

I fumbled around trying to delay, but a Filipino manservant swiftly stepped forward and his fleeting hands stripped me naked. I burned with shame.

Not content simply to look, the Master tugged and prodded provocatively at my manhood, which had the last traces of Tahani's virginity, the rosy blood of her maidenhead, still clinging to it. 'I'm entitled to check for myself the thickness of the stick that will chastise my enemies, right?'

He pulled and tossed my member this way and that, making his own assessment. He flipped it to the right, then to the left, raised it, lowered it, pulled and stretched, and finally released it as nonchalantly as if he were examining a fish for its freshness.

'Do you always walk around with visible traces of your aggression?' he asked with a nauseating laugh.

I burned with shame.

Then he looked towards Issa and issued his verdict: 'He'll do.'

I pulled up my clothes while the Master, with a sneer of distaste, reached for a tissue from a box on a marble-top table and began to wipe his hand. This was a signal to the Filipino, who nodded eagerly and flashed a wooden smile as he jumped into action.

Issa was just as obsequious. As soon as the Master had uttered his opinion, Issa left the room, nodding deferentially as he went. I was left in the care of the Filipino who walked me down the corridors of the Palace, sometimes a few steps ahead, sometimes propelling me from behind, as we went through a series of doorways. Whenever I slackened the pace, he stopped smiling and urged me on, until we came to a comfortable-looking bedroom flanked by a small antechamber and a bathroom.

He told me to step into the bathroom and, when I remained rooted to the spot, he substituted miming gestures for his pidgin Arabic, indicating I should undress fully this time. Seeing me hesitate, he came up to me and took the matter into his own hands, stripping me of one item of clothing after another, smiling all the while. I grabbed his hand forcefully, but he treated me like a poorly disciplined child making a fuss over bath time. His features clouded over as the hint of a threat hung in the air.

I submitted to a thorough scrubbing. Every dead and dry cell on my body was exfoliated, my skin was conditioned with almond, walnut and pomegranate oils, lotions and ointments were rubbed on and, finally, a dusting of warm-scented powder was applied to attenuate the shine. I glowed.

I put on a cotton robe and the Filipino servant left me to lie down, my head swirling with unanswered questions. Issa had communicated no details about my prospective work beyond urging me to demonstrate total compliance with any command I was given. The image of Tahani's tear-stained face overshadowed any other thought and her pleading cries crowded out every concern I had. I could not imagine what was about to happen nor anticipate that what I had just been subjected to was a harbinger of things to come.

The sound of approaching voices put an end to my reverie and the Master burst into the suite accompanied by four men who laughed and jostled raucously as a fifth man was dragged in wailing and flanked by two black manservants. The man was imploring the Master, swearing on his life that he would never again be guilty of insubordination.

His pleas for mercy mingled with Tahani's and their two voices reverberated through my mind.

Working quickly together, the servants stripped the man naked and threw him on to the bed where I lay. The Master seated himself across from the bed, flanked by a stony-faced acolyte on either side, while the other two busied themselves setting up a video camera and the African servants stood at attention by the door.

'I want to hear him screaming at the top of his lungs,' the Master said.

Only then, seeing the naked man on the bed, begging for mercy, did I finally realise with rising dread what was expected of me – the nature of the work I was to do at the Palace. I could not conceive carrying out the task expected of me, especially with all those eyes following my every move and being recorded on camera to boot.

'I can't do anything under these conditions,' I said, the vexation I felt showing in the words that tumbled from my lips.

The Master looked pointedly towards the figures of the two black manservants looming at the door and winked at me. 'Those two will take good care of you then … and you'll end up being known as a whore.'

At that moment, the door opened and a smartly dressed waiter stepped in with a trolley filled with an array of alcoholic beverages. I had never seen anything like it. He busied himself mixing drinks for the Master and his acolytes, and complied with an order to pour one more drink, which he thrust towards me.

'This should help you take care of business,' the Master said. 'But don't make it a habit.'

The victim's skin was as soft and clear as that of a woman stepping out of a scented bath; despite that, I imagined that he would not be easy to handle. I was not used to docile prey. He had not stopped pleading for mercy, his face streaming with tears, swearing he would be as a ring to the Master's finger. His entreaties fell on deaf ears, however. I too felt like crying out to be spared the task that awaited me. Notwithstanding the general mirth the pleading seemed to induce, the Master's sharp glances clearly indicated that his patience was exhausted.

I needed a few moments to recover myself, but with the threat of being administered my own medicine by the two Africans, I quickly complied, following the directions of the cameraman who seemed experienced at filming such scenes. He asked me to repeat several moves as if he were producing a film to be entered into some competition.

That night I was overcome with disgust at what I had been doing all these years in the dark alleyways of the neighbourhood. I had abused many young boys, completely indifferent to their suffering, and here I was about to get a taste of my own medicine. Even though I had engaged in countless acts of sodomy, I felt as if it were I who was being raped – that I was the one vainly begging for mercy.

I learned that my position at the Palace was an important one and that I was replacing someone whose 'flame' had gone out and who had served the first Master – *Sayyid al-kabeer* – in the same capacity. All indications were that the old-timer, Uncle Muhammad, was the retired punisher. I yearned to verify this but it was many years before the opportunity presented itself – or, to be honest, before I summoned up the courage to ask Uncle Muhammad directly.

Life inside the high Palace walls was something else entirely. Principles and values had no place there; we espoused whatever values the moment dictated, whichever ones best suited the Master's mood.

Whether it was an inability to say 'no' or inherent depravity, it took me many years to understand fully the extent of my debauchery. Worldly pleasures are worthless when we do not choose them ourselves. In my view, that is the reason for boredom. The Palace devotees thought otherwise, however. Their hedonism knew no limits and they were forever searching for some new form of gratification – turning to perversion if all else failed. Perverts and deviants are basically motivated by boredom: tired of what is socially acceptable, they seek whatever is novel or uncommon to break the monotony of routine pleasures.

The Master was so jaded that he had a special reward for anyone who could entice him with a new distraction. He had grown disconsolate about most worldly pleasures and felt there were no carnal delights left for him to experience. He enjoyed mutilating servants as much as he delighted in trading jokes with his brother or bringing in dancing-girls and singers from far-flung places. He also indulged in several marriages to celebrities, pretty news anchorwomen and the like, and frequented the world's biggest casinos. Watching his rivals being sodomised was his latest thrill.

On my very first night at the Palace, before I had even met the Master, Uncle Muhammad had taken me aside and said, 'Mark my words – don't hang around here too long.'

I was sitting, waiting to be shown in, when he offered me a cup of coffee in the traditional manner: bowing, as he had done faithfully for the first Master of the Palace. He poured the coffee ceremoniously into my cup and accompanied his cascading gesture with a small torrent of words that I did not fully grasp at the time.

'You'll get singed,' he warned, 'like a moth dancing too close to a flame. To the high and mighty of these halls, we're just a temporary convenience. Just like a tissue for a snotty nose, you'll be discarded soon after use.' When I responded with silence, he reminded me that money was the root of all evil.

A life of destitution is holier than anything I encountered at the Palace, where nothing was sacred and everything permissible. Without limits to freedom and nothing to push against or to hold us back, freedom is meaningless. I learned late in life that without obstacles or barriers, freedom is a mirage.

On Friday evenings, Aunt Khayriyyah would sit behind her lattice-screen window hoping for a little breeze to dry off her weekly henna application. Whenever she caught sight of me hanging around aimlessly on the street, she would launch into her usual vituperation. 'Mind you don't scrape that rear-end of yours sitting in the dirt!'

We thought we would die, as we had lived, drowning in rubbish. The filthy neighbourhood was a Babel of residents who hailed from every corner of the earth and who trickled into the streets every Thursday night like cheap dye that stains everything.

Only one area of the neighbourhood had retained any social cohesion and was still inhabited by the original settlers.

The other districts were populated by more recent arrivals, a motley collection of people from the southern part of the country – the Ghamad, the Zahharis, the Qahtanis, the Shahranis, the 'Asiris, the Yamis, the Jazzanis – and a hodge-podge of Bedu from outlying desert areas. There were also expatriate communities of Yemenis, Levantine Arabs, Egyptians, Sudanese, Somalis and Eritreans, as well as Indians, Afghans, Indonesians, Chadians, Chinese and Kurds, and Bokhari Uzbeks, Turkmen, and Kyrgyz who had fled the hell-hole of the Soviet Union.

Catapulted together, this multifarious assemblage of human-ity spread deep into the neighbourhood, sharing the daily grind of life all the while dreaming of escape. Soon, it was no longer enough to say that you lived in the Firepit because dozens of smaller contiguous neighbourhoods had sprung up that were named after some event or community. The Firepit had its own elusive history, one that its inhabitants had colluded in writing. Every event in that history – good or bad – could be attributed to someone who lived there.

The Hadhramis from Yemen were the most numerous and were well-regarded by the wider community. The next largest group were the Africans, mostly Somalis, Chadians and Nigerians who were known for their unflagging vigour and unrepentant licentiousness. No one, whether newcomers or long-established residents, was interested in further classifying the residents of the neighbourhood.

The award for manliness would go to whoever took on one of the Africans. If you backed down from the contest, your friends would consider you a coward and it was then best to make yourself scarce and not stray too far from home.

That was a life lesson that I learned early on. I had lain in wait for the least spirited among the African boys and assaulted him right in front of his peers. I laid into him and did not back off until I had secured my reputation as a tough guy.

We did such twisted things in the alleyways that we were often shunned and sometimes beaten by elders in the community who hoped to reform us. In their view, our actions were beyond the pale, and this only drove us to greater secretiveness.

Our depravity exposed us to imprisonment, banishment or a thrashing at the very least. It was like a red light. The opposite was true at the Palace, where no vile act committed within its towering walls would ever be exposed.

The Palace comprised two distinct wings: one for the Master's family, including a retinue of nannies and concubines, and the other for guests. The two areas were not completely separate since various structures within the compound were common to both, notably the halls, foyers, lounges, gardens and recreational areas.

Only a handful of people ventured into the wing that housed members of the Master's family, foremost among whom was Issa. He was responsible for seeing to the requirements and needs of the women. It was rare to have any news of that side of the Palace and no one knew exactly the connections between the Master and the various women who emerged from a door deep inside.

The women were assigned chauffeurs from a host of Islamic nations, each of them a paragon of honour, temperance and piety. The cars that conveyed the women used one of two roads: one that ran right through the middle of the compound, which was closed during celebrations and festivities, and a back road that followed the perimeter of the Palace along the seafront. This was the preferred route when there were too many visitors and during wild parties.

A luxury car glided to a stop near the family compound and a woman with bewitching eyes rolled down the window. Her *niqab* slipped momentarily off her face to reveal a lustrous complexion and to suggest many other charms besides those distracting eyes.

'Isn't Issa back from his trip yet?' the beguiling young woman asked.

When Issa was away, everything was topsy-turvy – at least that was how it felt. I realised that the young woman was repeating the question and that I had been staring at her the whole time. I was flummoxed.

'Is Issa back from his trip?' she repeated.

She was annoyed by my staring into her eyes and urged me to respond as I searched for the ineffable charms that might lurk behind that veil.

'Lower your gaze or say goodbye to your eyesight!' she snapped.

Coming to my senses, I mumbled a halting apology which she ignored. She raised her hand against the tinted window and the car resumed its stately passage through the compound.

When I was younger, a sure path to stealing a woman's heart – and body – was through her eyes. The secret was to gaze into a woman's eyes longingly and then make all the other moves to reach what lay behind them. It was a lesson I had learned from Mona. 'Women love being looked at,' she had told me. 'They love feeling that you are entranced by them. It gives them a heady sense of their femininity.'

The only woman I have ever known to dislike being

looked at was Aunt Khayriyyah. Finding herself being stared at was likely to bring out her most warped traits and spark uncontrolled rage. The merest glance at her would ignite whatever fire lay smouldering inside her. If you wanted to see her enraged or find out first-hand what a mean and spiteful person she was, all you had to do was stare into her eyes.

The men in the neighbourhood knew that looking her in the eye was likely to set off a torrent of obscenities and went out of their way to avoid her, stepping briskly out of view if they happened to come across her in the street. No suitor ever darkened her doorway for fear of that inextinguishable wrath.

Since she was unable to spark anyone's interest when she was still of marriageable age, she remained a spinster. Knowing that men would always flee from her, she began pursuing women. She did this openly, but the women she approached fled her as much as any man had done and alerted all their friends to my aunt's perversion.

After everyone was gone, only she and I were left in the house, with our grudges and watchfulness. Whenever she suspected I might uncover something she wanted kept secret, she would start gossiping about me at her women's gatherings, excoriating me for what she described as my perversions.

My aunt had watched my every move ever since I was a child. She was responsible for running the household and my mother had no say in my upbringing.

'Aren't you coming home?' she called out one day, craning her neck from the window looking out on to the back alley. I heard her but deliberately ignored her. I was chasing a boy who had snatched a wooden toy Tahani had been playing with in the alleyway next to his.

Aunt Khayriyyah resumed her conversation with the neighbour, the imam's wife. Water levels in the storage tanks were at their lowest level and another poor rainy season was in sight. Prayers for rain had been fruitless; not a rain cloud had appeared despite the oratorical skills of the mosque's imam.

Three whole years had gone by without a drop of rain. Whenever the imam's wife heard him imploring the Almighty for a shower, she could not help but recall how boorish and nasty her husband was to her and thought about how mercy should begin at home. 'The All-Merciful shows no mercy for the merciless,' she repeated like a refrain.

Tahani was leaning against a motorcycle that had been abandoned on our street ever since its owner had been run over and died. She held out her hands, smiling, as I returned the toy to her. But she ran off as soon as she heard her mother screeching about her playing with me.

Aunt Khayriyyah began complaining to another neighbour about her hair falling out in great big clumps. She lamented the loss of the locks which, she claimed, had drawn every boy in the neighbourhood to flock under the windows of her father's house.

'You mean that the windows in your day had no lattice-work?' the neighbour asked.

'Just as bitchy as your mother, aren't you?' Aunt Khayriyyah shot back, bristling.

She went back inside the house, muttering about the curse that had been cast on her and that had resulted in a wasted life, imprisoned inside her brother's home.

Hopping over the piles of rubbish lying in front of our house, I stepped through the rotting, termite-ridden doorway whose squeak was as shrill as my aunt's voice. To me, she was as decrepit as the old door and I wished she would give up on her mite-ridden situation.

Aunt Khayriyyah frowned at my empty hands. 'Didn't I send you to fetch water?'

'There isn't a drop of water to be had anywhere.'

'That's how it is with the likes of you,' she snapped, slapping her thighs in frustration. Then she reached over to grab my ear. 'Now go,' she said, pulling me down, 'and don't come back until you've got some.'

I found a water-bearer willing to deliver. Almost immediately after his donkey cart pulled up at our house with the order, there was an altercation that brought out all the neighbours.

My aunt started screaming bloody murder and hitting the water-bearer with a broom, claiming that he had been ogling her. When his screams rose to counter hers, the neighbours came running to the rescue. They burst into the house, pinned his arms behind his back and started to thrash him. As the blows rained down, the water-bearer collapsed unconscious on the floor and his attackers switched to delivering first aid instead of punches. They propped him up and splashed water on his face until he regained consciousness.

Before the poor man had even caught his breath, my aunt was inciting the neighbours to give him another thrashing. She began hollering as soon as the man was able to sit up. 'Look at him!' she screamed. 'Look! He's still making eyes at me!' She threw the broom at him.

The crowd looked at him and realised he had a tic which made him look as if he were constantly winking. They could barely conceal their amusement and helped him out of the house, apologising for their behaviour. All the man wanted was to be gone. He struggled to his feet and jumped up on to the seat of his donkey cart with a practised hop, cursing my aunt and the men who had come to her aid.

'By God, I wouldn't glance at that thing if I were a donkey,' he exclaimed. 'I'll be damned if that's a woman.' He was already moving away at a lively trot and had to turn his head back to deliver the parting shot: 'That's a woe-man!'

Unbeknownst to my aunt, the water-bearer's name stuck. Following the incident, it gained wide currency among the women of the neighbourhood and no man ever cast the shadow of a glance at the woe-man.

10

I COULD NOT STOP THINKING of those bewitching eyes peering from the window of the luxury car. Eyes like those could launch a thousand ships, and it would not matter if you drowned inside them.

I had never seen a *niqab* that framed a more entrancing pair of eyes: wide and deep and black, bordered by thick lashes and arched brows, their gaze aloof. In the days that followed, I lay in wait for her, hoping that she would reappear in the same spot. But her passage, like life itself, was not to occur twice.

I decided to imitate the water-bearer. I began practising and people were fooled into thinking that my right eye had suddenly started to twitch and blink involuntarily. My act was so convincing that I was advised to consult an eye doctor, which I promised to do. Meanwhile, I hoped that the woman with the bewitching eyes would pass me again so that I could try my winking trick on her. But she never reappeared and I dropped the tic before it became genuine.

Whenever I thought of my aunt, I could not help but snicker at the idea of a woe-man: a male seed that had rotted during gestation. My father had been infinitely more tender-hearted and gracious than his sister, for whom I felt only the

138

deepest hatred. My imagination often overflowed with visions of revenge: when the time came, I would reduce her to a babbling idiot who could never again raise her voice.

Only after we have lived our lives do human beings actually see clearly. The past is the record of a life and its assessment can confer wisdom. My aunt's was a record of sharp and piercing jabs, like nails strewn on my path, and every venomous word that dripped from her lips led me to some form of delinquency or another.

I have experienced both poverty and wealth and have concluded they are equally limiting: poverty pushes us to seek riches while wealth pulls us toward immorality. In either case, our lives are determined by our earliest actions.

Many years have passed since my early childhood, a time when the night became my constant companion.

I have been a night owl ever since I was a little boy. The neighbourhood commons was a welcoming space for children desperate to get away from their cramped and overcrowded homes. We gathered there, lining up in formation to play all sorts of games, with different teams selecting their players and passing over kids we had been warned to avoid.

Issa was one of those kids. Excluded from every group, he shunned all of them in return and took to hanging around drunks, homosexuals, sheep rustlers, chicken poachers and the petty thieves who stole bicycles and motorbikes. He acted much older than his age – just like Osama did – and he was not afraid of being jumped as he wandered around the dark alleyways with his older companions.

We became friends one dark night when I was crossing the Kuft, an alley notorious for sexual predators, where young boys were lured by fear or desire. I had gone there to meet up with a boy named Yasser Muft, who had asked me to arrive early because he had received threats for responding to my overtures.

As I waited for Yasser Muft to show up, I began pacing up and down the alley. Suddenly, a torch was trained on my face and I heard a little ditty: 'Pretty boy's gone away, gone, gone pretty boy.' I recognised the voice of Mustafa Qannas.

He stopped singing and bluntly told me to undress.

In the beam of the torchlight I looked for a stone with which to crack open his head and when I sighted one and lunged for it, his blade pressed into my back and his left arm had me in a stranglehold.

'You do as I say or you're dead,' he hissed.

Issa appeared out of nowhere like an angel descended from heaven. Taking in the scene, he laughed and tapped Mustafa on the shoulder, saying, 'Couldn't you find someone else to threaten other than the Hammer?'

I slipped out of Mustafa's grasp and picked up a good-sized stone with which to split his head open.

'Don't do it,' Issa warned as he grabbed me, 'or else he's sure to ride your arse, sooner or later.' He turned to Mustafa almost playfully and told him that I was his closest friend.

The tension lifted immediately.

'The Good Lord took pity and sent you Issa,' Mustafa said, patting my cheek.

Issa chuckled, his laughter ringing in the night. 'If you knew the Hammer like I do,' he said, 'you wouldn't even have tried to have your way with him.' He went on to regale Mustafa with tales of my voracious sexual appetite and how it stopped at nothing, whether human or beast.

Mustafa began to laugh and put his hand on my shoulder. 'You and I are kindred souls, eh?' he said with a twinkle.

At that moment, Yasser Muft came out of the shadows and all three of us dug into him.

I was spellbound by the eyes in the *niqab*.

My position at the Palace prevented me from seeing women, much less mixing with them. Initially, I did not understand the reason for this total prohibition, but it became clear that it was to keep me from slackening – so that my pent-up lust would have me drooling at the prospect of riding yet another victim.

On a whim, the Master decided to create a team dedicated to humiliating his enemies. He began to plan for the venture and put me in charge of recruiting for what came to be known as the 'Punisher Squad'.

The more sexually repressed a recruit, the better suited he would be to perform the job. That was the Master's view and he wanted me to pick the cream of the crop.

After my designation as squad leader, Issa no longer had anything to do with this aspect of work at the Palace. But he suggested that I would be able to find the kind of men I needed at the Dreams Café behind Tahliyyah Street, where all the deviants and perverts gathered. Just one visit there made me blanch.

In the event, I recruited the squad members from the wretched and impoverished residents of the densely populated neighbourhoods of the city, where people were ready to chew on whatever fodder was thrown their way – no questions asked.

I rounded up a few contenders and told them all the

activities that would get them expelled from the squad if they were caught doing them. The most important prohibitions were mixing with or even looking at women, watching television outside the approved channels, using mobiles or any other kind of telephone, bringing women's magazines into the Palace and, finally, masturbating. The last would be enforced through spot checks, including lab tests of seminal fluid if necessary.

After everyone had agreed to these conditions, the squad was housed in a secluded area of the Palace, which the team members could leave only to perform an assignment, returning to their quarters once they had finished.

The only member of the group able to transfer to another area of the Palace was Osama. Though I had recruited him, Issa assigned him a position that he felt better suited him and that had only recently come to light. Thus, Osama was seconded from the Punisher Squad and no longer reported to me.

In any case, the squad was short-lived because the Master's rules and regulations proved impossible for most recruits to follow. Before the squad was disbanded, all its members were subjected to the same treatment they had meted out to the Master's adversaries, with photographic evidence as back-up. They were duly warned to forget what took place in the Palace on pains of some unspecified punishment. All understood the veiled threat and the consequences of breaking the team's vow of silence.

Only I was retained to carry on with the punishment assignments. I was less worried about my manliness being violated than by the numerous prohibitions the Master had decreed. To ensure my unflagging performance in servicing the billy goats, I was denied access to the nanny goats.

After almost seven years of formal requests, as well as numerous pleas and entreaties, the Master eventually granted me permission to move out of the Palace. I wanted to live in a place of my own, ostensibly to take care of my aunt, who had no one left to look after her in her old age.

Of course Aunt Khayriyyah's life was of no interest to me and I was certainly not keen to relive what I had experienced with her. But it was a valid excuse that would allow me to have at least one foot out of the Palace. The idea came to me when, after one of his nightly seduction acts to lure young women to the Palace, Osama whispered, 'Your aunt is on the verge of starvation.'

We had just finished setting up for a party and several young women had swooped down on the Palace intent on snagging a man who would prize their beauty and shower them with gifts. The Master had recently granted permission for me to leave my quarters between assignments. Osama and I secluded ourselves at the back of the hall, watching the young women sashaying about before the predatory eyes of the Palace guests.

'Look, over there,' he whispered urgently. 'It's Tahani!'

Osama dropped the bombshell as he gestured toward one of the girls. I could practically hear my heart pounding inside my chest.

'Where? Where is she?' I looked around feverishly.

'Over there – dancing.' He pointed vaguely at a small group of young women swirling around a fat guest.

'I don't see her,' I said. 'Tell me exactly where you're looking.'

'The one wearing the dress with the slit in the back.'

My eyes zeroed in on the girl like an infrared missile. Could

143

it be that she was making good on her promise? Had she finally caught up with me in the middle of all this debauchery? If so, I would have to kill her, plain and simple.

I was on the point of getting up to go towards her for a better look, but he stopped me.

'I mean, doesn't that girl *look* like Tahani?'

I broke into a cold sweat and felt faint.

Whenever the past wants to reclaim us, it lures us with its finely wrought enticements. The one thing I dreaded above all else was to find myself face to face with Tahani. I became convinced that she was concealed somewhere within the walls of the Palace. It upset me whenever I thought about it as I would imagine her standing in the punishment chamber watching me. I imagined myself justifying my abject state and the time I ravished her.

Oh, dear God, what if Tahani *had* landed here? Could she have come here, like the rest of us, to be immolated in this infernal paradise?

Or maybe she was exactly where I had left her, wiping away her tears and the traces of blood. Maybe a statue of her had been erected to remind passers-by of the victims created by the firestorm of love.

I was still staring at the look-alike when Osama plunged in the stake.

'What did you do to Tahani?'

When we do not right our wrongs, we are continually haunted by regret. It is futile to feel guilty about the past because we cannot make whole that which is broken. That is why I needed to escape.

Osama launched into a long discussion of Tahani and only then did I realise the extent of the torment I had caused him.

144

At the time, Osama's position at the Palace allowed him to come and go as he wished and he would bring me news of the neighbourhood, inserting titbits about Tahani in the hope that I would react or come clean. He was on a mission to find out what had taken place.

When I remained mute over Tahani, Osama changed tack and hissed in my ear, 'Didn't you hear what I said about your aunt? She's on the verge of starvation.'

There and then, I decided to use my aunt as a pretext to end my enforced isolation in the punishers' quarters.

I had left the old neighbourhood in the middle of that darkest night, and I slipped back into the Firepit at night, almost seven years later. I was a changed man. I had nothing left in me. My equipment was worn and slack with overuse and my body was weary from the excesses of my depravity.

The neighbourhood had barely changed. There were still heaps of rubbish everywhere. There, too, were the familiar burnt-out street lights and the kids in dirty clothes, playing and cursing at each other. Women selling almonds and roasted watermelon seeds still sat listless and resigned behind their merchandise, while pedlars plied the alleyways with their trolleys of cotton candy, pulses, spices and pastries. More flies swarmed about their wares than all the neighbourhood kids put together.

The Firepit seemed less animated than I remembered it. There were no women calling on one another any more, and all the windows overlooking the streets had been sealed. Houses were more secluded, doorway curtains had disappeared, and even the newer houses that I did not recognise already seemed old and worn.

I heard the evening call to prayer and immediately recognised my half-brother's voice – Ibrahim's dewy call drifted in from the loudspeakers in the Salvation Mosque. Soon, the higgledy-piggledy neighbourhood settled to a tranquil calm. As the old men responded to the call, their ablutions completed and water still dripping from their full beards, I walked by quickly with my eyes fixed to the ground and the loose ends of my *keffiyeh* wrapped around my face.

I entered the alleyway leading to our house and glanced up at Tahani's window. It was boarded up, with rust-encrusted nails for ever sealing the latticed shutters. I caught sight of her older brother outside their house, who initially followed me with his eyes and then turned his face the other way, pretending not to see me. I wished to ask him about Tahani, but when I looked at him again, he spat in my direction several times without ever looking me in the eye.

I looked up again at Tahani's boarded-up shutters and realised with a sharp pang that I would never again see her at her window. I would find nothing there but seething rancour amplified many times.

My visions of Tahani were invariably mixed up with those of my mother. I felt my mother had abandoned me when she agreed to marry Ghayth Muhannad and moved out of our home. Instead of keeping the flame of maternity burning bright for me, she had betrayed it and granted the breasts that had nurtured me to another man.

Whenever I thought of him thrusting inside her, I would imagine her being stoned like a common adulteress. I pictured ever more stones being hurled at her as she cried for mercy. But the wishful thinking would collapse when I remembered that she could not plead for anything – as it

146

was, she could barely stammer intelligibly, managing only simple grunts and moans.

Then another picture would come to mind: of Tahani, lashed to a wooden stake in the sand and surrounded by a crowd of people pelting her with stones and screaming 'adulteress' at her. Her clothes would be soaked in blood and, when they removed her blindfold, she would catch sight of me in the midst of the stone-throwers. The vision always ended with Tahani being led away to some jail for sexual offenders and crying in desperation, 'Why have you forsaken me, Tariq?'

I blended visions of Tahani's possible fate with the stories of the Palace girls. So many young women had found sanctuary in the Palace. Many had been arrested after their very first sexual adventure and had become prostitutes on being released from jail. It was their only means left to earn a living outside the rank-smelling jail where the female warders had their way with them. Some of them were able to parlay the profession into positions of influence and get their way with prominent men. I had heard of, or observed, so many young women losing their virginity and speaking about their first sexual encounter in such a nonchalant way that my feelings about the treatment of women were wrapped in a thick layer of indifference.

With a final backward glance at her window, I wondered if Tahani had followed the same path. This was why I always looked for her in the Palace – and always dreaded ever finding her there.

Reaching my destination, I knocked on the door repeatedly and waited.

'Who is it now?' screeched a familiar voice from inside.

'The devil take you! You're going to break my door if you keep knocking like that!'

When she saw me, she could not believe her eyes. She was so taken aback that she practically swallowed her words.

'I should have known,' she finally managed to say. 'Nobody but you would pound on a door like that.' Her eyes were still wide in disbelief at seeing me there after almost seven years. 'What brings you here?'

As she stood holding on to the door, I kissed the top of her head and inhaled the familiar smell of congealed aromatic oil in her hair parting. She pushed me away and put on a show of tearfulness as she avoided my embrace and bemoaned the cruelty of an existence that had left her alone and poor, with no one to care for her.

She was even more withered than she had been and everything about her had shrunk – except, that is, for her tongue, which had lost none of its agility. Past the shock of seeing me again, a stream of the old invective burst forth once more, and my long-buried loathing was reawakened just as swiftly.

As I was reminded of my hatred, Aunt Khayriyyah dredged up her own loathing for my mother. 'What else can a snake give birth to?' I, too, had not seen that serpent mother of mine since she had moved out to live with Ghayth Muhannad.

'So what brings you here?' she asked directly.

That was the question. Standing there, I could not fathom the overwhelming urge I had to bring this woman back into my life. She was like the germ of an eradicated disease that I had locked up in the laboratory of my emotions. I was back to show her how well her scorn had borne fruit and to give her a taste of her own medicine. I asked myself the same

148

question: was I here to give the lie to all her dire warnings or to confirm them?

She kept asking why I was there, like a broken record, and I was tempted to give up on her. I had already had enough of her and of everything I had gone through with her. But I hesitated, remembering that I needed her for two reasons: as a means to escape my quarters at the Palace and to satisfy my thirst for revenge.

'Would you like to come with me?' I asked her, and immediately regretted it as it gave her an opening to refuse.

What if she turned me down? Then it really would be impossible to budge her. Before she could waver, I quickly pointed out the miserable condition she was in and the decrepit state of the house. The ceiling in the living room was caving in and there were deep cracks in the walls of the courtyard. I followed her around the house where I had spent such a significant part of my life, taking in the interior doors that had come off their hinges, the carpets and curtains that had faded and the light switches that no longer worked.

For her part, Aunt Khayriyyah was taking *me* in, without giving voice to the questions she had for my sudden and unimagined appearance.

'Would you like to come with me?' I asked again.

Perhaps she had been pondering my question quietly to give me a chance to consider her own counterproposal.

'Your mother is in greater need than I am. Why don't you help *her*?'

'Because she has a man. She doesn't need me,' I said pointedly. 'I don't have anyone in this world except for you now.'

All she needed was a little insistence on my part to wear down her pride. She had a litany of complaints: from

149

loneliness, to the bureaucrats in the social security system procrastinating over her papers, to having to live off the charity of others. I persisted with my offer as much as I felt she needed me to, despite her graceless temporising. I promised her a comfortable existence with servants at her beck and call to take care of her.

I had to keep myself in check often in order to disguise my deep-seated loathing for her. I put my arm around her and told her that I wanted someone from my bloodline to care about me and keep me company.

'Why aren't you married?' Aunt Khayriyyah asked suddenly.

She was trying my patience with endless questions I was unprepared for, but I managed to deflect her by saying, 'Will you be the one to pick my bride?'

She laughed and I think it was the first time I ever saw her teeth. Despite the filth of her tongue, they were a brilliant white, pristine and without decay.

'What do you think of Tahani?' I asked her.

'Which Tahani? Do you mean Salih Khaybari's daughter?' I nodded.

'So you're on the lookout for a slut who is like your grandmother, Saniyya,' she stated viciously. She paused. 'They say Salih took her back to his village one night and married her off without a wedding.'

I was too stunned to say anything.

'Apparently Tahani did something shameful and brought disgrace to the family. The only way her father could conceal the scandal was among his own people in his village,' Aunt Khayriyyah said. Pulling her dishevelled braids together, she carried on, now in true form. 'Saniyya's blood runs in your veins, boy, that's why you only go for whores!'

I took the double blow about Tahani and my grandmother, and swore to myself that I would silence that tongue once and for all when the time was right. I had no outlets to vent my rage and dispel my fury other than the cesspit where I had learned to swim amid streams of rubbish.

My patience reached its limits when she went to her closet to collect some tattered old clothes. I tried to stop her short by promising that we would go shopping and that she could buy whatever she needed. But she insisted on taking some of her rags, along with a small wooden jewellery chest where she stored the rings, earrings and gold chains that she had accumulated over a lifetime.

Whenever I tried to hurry her, she would remember one more thing that she needed to take along. Finally, remembering her headcovering, she went through the clothes piled up in her closet. Swearing she had not been out for over a month, she went from room to room looking for her *niqab*, furious that it had disappeared.

'You don't really need the *niqab*,' I said, which immediately sparked off her hostility again.

'The likes of you would poke their thing up a hole in a rock if they could,' she shot back, punching me in the chest.

She was getting worked up and I feared she would change her mind. I cajoled her and pretended to be joking.

I was just about ready to strangle her when she shuffled over to the neighbours' houses to bid the women farewell.

'I'm off with my nephew, Tariq. Goodbye!' she shouted, knocking on each and every door.

The farewells to the various neighbours were long and drawn-out despite my repeated calls for her to hurry up.

To her closest neighbour, Aunt Khayriyyah said, 'If Ibrahim comes looking for me, tell him I've gone with his brother.'

Women crowded around to bid her farewell and convey a few parting words. As we took our leave she asked me whether she should leave the keys with one of the neighbours to look in on the place. I told her she could come and do so herself any time she wanted.

It was only when she was seated next to me in the car and we drove away that I knew for sure that I had finally prised her out of the Firepit. Her eyes were practically popping when she saw the car, and she fired off a salvo of questions at me.

'Where in the world did all this come from?'

I had to field a stream of phone calls from women at the Palace and Aunt Khayriyyah eavesdropped on the conversations. She tried to get a question in at the end of each call but was interrupted every time by my cell phone ringing again.

I drove to my new villa and when Aunt Khayriyyah stepped inside, she was visibly astonished and her eyes scanned every inch of the place.

'Is all this yours?' she wondered. 'Only thieves and drug dealers have stuff like this.'

There was an uncomfortable silence while she looked searchingly into my face. Eventually, she asked, as if dreading the answer, 'You've become a pimp, haven't you?'

Hatred has an odour, just like love.

Smells are alive. They are born and grow in our memory after becoming associated with a specific time in our lives. Regardless of its nature, a smell is for ever linked to the time we first experienced it. Smells can be associated with all sorts of things, a sweet from childhood, new holiday clothes, the chairs in a particular classroom, even a teenage song or our first love. When a smell triggers our memory, we recollect all the attendant history and context of its first occurrence and are left aching with grief or sorrow.

I had forgotten how much I hated my aunt. The full extent of my loathing and hostility came back to me as I breathed in her smell.

Whenever I came home to the villa, the air inside was redolent of my aunt and hung so heavy I felt suffocated. Our past history lurked in every corner of the house like swarms of locusts, aggravating me as I tried to cultivate patience and a measure of goodwill towards her. After all, the reason for coming to my aunt's rescue had been to give myself a little breathing room, a place I could escape, even if only momentarily, from the Master's clutches.

At the Palace, I hated the smell of the victims. I loathed the smell of the Master and of Osama. I hated my own smell and was sure that to someone, somewhere, I also smelled revolting. Would Tahani be nostalgic for my smell? Nothing remains fresh for ever, whether real or remembered.

After six years of uninterrupted service at the Palace, I had felt stuck and had turned to Issa for help. He said he would do whatever he could to help me move into a place of my own. I had to remind him more than once that my aunt's situation was becoming urgent, and he finally obtained exceptional leave for me to go and live with her.

'But I can't go back and live in that neighbourhood,' I protested.

'You don't have to,' Issa said. 'You can rent a villa in Zahra or Naeem. Or buy one.'

'That would be nice.'

'OK, let me speak to him.'

Months passed and Issa was frequently away. I followed up with phone calls and text messages until he finally got back to me.

'I've spoken with the Master about your situation, and he too thinks you need a break. However, his stipulation is that you must find a substitute and that you remain on call. And the list of prohibitions stands.'

'That's fine.'

'Have you thought about who could replace you?'

'Yes, Osama.'

'He's been given other duties. Forget Osama.'

'Don't worry,' I said. 'I'll find someone.'

'Of course, you can only live with your aunt and no one else,' Issa reminded me. 'You understand that, right?'

Looking for a substitute who would satisfy the Master was not going to be an easy matter. I had to rack my brain to think of someone who could do the job without complaining. It occurred to me that I could approach the former members of the disbanded Punisher Squad. But after what they had endured as a pre-emptive punishment, it was unlikely any of them would even consider an offer from me. They would probably want to give me a taste of my own medicine before listening to what I had to say.

I was able to arrange the purchase of a villa and to move there with my aunt. I spent the next few days looking for a substitute and settled on someone from my sordid past.

I found Mustafa Qannas just as I had left him: nursing his moonshine in an alleyway and improvising poetry about the boys he was infatuated with. He was not working and spent his time loitering around the neighbourhood schools, feigning interest in the young boys' progress in class and exhorting their teachers to take good care of them, like some kind and attentive uncle. He had a love interest in each school, whom he wooed with his verses and protected from other predators in the area.

'Hey there, Mustafa,' I called to him.

He was leaning against a wall, eyes glazed.

At the sound of my voice, he squinted to see who it was and jumped to his feet to welcome me. We fell into each other's arms; it felt like he had not embraced anyone in a long time. I noticed how he still smelled the same. Our lingering hug revived the memory of that night when we had our way with Yasser Muft. He stepped back, keeping his hands on my chest, and looked into my face, smiling broadly.

'It's been a long time, kid,' he said.

'Not much of a kid any more,' I laughed. 'Don't you see how old we've grown?'

He shook his head. 'We're young at heart no matter how much we age.'

I told him why I had come to see him but he seemed unable to grasp what I was saying, as if he had gone soft in the head. I wondered whether he had any juice left in him. But my job was to find a replacement, not to assess his potential to perform.

Mustafa came with me to the Palace and I handed him over to the Filipino manservant, pleased that I could now go and enjoy my life relatively unburdened. But my elation proved to be short-lived; Mustafa categorically refused to do what was expected of him with a video camera running. I never saw him again and went out of my way to avoid him after that, since he swore he would kill me if it was the last thing he did.

With my move into my own living quarters, I began to believe I had escaped from the Master's clutches.

I started to host soirées at the villa to which I invited people who could be trusted to be discreet. I stopped attending Palace parties on the pretext that I was having trouble with my old aunt.

One night, the Master stopped me and, looking me in the eye, asked, 'So, how is your aunt these days?'

'Very well, thank you. She is grateful to you and always singing your praises.'

He started to laugh viciously. 'Singing my praises, eh?' He found that so amusing that it took him a while to stop. 'Singing my praises,' he repeated with a final chortle. 'Tell me, did you have to reattach her tongue so that she could sing my praises?' That set him off again.

I was nailed to the spot. His sarcasm had undone me and I felt panic-stricken. How did he know? No one was there when I did what had to be done.

Her tongue-lashings had become intolerable.

Every one of her body parts had deteriorated with age except for her tongue. Aunt Khayriyyah would launch her invective in the midst of social gatherings, insulting the women in the room and showering me with obscenities.

Initially I had wanted to show her who was boss and that I could do whatever I pleased. I would bring her down from her room so that she could witness the posse of young women at my feet. I even went so far as to kiss and flirt with them while she looked on. I regretted that later, though, because it only provided more ammunition for her vile tongue.

No sooner did people arrive in the evening than she seated herself with us in the reception area and let loose on the poor guests. I would tell her to return to her room but she would ignore me and continue to buzz around like a mosquito on the trail of fresh blood.

Some of the women would leave early, unable to stand her constant griping. The less sensitive ones simply moved to another part of the room or to another part of the house. Those sitting by the swimming pool outside swore they would not come back inside until she had been silenced. They hovered around listlessly just long enough to be paid.

Even without women visitors in the house, my aunt's tongue overflowed with venom. She would attack the men for their conduct and call them pimps and perverts. She often tipped their drinks on the floor or threw them in their faces, threatening to report their debauchery to the authorities if they did not leave immediately.

My patience was running out.

One night, Aunt Khayriyyah hurled an ashtray at a guest, inflicting a deep cut in his forehead. On the pretext of having to take him to the hospital, most of the guests fled the scene. A few women stayed behind just long enough to collect their pay, swearing never to return even if I offered them their weight in gold.

Once the house was empty and Aunt Khayriyyah had spat out every foul word in her lexicon, she crawled up to her room like a snake returning to its lair. She had tasted blood. Feeling no remorse for injuring the guest, she threatened that

157

anyone coming to the villa from now on would be taking their life into their hands.

I was livid with rage and went after her. I burst into her room, grabbed her by the hair and threw her on to the floor. Ignoring her screams, I tied her hands behind her back with a telephone wire and stuffed a wad of tissues into her mouth.

I was determined never to hear that voice again. I ransacked the bathroom for a razor blade and came back into the room with a handful of them. I propped her up across from me.

'This is your day of reckoning,' I shouted in her face. 'You do remember what you did to my mother.' I showed her one of the razors. 'I'm going to put your tongue in the freezer – that way you can stand in front of the mirror every day and dream of reattaching it.'

I had never seen her in such a state, her eyes bloodless and bulging with terror.

'No, better still. I'll get a cat, starve it for three days and then give it your tongue.' I leaned in towards her and hissed, 'Poor kitty will have to swallow all your bile.'

I pulled the wad of tissues out of her mouth and she immediately started to scream, 'You stink to high heaven. You came from a filthy belly. That's why you stink to high heaven.'

This was the last thing I ever heard her say.

I slapped her and clamped a hand over her mouth to stem the flow of bile pouring out of it. Any more of her insults and I would lose my mind completely. Still she carried on and, despite the words being muffled and unintelligible, I knew she was cursing everyone who had anything to do with my coming into the world.

I had hoped that she would finally relent and invoke our family ties – that she would beg me to honour my father's memory, show remorse or say something, anything, rather than carry on with her insults. But only venom poured out as if she feared that if she did not get it all out of her system, she would never have another chance.

I moved my hand off for barely a second and, with her mouth gaping open in mid flow, I reached in deftly to grab hold of her tongue with my fingers. I held on tight, making sure I had it firmly in my grip. Then I pinned her head down with my leg and, in one swift motion, I used the razor in my other hand to slice off her tongue.

I held on to the amputated portion as blood bubbled out of her mouth and streamed down her face. She lay completely still.

I thought I had killed her, and for a while all I could do was stare at the body, terrified. I flipped her over and felt her frail bones but was unable to feel the slightest sympathy for the old woman. I wanted her to wake up and listen to what I had to say without, for a change, being able to talk back. I did not want her just to go and die like that. I needed her to hear me out, to hear what she had never heard before. Now what was I going to do?

My meeting with the Master occurred several weeks later, well after the doctor's visit to administer first aid and soon after I had hired two women to look after Aunt Khayriyyah.

The Master had stopped laughing. 'She wasn't really the type to sing praises, was she now,' he commented as he handed me a video tape. 'She had a filthy tongue and it deserved to be cut off.'

I was rooted to the spot.

'It's not what you did to your aunt that upsets me.' He paused and then added, 'Actually, you've got talent for crime.'

159

Head lowered, I silently awaited his next command.

'I'm upset that you violated the conditions of your employment. So long as you work for me, women are strictly off limits.'

This time there was a longer pause as though the Master was considering an appropriate punishment for his disobedient servant.

'I thought I might have you castrated,' he said slowly, 'but then you would become utterly useless to me.' Indicating the video tape in my hands, he warned, 'I have my eyes on you – always. Another slip-up and it's over. Do you understand?'

I nodded weakly.

'Good. So go back to your aunt now,' he said, 'and please give her my best.'

His laughter pursued me to the end of the hallway as I walked away, drenched in sweat.

I began watching the video the moment I stepped into my room.

It was an edited recording of everything that had taken place in the villa, in perfect video and audio quality.

The film had captured everything I had given vent to that night and I was thankful that I had not said a single word against the Master. The camera work was professional, shifting seamlessly from the reception areas to my aunt's bedroom, through the hallways and into the bathroom. It documented all of the main highlights of that evening: the ashtray hurled at the guest, the women who left early and those who stayed on to collect their pay, and the curses streaming from my aunt's mouth before I grabbed her by the hair and she lost her tongue to the razor.

The camera moved on to focus on me in the kitchen, placing the piece of tongue in the freezer and then, the following day, on the servants changing shifts and the doctor's visit to administer first aid. His subsequent visits and treatment suggestions were also recorded, as was my recruitment of two women to look after her, with my explanation of how my aunt had fallen and bitten off her tongue.

I had captured a cat outside, but the film showed how I kept it locked up in the house for a couple of days to starve it and to allow extra time for my aunt to recuperate. Then, finally, the closing scene was me sitting my aunt down across from me, chopping up her tongue into tiny pieces and feeding them to the cat one by one, as she watched with horror.

My crime was fully documented, in perfect video and audio quality.

II

I HAD GONE TO STOCK up on groceries for the prisoner in my villa but before I could drop them off, I received an alert message on my phone telling me I needed to rush back to the Palace.

The Palace staff and servants had no set time to sleep. We were supposed to remain awake and be on call whenever the Master was up; he was in the habit of asking about his staff day and night, and if he ever found out one of us was asleep or absent he would fly into a rage and promptly fire the person. That is why we stole a wink here and there whenever he was asleep.

There was a trade in these furtive snatches of sleep: his personal attendants would message the other staff that the Master had dozed off. This was especially useful to those who worked the following shift, since they also got a message to alert them that he had woken. To avoid detection, the phone alerts were written in code and sent only to subscribers of the service, which was called 'Ever Ready'. For added security, the body of the text messages changed every day, and only the keyword 'ready' was retained in any message that went through the service.

The network was headed by Joseph Essam, who was so

afraid of being found out by the Master that he operated the service with great subterfuge. In addition to discretion, considerable financial resources were required to join the network. The Master's personal attendants found this service highly lucrative. They shrouded the enterprise in secrecy and competed with one another to create additional, fee-paying services that they could offer the Master's acolytes and guests.

My despondency provided Joseph Essam with an excuse to attend to my spiritual health; he wanted to save my soul from eternal torment and bring me closer to God. But he was more interested in converting me than in being my friend, and once I understood that, I stopped being irritated by his futile efforts.

I read the alert message on my phone and called Joseph Essam. 'That's right. No going out tonight,' he warned. I decided to follow his advice and dropped the idea of going to check on my aunt. She could go to hell for all I cared.

The women brought into the Palace to satisfy the voracious lusts of the Master's guests came in every shape and form. Each had a miserable past buried under a cheery and lively façade, since the men sought them out for their bodies and not their miseries.

Outside the Palace, there was another tumult of women who swarmed the gates. They fluttered around like ravenous crows and were kept out of the grounds since they were destitute. They hitched their infant children to their hips in the hope of a handout, however modest, that would compensate them for the grief meted out by the guards and the unrelenting pounding of the sun on their heads.

The Palace regulars wanted nothing to do with them; they

harangued and chased them off as if they were some sort of plague that would spread unless it was swiftly eradicated. When they brought the matter to the Master's attention, he silenced them with a gesture of his hand. He had heard enough, he indicated.

There had been only a few beggars to start with, but one Eid the Master had been so generous that they were soon joined by others who had heard them bragging about their good fortune. Hundreds of beggars set up camp outside the Palace gates and the swelling din of supplications and crying infants became a source of thrill for the Master.

The sound gratified him because he was experiencing a new pleasure, one he had not encountered before. He instructed the guards to allow the beggars their rugs and cushions but to keep them confined to the area immediately adjacent to the gates, and to placate them with assurances that handouts would soon be distributed.

The Master went in and out of the compound repeatedly, and every time his car passed the ragged figures intoning blessings and prayers for his prosperous life, he felt he was in heaven. The sound of those beggars was so different from anything he had ever known, it went straight to his heart. He made up his mind to distribute the alms personally.

He went out to where the beggars were gathered and began scattering banknotes of every denomination about their heads; the crush of people very nearly tore him to pieces as they clawed at the paper money in the air. He felt so rewarded by this experience that, for a while, he became a serious philanthropist, donating to charitable associations and homes for the elderly and insisting on the media's presence whenever he did so. The depictions in mass-market newspapers were invariably angelic, portraying him as one who relieved the suffering of the huddled masses in the swoop of his wings.

However, like all his previous pleasures, this one also proved short-lived. He soon grew tired of the beggars, whose numbers augmented daily, and he became so irritated with them that a vehicle from the city's anti-vagrancy agency was stationed outside the gates so that the approaches to the Palace could regain their stately splendour.

Now, instead of decrepit and haggard bodies at the gates, there were supple and vivacious bodies crossing the threshold of the Palace to deploy their charms, passions and resonant laughter in the pursuit of fame and lucre.

It was a transaction pure and simple: the women bestowed light – or heavy – favours and in return were paid handsomely. They left at the end of the evening, hoping for similar opportunities in the future. A single evening of lascivious dancing at a Palace party typically earned a woman more money than it took to silence all the beggars outside.

Maram was sexy and provocative.

She belonged to a group of dancers who had been brought in to liven up the evenings at the Palace. Though young, she showed early promise as a professional seductress.

Maram was reserved and coy to begin with, but when she saw that her takings paled in comparison with those of the other dancers, she dropped her demure manner. She would take the dance floor by storm and flash plenty of flesh to fire up the men watching. Whenever she felt she had been short-changed, she negotiated a private deal with a guest to make up the difference. However, unlike her charms, which were stunning, her negotiating skills left a lot to be desired; had it not been for the Master's eye falling on her, she would have worn her body out for piastres.

I was reminded of young Souad and how the child-sized seductress haggled over one riyal before accepting my nail in her plank.

I had encountered Souad again more recently, when I was sent to the Palace gates to organise the mêlée of beggars. I was told to count the people and collect their requests after the Master had lost interest in going out to scatter money over their heads.

Souad was begging for charity with the other destitute women and had a child with Down's syndrome beside her. I saw her standing there, holding a piece of cardboard over the boy's head to shield him from the scorching sun, giving him sips of water from a half-empty water bottle. I asked one of the guards to show her into the reception lobby and she picked her son up off the ground and ran in carrying him, ignoring the snickering comments of the women around her.

As the cold air from the air conditioning in the lobby hit her face, she exclaimed, 'Dear God, may our graves be as cool as this.'

One of the guards blocked her path and asked her roughly, 'What do you want, woman?'

'Bread. What else do hungry folk dream of, brother?' she replied. Seeing that he was about to push her outside, Souad added urgently, 'Someone here sent for me.'

I told the guard to let her be and as he went on his way, Souad inched closer and launched into her fevered entreaties, seemingly unconcerned that her face was not properly covered or that her shrivelled breasts were visible from the opening of her tattered dress.

How she had aged! Her two front teeth were broken, her hair parting was streaked with grey and her eyes were set deep in their hollows. Some women wilt like weeds.

I expected her to be at least surprised to see me again. But she just kept mumbling the prayers and pleas of beggars everywhere.

'Is this your son?' I asked, interrupting her.

'Yes,' she replied, 'and I have three others who are older than him.' Then she proceeded to itemise her long list of needs, starting with her electricity bill and ending with her youngest son's costly treatment.

'Doesn't your husband work?'

She shook her head. 'He's in jail. He got ten years and he's got six more to go.'

Our lives are full of ups and downs. Some of us rise and some fall. I had always known Souad to be close to the bottom of the pit, and I was not that far behind her. She and I were alike in that we were both fallen. The only difference was that she had hit rock bottom, while I was still falling and could see myself falling much further.

I pulled out my wallet and handed her 4,000 riyals. She gasped and bent to kiss my hand, but I withdrew it. 'This isn't charity,' I told her. 'This is to pay back my debt to you. It's taken a very long time.'

Souad was bewildered. She held on to the money with both hands while her son squirmed at her feet.

She looked down at the banknotes, unsure. 'I've never lent anyone money,' she said. 'Are you making fun of me?'

167

Holding out the wad of cash, she choked back a sob. 'Here, take back your money!'

'No, Souad, this is a very old debt,' I insisted.

At the sound of her name, she peered into my face and asked, 'Do you know me?'

'Don't you recognise me?'

Gathering her abaya around her and shrinking further into her already shrunken frame, she apologised profusely. 'I'm far-sighted,' she said. 'Life has worn me down … I can't afford glasses.'

'I'm Tariq. Tariq Fadel.'

'Tariq?'

Slowly her face brightened and she flashed a grin. 'Our child-hood – what a wonderful time that was,' she said earnestly. 'Since you owe me a debt and if you are able to, could you get my husband out of jail?' She pulled out a piece of paper document-ing her husband's charge and showed it to me. 'They say that if someone vouches for him, he'll be out the following day.'

I read the name: Yasser Muft. The boy Issa, Mustafa and I had taken turns with all those many years ago, now in Breeman Prison on drug-peddling charges.

'Of course, Souad,' I said. 'I will do my best.'

She picked up her son and went out through the doors, turning back to look at me while I stood watching her against the glass pane of the reception area. She clutched both her sick boy and her abaya in an attempt to hide the tear at the back. I watched her as she stepped outside, saddened at how diminished she had become. As she vanished into the crush of bodies milling about the Palace, I wondered where that little girl who used to play bride had gone.

★ ★ ★

I was invisible to all the Palace VIPs except for those unlucky enough to cross my professional path. I was as unseemly as a genital wart kept hidden from view.

I had been hired for one specific purpose. Though over time I took on other, smaller assignments, the Master always made sure I would never forget that these were secondary functions.

One of these functions was to remunerate the women who attended what came to be called the 'Red-Hot Nights'. I would stuff wads of cash into envelopes at the end of the evening and hand them over to the women in accordance with the Master's specifications. This afforded me an even more important role, that of go-between: many of the guests were desperate for the services of the Palace women and equally keen to have their affairs kept secret from the Master.

It was here that the city's most influential men shed all pretence of personal dignity and forsook every shred of self-respect in their pursuit of novel pleasures. Before the night was even over, they would be anticipating the next opportunity for quenching some unfulfilled desire. I became the point-person whenever one of the girls was not responsive enough to the advances of the guests. As I had a list of all their phone numbers, I could provide the guests with their contact information or my services as a discreet go-between. If the Master had learned I was dishing out his Palace girls, I would have been hanged, drawn and quartered.

I started keeping records after I realised I actually knew next to nothing about the girls, who were, in effect, like my personal and much coveted clutch of golden eggs. This was brought home to me when a prominent businessman took me aside one evening and intimated he wanted the phone number of a girl he called Dalia. The women all had aliases which they switched as easily as they changed evening gowns, and I had not memorised their names. Although he laboured to describe the girl, I was unable to help him.

After that incident, I became diligent about keeping files on all the girls, with their names, brief biographies, pictures if available, interests, and family and socio-economic backgrounds. Since most of the girls provided false information, I double-checked their stories with their friends. They all delved into the minutiae of each other's lives and whenever I came across information that seemed contradictory, I would check it against someone else's account. The files were not for the Palace guests to see but for my own use.

On party nights, luxury cars would glide through the Palace gates with their consignment of girls. These had been carefully selected to appeal to a wide range of tastes in a process akin to a beauty contest. Girls nominated for the so-called elite brigade were subjected to an even more meticulous inspection, although they were not aware of it.

The elite brigade consisted of women from every race and breed, each of whom had a unique characteristic that set her off from the others, and they were reserved for private functions attended by select guests. These men had to be lavish spenders as well as lechers. The young women who attended the bigger events aspired to enter the exclusive circle of the private functions. Such an accomplishment indicated that a girl had attained top ranking and could name her own price and make plenty of easy money.

Maram was like a vast ocean whose surging waves could drown you if you stayed in too long. She caught my eye the very first time I paid her for attending an event.

'Am I missing a leg or an arm or something?' she had objected, when she realised that she had earned less than the other dancers. 'Why am I being paid less?'

Normally I would respond roughly to this type of petulance, but she possessed such vitality that it was difficult to counter her. I explained that I was willing to increase her share of the takings but that I had strict guidelines from the Master. Maram faced me, her eyes glinting and without the trace of a smile on her lips.

From then on I began watching her and waiting for an opportune moment to be with her. She could sense that I was all eyes for her, and responded to my eagerness with every cell in her body.

We had several phone conversations before she became the Master's trophy-woman, his dazzling beauty. She appeared naïve and unfamiliar with her new setting and did not seem fully aware of what lay ahead. Seeing myself as something of a guardian angel who could protect her, once I called her and expressed concern for her future and reputation. She hung up on me with a choice phrase spoken like a true whore.

Whenever she attended one of the Palace gatherings after that she noticed me watching her. But the Master staked out his own claim before I could make my move and once she was his, she became off limits to all other men.

Once she had possession of the Master's heart, there was no need for Maram to come by the cash register to get her money. Now she only had to say the word and whatever sum she desired was in her bank account.

The new arrivals, especially, appreciated my role. Whenever they got embroiled in relationships at the Palace, I was their man – not so much the key to the door but rather a well-worn threshold that had to be crossed. I knew where everyone fit in the scheme of things and I could help a girl take her first step into Paradise.

A different roster of women and girls attended each function. They hoped to attain permanent status in the constellation of favourites and sought out their recruiters and minders for information on the Master's state of mind, wanting to anticipate his every mood.

The girls were never handed any money in front of the Master. It was his prerogative alone to bestow largesse on the women who attended his functions, including those lucky enough to be his friends. He was generous with the sums he handed out and it was understood that the guests were forbidden to rival him in such matters.

One particular VIP, who had made his fortune in the telecom sector, had not been made aware of this interdiction. At his first Palace function, after he had become good and drunk, he pulled out his chequebook and wrote the girls a cheque for 50,000 riyals each. He looked pathetic as he bent down to get each girl's full name, writing out the cheque and stuffing it into her cleavage before moving on to the next.

Knowing how the Master would react, the girls ridiculed his gift to his face. No sooner had the telecom mogul stuffed his cheque into her cleavage, than each would swiftly pull it out, tear it into little pieces and scatter it about his head. The Master was delighted by the sight of this repeated scene. He laughed heartily and instructed the servants to carry the drunkard away and throw him out of the Palace.

The matter did not end there. The Master wanted to know who had invited the man to his private function and since Joseph Essam was in charge of the guest list, he got a drubbing. This was all done for the benefit of the guests, however, because the Master knew perfectly well who had been responsible for inviting the wayward guest.

'Anyone who had anything to do with inviting this moron needs to leave the Palace right away – and stay out of my sight,' the Master barked.

The guests were silent as if to deny knowing any such person.

The Master pointed to an individual called Hisham Jawharji. 'Son of a bitch,' he roared. 'Who invited scum like you here?'

Hisham said nothing, knowing that to respond to an outburst, even if it was to apologise, would be courting trouble. The Master came up to him slowly, grabbed his ear and spat in his face.

'I never want to see you here again. Is that quite clear?'

Hisham nodded but did not attempt to wipe the thread of saliva dripping down his right cheek. As soon as his ear was released from the Master's grip, he turned to go on his way.

'How dare you turn your back on me?' thundered the Master.

Hisham stopped dead in his tracks, terrified, and adjusted his posture to face the Master. He backed out of the room, apologising profusely as he went.

Gloom descended on the guests who remained frozen in place for fear of provoking a new outburst. The Master returned to his seat as his entourage crowded around him, bowing and scraping and wondering what to do next.

There was a prolonged silence and the guests shifted uncomfortably in their seats, looking everywhere except at the Master.

Whenever Maram was late, the Master would be irritated

and the most trivial thing could set him off. She would know how to calm him when she arrived. After an interminable few minutes, Maram swept into the hall with self-assurance.

'Where have you been all my life?' the Master asked as he jumped up to greet her. He kissed her on both cheeks. 'What kept you, dear one?'

'My mother was not well.'

'I'll have every doctor at her bedside – right away.'

Maram laughed, her face up against his, and wrapped her arms around him.

'May I never be deprived of you,' she sighed contently, kissing him between the eyes and whispering endearments. The tension fell and he relaxed. He turned and whispered something to his chief accountant, who ran off and returned moments later with two briefcases. Grinning from ear to ear, the Master turned towards the girls who had torn up the cheques and announced that they would each receive 100,000 riyals. He grabbed the briefcase closest to him, opened it and scattered more than one million riyals in banknotes at the girls' feet. They shrieked with delight and stepped out on to the dance floor shaking and shimmying seductively to a song called 'You Know What's the Nicest Thing about You?'

Until that moment, no one had uttered a word; everyone knew to wait for the go-ahead, for a hand gesture, from the Master. He was generally ill-tempered but there was money to be made from his company.

Discussing politics was strictly forbidden. He was adamant nothing should mar his enjoyment of alcohol and women. No one was allowed to bring up anything connected to current events, whether inside the country or abroad. But before every function the Master was briefed on world events by his media adviser and sometimes, when the conversation turned to the stock market, a news headline would be talked about because it impacted share prices. It behove whoever was speaking to disregard current events and focus on predicting market trends and outlining how the Master's affiliated businesses could influence trading, whether upwards or downwards.

One night when he was quite drunk, the Master overheard Uncle Muhammad talking about the trial of Saddam Hussein. As a long-standing and ardent Arab nationalist, Uncle Muhammad was following the trial closely. 'Saddam, the hero, will expose the truth of events in the region,' he opined.

'Your job is to serve coffee,' snapped the Master, 'not to pontificate about politics, you ass!' He pelted Uncle Muhammad with a shoe, cursing both the old man and his hero.

After that, Uncle Muhammad took to his room. Rumour had it that he was upset at being humiliated in his old age and despondent at the fading of his youthful dreams. In any case, no one really cared whether Uncle Muhammad stayed in his room or not.

Uncle Muhammad felt the indignity of old age was ruthless and that time had trapped him in the torment of a long life. On the morning of Saddam Hussein's execution, he cursed all of mankind and refused to attend prayers for Eid al-Adha.

Uncle Muhammad fashioned a noose out of nylon cord, tied it to a metal hook hanging from the ceiling, looped it around his neck, made a blindfold out of his *keffiyeh* and climbed on to a chair. He had tied the chair legs to the door handle; since the door opened outwards, anyone coming in to his room would cause the chair to be dragged from under him and propel him to his death.

Several hours went by but no visitor came to his door. Uncle Muhammad pulled the noose off and wept, realising that he lacked the courage to take his own life and that he would have to wait for death to come of its own accord.

12

IT HAD BEEN A riotous night at the Palace and the Master and his companions were wasted.

The ashen threads of dawn seeped into the large hall strewn with bodies. Revellers were sprawled out everywhere, bloated with intoxication and slurring their words.

The evening had begun in a large circle that gradually disintegrated and scattered to the loud music of the band. The guests had shed their stiffness as a Khaliji ensemble, brought in especially for the occasion, belted out rhythmic dance tunes and the lead singer whipped the crowd into a wild frenzy. The girls shimmied and shook their bottoms skilfully while the men, their joints loosened, leapt around them gracelessly. By the closing number everyone had shed the last of their inhibitions and sprung to their feet. The excitement abated when the performance was over and the musicians packed up their instruments and left quietly with the singer.

The languid and dewy breeze had not yet dispelled the last of the night, and the Palace lights shimmered against the glassy surface of the sea, tinged with the first light of dawn. The glow cast by the lanterns suspended from the Palace balconies turned the waters into a vast turquoise canvas streaked with gold.

Fighting his hangover, a guest called Jalal Ma'eeni struggled to a half-standing position from his stupor. He turned his feet in the direction he thought was due east and his musical voice lifted in the morning call to prayer. By the time he was done, he had called the prayer in all four cardinal directions and was now facing north.

Still pitched on their stomachs, the other guests responded with almost involuntary motions. They could hardly move in their drunken daze. Joseph Essam, claiming he wanted to break down the barriers of religion, asked someone to demonstrate what he needed to do to join in the prayer. He lined up next to everyone else and began reciting from the Holy Bible until someone silenced him and suggested he should stand away from them if he wanted to pray.

Everyone lined up in two crooked rows behind Ma'eeni, who looked right and left and invited the women to form their own separate row next to Joseph Essam. Before he had completed the very first words of the prayer cycle – the *takbeer* – the Master struggled to his feet.

'The only one who leads prayers around here is me, you ass,' he exclaimed, grabbing Ma'eeni by the shirt-collar.

Ma'eeni sank to the ground and did not try to pick himself up. Sprawled on his back, he reached out for the closest liquor bottle and slugged whatever was left in it.

The Master stumbled through the Qur'anic recitation: he wrestled with his memory to dredge up the verses of a particular *sura* and came up with those from another *sura* instead. He faltered through the opening words, 'Have We not soothed your heart, and relieved you of the burden—' He stopped abruptly, unable to remember the rest.

The Master roared, 'Help me out, sons of bitches!'

178

Since none of the congregation could complete the Qur'anic *sura*, he bowed and sank to his knees, not in reverential prostration but simply keeling over drunk. He fell asleep on the spot and began to snore; he was soon joined by several guests, with their mouths hung wide open.

Servants picked their way carefully around the sprawling bodies to collect bottles and glasses. The few remaining guests who had not dozed off fought their torpor and staggered off to their bedrooms to see if they could rekindle their pent-up lust.

In addition to my original crime, there was now another – one that could see me hang if it were ever discovered. But what bothered me more and plagued me with doubt was the video tape the Master had handed me. I remained baffled by it and assumed that, somehow, a spy with a camera had been hiding inside the villa and following my every move.

One day, out of the blue, the police raided the villa. Thankfully I was there when it happened.

It was during the summer holiday when the Master and his family were away on a tour of Europe. Before me lay the prospect of three months of freedom in which to do anything I wanted. I considered a trip to Casablanca, where a group of Palace employees had arranged to spend their holidays, but felt hesitant about leaving my aunt alone at the villa.

I toyed with the idea of taking her back to her house in the Firepit. It offered the prospect of getting rid of her once and for all since she would never be able to tell anyone what had happened to her and it would be practically impossible to convey the story in sign language. But I thought better of the idea when I recalled that the two women I had hired were able to communicate with her perfectly well. They understood all her hand gestures even when she was so angry she was fit to be tied.

It was one of those women who came to tell me the police were at the door.

I took my time going downstairs, trying to think of a reason for their visit. I momentarily panicked at the thought that the Master might have gone ahead and handed a copy of the video tape to the authorities in order to get rid of me. I thought of a whole host of possibilities but decided that delaying would just further complicate matters.

I came down the stairs pretending to have a stomach ache and apologising for keeping them waiting. I was at the door, talking to three policemen and I could see two cars in the driveway. As soon as I appeared, a higher-ranking officer hopped out of one of the cars. I introduced myself and told him where I worked. For the first time ever, I used my work address and the power of the Palace for a private purpose.

'How can I help you?' I asked politely.

'Maybe you can tell us why we keep getting emergency 999 calls from here,' the officer said. 'But there's never anyone on the other end of the line saying anything intelligible. We just hear stammering and shrieking.'

'My sincere apologies, sir,' I answered quickly. 'I stored the number on my phone in case of an emergency. Looks like some of the kids figured out which button to press and have misused the phone.' I apologised again and began shouting out random names that came to mind. 'Hattan! Ghassan! Ma'een! Get over here!'

We waited in silence.

A few moments later, I tried again. 'Hey kids, come here!'

180

I worried that I would have to keep on calling fictitious children till I turned blue in the face. I apologised again and praised the police for their vigilance. Then I realised it was a grave mistake to suggest that children were the culprits. The police had probably investigated beforehand and would know that a bachelor lived in the villa. Now, I thought, their suspicions would be aroused and I would be found out.

So I stopped calling out any more names and decided I would tell the officer it was my nephews or the neighbours' pesky children or maybe a friend's brats. But I did not know anyone who had relatives with those names. I was getting more and more worked up, and decided the best thing would be to say nothing.

Luckily the officer took his leave and left it to me to warn whoever was dialling the police station to stop. He concluded by reminding me that it was unnecessary to store the emergency contact in my phone since it was such an easy number to remember.

I took a long and deep breath as I watched the two police cars disappear into the distance.

Cutting off her tongue had not been punishment enough.

While I was talking to the police officer, I could see her watching us from the window. As soon as the officer climbed back into his vehicle and shut the door, she began pounding on the shutters. She was crying and whimpering, but the sound was fortunately very faint. After I had made sure the police were on their way, the first thing I did was to call the phone company and request a temporary suspension of service. The customer service representative told me apologetically that he could not process my request and that I would have to go and fill in a form at the main office in person before service could be suspended.

I ended the conversation hurriedly, fetched a pair of pliers, and disconnected the phone line on the outside of the villa. I called in the two women who helped with my aunt, paid them a full month's wages and then dismissed them.

They were taken aback and asked nervously if they had neglected any of their duties with my aunt, but I reassured them that all was well on that score and that my concern was for them. The police had been checking on domestic workers who had overstayed their visas, I said, and they were returning momentarily with a female officer who was going to search the house. The two women thanked me profusely for my consideration, gathered their abayas about them, and left the house hurriedly. I instructed the driver to drop them off wherever they wished.

After locking the door, I went up to my aunt's room and found her crouching in a corner, under a big pile of clothes. I pulled off the top layer that covered her head, grabbed her white hair and pulled hard. She gasped, her eyes widening like saucers. As I had done the previous time, I tied her hands behind her back with telephone wire, stuffed a wad of tissues in her mouth, and sat on her, bearing down with all my weight. Her bones practically snapped under me and she groaned and growled as her eyes fixed on the pliers in my hands.

'Which of these fingers dialled the phone, eh?' I demanded as I held her fingers and examined them. 'It seems to me that you're looking for more punishment.'

Her muffled scream was barely audible.

I placed her right index finger between the pliers and

squeezed hard, but not so hard as to sever it. Then I moved on to the other fingers: her pinkie, her middle finger and her ring finger. I squeezed each one until I heard the snap of a bone breaking, before proceeding to the next one.

She had stopped screaming and lost consciousness. I untied her and left her lying where she was.

How I wished she would die. If she did not, I would have to kill her. In the meantime, I was well and truly her prisoner.

Life at the villa had become intolerable: I was stuck with this aunt who, though she was a near-corpse, refused obstinately to take herself off to the next life. I was restless and consumed by the idea of getting rid of her before she could do any further damage and have me hang for it. I brought in a succession of women to attend to her, rotating them before they could bond with her or develop any empathy for her.

Aunt Khayriyyah had grown used to dressing her own wounds and was so exhausted she no longer did anything besides moan, grind her teeth and chew on her palms. Her eyes had lost all their ferocity and she kept them mostly closed. It was as if the years of her life were gathering themselves for the final journey.

The Master returned from his tour and was greeted by a line of servants and staff welcoming him back. I was among them and he asked me explicitly to stay behind.

I felt I could not stomach one more ignominious act of sodomy. I was so dispirited that I would have gone to my death willingly and was steeling myself to refuse his next request.

He busied himself with the well-wishers, discussing the

183

various cities he had visited and other things he had enjoyed seeing.

I stood there for a long time, like a guard from the Abbasid era at the sultan's disposal day and night, primed and ready to plunge his sword into whichever miscreant was at the execution block. I stood there, seething with resentment, certain that I was about to be tasked with another assignment.

The Master gave everyone a beautifully wrapped gift and then dismissed the other members of the staff. They began to disperse and the accompanying hubbub died down.

When we were alone, he handed me my gift and said cryptically, 'You need to get rid of your aunt before she dies on you.'

I accepted his advice unquestioningly, relieved that this was his reason for asking me to stay behind; there was no other business, no punishments scheduled for that day.

Later, I unwrapped my present to find three things in the package: sexual enhancement pills, a bottle of cologne and a video tape. I hurried home and inserted the cassette into the video player to witness the entire sequence of my aunt's fingers being crushed.

Aunt Khayriyyah had become frail and withdrawn, and spent the entire day moaning plaintively.

She paid no attention to me when I got home and I no longer provoked her terror. If I ventured near her, she just shut her eyes and wrapped her arms around her head, and her body tensed with apprehension.

I had given up hurting her.

I had also figured out the mystery of the two video tapes.

I was checking in on Uncle Muhammad, who was still holed up in his quarters. I broached the subject of the Master's uncanny ability to be aware of everything that happened around him. Uncle Muhammad interrupted me and launched into a eulogy, praising the Master's treatment of his staff, his pursuit of their well-being above all else and his vigilance in protecting them from mistreatment by others. Then he changed the subject completely.

'They say that Sheikh Omar is in a really bad way,' he said, 'and that he's dying. Is that true?'

I was not interested in talking about the former head fisherman. 'But I'm asking you—'

'I think I should visit him right now,' Uncle Muhammad interrupted. 'You can come with me if you like.'

For the first time since the night he was humiliated by the Master, Uncle Muhammad left his quarters, pulling me along as he negotiated the meandering hallways of the Palace.

He was clearly uneasy, but this discomfort was not linked to his advanced age. After a while, he leaned in towards me and hissed, 'All this time and you haven't learned a thing.'

'Learned what?'

'If you come to my room to talk about him, what do you expect me to say? Don't you know that all of the staff quarters are bugged and that there are people whose job it is to film everything and pass it all on to him?'

I did not respond.

'You're never going to get it, are you?' he exclaimed and was seized by a sudden coughing fit so acute he practically choked.

Around me, my aunt was completely silent. I felt nothing but revulsion when I saw her. It was as if her tongue had been the source of her vitality, and all that was left now was this decrepit, old and emaciated hag. Just as her screaming had been a form of torture, so now her silence was a torment. She avoided me and I avoided her.

The villa became a wasteland in which two housemaids and a Filipina nurse roamed with nothing to do but watch my aunt. They made sure she kept to her room and prepared food for her if she requested it.

I could no longer invite anyone over and the huge villa became a hotel where I spent part of the day sleeping and left at three o'clock in the afternoon without seeing anyone.

I needed to get away from the twenty-four-hour surveillance.

I had become cautious and was circumspect at all times. I moved like a rat trying to get across an open space full of hungry cats: security precautions preceded my every step. I became increasingly desperate to leave the villa.

The only obstacle was my aunt, a constant thorn in my side; I could not just pack up and leave.

Then I hit upon the idea of transforming her room into a prison cell – a jail without warders or guards who might inadvertently let their captive escape. Since I did not know where the hidden cameras had been planted, I decided to cover the walls and ceiling with wallpaper.

First I dismissed the guard who watched the villa, as well as the nurse and the two servants. After going about the rest of the day as usual, once night fell I switched off all the lights and applied layers of wallpaper. I brought in crates of water, milk, canned goods, biscuits, and dried fruit and vegetables and stashed them inside the room with her. I locked everything up, including the front door, and drove away.

I stayed in hotels and beach bungalows, after having

obtained the requisite family ID card as evidence I was not a bachelor. Normally, an unmarried man would not be able to check in to those establishments.

I had learned that the hard way. Whenever I had snagged one of the girls at the end of Palace parties, there was never anywhere to take her. I would do this typically by the end of the evening when the Master was so drunk he could not tell which way was up. I would pick up some woman who had not been selected by any of the guests and find myself circling every street in Jeddah looking for somewhere to take her. Every establishment required a family ID card before they could offer a room, even for an hour, and so I lost my catch every time.

I had never thought of obtaining a family ID until I realised that women could provide escape from my deep depression. It felt as if a weight were pressing down on my chest, and the feeling worsened whenever I thought of my aunt, of Tahani and of the punishing assignments the Master set up for me.

All of this was weighing on me so heavily that I began to have trouble breathing and found that, no matter how wide I opened my mouth, I could not inhale sufficiently deep breaths. I thought I had asthma or that my lungs were sick, but after several inconclusive tests, I was referred to a psychiatrist.

He wanted me to go over my entire life in detail. I would not agree to do that, but he did say something that resonated with me. Human beings need to nurture their souls with positive feelings and to rid themselves of negative emotions, he said. Just as you sit down to lunch every day and later discard the waste, so too you have to sit down and feed your soul and clear out toxic residues. Life, he said, was nothing but nourishment and excretion.

I agreed with this notion and so began searching for some positive nourishment for my dispirited soul.

Thinking of Maram made me feel good and all I wanted to do was to take refuge in that image which came to dominate my thoughts. Before becoming the Master's favourite, her candour during our conversations had verged on salaciousness. She had rejected the possibility of love but offered sexual bliss if I wished. Just as I began exploring the most effective approach to pick her ripe fruit, the Master set his sights on her and she became inaccessible.

I turned to other Palace women for solace.

But in order to be alone with a woman, I needed an official permit that would allow me to move freely in her company. That is why I had to get married: I needed that family ID status.

I quietly approached a family from the countryside and negotiated a marriage contract where my name would not appear in full, on the off-chance that the Master had spies in the marriage courts. The clerk who drew up the contract was an easy-going fellow and, for an additional fee, was sympathetic to my predicament – my lie, that is, that I wished to protect my current wife and children from finding out about this additional marriage.

The marriage was a mere formality. Once I received the certificate, I could divorce my putative wife without ever having set eyes on her. In the meantime, I completed the paperwork for the family ID, which enabled me to cruise unhindered around the hotels and beach bungalows of Jeddah.

I settled into a bungalow in a hotel compound. One

afternoon I felt the need to wash away any lingering thoughts of my aunt sealed in her cell, and had a few hours before I was expected at the Palace. I ran a bath and even though the water was only lukewarm, I submerged myself. Thoughts of Tahani began trickling into my head as I watched the drip-drip-drip of the water from the tap.

How close past events seemed even when they had taken place decades earlier. Tahani was the springboard from which I leapt into the inferno.

We had liked to quarrel because it stoked our passion. After we disagreed about something, we would have to make up; we would get close and, one thing leading to another, we would be ablaze with desire.

We bickered over trivial things: seeing her standing in the window and looking at the young men hanging around the neighbourhood, some scurrilous rumour she had heard about me which had made her angry, her refusal to come out in the evening to meet me in secret, her failure to respond to one of my letters, her anxieties about my past, my irritation whenever she told me of suitors knocking at her family's door.

However, there was never a time we did not make up and forget our quarrel. The Egyptian diva, Najat al-Saghira, could always be counted on to break the logjam, particularly her soulful 'A Night to End All Nights', which seemed to have been written just for us.

I recalled the night of my senior school graduation, when Tahani appeared at her window and waved. Both Osama and I had noticed that wave. Later, she told me that her aunt, Osama's mother, had approached the family to arrange for a betrothal. He had expressed an interest in her and had promised that, if Tahani agreed to marry him, he would work and study at the same time. I had said nothing that day and had slipped away, realising how much I hated Osama.

Where was she now, I wondered.

Even when I hit rock bottom, Tahani remained a ray of light.

When we fall, we are not conscious of our screaming and shouting, nor do we remember how we scrabbled desperately to grab on to something or someone to prevent our fall. We are not aware of our bleeding wounds; all that we can do is try to stop that fall. It is only once we hit the bottom that we can take stock of both our injuries and the pit we find ourselves in. I had sunk as low as possible and had nowhere left to go.

As the tap dripped, I took stock of my wounds and how much they hurt.

I had not been aware of the depth of my love for Tahani. Did I love her because I had ruined her, and were my feelings in fact closer to pity or self-reproach? When we slaughter an animal and make a mess of it, the creature, foaming at the mouth in agony, ends up haunting us. Tahani was my botched sacrifice.

Thinking about Tahani invariably led me to thoughts of Maram. Maram dominated my mind; her spirit was so radiant that she could brighten the darkest gloom. And I needed someone to help me out of my gloom.

In our neighbourhood the practice of sodomy was not considered inherently perverse. It was a way to acquire a reputation for virility and was looked upon as an expression of one's sex drive rather than one's sexual preferences. It helped to classify one as either predator or prey.

Sodomy became my bread and butter at the Palace, and

with the greater availability of women, less perverted sex also became commonplace and banal.

'Maybe I need to open an academy for budding queers,' the Master had said one day, laughing, after it was brought to his attention that his victims hankered for more of our punishment. The Master did not disband the Punisher Squad because the group had been unruly or unwilling to accept the strict regimen he enforced, but because many of the victims had started to crave more punishment.

Foremost among those was the businessman Mamdouh Suleiman, who bid on a large project when he knew only too well that the Master was also in the running. Despite several warnings, he persisted and made sure that he undercut all other bids.

The Master arranged to have him brought in and punished, and specifically instructed that he be broken. However, after being thoroughly chastised, instead of behaving as the Master had expected, Suleiman just persisted in bidding on projects to compete with him.

The Master switched to punishing his rivals by stripping them clean of their wealth. He did this by luring them into various scams, including money-losing deals, shady real estate schemes and fictitious joint ventures. Eventually he struck where it hurt them and their shareholders the most and he celebrated their declines in the stock market. He played his hand masterfully thanks to the advice and acumen of an army of economic and media advisers, planners and policymakers, bankers, brokers, middlemen and fund managers.

Once the Punisher Squad was disbanded, I was freed of the vile responsibility of recruiting for it. Instead, I was charged with distributing gratuities to the girls who provided the entertainment at the Palace gatherings.

Maram was the choicest among them.

She knew how seductive she was and thrived on the attention of the men who lusted after her, albeit discreetly. They had to be careful that the Master did not notice their eagerness when their gaze lingered on her cleavage, her majestic ivory neck rising out of the vale between the rounded hillocks of her breasts. His drinking companions stole only surreptitious glances at her whenever she swept into the room to take up her place beside him.

I had become adept at the furtive contemplation of women during my adolescence. They hurried through the alleyways and little markets of the neighbourhood and I filled my imagination with whatever I could steal without them noticing my marauding eyes.

There was nothing furtive or oblique about the way I looked at Maram. Women are very responsive to a man's lustful stare, which generates an almost electrical charge inside them. When a man looks at a woman with desire, she responds with every pore and cell of her body and wants more of it.

Maram often caught me with my eyes latched on to her breasts, and she tripped me up time and again.

On dancing nights, Maram would remain seated until she was specifically requested to dance, and then she would get up and do so only if she had the entire dance floor to herself. The other girls knew this and as soon as Maram stood up they all made way for her.

The men, for their part, launched into conversations with their neighbours and averted their gaze. They knew it would mean the end for them if the Master caught them ogling her.

They would be summarily expelled from the Palace and would be lucky to escape with their eyes intact.

Maram was gifted in both the Khaliji style of dancing as well as in the more boisterous Egyptian rhythms. She would begin by kicking off her shoes and stepping coyly to the centre of the dance floor. Then, wiggling her bottom provocatively, the rippling movements progressed to her waist and from there her whole body shook and undulated. All of her seductiveness was concentrated between her torso and her buttocks and she swung her cascading hair enticingly from side to side. She moved ever so lightly on her feet, painting sways and bends with her body in waves that revealed her breathtaking femininity. Like a priestess in a sacred dance, every limb and joint shimmied and trembled. Finally, with tiny intertwined steps and snaking legs, she would sidle up to the Master and let her hair cascade over his face.

Unable to contain himself after such a bewitching performance, the Master would envelop her in his arms, kissing whatever part of her his lips could reach. Then he would lead her off to one of the Palace bedrooms.

More often than not Maram would later return to the hall without him, smiling radiantly, to look for her purse or phone or shoes and to bask in the pleasure of the guests' lechery. She was careful to avoid looking directly into any of their covetous eyes after they had ravished her body.

Before the videos of my crimes came to light, I had thought of luring Maram to the villa. The Master beat everyone to the draw and snatched her up. She sowed the seed of a passionate love in his heart. However, it became apparent that she was not as enthralled as he was. She would invariably leave whenever he was at the peak of his pleasure, claiming she had to return home.

It became so intolerable that he told her she had to make a choice. Maram chose him, and he took care of all the impediments that had kept her from being with him night and day. She later told me that the Master enlisted the help of people in high places to get rid of her husband, who ended up institutionalised in a psychiatric facility after a judge obligingly issued a court order.

Ever since her first night at the Palace, when she had complained about making less money than the other girls, I had been baiting her with flirtatious remarks. She responded to my overtures with a broad grin but continued on her way, sweeping through the Palace majestically, like a ship cutting through the waves on the high sea.

One day, before she had become the Master's exclusive preserve, I took my courage in both hands and confided that I was in love with her.

'And what exactly are you after?' she replied, laughing.

'I just want you to know that I love you.'

'Do you not think that's what I've heard from every man I've ever known? Love is just a word and I'm not looking for words.'

'I can give you whatever you want,' I tried again.

'You think love can be bought, just like a body? Look around you,' she went on. 'There is not a loving man or woman in this place. There is only lust, extinguished as quickly as it's ignited.'

I remained silent.

'But if you're looking for something else,' she said, 'a little bit of bliss, maybe, I would consider it. Just don't ask for more.'

Whenever I saw her after that, she held my gaze and it was clear in the way she moved that it was a promise deferred but not forgotten – even though she had become the Master's chattel.

Where was Tahani now? What abyss had she fallen into?

I erased every act of wrongdoing with a more egregious one, and had no qualms whatsoever about it. For good measure, I was careful never to look my victim in the face. Such abdication of responsibility came at a price – as I found out for myself.

Tahani lurked on the periphery of my mind, but I managed to keep thoughts of her at bay until Osama joined us in Paradise. With him around, I could not help being reminded of her and of our rivalry.

The wild nights at the Palace were of no interest to Osama. Once his job setting the parties up was done, he would disappear and return only at the end of the evening. He would slip off to his room and keep his cell phone close by in case he was needed.

One evening we began reminiscing about events both recent and long-gone.

'Would you feel sorry if I told you that you ruined my life?' he asked with a deep sigh, as if some heavy burden was being lifted off his chest.

'We all ruin each other's lives without meaning to,' I answered, patting him on the shoulder. 'Should I blame Issa for ruining my life? If I hadn't gone along with him, I wouldn't be stuck here now. Nor would you, had you not chosen to follow suit.'

'I wasn't talking about being here,' he said.

'I know we made a dirty choice, but it's too late to clean up our act now,' I cut him off.

'I'm not talking about the Palace, Tariq,' he said, adding with resentment, 'I'm talking about Tahani. Tell me what's become of her.'

I said nothing. Her face loomed before me, tender and sad as if from behind a veil of dust. I had covered her tear-streaked face with layers of dust in the years I had spent putting her out of my mind.

Osama stood up and faced me. 'I came to the Palace to kill you,' he confessed. He buried his face in his hands as he added, 'And to kill Issa – and to kill myself.'

There was a long, strained silence.

Eventually, Osama asked me bluntly, 'What did you do to Tahani?'

Just then, a servant approached to let us know that the Master was asking for us. We were both worked up, but we set aside our animosity, jumped to our feet and hastened to the Master's side.

'Get ready,' the Master said, addressing us both. 'There's an arse that needs whipping into shape.' He rose and headed to the private quarters where his family resided, adding glee-fully as he reached the door, 'I'll be watching you. Don't let me down.'

We took care of business, the Master watching us closely, and when we were done we went back to our seats as if noth-ing had happened.

Tahani was right there where we had left her, waiting to torment us both.

13

BEFORE COMING TO THE Palace, I would sneak off in the dead of night to the Kuft to enjoy the tenderness of young flesh and unburden myself of my infamous sex drive. Like well-worn steps, those alleyways were beaten smooth with stories and allegations of transgression. Every boy in the neighbourhood had left some trace of himself smeared against the ramshackle houses wedged together there.

I would walk the familiar twists and turns all night. The paths were as intertwined as the spilled guts of the run-over cats I would stumble upon, their bulging eyes a stark testimony to the fatal impact.

Early on, life in the neighbourhood had been a stagnant and putrid morass from which no one thought to raise his head or venture away. Residents were content and accepted their lot. The first person to disrupt the placidity was Issa, who set off in search of excitement and planted the idea of the easy life among us boys hankering for a little more glamour.

Issa lured us to the Palace one after the other, slipping golden spoons into our mouths and tickling our palates. Unfamiliar with the sight of gold and the other bounties on offer, we responded eagerly and did whatever was necessary to feel those delicacies were meant for us. We were brought into the Palace to decorate it with our shabbiness like so many antiques or bric-a-brac acquired at a flea-market.

The Master scattered us about the Palace like a novice collector who regards tattered old things as priceless gifts. In each of us, he found some distinctive feature to play up which allowed him to demonstrate to his entourage that even the poorest districts harboured hidden treasure – in our case, untold riches of deviancy to fulfil every imaginable desire.

It was Issa's job to hunt down such treasure. I was the first to be drawn in. After me was Sheikh Omar al-Qirsh, formerly the head fisherman, who piloted the Palace yacht on sea excursions and fishing trips. After him, blind Ali Madini was hired to tell dirty stories and gossip about the women he followed with his nose thanks to the overpowering perfumes they favoured. Jameel Badri was hired to plant trees and Bakr Adam to cook popular dishes. Ibrahim Dana instructed guests in the performance of the stick dance, or *mizmar*. Hamdan Bagheeni, who still struggled with the alphabet, was hired as a guard and Hassan Darbeel trained the dogs. This long line of people made its way into the Palace at Issa's behest: they were selected for a particular attribute or because Issa nursed some old grudge he needed to settle.

Of them all, I was the most dishonourable. Only I was truly despicable.

I was the second one to enter service at the Palace after Issa. Osama joined us three years later. He was hired to assist me in punishing the Master's rivals. After him, all kinds of characters streamed into the gilded cage.

Osama distinguished himself from the very first day he worked at the Palace and the Master was so pleased with him that he appointed him to the Punisher Squad immediately. I had noticed him enjoying it whenever we had shared the spoils of our hunt through the dark alleyways, and only later did I realise that he had been faking it.

At the end of his first day at the Palace, Osama frowned when our eyes met.

'You still nursing that grudge of yours?' I asked him.

He left the room without saying a word. He was gone long enough to splash his body with water and came back, hair dripping wet and carrying a copy of the Qur'an.

'Place your hand here,' he said, facing me, with the holy book open.

Though I was ritually unclean, I stretched my hand out to place it on the open pages, but then a shudder rippled through me and I was covered in goosebumps. I could not go through with it and drew back my hand.

'If you want to end the ill will between us, just place your hand on this page and take an oath,' he urged.

'What kind of oath?'

'First, place your hand on the page.'

'I'm unclean.'

'Then go and wash,' he said. 'I'll be waiting here.'

I was gone for two hours and hoped that if I dawdled long enough he would get bored and leave. But he remained rooted to the spot like an old tree. He jumped to his feet as soon as I came into view and opened the holy book to the sura entitled 'Repentance'.

'Place your right hand here,' he insisted.

I did as he asked. He closed the covers over my hand and

told me to repeat after him: 'Say, "I swear by Almighty God, Lord of the Heavens and Earth, that I do not have and have never had a relationship with Tahani."'

I could not bring myself to take the oath and tried to think of some way to wriggle out of it. Then it struck me, of course, the word 'say' was just the subterfuge I needed. If I uttered 'say' silently and kept it to myself, I could complete the oath.

Osama snapped the holy book shut after kissing it, brought it to his forehead and looked at me warily. 'I don't know why,' he said, 'but I feel that you've just made a false oath.'

He was determined to get to the bottom of the matter and kept making veiled threats. 'I could swear that you are the culprit,' he said. 'I could kill you, although killing you wouldn't satisfy my thirst for vengeance.'

I did not respond.

'But I'll find a way to make you sorry for what you did as long as you live,' he warned.

When the Punisher Squad was disbanded and Osama went to work for the Master's brother, Nadir, there were fewer altercations and we stopped stoking the embers of hatred between us.

When we graduated from school, Osama said he wanted to start working right away so as to improve his chances with Tahani. He felt he was old enough and his desire to marry her became so intense he could no longer contain it.

The day results were announced he went to his maternal aunt, Tahani's mother, and asked for her daughter's hand in marriage. His proposal was apparently accepted because when he returned he was ecstatic, and set to hugging all the young boys in the neighbourhood. His joy was plain to see; when he told Issa and me about his marriage proposal, it was obvious he had no idea of my relationship with Tahani.

That was the day Tahani appeared at her window and waved at me. Thinking the gesture was meant for him, Osama vowed to make a break from his wayward past. Osama was going to make a fresh start and lay the foundations for a lifetime of happiness with Tahani.

He was very practical about it: when he realised his marks were not good enough for a place at university, he applied for a job with Saudi Telecommunications. He was hired and immediately began to prepare for his betrothal to Tahani.

He bubbled with joy as he planned for the wedding. He looked into all the costs, calculated expenses and left no stone unturned in his efforts to obtain the necessary funds for that dream. He considered selling the family home but decided against it. He even thought about claiming compensation from the government for his father's death in the hostage incident in Mecca, but he soon dropped that idea for fear of running foul of the authorities, going to jail and never again seeing the light of day.

He settled on taking out a loan. Although he did not have all the wedding expenses quite covered, he remained buoyant with joy.

In a matter of days, however, his face went from utter exuberance to abject misery. Tahani had told him frankly that she was not interested in him and that she was in a relationship with another boy. Osama's hopes were dashed and he repeated, bewildered, to anyone within earshot, 'Who is this boy?' He had no idea that the one he was looking for was among his closest friends.

Issa tried to comfort him but was not around for very long

as his own relationship with his father was heading for a crisis. Abu Issa had noticed that his son had become flush with money and he began to suspect that Issa was selling drugs. He enlisted the help of the counter-narcotics agency to spy on his son.

The agents watched Issa for a time but could not find anything to charge him with. At Abu Issa's insistence, they raided the house one night and went through all of his son's possessions. They found nothing and left after mumbling a half-hearted apology. For Issa, that was the straw that broke the camel's back. He left home and returned just once, a week later, and only in order to get his mother out of the house.

That left *me* all alone with Osama. I tried to summon the courage to tell him about my relationship with Tahani but could not bring myself to do it – the boy was lovesick and inconsolable. Osama met his match in misery with Kamal who was also grieving because his sweetheart, Samira, had just been married off to the old wretch, Abu Musharrat. They were like a pair of mourners with their lamentations, and while I dispensed vacuous words of comfort, all I wanted was to knock the infatuation out of them, especially when Osama went on about the boy Tahani was involved with.

After the terrible night Samira died, Kamal became obsessed with visiting Samira's grave, turning what had been nightly trysts into a passion play for the dead. Kamal would set out in the afternoon and remain at her graveside talking to himself until sunset; when he was finished, he would slip out of the graveyard furtively, like someone trying to cover up an illicit relationship.

For his part, the broken-hearted Osama started to drink. He stumbled around the alleyways at night swigging straight from a bottle of cheap wine with the other drunks and lamenting his unrequited love and back-stabbing friends. Tahani, he predicted, would bitterly regret having driven him to perdition.

Osama followed me into the Palace and it was there that our hatred blossomed.

I had decided to break with my past when I moved to the Palace. I wanted to put everything behind me, first and foremost, Tahani's blood on my conscience. I had managed to forget about her until Osama showed up at the Palace three years after that fateful night. He had apparently spent the entire time searching for Tahani and the young man she loved.

His aunt, Tahani's mother, had promised her daughter in marriage but her promise had been nullified by Tahani's banishment to the village following the fateful night of the intruder. Osama looked for her everywhere and even accepted the idea of her marriage to another man; he just wanted a glimpse of her to regain some peace of mind.

He eventually made his way to me.

Initially, I thought he knew what I had done to Tahani and was guarded. But his reproaches centred on my having kept our relationship a secret. After Osama told me that her father had whisked her off to his ancestral village, I denied having any feelings for her. I convinced Osama that I had never carried on with her and that rumours of a relationship between us were unfounded. She might have said so, I told him, though I doubted it, but as far as I was concerned, Tahani and I had never been together.

At that stage, he still believed me.

This disavowal gave him a new lease on life. He started his search all over again. He returned to the village and even stayed with some of her father's relatives but found no trace of her.

His aunt, Tahani's mother, had no idea where her daughter had ended up. When Salih Khaybari had returned from the village, he told her that he had married their daughter off to one of his relatives and that she, the mother, was never to ask about Tahani again.

It took her twenty years to discover her daughter's fate; when it emerged, the news shook the neighbourhood to its core.

The day Salih's soul gave up the ghost, his eyes welled up with tears as he asked his wife and children for their forgiveness. He told them in short, halting sentences that he had cleansed the family honour with his own hands the day he had travelled with Tahani to his birthplace because he was not prepared to let her maidenhood wither as he searched for its raptor. He gave no one the opportunity to rebuke him; closing his eyes, he breathed his last breath.

Tahani's mother screamed with grief, but not for her husband. His corpse was left lying in the room for two nights while Osama's mother remained at her sister's side, consoling her. It was she who later related all this to her son.

Those twenty years later, people still had no inkling about Tahani's attacker. Now, speculation was rekindled as the women of the neighbourhood tried to figure out who had ruined the young girl's life.

They remembered that it had been the night of the condolences for Samira, when Salih Khaybari was heard shouting at the top of his lungs that a thief had broken into the house and robbed him. As word of his final confession began to circulate, everyone understood just what had been stolen and that the thief in question was ultimately responsible for sending Tahani to her death.

14

FROM OSAMA'S PERSPECTIVE, EITHER I was innocent of the crime, in which case he could share his woeful story with a friend, or I was the thief in question, in which case his story would weigh down unbearably on a guilty conscience. Either way, he finally divulged every detail surrounding Tahani's death.

When Salih told his wife that he had married off Tahani to one of his relatives in the village, she believed him. She also bowed to her husband's wish, albeit reluctantly, never to mention her name; she was sure that given enough time, Salih would change his mind and she would see her daughter again. She knew that the family honour had been defiled and that the culprit had vanished into the night. She was more than willing to accept whatever course of action would spare her family further disgrace.

She would never have believed that her sweet and gentle husband had a rock for a heart. His harshness and cruelty came to light on his deathbed when he revealed the bloodletting he was responsible for in his village, unbeknown to anyone there.

With his last remaining breaths, Salih claimed that all he had wanted was to hold his head up high, and that there would have been a different ending had Tahani been willing to reveal the identity of the scoundrel who had destroyed her life and run away.

It hurt Osama to think that she had loved the intruder so much that she had said nothing, despite the severe beating she had to endure. Tahani swore she did not know him and that surely her cries for help were proof of her innocence. Salih interrogated her all night and thrashed her so hard that she lost consciousness several times. But she stuck to her story. Salih was so furious that no one in the family dared to intervene.

In life, Tahani's mother had loved her husband; in death, she came to despise even the mention of his name and regretted every last bit of love she had shown him. She hated him for dying before she could vent all her fury and, with her heart ripped by the waves of hatred swelling inside her, she started to hate herself for acquiescing to his wish and waiting for twenty years in the vain hope of seeing her daughter again.

She did not observe the requisite mourning period or receive the mourners who had travelled all the way from his village for the obligatory condolences. Rather, she went to the village to take proper leave of her daughter. She wanted her sister – Osama's mother – to go with her and so Osama offered to drive them.

None of her own sons came along because she did not want to be reminded of Salih in any way. She cursed him throughout the long journey to Salih's village, begging God to show him no mercy. Every time her tears subsided, she would pray for the mercy of Tahani's soul and for the eternal damnation of Salih's.

They took the coastal road and avoided going through any towns or villages. She refused to let Osama stop for anything besides fuel. 'Tahani is waiting for her mother to grieve,

Osama,' she wailed. Tahani's death was still raw even though she had died twenty years earlier.

The closer they got to her husband's village, the more hysterical she became. She cursed anything and anyone to do with Salih: his background, his village, his tribe, his children and even herself, his wife.

They stayed with a distant relative of her recently deceased husband and as news of her arrival reached the women of the village, groups of them who had not been able to make the trip to Jeddah came to offer their condolences. They were greeted with the same response as those who had made the trip to the city.

'Whoever has come to mourn Tahani is more than welcome,' she said, adding sternly, 'but if you've come for Salih, then you'll need to leave now.'

This caused a scandal and the women started to say she was mad for coming to the village and expecting people to condole with her over a daughter who had been dead for decades.

There were so many different accounts of Tahani's death that it was impossible to know what to believe. There was no one left who had a clear recollection of her passing. According to the older folk, Salih had come to the village with his daughter to visit relatives and family; he was seen the next day taking her corpse to be buried on the northern outskirts of the village with only his brothers and nephews in attendance. He left for Jeddah immediately without hosting the customary condolence gathering.

According to the oldest of Tahani's uncles, she had died in an unfortunate accident, choking over a piece of meat. He recounted that Salih had shown up unexpectedly with his daughter and that he offered them hospitality in a room off the main hall of the house. When he called them to join him for dinner, they declined and asked to eat in their room. Moments later, the uncle heard a choking cry and the clatter of falling cutlery and of plates shattering. He knocked on the door and when there was no response, he and his brothers forced their way in. They found Salih holding his daughter against him, smoothing the hair from her brow to either side of her face.

Salih was weeping copiously and his brothers could not ascertain what had happened. After the burial, he gathered them together and pleaded that the news of Tahani's death should not reach her mother or brothers. His wife, he said, suffered from heart trouble and if she heard that their daughter had died, her heart would not withstand the shock – and he would then have lost both his daughter and his wife in less than a week.

Tahani's mother listened to that account and swore that her husband and his people were uncouth and barbaric, so devious and cunning in fact, that they did not deserve to be considered men at all. They, for their part, could not for the life of them understand what had prompted Salih to marry a woman with such a sharp tongue.

The women of the village were particularly outspoken and critical of her behaviour. They were outraged by her refusal to receive their condolences and for speaking to them so condescendingly. They condemned her for her city ways, which they considered contrary to hallowed traditions and in defiance of the natural order. Only a woman from the city could abandon her duties as the wife of a recently deceased man and go off to visit a grave that had been filled for twenty years.

In the village, they referred to Tahani's resting place as the 'grave of the damned'. No one could explain why the grave was in a remote location on the outskirts of the village. A stone's throw from an abandoned well, it was overgrown with thorn bushes and bounded by sand dunes as high as ramparts. The villagers claimed that the well had dried up some twenty years earlier, soon after Tahani's burial there.

Some of the women had wanted to visit the grave, but Tahani's mother declined the offer. She gathered some basil plants and a couple of jerry cans of water and the three of them – she, her sister and Osama – set out for the gravesite. They had to go on foot, scrambling up two large sand dunes, and then down to a level area that was scattered with bushes and scrub. Tahani's grave was off in an isolated corner.

Osama could swear that Tahani's presence was almost palpable, as if she had come back to life. They wept before the packed mound of earth enclosed by a wooden frame as they imagined her rising to greet them, with a reproachful look for the long absence. As they stood there at the foot of her tomb, a desert wind stirred up whorls of sand from the surrounding dunes.

Tahani's mother was convinced that it was her daughter's spirit howling. 'That's Tahani breathing and cursing us,' she moaned and, slapping herself, she started to scoop up handfuls of sand to pour over her head. She would subside for a few moments and begin again as soon as another gust of wind stirred up the sand, scooping up the dirt and slapping it over her head.

When the wind finally stopped, she asked Osama to fetch the basil plants and the jerry cans of water from the car. She poured the water over the grave and laid out the basil plants, and then she took out a handful of flower seeds from a pouch stuffed in her cleavage. 'These will grow for you, Tahani,' she said, scattering the seeds.

'Poor Tahani,' she continued tearfully, taking in the barrenness of that wasteland. 'Even your final resting place is withered.'

A few villagers stood a little way off and stared from behind the dunes at this scene of grief over a long-gone corpse. Tahani's mother hurled sand at them, cursing, and then threw herself down on the grave and clawed at the dirt.

Osama pulled her away with his mother's help, and they got in the car and drove straight back to Jeddah.

15

Pain is like a mythical creature. It subsides but never dies, and when it returns, it comes back with a vengeance. It is compounded as we endure the pain of both the original event and its recollection. Pouring salt over a rival's wound reopens our own wounds.

That is how I became afflicted with Tahani all over again.

Whenever his boss, Nadir, was around, Osama could not leave his side. But when Nadir, who was also the Master's brother, went out of town, Osama would spend the entire time tormenting me with the memory of Tahani.

When Osama disappeared for an entire week, I assumed Nadir had sent him on some business outside Jeddah. He wore a stony expression when he resurfaced at a function put on by the Master for a group of businessmen. He sat at the back of the hall with his sunglasses on, fingering gold prayer beads. He remained impassable as waves of enthusiastic applause greeted the Master's speech. Reclining in his chair with his legs stretched out, it was impossible to tell exactly where he was looking because of the dark glasses.

'Why is Osama wearing sunglasses at night?' Uncle Muhammad asked.

It went without saying that our employers paid us no heed;

it was up to us to look out for one another. Uncle Muhammad's remark shamed me. I certainly had not been paying much attention to anyone and I was generally indifferent to people's actions. I interacted with others like a casual passer-by whose only purpose was to reach his destination. Not that I had a destination. I did not know where I was heading, but I kept going like a robot and my heart kept pumping blood through sclerotic veins, unaware of how tainted it had become.

Osama seemed impatient for the party to end. As soon as the guests jostled to gather their belongings and bid each other goodnight, he sprang to his feet. As he passed me he whispered urgently, 'We're hanging out tonight.'

It was more of a command than a suggestion. He did not wait for my response and turned to attend to his boss. He leaned down slightly to hear Nadir's instructions and then stepped aside so that the two servants assigned to him could pick him up and carry him to his wheelchair.

Osama did not want to stay indoors, so we stepped out together.

The humid air of the night was somewhat relieved by the movement of the waves lapping against the earth-moving equipment parked across from the eastern wing of the Palace. There, a large sandy expanse had been levelled and planted with date and coconut palms. Spiralling beams of light bathed the tips of the trees with a glowing radiance that spread all the way to the surface of the water.

Osama's eyes were puffy and red, and when I asked him if he had been crying, he did not answer. He just led me by the hand and walked in silence towards the seashore, clutching a small bag against his chest.

'You're not worried about getting your clothes dirty, are

you?' Osama asked, inviting me to sit down on the ground next to him.

Opening the bag, he reached in for a half-empty bottle of Black Label and took a swig. As he offered me some, he said almost casually, 'They say you were the thief in Tahani's bedroom.'

He was looking for some certainty that would put his suspicions to rest, but I did not oblige him. 'Who's *they*?' I countered immediately.

'For the last time, I'm asking you, was it you?'

'And for the last time, I'm telling you, no, it wasn't me.'

'OK,' he said slowly. His words now came out haltingly, as if he were having trouble breathing. 'I have been crying,' he admitted, 'and I'll tell you why so that you can help me look for that bastard who took Tahani's life and ruined mine. And then we'll kill him together – you and me. OK?'

I had no choice but to nod.

He put the bottle to his mouth and gulped down enough whisky to stun a camel. He was about to hand it to me when he stopped himself. 'No,' he said, 'I want you to stay awake so you can hear what I've been doing this past week.' He placed the bottle back in his lap and told me of his trip to Salih Khaybari's village and how he had sensed Tahani's spirit in the barren wasteland that was the 'grave of the damned'.

When he reached the end of his story, he picked up the bottle from his lap and emptied its contents in one gulp. 'Don't you think that whoever destroyed her life deserves to die?' he cried.

I was concerned that the Master would hear us so I tried to cover his mouth and said in agreement, 'If I get my hands on the culprit, I'll rip him to shreds.'

In the distance, there was a steady stream of cars coming and going, and the silhouettes of Palace servants scurried about arranging seats for a gathering not far from where we were sitting. They were rushing to prepare an impromptu barbecue in accordance with the Master's instructions.

Osama had begun slurring his words and was moving unsteadily. I pulled him up to a standing position and braced him against me.

He started to chuckle loudly. 'You know what's funny?' he said. 'Here I am looking for the man who raped Tahani so that I can kill him, but I do exactly the same thing every day to other girls.' He looked ashen and it was clear the alcohol had seeped into every neural pathway of his brain. 'You suppose they have families and sweethearts?'

With my arm around him, we walked slowly back to the Palace.

Osama slapped his forehead as though struck by a revelation. 'Guess that means one of them will want nothing better than to rip me to shreds!'

I could not tell whether he was laughing or crying.

I took him to his quarters, put him to bed and covered him with a blanket, hoping that neither the Master nor his brother would be needing Osama any time soon.

Just before I turned to leave, he grabbed my arm and said drowsily, 'I'm thinking about moving. So that I can be close to her and share her loneliness. It's so desolate out there.'

I patted him on the shoulder. 'Sleep now. We'll talk tomorrow,' I told him.

'At least if I'm there, I can water the seeds my aunt planted. Don't you think that's better work than the despicable things I do in this palace of the damned?'

I quickly clamped his mouth shut to stop him from uttering another negative word about the Palace, which the cameras and bugs everywhere would relay at the speed of light.

I reached down to kiss the top of his head.

His eyes were shut and he was probably already half asleep when he mumbled, 'Are you sure you're not the bastard I'm looking for?'

Until her husband came to see me, my mother had been the furthest thing from my mind. As far as I was concerned, she was as good as dead once my father passed away and she moved in with another man.

'Your mother wishes to see you,' Ghayth Muhannad told me.

'And how, may I ask, did she communicate her wish?' I retorted.

As was his wont, Ghayth remained calm and composed.

If he had been expecting me to refer to him respectfully as 'uncle' or use some other kind of honorific to acknowledge his venerable status, my rudeness soon dispelled his expectation.

'Please don't forget that your mother is still alive,' he said. 'Showing me respect is part of respecting her.'

'My mother died when she married you,' I replied swiftly. 'And for your information, no one in this life is worthy of my respect.'

'Talking that way isn't at all helpful. So long as she is alive, be kind towards her.'

I was rude because I wanted to humiliate him. But his patience and generosity of spirit allowed him to let my abuse go unanswered until I had run out of nasty words. He cleared his throat and praised and blessed the Prophet as he wiped a beautifully embroidered handkerchief across his face. Ghayth noticed me staring at the handkerchief and lifted it to my face with a friendly smile.

I immediately recognised my mother's handiwork; her reputation as a skilled embroiderer was unequalled among the women of the neighbourhood. I knew why I felt really provoked by the handkerchief. She had always embroidered things for my father – handkerchiefs, *keffiyehs*, traditional loose-fitting *sirwal* trousers – and now this man was wiping his brow with a handkerchief she had lovingly sat and embroidered for him.

I fought off all his efforts at weaselling his way into my heart and sent him on his way as I had greeted him: with a stream of abuse.

He left, muttering that he had done his best and that, having washed his hands of the matter, it was now in God's hands.

I had never forgiven my mother for marrying Ghayth. Filling me in on some of the history, Aunt Khayriyyah had said, 'Your mother is as slippery as a snake. Although she was betrothed to your father, she loved her maternal cousin, Ghayth.'

At the time, I thought my aunt was simply being her usual venomous self and paid little notice. But my mother's move to Ghayth's household so soon after my father fell to his death came as a shock and it poisoned my feelings towards her. Offering her condolences, Ghayth's senile mother had managed to hobble over to our home and confided that her son, the cousin my mother had been in love with as a young woman, still hankered after her.

My mother prepared for the move immediately and was

betrothed while my father's blood was still warm. I had trouble understanding how she had managed to give her consent with her severed tongue.

I had watched her sitting night after night trying to enunciate my father's name. Back then, she seemed to me the epitome of a woman in love with eyes only for her beloved. How rapidly those eyes had shifted their focus; my father's grave was barely covered with earth before her love for Ghayth sprouted from its surface.

But perhaps I had been mistaken all this time. Just maybe she had been desperately trying to pronounce her lover's name, not her husband's. I started to convince myself that it was indeed the case since how else could she have said it on the night of that long-postponed wedding if not through nightly practice. Perhaps, too, if my father had not got in the way, the enchantment that had bound their hearts since earliest childhood would not have been disrupted. My recollection was that she had married my father out of love and that the dark horseman of her dreams had overcome all manner of obstacles to win her heart. Which of the two men did she love? What if Tahani had also been leading the two of us on, Osama and me? Maybe there was a third or even fourth man?

That was the way women operated, as I had learned at the Palace. I saw how fickle and inconstant they were, and how volatile. A woman would grant her body for pleasure but would deny her heart; she kept her beating heart for her children, on whom she lavished all her feelings. As for my own mother, my memories were confused. Every time I found out something new about her life, it shed a different light on what I remembered.

I was starting to wonder whether Aunt Khayriyyah had

been right all along that my grandmother's womb had borne nothing but rotten fruit. If she was, then cutting off her tongue had been pointless, just a stupid impulse rather than the fulfilment of some preordained fate.

I even began to worry that my punitive act against my aunt had been less about seeking retribution for my mother and more about being vengeful towards women in general. Could that explain why I had cut off my aunt's tongue, taken Tahani's virginity, rejected my mother and had sex with men? Was it all so that I could do away with women?

We all fall, in one way or another, because gravity cannot be defied. Every one of us must fall, whether we like it or not. But falling is incremental: each stage in the process leads to the next one, and on down all the way to the bottom.

Dr Bannan loved the concept of transference. One night, he overheard Joseph Essam and me having a discussion about the ephemerality of life. Not one to miss an opportunity to flaunt his knowledge, Dr Bannan lectured us at length, analysing the vagaries of our lives in the process.

I had been feeling particularly gloomy that night. It seemed to me that I was beginning to fall apart but I consoled myself with the thought that in any case it was all beyond my control. Wanting to be supportive, Joseph Essam had taken on the role of therapist.

He told me about the importance of confession in the process of self-purification. I tried to stay open-minded as he strove to instil in me some basic Christian notions, perhaps in the hope of converting me. He liked me because I listened and did not get combative with him, and he probably thought that I was ready to be saved.

I became the repository of his past mistakes as he

proceeded to tell me about his own troubles. There was a young woman he loved but had abandoned. He did not say anything about her appearance, concentrating instead on her character traits. She was delicate and sweet, and her love as pure as that celebrated by Solomon, whom he quoted: 'As the apple tree among the trees of the wood, so is my beloved among the sons. I sat under its shadow with great delight, and its fruit was sweet to my taste.' He needed nothing besides her sweet chastity, he said, and wanted nothing more than the purity of her soul to dissolve all that was bitter in him.

At this he launched into a spiritual discussion of the passions and distinguished that which is sanctioned from that which is prohibited. It was the burning flame of faith that had finally led to his enlightenment and prompted him to flee the object of his love: the young girl in question was his niece, his sister's daughter.

We are all bound to fall at some point or other; only we know when we hit bottom. It is a gradual process and we are gripped by such emotion every step of the way that we are completely confident of our assessment of our situation. It is only when our emotions subside that our certainty falters.

And now my mother was asking about me, as if she suddenly had remembered after all those years that a creature she had given birth to still existed.

They say that children are the crutches for parents to lean on in old age. A childhood spent without support results in repeated stumbles; I certainly had fallen many times as a child without anyone lending me a hand.

In the face of conflicting feelings, we discover that we are like strangers or casual bystanders standing before an incorrect road sign. We can neither go back nor continue on towards our destination.

That is how I found myself still mired in my past, after all I had tried to put it behind me.

One of the Palace guards came to let me know that my half-brother, Ibrahim, was at the gate. I made my way there and saw him being subjected to a barrage of questions by the security guards.

'Who knew that just coming to see you would lead to my detention,' he exclaimed, visibly upset. 'I'll never do it again!'

He had been trying to see me for three days, he explained, and then set about questioning me about Aunt Khayriyyah. 'How is she?'

'She's fine. I'll fill you in later with all her news.'

'That's it? Just "fine" after all this time? You have no idea how worried we've been.'

'Let's hold off on the blame until we're alone,' I told him.

I did not have permission to let him enter the Palace and, since I was busy, I promised we would meet later at his home in the Firepit.

It would take me several years to keep that promise. I was determined to sever all my connections to the past – whether people, places or specific times – and refused to see anyone who came looking for me.

But Osama was the hook that snared me, drawing me back to the neighbourhood that had launched me on my journey. It was as if my attempt to make a final break with the past had left me charged like a magnetic field, subject to the forces of attraction and repulsion.

The force of attraction was the stronger of the two. All of

my memories and all the people that I had fled were being drawn back towards me, or I towards them, and the charge had me looking for an escape.

First and foremost, there was Tahani, who was never far from my mind. Then there was my aunt who was embedded in my life like a rusty nail in a festering, stinking wound. Souad, too, with her plea to help her husband, Yasser Muft, reawakened memories of my earliest delinquency. There was Mustafa Qannas, whose masculine pride I had trampled and who left the Palace in humiliation to resume cruising the alleyways, vowing vengeance; and Osama, who watched night and day for any sign that might confirm that I was that marauder in Tahani's bedroom. And then there was my mother, Ghayth Muhannad, Ibrahim and Issa. Damn that Issa!

They were all embedded in my flesh and in my memory like so many hooks, each one tearing at some part of me. I was unravelling and felt myself being propelled into the abyss.

After the encounter with Ghayth Muhannad, I resolved to call on my mother and to make good on my promise to visit Ibrahim. Day after day, however, I postponed and procrastinated to the point that a year, and then two, three and eventually seven years went by.

At the stroke of noon on a blazing-hot day in August, Ghayth Muhannad stood at the Palace gates pleading with the guards to send for me. They denied any knowledge of my existence.

'Have you no fear of God?' Ghayth railed at them. 'His mother has died and he must not miss the funeral.'

I stood in the observation room and watched and listened as he pleaded, begged and enumerated all the ailments that prevented him from standing there too long.

So she had finally died and I was free of at least one commitment I had made years earlier.

The guards seemed more upset by the news of my mother's death than I was. One of them seemed on the point of telling Ghayth that I was there, listening to his every word, and had he not been afraid of losing his job he would have dragged me by the scruff of the neck to relieve the old man of his discomfort.

'I can't stand here for very long. I have diabetes, high blood pressure and heart disease,' said Ghayth. 'Just tell him that his mother has died and that we will pray for her soul during evening prayers at Al-Khayr Mosque. He'll know where that is – if he hasn't forgotten the houses of the Lord the way he forgot his mother. If he doesn't make it to the mosque, tell him we'll be burying her at the Cemetery of Our Mother Eve.'

Ghayth struggled to straighten up his back and then turned to leave.

The senior guard offered me his condolences formally. 'A mother's passing is the hardest of all losses, you know. When a mother dies, God Almighty tells the angels, "Close the door we had kept open in her honour."'

I cut him short and told him the deceased was just my wet-nurse. Undeterred, he went on, 'She was still your mother. May God comfort you in your loss.'

I was sure that my absence at both the prayers and burial would be sufficient to put off anyone from trying to reach me ever again.

Two years after my mother's death, Ibrahim showed up one day at the gates and insisted he needed to talk to me. I am not sure why, but I agreed to see him in the main reception area. I suppose we fulfil our destiny, whether we like it or not.

'Do you know what I had to go through to reach you?' he exclaimed. 'I need your help with something urgent.'

I pulled out my chequebook with a flourish as I looked him up and down. 'How much do you need?'

'I don't want your money, Tariq,' he said crossly. 'Foul money has a foul smell.' He paused briefly and added more evenly, 'I want you to help our sister.'

'Our sister?' I repeated. 'And what sister might that be?' I was being deliberately obtuse; he was referring to our half-sister, the fruit of our father's last wife.

'Have you even forgotten that you have a sister?'

'Well, I don't know her. I've never seen her.'

'That's beside the point,' Ibrahim stated. 'She's still your sister and she needs your help.'

That reminded me of Souad's plea for her husband, Yasser Muft. 'Is she in jail?'

'God forbid. No, she's not in jail – but she's in trouble.'

'Fine. I'll come and see you and we'll talk.'

That caused Ibrahim to chuckle, which somehow seemed at odds with his dignified bearing. 'Have I not heard that before?' he said with a sad shake of the head. 'You think I've forgotten that you promised the same thing seven years ago?'

'Life is busy and I have a lot on my mind, Ibrahim.'

'Listen, Tariq,' Ibrahim insisted. 'Our sister has no one but us. At the end of the day, her honour is bound up with ours. I don't have the means to help her. If you can't help her either, just tell me and I'll ask someone else.'

'How am I supposed to help when I know nothing about her?' I argued. 'You haven't even told me what her problem is.'

224

'Families have their secrets.' Ibrahim looked around the reception area and the flow of people entering and leaving the Palace. 'Either you take me somewhere private where we can talk, or you come with me.'

'I can't right now. Expect me tonight – no, wait, I'll be there tomorrow.'

Ibrahim nodded slowly.

This time, 'tomorrow' took another two years.

I really wanted nothing to do with the quagmire of the past. All I wanted was to run from the hooks that were embedded in my flesh. I certainly had no desire to meet a sister whose birth I had only heard about and who might end up being drawn to me like iron filings to a magnet.

After that, Ibrahim never came to see me again at the Palace.

The night my mother died, black clouds rolled into the sky above Jeddah. Bolts of lightning sliced through the heavens and unleashed a torrential downpour. Feelings of self-reproach and guilt ripped through me with similar force and I was overcome by a flood of tears.

It had been years since I had cried – at least for as long as I had been at the Palace. My spirit was as parched as the arid dunes and scrub of the wind-swept desert.

Everything about the Cemetery of Our Mother Eve was unwelcoming. Eve had gathered her children on their journey to oblivion inside, and the earth had been made earthier with the decay of their bodies. It was our mother who had led us, her children, out of Eden to roam the earth like errant cattle. When we tired of roaming and mooing, we went back to the earth, as she had done before us. We did not go to be

225

held in her embrace but only to follow in her footsteps, for she was the archetype, the one whose actions constituted the blueprint for ours.

I ended up walking around the cemetery wall because the gate was locked shut. Bolts of lightning crackled before my eyes and accompanied my steps as if chasing a wayward cloud. I surrendered to their power and wept – my tears as futile as a torrent of rain in a swamp. For what is the use of water to unhallowed and barren ground, and what good are tears to the dead?

On this first night of my mother's rest in the earth, I thought of jumping the wall and hurling myself inside the cemetery. I wanted to scale the wall and find that freshly dug grave, give vent to my grief and leave. It would be my final apology to her for all my years of absence. Just something to lighten the desolation of her first night.

But the downpour put paid to that idea. I would now never find her grave. After the torrential rain, all the graves would look equally fresh, as though all the cemetery's dead had been buried on the same day.

I had never seen her again after she remarried. I had forgotten what her face looked like. I did not know whether she had gone grey or lost her teeth, whether her back was bent with age or she suffered from any ailments. I wondered if she had given birth to other children whose fate might be the same as mine, especially if Aunt Khayriyyah was right that my mother's womb could bear nothing but rotten fruit.

I needed tears to wash away the corrosion at my core. As I walked around the cemetery, I grieved over this ultimate of separations as the drenching rain obliterated her final resting place. My mother had gone to her grave and my delayed grief devastated me, like the bare limb of an old tree that had been shorn of all its leaves.

I remembered an episode from my childhood, when I had come running home crying my heart out for some forgotten reason. 'Men don't cry,' Aunt Khayriyyah had scolded. 'And crying is no use anyway, so be a man.' She had slapped me hard on the cheek for good measure.

In all my years at the Palace, I had not shed a single tear. Whether I was responsible for them or not, I had swept aside all my dreadful experiences and carried on with day-to-day life mechanically, like the unthinking hand on a clock.

I stopped at the cemetery gate, wanting to pray for her soul and the souls of all those buried with her. But I could not recall any of the prayers for the dead. So I muttered a few garbled phrases that sounded pathetic in the rain and beside the solemnity of the place. I cut my prayers short and wiped away whatever remained of my meaningless tears.

Just as the skies above Jeddah were overshadowed by thick clouds, my mother's death had overshadowed my day. I was not used to being in a state of emotional turmoil.

Before her death, my mother had made that sole attempt to reunite us by sending me her decrepit old husband. She had never tried again; now I wished she had insisted, like one would with an obstinate child: first voicing a wish, then making a request and finally giving it one last try. I would have liked some determination on her part, a little persistence.

She died suddenly and deprived me of the chance to blame her for what she had done. I wanted her to know how abandoned I had felt, betrayed by my own mother, when she had taken up with a man she had been in love with as a young woman. He had waited years for her without marrying and I imagined that he had actively wished for my father's death to get her back.

But I did not hate her – or him – the way I despised my aunt, who was like an unrelenting buzzer that went off the moment my hatred started to wane.

I drove to the villa and as I travelled north, the rain began to subside and the lightning had already moved on. My tears dried up and my heart returned to stone.

I turned the key in the rusty lock of the outer gate and the loud squeak punctured the tranquillity of the night. Even the plants seemed startled by this sudden visit, as if they had been caught unawares with their leaves withering.

Inside, the smell was suffocating. From the moment I set foot in the villa, I was assaulted by a putrid smell. I turned on the lights and went up the stairs, hurrying through the hallways that led to my aunt's room. I had not brought anything for her and it had been at least a month, possibly two, since my last visit.

The stench of decay became stronger the closer I got to her room. I wondered whether she, too, might have died.

If that were the case, I would be visiting the cemetery two days in a row. My mind was already reeling off a series of images: I would place them next to each other, she and my mother, so that they could continue quarrelling and arguing until Judgement Day – both mumbling unintelligibly with their clipped tongues.

The stink was thick in the hallway leading directly to my aunt's room. It was a rancid mix of excrement, urine, mould, sweat and putrefaction.

With the house reeking like that, her death would arouse

suspicion. It would be best to delay the announcement. There was no one whose heart would be broken by her passing, in any case. Besides, no embalmer would be willing to carry out the ritual washing in this stench. By postponing the news of her death, I also would have the chance to air the place and allow the stench to disperse in the fresh air after the rain.

The only thing I was afraid of was that her body had already decomposed and that her bloated remains had exploded and scattered everywhere.

I held my nose, closed my mouth and opened the door warily.

It was a scene from hell: the room, plunged in darkness, reeked to high heaven. With the fingers of one hand still pinching my nose shut, I felt for the light switch with the other. As the light came on, the full horror of what lay before me was revealed. The room was one big mound of rubbish, piled with clothes, cartons, cans, bottles, lids, food scraps, bedding and blankets. The bed was overturned, the wardrobe was broken, and I could see faeces and dried-up blood everywhere.

As I took in the scene of mayhem, I scanned the room for her corpse but there was no trace of one. I carved a path through the debris, holding my breath against the stench. Every time I pushed something aside, the smell of decomposing food and excrement would rise into the air. I was beginning to wonder whether her body had completely decomposed under the heap of rubbish and all that remained was the smell of putrefaction.

Dreading that I might step on her corpse or bones, I moved hesitantly, with visions of my feet sinking into her viscera, or crushing her skull or rib cage.

229

All of a sudden I felt a blow, and my heart began pounding.

I had been so convinced that she had died that I did not expect her to leap from under a pile of cartons like a fury. She lunged at me with metal coat hangers she had filed to dart-like points and drove them into whatever part of my body was within reach, moaning and groaning loudly.

I pushed her away with all my strength and sent her flying into a wall, crying out in agony like a wounded animal.

She looked monstrous.

Aunt Khayriyyah was so emaciated her bones protruded from under her clothes, and her skin was so wizened that the criss-cross of wrinkles looked like a scorched river bed. Her front teeth were chipped, her fingernails were black with filth and long as talons, and her white hair stood on end like a mass of carded wool. Only her sunken, hollow eyes retained their fierceness.

She tried to get up but could not, as if she had exhausted every last drop of energy to pounce on me. Staring at me wild-eyed, still clutching one of her darts, she seemed to be pulling herself together to resume combat. She struggled to her feet and made for the light switch. Darkness descended on the room like a blanket, with only a faint ray of light trickling in from the cracked door.

She was used to the gloom. I could sense her approaching, making stabbing motions in the dark, hoping to get me in the chest before I could reach for the light switch. I backed away slowly and felt my way to the door. I moved faster than she did and reached the door before she could get to me. I slammed the door shut and ran.

She, too, had been honing her hatred. She had sat in that ruin of a room and manufactured weapons to sink into my chest and finish off the foul offspring that had sprung from my mother's womb.

I made my escape and, getting back into my car, drove away.

I was beset by the nagging thought that, in my rush to leave that vile place, I might have forgotten to lock the door. I almost turned back, but my dread of seeing her rise from the wreckage like a ghoulish monster was stronger than my desire to find out.

I also began to worry that the Master's cameras might have captured that scene from hell.

16

DRAWING ON HIS ARMY of assistants – his advisers, analysts, speculators, investment fund managers, media specialists and individuals involved in insider trading – the Master became an expert at manipulating the stock market. Acting on his behalf, the assistants dug deep pits into which greedy investors and rivals would jump and, subsequently, drown, bewildered by their sudden loss of fortune.

The Master's gambling addiction had taken root early on, when he began frequenting casinos in European capitals. He distinguished himself from his countrymen by his civility whenever he lost at the tables, for he was keen to maintain his good reputation.

He never recovered from the addiction. His life was one never-ending wager. His own friends placed bets on whether he would continue to pull off the gambles he seemed perpetually enthralled with, as if the thrill alone gave meaning to whatever he did.

Every aspect of life was worth a wager: horses, hunting expeditions, the card game *balut,* procuring a celebrity singer, marrying an actress. The winnings were sometimes purely symbolic. It could be something as mundane as getting an opponent's *iqaal* – the black headband that secures *keffiyehs*

– or getting them to meow or bark. He got his thrills from one gamble after another.

The stock market became a substitute for the casinos and turned him into an early riser. The start of trading early in the day lessened his enthusiasm for carousing until the break of dawn.

I hoped that this infatuation with stocks would last and that punishing his rivals on the floor of the exchange would continue to relieve me of my duties. My only fear was that he would grow bored with this, as with all his other pursuits, and that when he started looking for some other thrill to provide the excitement he craved, it would somehow involve me. For now, the Master was enthralled with causing wild fluctuations in the market, relishing both the anticipation and the actual excitement of trading.

His advisers had found a novel way to make even more money, and he sent out invitations to a select group of powerful businessmen to meet and discuss how they might expand the financial market by selling individual loans. The idea was to encourage local banks to extend personal loans that were many times greater than the borrowers' annual salaries. This required a consolidated corporate front and a strategy to convince government policymakers.

The meeting took place on the cement jetty extending out to sea. The small and select group of businessmen debated a variety of credit schemes that would enable them to manipulate shares. The goal was to buy up a particular stock in its entirety and then unload it when the market was favourable, thereby making a killing.

Servants were passing around all manner of elegant appetisers and salads to whet the guests' appetite for the main meal, which would be served later to celebrate their already substantial profits. The discussions held no appeal for the young women present. They grew restless, stretched their legs and shifted in their seats with boredom. One of them got up to lean against the railing, watching distant ships on the horizon while holding up her cell phone to listen to the latest hit by the singer Sherine. Two others joined her and they began to discuss plans for a trip to Paris over the weekend.

The slowly sinking sun reflecting off the surface of the water lent the setting a romantic aura that contrasted with the dullness of the exchange between the Master and his guests. Their excitement at the prospect of huge profits made them oblivious to the young women, and not a hint of passion stirred in their loins.

Maram was also there. Standing directly across from her, I was examining the low-cut sleeveless black dress which showed off her cleavage while keeping her unruly breasts in their place. She caught my lingering gaze and held it. My eyes pleaded silently for her breasts to break the hold of the enveloping fabric.

I had desired her from the start.

She was unique in that she could weave a sultry web of seduction regardless of the setting, with a deliberation that was well beyond her years. Both Maram and the Master conspired in the air of ambiguity surrounding her. No one knew where she was from or how she had come to be in Paradise.

There were rumours that her husband had 'gifted' her to the Master as part of a commercial deal and that, having become used to the lap of luxury, she had been unwilling to leave it. According to another rumour, the Master had simply wrested her from her husband with the force of a court order. There was also a story that went around that she was the daughter of a wealthy merchant who had offered her up in exchange for a substantial bailout that he needed to get out of some financial trouble. And lastly, it was said that she was simply another of Osama's catches. There were countless stories that followed Maram wherever she went because no one knew for sure.

All I knew with certainty was that the Master saw her in the Palace one night and fell for her.

There had been a lottery and Maram was supposed to be the prize of one of the millionaires that evening. The idea of drawing lots for the women who animated the Palace parties was the brainchild of Joseph Essam, and the Master quickly saw its erotic potential. At the end of an evening, a large silver bowl would be filled with alcoholic punch and the contenders would drop their car keys inside the bowl. The bowl was then passed around, and each young woman fished out a set of keys. Their owner got to claim her as his prize for the night.

The lottery ritual had become quite established but that night, the Master disputed the result and claimed Maram for himself. She was never again entered in such lotteries and soon became the Master's favourite.

There were many desirable women who roamed the corridors of the Palace, and they were all off limits to the staff who worked there. Our job was simply to escort them to designated bedrooms and await further instructions from the Master.

Every day, a chauffeur was assigned to go and fetch the

girls. After dropping them off, he would relieve the lust they had aroused in him by seeking out one of the female migrant workers scattered about the Palace. Negotiating with whoever was most responsive, he would bed her, fast and furious, while still aroused.

While falling asleep, I would often conjure up Maram in my mind's eye and feast on her. I would go over her inch by inch – her face, her laugh, her cascading hair, her voluptuous curves, her statuesque bearing, her graceful neck – and then whisper longingly as I held her close and drifted off to sleep.

I would picture her lying there with every cell of her body unfurling before my eyes which were hungry for anything she might reveal of herself. I imagined her beside me singing a few snatches from a favourite song, her beautiful lips in an imperceptible pout.

The Master's intense focus on the discussion of the planned stock market manipulations gave me the opportunity to devour Maram with my eyes. I watched her every move as she flitted around humming her favourite songs. Whichever way she turned, she knew my eyes were on her.

She leaned and whispered into the Master's ear. He looked up sharply and his eyes followed in the direction that she was indicating. Of all the members of staff on permanent standby to respond to any request or instruction, she gestured boldly towards me.

'Hey, you,' she yelled, pointing.

I was seized with panic. My eyes, lost in the splendour of her cleavage, snapped to attention and met her gaze for the flash of an instant.

The Master's eyes scanned a number of faces. Had she just

236

told him that I had been undressing her with my eyes? I wondered with dread. I deliberately ignored her pointing finger and looked around, pretending to search for the person she was pointing to from among the people standing near me.

'Don't you hear me calling you, you idiot?' Maram called out, her finger still pointed.

'Who? Me?' I stammered.

'Yes. You!'

She signalled for me to approach and I obeyed nervously.

The Master punctured what little dignity I had, saying, 'You sure hit the nail on the head calling him an idiot.' He started to shake with laughter.

There was a sudden lull in the conversation as the guests stopped and turned to see which particular idiot Maram had singled out.

My steps were leaden and my heart was beating furiously.

The Master stared at me for a second and then ordered, 'Get the black Bentley ready for the lady.'

My heartbeat slowly returned to normal, but my legs remained frozen.

'Move yourself, you ass, and get the car ready for the lady,' he shouted.

I did not understand what he meant by getting the car ready. Did he mean for me to summon one of the drivers? This was not normally something I did.

'All of the drivers are ready, sir.'

'You really are an ass, aren't you,' said Maram with contempt. 'You've been told to accompany me.' She picked up her handbag and told one of the servants to fetch her abaya.

237

'I'm sorry, ma'am,' I said, 'but I'm not a driver.'

The Master was now furious. 'You do what you're told,' he roared. 'You're not here to object. Is that understood, you imbecile?'

I nodded apologetically; I knew better than to try to explain what I had meant.

'Now take the lady to the hair salon and wait until she's finished.'

I led the way and thanked my lucky stars that it was over.

I was sitting behind the wheel, eyeing her in the rear-view mirror.

Maram was no longer the girl who had been short-changed on her first night at the Palace. She was now a woman, the mistress before whom everyone kept their gaze averted and whose wishes no one dared question. Her wishes were commands to be carried out in the precise manner she stipulated, without delay or hesitation.

To desire her was to revisit the fate of humankind in the Garden of Eden; gazing upon her carried the penalty of eternal banishment. The Master had broken off a long-standing friendship over a few flirtatious compliments a friend of his had made once. He had been so incensed that he had driven his former friend to bankruptcy through a fraudulent real estate scheme.

Going near Maram was like touching a live wire – the prohibition was categorical. Untold misery awaited anyone caught glancing her way when she was in the Master's company or when she stepped out on to the dance floor.

Maram slid into the back seat of the car with a toss of her head, fluffing and then pulling her hair back behind a gold headband.

238

'Keep your eyes in front of you, jackass,' she warned.

I looked away quickly.

'First, you'll take me to Souk al-Bassateen to get some things.'

'But the Master instructed me to take you to the hair salon, not to the souk.'

'What I'm buying is connected with where I'm going, you jerk,' Maram said with clear irritation. 'If the Master got wind of this, he'd string you up and cure you of your cheek.'

'Still, I—' I began.

'Stop or I'll have you fired on the spot.'

'I'm sorry, I just wanted to—'

'Not another word. Just shut up and drive.'

I set out across the main road leading to the city. A deafening silence hung in the air along with her scent which permeated every cell in my nostrils.

She sat back in her seat as I desperately tried to catch her eye in the rear-view mirror, pretending to look at the traffic coming up behind me.

How could she suddenly turn into such a fierce and cruel tigress? The silence was making me nervous. I wondered why she had chosen me to take her into town when she had her own driver. Maybe it was a warning to desist from my boldness since I had been watching her every move.

After a while, I asked her if she might want to listen to a CD.

'I already told you I didn't want to hear another word out of you,' she snapped.

When we arrived at the souk, I stopped the car and

waited for her to get out, but she did not move and remained seated.

'We're at the souk,' I prompted, waiting for her to disembark.

'And you think I don't realise it, you ass?' she shot back. 'Now come open the door for me and be quick about it.'

'The door is unlocked. You can let yourself out.'

She was enraged by this and a stream of abuse followed. 'How dare you? Get out and open the door now! Do you hear me?'

I stepped out, fighting off an intense urge to pull her out of the car by the hair and drag her down the street. I opened the rear door and she stepped out daintily in a cloud of scented charm.

'And now, come with me,' Maram ordered.

She walked into the souk, swaying her hips seductively, as I followed behind. A group of young men milling at the entrance of the market ogled her, jostling with each other to see who could come up with the most flirtatious comments. Some of them were downright lewd.

Maram slowed down until I caught up with her and then leaned in towards me, her shoulder brushing against mine. 'I apologise for all the insults,' she said, suddenly coy.

I could not believe the reversal; barely a minute earlier, I could have wrung her neck, and here she was being as sweet and gentle as a breeze on a hot day.

'I'm really sorry,' she repeated. 'I thought the car might have been bugged. You know what I like about you?'

She pretended to be interested in the jewellery and cloth-ing on display. 'You're bold. The way you look at me as if you couldn't care less about the Master. No one ever looks at me any more! There's no excitement in that. Everyone looks away when I try to meet their gaze. You're the only one who still makes me feel desirable … your smouldering glances make my heart race.'

She paused. 'Do you remember what I told you once? Didn't I promise that one day … All you had to do was set the time and the place, and I'd be yours!'

Every fibre of my being began to sing. I could feel the heat of her body as we moved between the shopfronts and her shoulder brushed against my chest every time we stopped. She went into a beauty supply store for various hair bands and coloured clips, and all eyes were on her.

'You know why I love coming to the souk?' Maram asked. 'Because here, at least, I can feel people looking at me.'

The fact that I was there helped to tone down the effrontery of the young men who lined her path and who would otherwise have made passes at her.

I overheard one of them say to his friend, 'Watch out – don't you see she's with her dad?'

Had I aged that much? Our lives flash by like sand in an hourglass. Deep down we continue to feel our youth is not far behind.

As we made our way back to the car, Maram leaned in towards me once more and urged, 'Please don't talk to me in the car. Just don't say anything.'

I stepped out and opened the car door for her and, as she swept in, she brushed her cheek against my lips. I felt as if an electric shock had just run through me. I wished she would step out again, and that I could open the door for her once more, and then again and again, one hundred times over.

I turned the key in the ignition and before I could pull out of the VIP parking space, I heard her bark out an order. 'And now, to the Oasis Hair Salon, you dolt.'

'Yes, ma'am.'

Second threshold

Terrorism is not just a matter of an explosion here and an explosion there. Terrorism is the corruption of society as a whole, the withering of its values and principles: that is the real terrorism. It is the inevitable outcome of grievances that are left unaddressed and of the relentless perpetration of injustices.

From a Friday sermon by
Sheikh Ibrahim Fadel,
Imam of the Salvation Mosque

17

Issa stood in the middle of the bank, shouting at the manager, Adnan Hassoun. He had just learned that all the money in his accounts had vanished into thin air. A security guard came running and the bank manager slipped behind him. The guard was already bristling and ready to pounce, like a newly trained hound eager to go after its prey.

Realising that his shouting was having no effect, Issa did the unthinkable.

He began by tearing off his *iqaal*, going on to remove one article of clothing after another until he stood stark naked and fully exposed, indifferent to the howls of indignation from customers and staff who pleaded with him to cover his shame. He dashed out of the bank, gesticulating wildly and babbling incomprehensibly as he ran up and down the streets. For those who knew him, his crazed ranting was evidence that the loss of his fortune had caused him to lose his mind.

He remained in this vagrant state, sprawled out naked and demented on the sidewalk of the city's upscale bank and hotel district for several months. Guests and customers had to step around him and the security staff of the banks and hotels waged a losing battle to move him away. As soon as they prised him out of one spot, he would set up somewhere else, brandishing a toy pistol in their faces. They detained him several times, but he would always get back on the street.

Passers-by who urged him to cover up were met with an avalanche of abuse and profanity so foul they hurried away scandalised. The guards got tired of dealing with him and would drag him away from the entrances of the plush establishments they protected.

The police got to know his story as he became a regular in the detention cells. They moved him out of the district, first to a psychiatric facility and then to an underpass on the outskirts of the city. But he came back every time.

I came across him a month after he first lost his mind. He looked pitiful, slumped on the sidewalk in front of a McDonald's in the bank district, naked and thrashing about in an assortment of *keffiyehs* that shoppers had thrown to him to cover up his shame.

When Issa had led us to the Palace all those decades ago, little could he have imagined that he would suffer a vertiginous fall that would leave him splayed out on a sidewalk, his genitals on display like a baboon in a zoo.

I had seen his genitals three times before, twice up close. All that remained of them now was atrophied and shrivelled, superfluous as used plastic utensils or napkins that have been discarded. It was only when I got down on the ground and stuck my face right up against his that he recognised me.

'Tariq!' he exclaimed. 'Look at me, stripped bare for ever!'

Before I was able to take it all in, he went on and asked, 'Will you help me kill him?'

I said nothing.

246

'I will get him one day, you'll see, even if my initial attempts failed.'

I had not been aware of any attempts to kill the Master.

It never occurred to me that I would end up doing what I did.

Whatever freedom of choice I might have had was lost the minute I set foot in that damned place. I did not realise how bad things would get or that my fall would be so precipitous.

If only I had shaken hands on it when Issa had suggested we kill the Master.

Issa was not the only person who had thought of it: people from within his own circle were loath to see him die a natural death. Some of them would have liked nothing more than to expedite him with their own hands; as far as they were concerned, death had tarried and he had hardened like a gourd withering on the vine.

At first I was daunted by the Master's influence and standing, but I gradually became obsessed with the idea of getting rid of him. I had few desires left in life and would have been honoured to guide the Angel of Death to his door. My priority, however, was to preserve my sanity and avoid doing anything rash: I lived in fear of emerging from the Palace stripped as literally bare as Issa.

The Master had now snatched thirty-one out of my fifty years. When I started working at the Palace, I had not wanted to listen to the warnings of those who had preceded me there and whose lives were already poisoned. I considered them ingrates, carping and complaining while living large. Uncle Muhammad knew the ins and outs of life at the Palace and the fate that awaited newcomers. He had tried to warn me.

'Rich folks are like little girls playing with their dolls,' he told me one night, taking me aside before one of my torture assignments. 'They don't care about the consequences of their acts and the mess they make.' He prodded me in the chest. 'As for the dolls, well, they're just dolls – they submit to being pulled and twisted without complaint. All they do is provide passing amusement for the rich.' He paused briefly. 'As for the Master – well, he's just like a kid who throws tantrums.'

He had advised me to leave the Palace. But back then, I had been too young and rash to understand. In any case, Uncle Muhammad had not listened to his own advice and even now, past his self-imposed solitary confinement, he still chose to spend most of his days holed up in his quarters, waiting for death to carry him off because he could not bring it on himself.

Slavery has not been abolished. It exists in many guises and lurks hidden behind all sorts of façades. How I yearned to be my own master. Wealth and power are the foundations of sovereignty: throughout history these alone have determined whether one belonged to the master class or to the mass of slaves. Without wealth and power, we are slaves even if it does not feel like it.

Dominion over others necessarily implies being surrounded by slaves, opportunists, sycophants and crooks who regard their master's word as gospel. There is no morality that is compatible with being a master: power cannot limit its own reach. The lust for power of the overlords is absolute and it has always been their practice to crush whatever and whoever comes in the way.

One of life's grievous lessons that comes too late is that we are all inextricably caught up in some form of bondage and are as accustomed to it as we are to our own skin – which is why we do not feel it.

I knew that there was not much left in the vial that was my

life, and what remained had become so stale and musty that even I turned away in disgust.

The murky outline of a bleak destiny was traced on that night, thirty-one years ago. I could only hope that in the future, others would be sufficiently liberated from the strictures of current conventions to look upon every shameful act with as much amusement as Issa did. It was with this notion that I calmed my anxiety.

I had begun to feel that I, too, would end up being kicked out on to the streets, and that I would have nothing to do but chew over my bitterness and spew profanities like overflowing sewage.

I had lost my closest friends and there was no one I could talk to about the terror that gripped me one day when the Master gazed down at me from his balcony that overlooked the deep blue. He fixed his gaze on me as if he could look into my very thoughts, probing for something with which to indict me. He had just returned from a hunting expedition in Equatorial Guinea, with his retinue of cooks, marksmen, entertainers, gamblers and other sycophants.

I was seriously considering taking the step on which Issa had faltered. His mistake had been to visit the lion just as it was waking; its jaws had snapped shut around Issa, chewed him up and spat him out. It was left to me to bleed the beast, drop by drop, so that as he watched his blood coagulate he might understand how many innocent souls he had destroyed.

I was only worried that he would read my mind before I had a chance to do what had to be done. I had also taken to repeating, almost like a mantra: 'It's either him or me.' It was almost unconscious, like a tic, and once I caught myself doing it right in front of his smug face.

'Who are you talking about?' he asked, spinning around.

He burst out laughing when I told him and then left the room with his customary swagger, with Maram by his side. She could steal one's heart in a flash and the assembled guests delighted in her disappearing derrière.

The towering walls of the Palace kept out all global and local news, whether the bloodshed in Iraq, Lebanon and Palestine, the terrorist attacks in the country or the roving patrols of the religious police. People came to the Palace bent on cutting a deal, or the promise of a deal, and nothing else mattered. Bloodshed and dignity were irrelevant.

In fact, the trickle of virginal blood was the highest form of pleasure for the denizens of the Palace. There was nothing like a thin stream of blood trickling between a woman's thighs to heighten their passion, while bloodshed around the globe was of little concern.

I awoke to the news of Osama's escape, which did not entirely surprise me since he had asked me to join him. I thought his plan was stupid and rash and had told him so.

'It'll be the end of you.'

'It's better than dying here,' Osama retorted.

Issa had ended up naked on the sidewalks of the bank district, and Osama was convinced that we were next in line. He wanted us to avenge Issa and was surprised by my indifference.

'What do you want us to do? We're just puppets on a string,' I said.

'This place is nothing but a charnel house,' he exclaimed.

'Calm down!'

'I came to tell you I've decided to leave,' he said abruptly. 'Come with me.'

'He'd pull us back in.'

'Not if we went somewhere he'd never find us,' Osama countered.

Tahani had been calling out to him in his dreams and he had decided to make a run for it.

'Maybe we'd find her killer,' he ventured.

'Whose killer?'

'I wish I could be like you, with a conscience that erases everything and remembers nothing. Have you forgotten about Tahani's killer?' He paused and then looked me straight in the eye as he added, 'Maybe *you* are the killer since you're always telling me to forget her.'

'Will you lay off with your accusations?' I said, but he had already turned away.

I was now the only one left.

When Osama escaped and had gone missing for a few days, his boss, Nadir, vowed unimaginable punishment when he got his hands on him. His desperate search for Osama and the near hysteria with which he spoke of him raised a few eyebrows. Speculation increased when he offered a financial reward to anyone with information on Osama's whereabouts. The amount increased steadily with each passing day until it topped out at one million riyals. He called me in and I finally realised what was causing him such agitation. He had recently taken on an entirely effeminate demeanour, and the old queer could no longer live without Osama's expertise in pleasuring him.

I was certain that Osama had decided to go and camp in the shadow of Tahani's grave, to water the seeds he and his aunt had planted and to wait for the seedlings to grow in that remote desert spot where no one would find him.

After Issa was gone, and with Osama's disappearance, there was no one left to turn to for company but Uncle Muhammad.

Uncle Muhammad never missed an opportunity to criticise my conduct but his sarcastic barbs did not upset me because I knew he was simply a gruff old man. His external demeanour belied his complicated and passionate feelings.

His severity resulted from the fact that since his earliest childhood, when his 'fingernails were soft' as he liked to say, he had been exposed to politics and had always followed the news avidly. He considered himself an heir to an honourable generation driven to the soul-destroying Palace by terrible reversals of fortune.

After the night the Master humiliated him by pelting him with his shoe, Uncle Muhammad had retreated to his room where he spent the entire time watching the news, feverishly switching channels and getting riled by what the Americans were doing in the region. 'Sons of bitches,' he would shout at the screen. 'Plundering is nothing but a way of life for them.'

Uncle Muhammad wept when he heard the news about Issa, and I went to see him around midnight after Osama's disappearing act. I had to knock on his door several times, asking to be let in. When he eventually opened the door in his underwear, he seemed like a skeleton that had shed everything but its ability to move.

Despite his spacious quarters, he sat in one corner of the darkened room, and the only source of light was the television that blinked images of a documentary on Al-Jazeera about the American bombing of Baghdad. He let me turn on the lights and found something to wear.

'One can't be too careful being undressed around you,' Uncle Muhammad chided. 'You're a dangerous guy, Tariq.'

He did not want to talk about Issa and his naked vagrancy in the bank district, and he had not heard about Osama's escape. So he just sat there quietly, watching the documentary, occasionally spouting a profanity.

He suddenly pressed on the mute button and swung towards me. 'It's not only in war zones that you find death and destruction,' he said. 'Even places carpeted with flowers and smiles can be killing fields. People are left with nothing more than physical movement – dead corpses shuffling between one morgue and another.' Jabbing his chest, he added, 'Zombies, just like me.'

He raised his finger to his lips to silence me and looked back and forth between the television screen and my face. Finally, he asked, 'Will your depravity never end?'

Before I could answer him, he had turned the volume up on the television set and his voice was drowned by the commentary.

I thought I heard him say, 'I don't want to see you any more.'

This seemed to be confirmed when he motioned me to leave.

I slipped out of the room quietly, wondering if he thought that I had caused Issa's fall from grace. But then, I reasoned, if he had suspected this, he would have let me into his room only to rip me to shreds, notwithstanding his false teeth.

Everywhere I turned inside the Palace, I could feel people's contempt. When Issa used to be there, he had bolstered my spirits whenever I felt their disdain getting under my skin. I had not needed to talk to anyone else.

The last time Issa would come to the Palace, the bullets from the Master's revolver could have been for me. But I never had the chance to find out. Everything happened so quickly. We had no inkling of what lay in store. Had we known, we could not have done anything about it with the Master there. Nothing ever happened against his will.

18

Issa told me how he had once saved the Master's life. He described a figure bobbing in the waves, desperately clinging to life, the same figure who later would welcome all of us into the Palace. Had he not been plucked from the water that day, we would have been spared our dark destiny.

I retraced every detail of Issa's life to remind myself of everything that had led to and sprung from that one event.

As boys, none of us in the neighbourhood had ever believed Issa when he swore he knew the Master personally and vowed to get us all into the Palace. Seeing him in operation later, we could immediately tell what a high position he held and that the Master had a special place for him in his heart.

The Master owed his life to Issa.

Back in the days when Issa hid on the remote islets beyond the reach of novice swimmers, the shadow of the Palace scaffolding danced across the seawater. One day there was an accident: someone fell off the cement bridge under construction that jutted out into the deep. The victim began to drown, his body bobbing in and out of the waves as people looked on powerlessly and screamed for help. The workers at the construction site rushed to the scene.

Like an angel swooping down from heaven, Issa dived in

and later emerged from the water after wresting that body from the tentacles of the deep blue sea.

Issa had heard the clamour and cries for help, and had jumped in to rescue the victim. He was nearly dragged under himself: twice, the panic-stricken victim had clutched at his neck frantically, practically choking him, and he had had to let go of him. The second time, he was able to dive under and grab him by the chin from below, and kept him at arm's reach so that he could swim unhindered.

With every powerful stroke of his arms bringing them in to shore, more people flocked to help. Many waded in, calling out at the top of their lungs, all vying for the honour of saving a drowning victim. They huddled around Issa as he dragged the body up the beach and literally snatched it out of his grasp to begin administering first aid. People were running helter-skelter, calling out for the Red Crescent to be summoned.

Startled by the sudden appearance of so many self-appointed rescuers, Issa turned to swim back to his island hideout. Before he could get very far, however, two men caught up with him as others called out to him. They told him that the Master of the Palace wanted to see him.

Issa was nervous as he stood bedraggled before the first Master – *Sayyid al-kabeer*. The old man paid tribute to the heroic rescue of his first-born son, and thanked him for his brave deed with a wad of one-hundred-riyal banknotes he pulled out of a pocket. A young girl, who looked no more than fourteen, looked on as Issa hesitated and she smiled encouragingly for him to accept the gift.

Issa refused to extend his hand and stood silently, looking back and forth between the girl and her father. The more he was pressed to take the money, the further he retreated until finally he felt his feet propelling him into the air, and he ran back to the concrete jetty and threw himself into the water.

'You can come back here any time you like,' rang out the voice of the venerable old Master.

That half-drowned figure was none other than his son and eventual successor, the person who ended up toying with our lives. Had Issa let him drown, we might have escaped the destiny that became ours.

As the child of an old salt in a long line of fishermen, Issa knew the secrets of the sea. He could tell when a fish had swallowed the bait even when he could not feel its weight tugging on the line. Maybe that was why he was convinced that he had been snared by the eyes of that spirited young girl, and she began reeling him in slowly but surely. He felt irresistibly drawn to her and took to swimming by the concrete jetty every day, his sinewy arms pushing against the waves, his eyes watching. He swam there at all times of day, lying on the surface of the water like a piece of seaweed impervious to the motion of the waves. He got sunburnt swimming there day after day and his back was covered in blisters. At sundown, he would wade out of the sea and go home to wash and soothe the raging sores with freshwater.

The construction of the Palace was nearing completion and as the number of workers began to dwindle, he was emboldened to sneak on to the grounds. Throwing caution to the wind, he roamed around the vast and spacious compound, awed by its imposing structures. He examined the atriums and mezzanines with their marble floors to match the colours of the walls, taking in the intricately carved cornices on the ceilings, and walked around the gardens dotted between the buildings. His sense of wonder grew with every new structure he came across; Issa had never seen anything like it before.

Lost in amazement, he did not hear the guards' approaching footsteps. He snapped out of his reverie when he heard them accusing him of vandalising the premises, blaming him for the dried-up human faeces and the stench of stale urine in several of the unfinished rooms. *Sayyid al-kabeer* had evidently blamed the guards, responsible for securing the construction materials and keeping the worksite clean, for dereliction of duty.

Issa was brought before the Master as the culprit. The young girl was there again and he felt mortified being accused of such disgusting conduct in front of her.

'Did you do it?' the old man demanded.

Issa's head hung low as he denied having anything to do with it and he became even more embarrassed when he saw her giggling.

At that moment, the foreman of the building site appeared and informed *Sayyid al-kabeer* that his workmen had been defecating and urinating wherever they could because the plumbing work had not been completed. Cleared of the charges, Issa regained his composure somewhat but the young girl kept on giggling.

As had happened earlier, his feet propelled him of their own accord and he threw himself into the waves from a little overlook above the water. Unfortunately, this time the water was shallow and he smashed against large pieces of debris lying on the seabed.

His whole body screamed in agony, but soon he was lifted out of the water and administered first aid. Issa noticed that the young girl who moments earlier had been giggling at him, was now watching with genuine concern and encouraging him to be brave. He vowed then and there to spend the rest of his life captive to her eyes.

He had been lacerated in several places by metal girders that protruded from the jetty's cement foundations deep in the water. The old Master called in a doctor to tend to Issa's injuries because he did not think the first aid administered was sufficient.

After he had examined him and bandaged him up, the doctor kept him under observation to ensure that there was no haemorrhaging. Issa was served refreshments and sat on the couch from where he could steal glances at the girl sitting next to her father. Her two brothers, shaken by the accident to which their father had responded with such compassion, were anxious to go home. The visit to track the progress of work on the Palace had gone on too long, and they started a game of chess to pass the time. Their father was engrossed in a book but every once in a while he peered over his glasses to check on Issa.

The young girl kept up her steady stream of smiles and also watched him. When she was restless, she would get up and go over to her brothers' game or look at the trees and flowering shrubs outside, planted to create a hanging garden effect from all viewpoints. Occasionally the girl would ask her father about the flowers and what they were called. She also stepped out to take a walk along the jetty, accompanied by her chaperone.

'Be careful on the jetty,' her father cautioned. 'Don't go far – the safety rails haven't been put up yet.'

When she did go too far down the jetty, he called her back and she returned to his side. He shut his book and conversed affably with Issa on the dangers of swimming in that particular spot with all the construction rubble that had been dumped there. Then remembering that this was where Issa had saved his eldest from a sure death, he did not pursue the thought. He tried to draw him into conversation, but Issa was guarded in his responses.

The chess match ended when the younger son gleefully checkmated his older brother. Smarting from the defeat and impatient to leave, the eldest turned to Issa and snapped, 'How long are you going to lie here sprawled out like this? Why don't you get up and get a move on?'

The old Master frowned at his son. 'When someone grants you life, you return the favour,' he reprimanded. 'This young man is the reason you're still alive. He snatched you from death's jaws and so he is now your brother.' He asked Issa for his name and turned back to his son. 'From now on, Issa is your brother. I pledge the two of you to life-long brotherhood. Betray this pledge and you betray me. Do you understand?'

The son nodded slowly and Issa got up to leave. The father ordered his two sons to embrace their new brother, which they were forced to do.

Issa bent down to kiss the old Master's hand; he had been moved by the man's compassion and surprised because he had never kissed his own father's hand. Before taking his leave, he turned to the young girl and held out his hand to say good-bye. Her hand in his felt completely relaxed.

Sayyid al-kabeer was at the Palace to lay the groundwork for the hanging garden that would be suspended in one of the internal courtyards leading to the jetty. He whispered something to one of his assistants, who quickly pulled out a stack of bills and handed it to the youth. Issa refused but the old man insisted. He accepted the gift and bent down, once again, to kiss his hand.

'This place is your home – its doors will always be open to you,' said the old Master, patting him on the shoulder.

The young girl's name was Mawdie.

I do not recall Issa taking up with any of the girls in our neighbourhood. The only woman from the Firepit he ever loved was his maternal aunt, Salwa, who was also his suckling sister. But he loved her as a sister, best friend and confidante. He could not bear to see her hurt in any way and it was the only thing that roused him to anger. Salwa was like his own soul in another body.

Issa had a number of interests. He played football with the local team and was one of the young ruffians who could not resist a brawl, whether with boys from our own neighbourhood or the ones nearby. He took part in musical evenings held at wedding halls, where he played the *simsimiyya* and sang plaintive sea shanties with a musical group. He raised pigeons and went out twice a week to fish or hunt rabbits in the wadis east of Jeddah and, at night, he looked for partners in the dark alleyways to play *balut*.

Nothing in his early life suggested he would achieve great things. In that respect, he was no different from all the other kids growing up in the Firepit: an uneventful life, with the expectation of a steady job on which to raise a family was the extent of their dream.

But Issa strayed early and began to keep company with older boys and men. Now when he looked for partners in the dark alleyways, it was no longer to play *balut*. He soon acquired two vices: chasing after boys and stealing.

His petty larceny included shoplifting from small neighbourhood groceries, pilfering from the carts of itinerant fruit and vegetable vendors, stealing the birds of other pigeon fanciers, and snatching motorbikes to go joyriding. But the theft that confirmed him as a crook in the eyes of his parents – and which became the talk of the neighbourhood – was the burglary of his grandmother's savings. That theft changed the course of his life and led him down the road to the Palace, and to Mawdie.

The moment he vowed to enter the Palace, a change came over him. He began to feel he was different from us and he spurned our company. All of a sudden, it seemed to us, he was no longer interested in petty theft – lurking about the small corner shops in the alleyways, scheming to grab produce off a pedlar's cart, or huddling together to plan the heist of a motorbike we would later resell to a bicycle shop.

His transformation was obvious the night he treated us all to a feast at a restaurant. He kept the tab open, letting us order whatever we wanted. That did not stop us from our cruel taunts as we voiced our suspicions that he must have robbed someone to be able to treat us all. He just laughed off our jabs.

Back then, none of us could figure out how he had come by so much money that he could spend it so liberally. Some of us gave him the benefit of the doubt and attributed his newfound means to the sale of the pigeons he had been raising for years.

His generosity extended to the local football club, whose expenses he basically underwrote: he paid for jerseys and balls, goalposts and nets, the clean-up of a vacant lot and all the planning work. Issa even bought the water and other refreshments that were distributed to the players at half-time. In recognition, the team nominated him to head the club, but he declined the honour. He was content to sit in his customary place at the nearby crossroad and stay out of the club's contests.

And at some stage during those matches, a luxury car would glide to a stop and Issa would hop in, spirited away to some unknown destination. Different cars would come and collect him at different times of day. Their models and designs varied but the cars were always gleaming. He swapped his garish outfits for fine and elegant attire. His sharp appearance and the succession of luxury cars lent credence to the rumour that he had given up petty crime and become a drug dealer.

He gave up all his hobbies. He no longer cared about rabbit-hunting in the wadis and stopped singing the old shanties and playing his *simsimiyya* with the band. His generous gifts and donations to community endeavours like the football club ensured that all the talk never got back to him.

Speculation that he was a drug dealer only grew after Crazy Jamal was run over by the Rolls-Royce. Issa asked me to accompany him to Crazy Jamal's house. Knocking loudly at the door, he had called out for Jamal's father and, once the old man appeared at the door, Issa handed him a wad of bills.

'A benefactor wants Jamal to have this,' Issa told him.

Crazy Jamal's father took the bundle of one-hundred-riyal notes, stared at it for a while and then flung it in Issa's face. 'I will not accept ill-gotten riches,' he shouted. 'Nor will I have them given to my children.'

News of the substantial recompense spread throughout the neighbourhood and soon everyone became convinced that Issa was selling drugs. This was when his father, Abu Issa, notified the counter-narcotics agency, which then came and ransacked their house. They went through all of Issa's personal effects and found nothing suspicious. Issa left home that night and only returned fleetingly, a week later, to take his mother away.

Salwa was the only person who knew where he had gone and she told no one.

Issa started working at the Palace before the death of *Sayyid al-kabeer*. That is how he was able to provide a detailed description of him when neighbourhood locals went and stood at the street corner to catch a glimpse of the first Master driving by.

That is also how money came to flow through Issa's hands.

For *Sayyid al-kabeer*, the incident with Crazy Jamal was a blemish on his conscience. Issa's arrival at the Palace alleviated his burden since he was able to entrust him with 50,000 riyals to give to Jamal's father.

When the Palace lights went out for three whole days and the usual car did not come and collect him, Issa was bereft. I saw him on the second day of the blackout making his way to the Palace on foot. He walked all the way around the wall until he reached the main gates and entered. He was gone a long time.

It was he who bore the news of the death of the first Master. The news was relayed from mouth to mouth without anyone ever knowing how it reached the neighbourhood.

We all thought that Issa came to leave the neighbourhood because of the dispute with his father. In actual fact, he had accepted the new Master's offer to move into the Palace in order to be closer to Mawdie. All he wanted was to be in her vicinity – ever since the day he had saved her brother from drowning. There was no other place on earth for him but in her bewitching eyes.

An innocent love had blossomed between them and nothing could keep them apart. He was to her as nourishment to a plant, nudging it forth through the soil and towards the sunlight. They were enamoured of each other from the first glance. It was as if the drowning that he had spared the young Master became his own beguiling fate: she lured him into the depths of her being with eyes he could die for and, like a diver, he plumbed her depths. Issa was spellbound, but did not dare to reveal what he felt. She had eyes only for him and he remained unrivalled in her estimation.

19

MARAM FINALLY CAME THROUGH on her promise.

Lying on the hotel bed and looking in the mirror directly across from her, she could see the curve of her hips outlined through the light bedcovers. She lifted the telephone receiver and ordered breakfast for two.

Her languor suggested she had just emerged from a deep slumber. Her hair had danced about her collarbones and neck until late in the night, until she had finally fallen asleep, exhausted.

She was mesmerisingly beautiful.

Like the other girls at the Palace, Maram had not expected to become the object of a derby for thoroughbreds. She had won the ultimate prize when the Master had placed her in his sights. When she finally came to me, she was like a parched field thirsting for rain.

'Slow down,' she had teased the night before, slipping into the bathroom. She was changing and her words were muffled. 'Wouldn't it be better if we spent the next two days at the bungalow?'

I did not want to respond to her question so that she would not know how much the Master had me on edge: he was always around and the further I tried to get away, the closer

265

he seemed to move. I tried going places where I thought he would not find me and spent time at different hotels along the seafront. But he always caught up with me with a phone call. 'Where are you, scum?' he would say.

I emerged from every escapade thinking it would be my last, feeling my neck gingerly to make sure I was still breathing. It is true that I risked death but I was watching my step. After a quarter century of confinement, I was calling the shots.

My reactions betrayed my anxiety. I was nervous when the receptionist asked with a knowing smile, 'Just a room, or a suite as usual, sir?'

He emphasised 'as usual' with that superciliousness that petty officials favour – it was their way of getting back at overbearing bosses who held them in their places.

I had seen far too many receptionists looking over the women who accompanied me, barely concealing their brazen thoughts.

'Are you going to spend the night in the bathroom?' I asked her.

She appeared in the doorway, striking a provocative pose, hands on her hips and torso thrown back. 'Now let's see how well you measure up to your passionate wooing,' she said with a laugh. 'But don't give up that charm offensive.'

She had me flustered. I checked that I had enough Viagra in my wallet, after I had not found any rifling through my pockets.

It had been a rough night, which I spent trying to meet her urgent needs.

Now morning, I watched Maram sleeping peacefully for a while and then moved to the bathroom. I really needed a warm bath to loosen my joints, which felt stiff and creaky. I stayed in the water, chewing gum to dissipate the smell of stale alcohol on my breath.

How I wished that some medicine had been discovered that could erase one's memory.

Like a slideshow, all the faces from the past clicked through my mind's eye. I saw Tahani, screaming for mercy as she squeezed her thighs together, holding her hand up to my face to show me the rosy blood that was evidence of her defilement. Aunt Khayriyyah appeared next, with her wild bush of white hair and rattling bones, shrieking hysterically despite her dwindling strength and stuttering gibberish in the torment of a never-ending life. Mustafa Qannas raised his head and roared like the grinding gears of a powerful truck engine, vowing to pound me to a pulp, dragging me stark naked through the neighbourhood's alleyways and squeezing the last breath out of me as he sodomised me in public. That image was replaced by Osama, who trapped me in a funeral shroud and exclaimed, 'At last, I've caught you, thief!' The Master's flushed and jowly face seeped into the picture and spread outwards like an oil slick on the surface of the sea, obliterating everything around, with his devious and cunning malice reflected in his features.

Those who did not know the Master were charmed by his smile and convinced that he would not hurt a fly. But those whose lives were bound to him knew that meekness and humility were only a veneer – and a very thin veneer at that. No matter how hard I tried to keep him at a distance, he would surprise me, worming his way into my very soul and boring into my skull. In my mind, I could always hear him say, 'I'll carve out a tight space for you in Jeddah's most pathetic cemetery.'

It had been a long journey.

It had taken more than a quarter of a century but I was proud of my financial success and willing to overlook the pact with the devil that it had taken to get there. With a pill to erase my memory, I could have forgotten all the unmentionable things I had been compelled to do throughout my life.

I was brought up in a humble home with a father who came back in the evenings half dead from work. His only reaction to hearing about my childish misbehaviour was to threaten me – but his threats were empty. With every vain warning, I gained more wiggle room to disregard the next one and to do whatever I wished with the full knowledge that the threats would never be carried out.

My ability to be a step ahead of him nurtured my recklessness. It never occurred to me that the strategies and escape routes that I used to get around my misconduct might one day bring on my downfall, or that I could lose my soul in the process.

Aunt Khayriyyah was like an affliction that had wormed its way into me and contaminated me with chronic hatred. She fed me an endless diet of animosity and thanks to her relentless and hostile scrutiny, I became a master in the art of deception and evasion from a very young age.

Once when the Master had phoned to see where I was, he had shouted, 'I'll send you back to the streets where you came from!' As long as he said such things, I felt I was safe. For if he had known that I was having a relationship with Maram, no street would have been punishment enough – I would have been chopped up into mincemeat then and there.

My love of the hunt, which I had acquired in the winding alleyways of the neighbourhood and on the reef islands strewn across our shore, had spurred me to go after his woman, even if it had not been easy to prise her from his grasp. I was able to get the better of him on one of those wild nights at the Palace, like so many others except that this playful young kitten had made that particular evening extraordinary.

She must have been trained by a true pro to arouse such powerful and simultaneous feelings of repulsion and attraction: one instant I felt that she had eyes for no one but me and the next I felt I was being flung into the rubbish bin like a scrap of meat.

I heard room service knocking insistently on the door of our suite. I quickly threw on a bathrobe, afraid they would barge in and feast their eyes on the charms of my reclining temptress.

I blocked the door as I opened it and grabbed the breakfast cart from the waiter. I was flustered and inadvertently exposed myself. He was mortified and muttered repeated apologies before closing the door.

I wheeled the cart into a corner and went to wake her up. I held her close and began nuzzling her neck as I considered how she too was risking so much to be with me. She shifted about, hoping to get a few more minutes of sleep, and I gave up trying to wake her.

I seated myself before the enticing smells wafting off the artfully plated breakfast and picked up a copy of *Okaz*, the local newspaper, that had been placed alongside. The first thing my eyes fell on was a photo of his jowly face under a banner headline. I paid no attention to the story and was fixated on the face staring out at me menacingly. I was shocked at feeling undone merely by contemplating his photo.

I looked into his eyes defiantly and before I could stare them down my cell phone began to vibrate. It was a text message from him. A wave of anxiety flooded over me. I read: 'Son of a bitch, you're not answering. Where are you?'

I jumped up and went out to call him from the balcony – if she said anything, he would surely recognise her voice. I was rehearsing all the excuses I would dole out but he did not give me the chance.

'Get over here, *now*,' he barked.

I shook her awake and told her we needed to leave.

'Didn't you say we were spending the day together?'

'I'll make it up to you later,' I promised her.

Osama's nightly sorties were anything but disappointing.

He was dashingly handsome and bold. Backed by the Master's protection and influence, it was not too difficult being bold. In any case, those two attributes greatly facilitated his job. All he had to do was wander about the souks and other recreational areas in search of attractive girls and then start flirting with them. If a girl did not respond to his overtures immediately, he would brazenly stuff his phone number into her handbag or hand it to her. He could be very forward when it came to doing his job.

I was worried that some day Maram and I would run into him at one of the places we liked going to. We had just started seeing each other in secret, stealing moments here and there, and she had begun telling me some of her story. It turned out that what I had on her in my file of Palace girls was inaccurate.

'Do you like Osama?' I asked her on one such occasion.

She bit on her lower lip, trying to recall who he was. 'Osama? Who's Osama?'

270

'You know, Osama,' I explained. 'He's the guy who brought you to the Palace.'

She burst out laughing at the suggestion and said she would tell me her story some other time when she felt more inclined.

I was pleased by that as it held the prospect of more surreptitious meetings.

We did the rounds of Jeddah's hotels, restaurants and beachfront bungalows for several months. We would steal out of the Palace once or twice a month after silently communicating our desire without ever looking each other in the eye.

'I feel so happy with you,' she once cooed with delight. 'Every cell in my body speaks of you, reminds me you are there. I can feel your fire even when you're gone.'

The imperious demeanour Maram maintained at the Palace completely vanished between the sheets. She became a sweet girl who craved affection and thirsted for any word that conveyed warmth. She loved it when I put my mouth over her ear and whispered my passion and longing for her, and she became wildly aroused and moaned urgently when I ran my tongue over her collarbone.

Once, in the Palace, she got up from her seat beside the Master and went to fill her glass. As she passed me, I whispered very quietly that I missed her. She was so disarmed, she practically fell into my lap, and began coming and going in the hope of hearing me repeat the words. She would sit down beside him and then spill her drink, or say that she got the wrong thing, or that she forgot the ice-cubes. I really thought she was going to give us away that evening. I kept my gaze averted but could sense her darting eyes looking for me around the room.

'I feel safe with you,' Maram said, quivering in my embrace

when we were finally alone again. I buried my head into her neck, inhaling her fragrance, and started to kiss her. Moving up to the top of her head, I planted my lips on her eyebrows and began kissing her eyes. She moaned and I took her into my arms.

'I've never known such tenderness my whole life,' she confided. Putting her arms about my neck, she looked deep into my eyes and asked, 'Would you like to hear my story?'

'Yes.' I pulled her head in close and ran my fingers through her thick hair.

She sat up, gave me a kiss, took a long sip from her glass of Chivas and began her story, with a distant and sad look on her face.

Maram told me how her father had died before she had laid eyes on him, which for her proved that her birth had been inauspicious. Her parents had only been married for a year and a half and her mother had been optimistic about the future when, out of the blue, her father dropped dead and they were left high and dry.

Maram's mother thought she had left poverty behind for ever after she had found a man willing to take her on and deliver her from the humiliation of being shunted around between her brothers. They had tossed her around like a ball, letting her spend a week here, a week there, and she was beholden to them. She wanted to settle down, and accepted Maram's father when he asked her to be his third or maybe his fourth wife. He was older than she was but she needed a way out of her predicament.

Not only did the marriage prove short-lived, but it took three months for her mother to find out about his death. She did not know his family or where he lived. He had set her up in a home of her own, that was what mattered, and he would come by and check on her periodically. Maram said her half-brothers – the sons by the other wives – had expressed no concern for them and withheld her share of the inheritance.

So now, they were two stray balls instead of one, and the last thing Maram's mother wanted was to be bounced back and forth between her brothers again. So she sold all her gold – the jewellery from her dowry – and bought a sewing machine. She opened her doors for business, making dresses, gowns and abayas for the women of the neighbourhood, charging them whatever they could afford.

Those were dark days. Maram was at school and looked forward to securing some kind of qualification that would land her a job and help her mother out. But as she approached her sixteenth birthday, suitors had started banging at the door. Her mother's stringent requirement was for a groom to be financially reliable and she settled eventually on a man who promised a villa, a car and a bank account in exchange for Maram's hand.

Her mother was overjoyed at the prospect and the marriage was arranged without Maram having any say in the matter. He was a stubborn and cantankerous man and, as it would soon transpire, also a swindler. He had informed them that he was a widower who had lost his wife a year earlier. Maram's uncles drew up the betrothal agreement in accordance with her mother's stipulations, the most important of which was that the dowry had to be sufficient for Maram's upkeep for life and that the deed to the house would be in her name.

The groom promptly wrote out a post-dated cheque for 200,000 riyals and promised that the title deed would be in his bride's hands as soon as she moved in to the villa. Even though the cheque was post-dated, Maram's mother and uncles were satisfied and the deal was sealed.

However, no sooner was the marriage concluded than he cancelled the cheque and Maram became his lawfully wedded wife with no dowry to her name.

On her wedding night, he took her to a cheap hotel and left her there. He would disappear for a whole day and come back the next, have his way with her and leave again before she could ask him where he was headed.

Once, Maram asked why they were in a hotel and he slapped her so hard that she never dared to ask again.

As far as he was concerned, she was just his whore. He would arrive, sleep with her and leave fifty or a hundred riyals under her pillow to pay for some take-away since the hotel did not have a restaurant.

This went on for almost six months during which Maram never saw her mother and could not contact the brother she had met the night the marriage contract was concluded. She felt totally alone but knew there was nothing she could do but ride it out.

At the end of six months, she began to show signs of pregnancy. When he saw her state, her husband thrashed her. Kicking and hitting, he accused her of conniving to get his inheritance. There was a loud knock on the door and he went to open it, muttering and cursing the hotel and its staff.

But it was a woman and his voice was immediately drowned by her screams and shouts of fury. She was called Salwa and when he asked her what she was doing there, she yelled that she had followed him and that he was a cheating bastard.

This woman stalked into the room, grabbed Maram roughly

by the hair and accused her husband of cheating on her for this whore.

He fell over himself apologising and asking for forgiveness, like a cat rubbing up against its master's leg. Still yelling, Salwa told him that she was not about to forgive him and that she would teach him a lesson he would never forget.

She still had Maram by the hair and forced her to move with her as she paced around the room furiously. It was at that moment that Salwa's brother stepped into the hotel room, prised Maram from his sister's grasp and eventually brought her to the Palace.

Maram sighed and took another sip from her glass. 'I think you know him,' she said slowly. 'He's your friend. I've seen you talking together.'

I frowned and shook my head.

'Her brother is called Issa, and he's very close to the Master.'

'Do you mean Issa Radini?' I exclaimed with astonishment.

'Yes, Issa Radini.'

'You mean that you were married to Waleed Khanbashi, the husband of Issa's aunt, Salwa?'

'The husband of his sister, not his aunt. You know him, right?

'She's his aunt and also his suckling sister.'

'It seems you know them well then.'

'I do.'

She chuckled ruefully. 'It's a small world, isn't it,' she said after a while and, looking directly at me, she added, 'That guy, your friend Issa, brought me to the Palace and I have vowed to get my own back on both of them, him and his slippery snake of a sister – or aunt.' She paused. 'I know the Master thinks very highly of him, but I'll get him one day, you'll see. Everything that's happened to me is Issa's fault – I'll get my own back, both for me and my child. How else will he ever be proud of me?'

She stopped suddenly, concerned she had said too much.

'Are you upset by what I'm saying about Issa?' she asked anxiously after a moment's silence.

'No, not at all.'

'It's been some time since I last saw him,' she said, changing her tone and adding, almost chattily, 'Is he away?'

'No, but his job is with the Master's family. He's responsible for their day-to-day upkeep. Most of the time he's in the lower section of the Palace, reserved for the family.'

I was keen for her to carry on with her story and I found myself wishing I had denied knowing her husband and Issa. As I feared, her need to unburden herself had been quashed by my ill-considered response.

She said one last thing and then no more. 'For those who can afford it, marriage is nothing but serial adultery. They can marry and divorce as often as they want.'

It was not clear to me whether she was referring to her husband or the Master. I waited for her to elaborate but she just sat there stiffly, looking stone-faced at the wall.

Issa dropped in on me unexpectedly and, grabbing me by the shoulder, told me excitedly that he wanted me to be his witness. He was dancing on air.

This was at the time when I felt trapped by my aunt's imprisonment and was considering the possibility of getting rid of her altogether.

'I want you and Osama to be the witnesses of my marriage contract.'

So much of our lives had gone by and not one of us had started a family or had any offspring.

I had spent my time channelling the life-force within me into barren land and it dispersed bearing no fruit.

Earlier on, I had yearned to free myself of the tyranny of the ogre that made me into an animal with no other purpose than to disgorge my warm and sticky liquid. When the ejaculation of that fluid became my livelihood, I yielded to its demands in the same way that a blind man submits to the darkness of the path before him, regardless of whether it is well or poorly lit.

Life had been quick to chew us up and expel us like so much excrement to be reviled by passers-by. Subsiding in us, life could grow elsewhere. But in truth, it was best not to reproduce and therefore not to bequeath our twisted destinies to offspring who would only become tormented by our sick baggage.

I wondered what had come over Issa. Did he want to reproduce before he turned into dust again? Was he not afraid of handing down his genetic legacy or did he really think he could just root out the past and start afresh with a home, a wife, children and a nice life? Was there still time for that?

Only demolition can widen a narrow street. The three of us were on a very narrow path and the further down the path we went, the more constricted it became. We could barely pick our way from under the bodies that we had strewn along the path. I seriously doubted that we still had it in us to raise families at such an advanced age.

It was only by standing in as his witnesses that Osama and I fully grasped the extent of Issa's grievous dilemma. He took us aside and told us of his secret love for Mawdie that had weighed on him these many years. He was at the point where he felt that he wanted us to bear witness to his very life, not just to his marriage.

The first registry clerk refused to draw up the marriage contract.

He shut his ledger and stood up, apologising. Mawdie's family name lay in the way of his pen. Fearing that news of his plans would get out, Issa took the clerk aside and nimbly spun him a tale of woe. It was sufficiently convincing for the clerk to agree to be sworn to secrecy.

Salwa and Issa's mother had to postpone their ululations while Osama went to find a marriage registrar willing to draw up the deed.

Issa and I chatted as we waited. I steered the conversation to Salwa and asked Issa how she was doing with Waleed Khanbashi. He had nothing good to say about Waleed, whom he likened to a stagnant bog compared to the lake of pure blue that was Salwa. Waleed was untrustworthy and he was oblivious to all that Salwa had done for him, Issa said. It would be his undoing and it would haunt him to his dying day.

I tried to get him to elaborate, but he would go no further. It was a disjointed conversation in any case because he had to jump up and attend to his mother whenever she called him. Mawdie also needed to be calmed. She was growing very anxious and was determined to have the contract drawn up that night.

Osama was soon back with a marriage clerk in tow who looked churlish and disgruntled. A very crooked set of teeth accentuated his fake smile and he grumbled about the absence of guests.

Issa greeted him expansively and explained that an

enormous wedding celebration was planned in Mecca as soon as the marriage formality was concluded. The clerk grudgingly accepted the explanation and began taking down the personal information of the bride and groom and their witnesses, after I had reminded Issa to provide him only with Mawdie's given name.

Just as he was finishing recording all the information, the clerk asked for the personal ID card of the bride's guardian. He was taken aback when he heard that the bride was an adult and could consent to her own marriage without a guardian. She was not a spinster and did not need a guardian, Issa told him.

The clerk scoffed and told Issa he was insufficiently versed in Islamic jurisprudence and that the consent of a guardian was essential even if a woman was wizened and her hair had turned grey. Any marriage that was not physically witnessed or verbally attested to by the bride's guardian would, he declared, be null and void.

'In whose religion?' Issa asked, his voice rising.

'Don't lecture me on religion!' the clerk retorted, rising to his feet and refusing to proceed.

Before leaving, he insisted on being paid for his trouble. Even though it had been a waste of time, he demanded the same payment as if the formality had been concluded. The man protested vehemently when Issa offered him 20,000 riyals to do the deed. Issa raised the amount incrementally with every outburst until he offered him 100,000 riyals. At that, the clerk changed his tune and the focus of his ire shifted; he began to lambaste the 'narrow-minded systems' that denied people their freedom of choice.

'I'd really like to help,' he said, now apologetic. 'But it is not within my power to conclude this contract. I'm so sorry.'

But Issa and Mawdie were determined not to let anything stand in their way. To overcome this latest obstacle to their marriage by hook or by crook, Issa went and fetched his mother's Indonesian driver and sat me in the middle of the room.

'You attended our neighbourhood mosque for a good period of time when we were there.'

'So?'

'You know some of the *suras* by heart, don't you,' he insisted, 'and some prayers, right?'

'Yes, I still remember a few, but—'

'Great,' he interrupted me, 'then you can conclude this marriage formality.'

I hesitated but he urged me on. Mawdie hastily sat down facing Issa and he asked me to begin. Unable to summon up the verses that are recited for such occasions, I substituted with other verses that I knew by heart.

I swore in as witnesses Osama and the Indonesian driver, and had Issa and Mawdie proclaim their acceptance of each other in marriage. The deed was done and I congratulated them warmly.

Now, Salwa's *zaghroutas* could fill the air, and his mother also trilled, although she sounded more like a rooster going to slaughter.

When I asked Mawdie if she accepted Issa as her husband, her *niqab* slipped – as it had the first time I ever saw her. Here before me were those same eyes in all their glory, the very eyes that had bewitched me that day when she had asked if Issa had returned from his trip.

Mawdie built him up like a tower, one brick at a time.

But before she could unveil her handiwork and proudly reveal his existence, Issa collapsed into a pile of rubble.

It was for her that he had single-mindedly pursued wealth and status, so that he could be considered deserving of her.

With the assistance of Dr Bannan, who had opened the university gates for several of the Master's acolytes, Issa had obtained a university degree. He endeared himself to his professors by offering them a multitude of services, from the simplest to the most involved. He provided them with gifts, aeroplane tickets, nights in world-class hotels, invitations to wild parties, anything that would help him get one step closer to his goal.

He obtained a Bachelor's degree with highest honours, and went on to get both a Master's and a Doctorate from Cairo University. He travelled there twice to defend his Master's thesis and, later, his doctoral dissertation, even though they were mere formalities both times, consisting of a welcome address and a presentation of the thesis chapters. There were no questions to answer nor any substantive discussions. He came away with a PhD in international law with the highest distinction and a recommendation his thesis be published.

As soon as the verdict was announced, he turned away from his well-wishers and got on his cell phone. He must have dialled more than a dozen times trying to reach Mawdie to tell her the good news, but every time he dialled he got through to a recording that the number was out of service.

All the congratulations and praise left him indifferent. The only voice he wanted to hear was hers, and hers alone.

He left Cairo University with an academic title and was irritated whenever people failed to address him as 'Doctor'.

Under the Master's wing, Issa had been able to invest in many projects which made him very wealthy. He often made use of the Master's name to open doors that would otherwise have remained firmly shut.

When his collapse came, it was sudden and unexpected.

No one had imagined that the Master would find out about Issa and Mawdie so quickly, and I felt that I had surely hastened his fall by divulging their secret. I had slipped up one evening when I was out with Maram.

Her silences bothered me and I would try and cheer her up with stories I embellished here and there. She was often sad and morose; when she was in that mood at the beginning of an evening, she would gradually become dejected and sink into silence. Maram would freeze up, like a beautiful but cold statue, as if all her vitality had been sucked out of her, leaving her to stare blankly into space.

When we are not strong enough to face the reality of our situation, we flee to our inner worlds and hide. There we can despise those we dislike and punish those who have humiliated us and who remain out of reach. We think that by fleeing we can obliterate whatever undermines or defeats us. When Maram fled to her inner world, I would try my best to bring her back and cheer her up although I myself was on the run from my own defeats and from those who had inflicted them.

Whenever the Master was busy, Maram took the opportunity to enjoy herself and do what she pleased, although she was cautious and circumspect about it.

'What's new with your friend?' she asked me that night.

As a rule, when she said 'your friend' she meant Issa. To lighten the mood I told her the story of Issa's wedding and how I ended up officiating at the ceremony.

Secrets spread like infectious diseases. I would later wonder if she had been with me simply because she wanted to isolate the virus that would take down Issa.

She planned our rendezvous and put together elaborate plans for us to meet without having to go to hotels and beach resorts where my presence would be noted. We started meeting in the homes of her girlfriends. She would have her driver drop her off at a friend's house and dismiss him; then she would change her outfit and have the friend's driver take her to another friend's home, from where she would call me to come over.

After we had had our fill of each other, she would reverse the procedure. Sometimes she would make a reservation for the entire wing of a hotel, using the name of her friend's husband. Then she would call me and I would drop everything and rush to meet her.

By the time I arrived, she would be laid out in all her splendour and I would plough her every furrow, from the top of her head to the soles of her feet.

I was sure she was besotted with me.

But every time we met, she would gather one more strand from the thread of Issa's story.

If not for Mawdie, I would not have known that the Master had found out. She had taken considerable risks to reach me, leaving the family wing of the Palace several days in a row and asking her driver to drive around the compound on the off-chance of running into me.

When at last they located me, the driver hopped out and called me over to speak to her. Leaning out of the window, she asked me if I knew what had happened to Issa. I was transfixed by her eyes, as ever, and said that I had no news of him.

'My brother found out about our marriage,' she whispered urgently. 'I don't know what he's done to him, but please, please find out and let me know.'

She ducked her head into the car briefly, opened her hand-bag and fished out a cell phone which she handed to me. 'This is a secure phone and I'll call you for news,' she said. She turned to the driver and told him to drive on.

The car had not gone a few feet when it stopped again and Mawdie leaned out of the window once more. 'This will be the last time I see you. I'm moving to the new palace in Sharm Abhar,' she said. Choking back tears, she added, 'Please tell Issa if you see him!'

I wondered if she had any inkling of what might happen.

20

OSAMA'S CONDITION HAD WORSENED. He was constantly in a drunken stupor, and as soon as his inebriation wore off he reached for whatever alcohol was at hand. Nadir's recently discovered sexual proclivities were to blame and Osama could no longer stand being fully conscious.

In his stupor, he would conjure up Tahani and express his longing for her as if she could hear him. He would say a jumble of things, some heartfelt and sincere, others corny; sometimes he recited love poetry or hummed a popular song. Then he would keel over and fall asleep as his inebriation got the better of him.

Osama found out about Issa's love for Mawdie before I did.

Issa had no one else to share his sorrow with but Osama. Even as he valiantly climbed all the necessary rungs, earning academic degrees and making untold amounts of money, Mawdie remained out of reach – and she would always remain so.

Mawdie had been made to marry her cousin against her will. Were it not for Osama's presence by his side that night, Issa might have died of a broken heart.

He had just returned from Cairo with his doctorate, confident that this highest qualification would supersede the class divide. Now, he felt, he could venture to approach her brother, the Master, and ask for Mawdie's hand in marriage.

The Palace was sparkling when he arrived. Every corner of the grounds was festooned with wedding lights and all the courtyards, gardens and the open plaza thronged with guests. Waiters circulated with refreshments, tables heaved with food and streams of musicians and singers entertained the crowd. As the bride could not be seen in public, well-wishers were lining up to congratulate the groom.

The city's elite would not have missed this wedding celebration for the world, especially as it provided them with the opportunity to pay tribute to the Master and congratulate him.

No one even noticed Issa still desperately holding his phone up to his ear and dialling repeatedly to get through to the number that had remained unanswered all week.

When he tried to enter the women's wing, there was such a crush of women shedding their abayas in the vestibules that they blocked all access to the family quarters.

He rapidly made a quick mental review of the women who inhabited the wing: the Master's mother, whom he called Aunt Shahla, Mawdie of course, the Master's wife, Nadir's wife, their two aging aunts, and the Master's and Nadir's daughters. With the exception of Mawdie, none of these women and girls were of marriageable age or status.

Had she been snatched up?

If she had, then the race he had embarked on all those years ago had been rendered meaningless. He had hoped to be able to stand tall and firm before her brothers and win them over. Now he felt worthless. Even if the differences in their social standing had narrowed over the years, whether he was a

286

pauper or a man of means, a rubbish collector or a PhD in law, it made not an iota of difference.

He needed to be sure, however, and he wanted confirmation that she had given up on him for a rival.

He was uninterested in mingling and kowtowing to all the VIPs, making obsequious noises and massaging egos. The only person who welcomed him was Osama, who embraced and congratulated him on the doctorate, and who sensed that Issa was reeling from the force of the blow he had just been delivered.

Sheikh Omar, the old sea captain, came up to them in search of solace after receiving some bad news of his own. He was tearful and even though he was brushing his tears away and sniffing audibly, neither Osama nor Issa enquired why.

'Uthman Kabashi has died,' he volunteered.

The news of the death of his old shipbuilding friend who had relocated to Port Sudan filled him with sadness and self-pity. Sheikh Omar rubbed his face with both hands now as he added, 'Oh, it'll be my turn next – I'm the only one left wagging his tail.'

The three men's grief and sorrow were drowned out by the wedding celebration, like a flash flood sweeping away dead tree limbs in its path.

As the night took its leave of the Palace, so did Mawdie. She slid into the back of the limousine, with her new husband guiding her in gently before sitting beside her, smiling. She was looking around at all her well-wishers when Issa came into view. Mawdie had no other gesture to offer but a parting wave.

Issa spent that night crying, with Osama by his side.

Osama was returning the favour from those many years ago when Issa had comforted him after the loss of Tahani.

287

Issa had no one left in the world now apart from Salwa and his mother, who suffered from many ailments. Asthma was her latest affliction and Issa had hired nurses and servants to look after her when he was busy at the Palace with the Master's wife and the other Palace women.

His life centred on three concerns: enlarging his fortune, caring for his mother and Salwa, and discharging his responsibilities towards the Master's family.

He ordered his life with the precision of a Swiss watch. He was unstinting with Aunt Shahla, the Master's mother, whom he loved almost as much as Salwa.

Sometimes unrequited love can turn a person into a demolition machine and the rubble created is commensurate with its roar.

When Salwa found out about Waleed Khanbashi's marriage she flew into a rage. Her only solace was Issa. He alone could provide some redress for her husband's crass ingratitude: after all she had done for him, lifting him up from nothing and providing him with untold riches to spend as he pleased.

Salwa and Waleed were about the same age and by the time they were in their mid-fifties, her body was droopy and his sexual appetites for perkier pleasures had grown commensurately with his bank account balance. Salwa no longer excited him and since Waleed did not want to commit adultery, he resorted repeatedly to *misyar*, a part-time form of marriage considered legitimate in some interpretations of Islam.

He never stayed long with one woman. Whenever he had an opportunity to consort with another woman, he would get rid of the previous one. He carried on in this fashion for over two years until he got to Maram. When he had approached

288

the family as a prospect, Maram's beauty had left him speechless and he had agreed to all their conditions for the contract,
foremost among them that it not be a *misyar* marriage. He put
on a lavish celebration and although it was sparsely attended,
he did not regret the ostentation: Maram rewarded him with
one of the most enjoyable nights of his life.

Waleed could not bear the thought of leaving her and, in
order to avoid being discovered, he rented a room in a cheap
hotel and went there as often as he could. After he took his
pleasure with her, he would go back home to his wife, around
whom he was stern and irritated because of her persistent
questioning.

This went on for several months until the night Salwa
showed up at the door of his hotel room, with Issa in tow,
and accused him of being with a whore. Salwa was even more
incensed when Waleed, trying to clear his name, told her that
he had done nothing prohibited in Islam and that Maram was
his legally wedded wife. When he refused to countenance the
idea of divorcing Maram, Salwa vowed to teach him and 'that
whore' a lesson they would never forget.

In the event, it was Issa who drove that lesson home, and
not Salwa. The best way to get the point across was to divest
Waleed of all his worldly wealth. Initially, Issa had tried to
have charges of insanity pinned on him but when that did not
work, he began to obstruct his commercial dealings. Waleed's
fear of losing his money turned out to be far greater than his
desire for Maram. He agreed to back down and divorce
Maram. To ensure that Waleed made good on his promise,
Salwa spirited Maram away to an unknown location and kept
her there until the divorce went through.

Maram, for her part, went through the bleakest days of her

life. By that stage, she had given birth to a son and Issa made them go hungry. By incarcerating them, with little to eat, he gradually broke down her defences until she agreed to become a Palace whore.

Once the Master had become infatuated with her, Issa could go ahead with the plan of stripping Waleed of his wealth. The Master agreed that Issa should take care of the bothersome fact that Maram had a husband and arrange for their divorce, unaware that Waleed and Issa were related. He gave Issa the go-ahead to do whatever was necessary and to be discreet about it.

Within two days, Waleed was committed to a psychiatric hospital where the medical advisory described him as a dangerous individual who should not be approached. By the third day, Issa was waving the psychiatric evaluation report in court requesting a judicial order declaring his brother-in-law to be of unsound mind and placing his assets under the control of Salwa, his first and permanent wife. A copy of the same report was submitted for the divorce filing of his ward, Maram.

Salwa was ecstatic. She embraced her suckling brother warmly and blessed his presence in her life.

Issa almost lost his mind.

Breakdowns were not unfamiliar to him. Before he ended up crawling stark naked on Jeddah's streets, he had had several temporary lapses of sanity owing to the stress that stemmed from the exacting nature of his work for the Master. Issa was never able to forget that the slightest mistake could mean the end of life as he knew it. He lived in constant dread of doing something that would unleash the Master's devastating fury.

One night when he had broken down and wept over

Mawdie, Issa reminded himself that he had to focus on his goals: namely, building up his savings and devoting himself unstintingly to the needs of the Master's family. Aunt Shahla, the Master's mother, had become very dependent on him. She relied on him almost completely; it was Issa who called the doctor when she felt poorly, Issa who administered her medicines with clockwork regularity, and Issa who brought in nurses to attend to her in her private apartments.

Issa was also the one who escorted her to perform Umrah, the lesser pilgrimage, in Mecca, and to visit the Prophet's Mosque in Medina. She trusted no one but him with distributing alms and charity on her behalf, and with supervising the charitable projects she funded. She would not countenance seeing him wronged or belittled, and her love for him had steadily increased with the onset of old age and its ailments. He had become her favourite.

It was during a visit to the hospital where Aunt Shahla went for specialised tests that Issa almost lost his mind. Such visits always turned the medical centre topsy-turvy as people fell over themselves to attend to her.

Issa had left her in front of the door to the X-ray room to make a quick phone call and when he returned, she was gone without a trace. Aunt Shahla had vanished into thin air.

None of the staff – nurses, doctors, administrators, hospital workers – had any knowledge of her whereabouts. The director of the facility was almost as distressed as Issa as they looked for her in the X-ray rooms, all the laboratories, the medical records department and emergency rooms, and each and every ward. Seeing them running through the hospital hallways and corridors, the entire staff, from the orderlies to the heads of department, set about looking for her.

Work at the hospital ground to a halt as staff left their stations to find Aunt Shahla, and the news spread among the patients, their visitors and their attendants. When someone asked for a description of the missing person, Issa became very agitated. He could not very well stop the news from spreading but he was also afraid that it would go beyond the hospital walls and get back to the Palace.

He almost reached the point of having to notify the Master that his mother had gone missing at the hospital. Two hours went by and no one had any idea where she was. They ruled out the possibility that she had simply walked out of the building since she was confined to a wheelchair. They wondered whether she might accidentally have been wheeled into one of the prep rooms by a nurse who might have mistaken her for an in-patient or, perhaps, that an orderly had wheeled her outside intending to help her to her car or even to the bathroom. This last possibility immediately gave rise to the hope that she would be found before the news got back to the Palace.

Everyone made for the hospital bathrooms, and female nurses and doctors went in to search the toilet stalls. When they emerged shaking their heads, Issa snapped. He began shouting and cursing everyone at the hospital and got into such a hysterical state that two psychiatrists intervened and volunteered to go with him, as well as the director of the hospital, and break the news to the Master of his mother's disappearance.

Just as they were about to leave, Issa spotted her wheel-chair. It was right where he had left it. Aunt Shahla was hidden from view by an old man, a patient, who was stooped over her figure, trying to settle her into the chair and to lift her feet on to the footrest. The man knocked on the door of the X-ray room impatiently; he had been waiting for his turn a long time. Issa raced towards them and she looked up at him smiling brightly.

'All this time, and still no one from X-ray has turned up,' she said with mild reproof, as the old man fussed over her again, making sure she was seated comfortably. Aunt Shahla thanked him profusely.

She refused to say where she had been all this time.

Some time after the incident at the hospital, Aunt Shahla said to Issa, 'Mawdie says hello.'

She conveyed the greeting while coughing. He had just given her the pill she took to regulate her arrhythmia.

He had not set eyes on Mawdie since her wedding two years earlier. He was careful never to be there when she visited. Aunt Shahla waited for him to respond but when he changed the subject, she handed him her cell phone and asked him to dial Mawdie's number because she wanted to speak to her daughter.

She could have made the call without his help and Issa wondered whether the old woman had sensed that there had been a relationship between them, or that she had known all along and had been watching them closely.

He called the number and after he handed back the phone to her, he slipped out of the room.

Aunt Shahla repeated Mawdie's greeting a month later and added, 'Do you know that Mawdie is having problems with her husband?'

Issa remained silent.

'Her brother forced her into it, you know,' Aunt Shahla said gently. 'You're aware of that, aren't you?'

Issa shook his head; he had not even had a chance to speak to her once since his return from Cairo.

'Do you know the stories of Clever Hassan, Sindbad and the Sad Lover? Although the princess marries Clever Hassan, she cannot marry the man she loves.' Aunt Shahla continued, 'Son, that's just the way it is and you have to endure the frustrations. I've told Mawdie the same thing.'

Aunt Shahla was a woman who had married against her will. Her wedding to the Master's father, *Sayyid al-kabeer*, had been a huge affair and she had no choice in the matter. While she had surrendered her body to her husband, in her mind she kept alive the image of the sweetheart she had been forced to give up. Now her daughter was repeating her history, almost to the letter, and all she could do about it was lighten the burden of the crossed lovers with words of comfort.

It was Aunt Shahla who kept their hearts connected. When she learned that her daughter's life was unhappy, she smuggled gifts and greetings from Issa and did the same for him.

A boy and a girl were the fruit of Mawdie's seven years of marriage.

Over that period, Aunt Shahla's health, already at a low, took a turn for the worse. Issa was nearby to comfort her.

'Life is passing you by, son. Shouldn't you be thinking of marriage?' she asked one day, taking his hand in hers.

'I'm too young to marry.' His playful response was accompanied by the laugh she so loved to hear.

'Are you waiting for her?'

He did not answer.

'Even if you spend your whole life waiting, you'll never get her,' said Aunt Shahla. 'Find yourself another woman to care for and who'll care for you. Let me tell you a story no one knows,' she said suddenly. 'Do you remember that day in the hospital five years ago when you asked me where I was?'

Issa nodded.

'Do you remember the kind man who was helping me back into the wheelchair?'

Issa brought to mind the old patient at the hospital. 'Yes.'

Aunt Shahla described the events in detail. The man had bent down to kiss her hand. At first, she thought he was one of their old servants, but his kiss went on too long and he would not let go. When she pulled her hand away, he whimpered as if about to cry. 'All I need is you,' he said. 'You are all I've ever desired, dear Shahla.'

That was the moment Aunt Shahla recognised him: he was her sweetheart. He had aged terribly, his hair was all white and he was very thin. But his eyes, with their thick, over-hanging brows that protruded like little parasols, were the same. He wheeled her into one of the inner waiting rooms and as he sat before her, all the years of separation fell away in one instant. He took her hand, looked at the wrinkles tenderly and singled out her ring finger. He told her how he used to dream of putting a wedding band on that finger and that he had waited his entire life to tell her that he had never stopped loving her. Not for a day.

He went on to tell her how he had achieved everything he had aspired to: learning, riches, standing. But he never stopped waiting for a time to come when they could be together again and so he had never married.

Aunt Shahla was hard on him. Time was short and she did not tell him how she, too, had suffered, how barely a day passed without her dreaming of seeing him. Just seeing him and nothing else. She said nothing, and he just wheeled her back to where she had been and left.

He disappeared right before her eyes, just as Issa and the hospital staff gathered around her and started asking her questions. Once inside the X-ray room, Aunt Shahla learned from a nurse that he came in regularly to get chemotherapy for cancer of the spine. So she started following his news from afar. There was no time left to have even one meeting or outing.

She had found out exactly a week ago that he had died. 'I could swear that if anyone had been there as he took his last breaths, they'd have heard my name on his lips,' Aunt Shahla said. She looked dispassionate, as if she had recounted the story of some other woman unconnected to herself in any way. She took Issa's hand and patted it gently. 'If you want to continue loving Mawdie, and be her one and only love, do so from afar.'

21

MAWDIE THREW A HUGE party to celebrate her divorce. She had vowed to herself that she would marry Issa or die. Her decision convinced Issa to follow his heart fearlessly. Issa did not follow Aunt Shahla's advice to continue loving Mawdie from a distance.

Their resolve to get married, however, brought them on a collision course with an immovable rock. The Master's anger awaited them, calculating and devious. He was not willing to renounce his anger as long as Issa remained at the Palace, living in the lap of luxury.

Issa was providing him with new excitement and it brought back the almost feline pleasures he so loved: toying with his prey, pawing it, only to disembowel it later with his claws. The certainty that his dominion was not diminished in the least contributed to his euphoria.

Issa was at a juncture in his life where he could have joined the ranks of billionaires, and the Master exploited his greed by placing a few choice temptations before him. He used the stock market to drive Issa into the ground. The bank manager, Adnan Hassoun, was tasked with luring Issa into the Master's snare.

Like the serpent that brought the devil into the Garden of

Eden, the Master ushered Adnan into Issa's life. The relationship was built up with demonstrations of affection, gifts and concern for Issa's welfare in a very volatile stock market. Adnan offered to manage Issa's portfolio in return for a percentage but Issa was reluctant to hand it over to his friend: he listened to his analysis of the market and followed his recommendations, purchasing shares in companies that were doing well. Issa's bank balance hit the 100-million-riyal mark.

Issa trusted Adnan to such an extent that he followed his advice to the letter and unswervingly. Adnan offered Issa a matching bank loan: these loans, offered only to the bank's most prestigious clients, were to enhance their trading potential and basically matched the client's balance held by the bank. What Adnan neglected to add was that the bank reserved the right to call in the loan following a fifty-percent loss in the value of the portfolio.

Issa showed up at the bank to complete the loan process and was shocked by the number of customers on the bank floor all trying to sign up for similar loans. These were people who had no other work besides trading. Construction projects were at a standstill and investors were opting to get into the stock market, adhering to the prevailing dictum that if you could not make it rich in days like these, you would never make it.

The bank was thronged with borrowers, investors and brokers glued to trading screens. They were all worried they might miss the gravy train. Issa pushed his way through the crowd and past groups of noisy men heading towards Adnan's office. He repeatedly apologised as he asked to be let through.

Adnan emerged from his office and came towards him, chuckling. 'As you can see, they all want loans,' he said.

'And does the bank have enough money for all these borrowers?' asked Issa.

'The bank is like a fountain, my friend,' replied Adnan. 'While funds allocated to credit may be fixed, they are distributed here and there and in the end, they all come back to the bank. Not a single piastre ever leaves the vault.'

'But at the end of the day those people's bank accounts are growing.'

'Yes, but that's just what shows up on the screens. This is a rare opportunity for all our people to strike it rich and it will never recur. In boom times, you have to grab what you can while the going is good. It's like running a marathon – you've got to have good lungs.'

'That's what everyone is saying,' said Issa, nodding.

'That's because it's the truth, and everyone can see it. Look around. They're all government employees, either borrowing or trading, that is, buying and selling. Everyone believes that the index will go up to 30,000 points,' he said. 'That's a five-to ten-fold growth in profits.'

Inside the office, Issa relaxed while two of Adnan's staff completed the paperwork for the loan. As the signature process began, Adnan held forth on the guaranteed profits that would accrue to Issa's portfolio and reminded him to be diligent about repaying the loan as soon as he had doubled his investment.

'The Master controls dozens of companies, so if you want the best yields, my advice is that you invest in those companies. Wherever he puts his money, just follow suit, eyes closed.'

This counsel bore fruit and Issa's profits were mind-boggling. His bank balance jumped to 250 million riyals – an astonishing return that he reaped in only four days of trading. Thus assured that Adnan was truly a reliable and sound source of advice, he finally entrusted him with managing his portfolio and just followed the progress of his fortunes. These soared day after day.

Issa's ambition had grown in line with his wealth and he would have taken over the country if he could have. He was willing to grovel and abase himself, and do whatever else was necessary to feed his ambition. The accumulation of wealth was predicated on abasing oneself, he felt; to do otherwise would be counterproductive.

Issa had already reached the point of prostration before Mawdie, ignoring the fact that prostration is an inescapable part of enslavement.

Financially speaking, he was already on his knees since the Master held him in a vice-like grip inside the stock market. When the bubble eventually burst and the value of shares collapsed, the bank hastened to liquidate Issa's portfolio and recover its loan. His entire account was wiped out in one stroke, down to the last piastre on the paper statement. Issa was left to wander the streets naked and deranged, hurling abuse at the high and mighty of the city.

By the time he was fifty-eight years old, Hamdan Bagheeni had managed to become a security guard at the Palace. While he would always have difficulties with the alphabet, particularly the letters *noon* and *jeem*, he felt that he had now made it in life. Hamdan swelled with pride as he stood to attention with his rifle propped up beside him, marvelling at the sight of the gates to Paradise, which, for most of his life, had been a distant vision.

The only thing that marred his enjoyment of this new position was that his father-in-law had not lived to see it. He would have liked to witness the old man's ridicule turn into pride: his father-in-law had little good to say about him and all the bad-mouthing had eventually driven Hamdan's wife to leave him. Had he lived just a little longer, Hamdan would have been able to repay him with a few choice words of his own. He had endured all the disparagement silently because the responses he would have liked to make would have been considered inappropriate to utter in front of a woman. So he said nothing and she had eventually given up on him.

After twelve long years of intellectual exertion and perseverance, Hamdan had finally obtained his primary education certificate. His motivation was very nearly destroyed by the repeated failure of several years, but he found new resolve every time he saw his father-in-law coming or going. With every passing year, his father-in-law got closer to the grave and when he died, Hamdan described him as a mean man because he had passed away before he could witness his success.

Hamdan had gone on to obtain his primary education certificate the same year, with a mark of 'fair'. When he proudly showed it to his estranged wife, he told her that her father had deliberately sought to annoy him by dying when he did.

He stood proudly in front of the Palace gates, with nothing on his mind besides gazing at the high and imposing walls, and occasionally allowing his eyes to stray towards the interior of the compound. He sensed that with a little more persistence he too would be able to get actually inside Paradise.

The guards were on notice to prevent Issa from entering

the Palace compound under any circumstance. Hamdan could not really get his head around that and he voiced his misgivings. 'Issa, who brought everybody in through these gates, is now forbidden from crossing its threshold? Why is that?'

No one knew the reason for this sudden reversal in Issa's fortunes and no one had expected it. Issa had kept his secret buried so deep that when he decided to act everyone was caught unaware.

King Abdullah Street runs through the heart of Jeddah, with more recent neighbourhoods flanking it on either side. It is the main thoroughfare into which secondary and intersecting streets feed and is plagued by permanent traffic congestion that only adds to the sticky humidity.

I wondered what the Master could want at this time of day when I set off to his other palace on the shores of Sharm Abhar.

I had stopped running like a racehorse that gallops off at the first sound of the firing gun and I had honestly contemplated not responding to his summons now.

I stopped at a cash machine to check on my bank balance and was relieved to find that it still stood at twenty million riyals. I was worried that it might just evaporate one day, as had happened to Issa. The Master's moods were erratic and unforgiving. This servitude had gone on too long.

I had reached the autumn of my life and had nothing to support me except for this bank balance acquired at the price of humiliation and abuse. Thankfully, I had been too slow and despondent to trade shares and had narrowly escaped the stock market crash – otherwise I would not have had a pot to piss in.

The main reason for my hesitation, however, was probably Joseph Essam, who had counselled restraint. 'Don't over-expose yourself,' he had warned. 'You know he'll skewer you.'

Seeing me perplexed, he spelled out what he meant. 'Look, you have no children, so why kill yourself to get even richer? You already have more than enough.'

His words also reminded me that I was wasting what was left of my life in unnecessary servitude. It was a reminder I did not want and I pushed it from my mind, clinging to my old conviction that nothing but rubbish would be dumped on my head regardless of whether it was a holiday or not. Once we are immersed in what is, to all intents and purposes, disgusting and filthy, no matter how much we yearn for something pure, we are stuck in the putrid rot.

I was not used to disregarding the Master's orders, no matter how onerous. I was, after all, at his mercy, and he could destroy me any time he chose to. I wondered what was stopping him. I had observed him for years and knew his vicious streak intimately: the people he surrounded himself with were kept on a tight leash and the day inevitably came when he simply crushed them.

He was careful to expose only one side of his multifaceted personality, whether in public or with the media. All of us who worked for him were bound to silence – you broke the rule of silence at your peril, for any leak of a word or deed of his would ensure you were permanently silenced.

Three of the Palace staff literally lost their tongues that way. Their enforced speechlessness resulted from relaying stories about Palace goings-on that only they could have known about. It was his chosen punishment that planted the seed in my mind to cut off Aunt Khayriyyah's tongue. I found out how one amputated a tongue with a razor and followed the process to the letter.

When it came to dealing with the Master, you could not be deluded by any sense of closeness you might think you had. He was like a wild horse that bucked and threw its riders as soon as they got in the saddle. I very nearly lost my tongue the first night we met: I had come out wanting to tell Issa what had happened and he had clamped my mouth shut, warning me not to breathe another word.

I remembered our first encounter on that ill-fated night. After performing the punishment as he had instructed, I had scrubbed myself clean to remove both the traces of Tahani's blood that were still on me and the filth of what I had just done at the Master's behest. He summoned me and when I appeared before him meekly, he was holding court with his cronies.

'You did an admirable job,' the Master had said as I stood facing him. 'Now just forget it ever happened – until the next time I call on you.' He motioned that I should leave but stopped me as I turned to go. 'You won't be leaving the Palace. I'm keeping you close at hand.'

Issa fell into step beside me and stuffed 1,000 riyals in my pocket. 'Now you truly belong at the Palace,' he whispered. 'It's a godsend – and don't you forget it.'

The Master's word carried as much weight now as it did back then and his influence was as unchecked. I had not imagined he could last this long. I had assumed that he would be diminished with age and that, like a rotting tree with termites at its core, the shadow he cast would subside and disappear.

304

I had hoped that he would be whittled down to size with time and that his old carcass would be relegated to a wheelchair, to be wheeled to the toilet by a disgusted Asian servant so that he could relieve himself after his gargantuan meals.

It remained a vain wish, at least as far as the Master was concerned. His brother, Nadir, on the other hand, did end up in a wheelchair after a traffic accident which left him a double amputee. Nadir was the spitting image of his brother, albeit an image that was smudged by his perpetually gloomy mood. He liked dirty jokes and was particularly fond of a joke which Osama had once told and which broke all records when 50,000 riyals was offered as a prize.

Nadir's companions flocked to his side to relay the latest jokes. He would handsomely reward the one who could tell him a joke three times in a row and still make him laugh so hard that he cried. This joke session would take place early in the evening, before the parties, and Nadir would then retell the jokes to the entertainment girls in his own sick and twisted way.

He was a lanky man with a long and lopsided face. The goatee he favoured further accentuated his crooked features, especially when he laughed. His unusual height was not hampered by the electric wheelchair he used, and even when seated he was as tall as a stocky man. His elegance, however, was distinctive and, so long as he did not speak, he appeared quite handsome. It was only when he spoke or laughed that his face looked contorted; he looked even more repulsive talking for any length of time because of his pointy stunted teeth and the saliva foaming at the corners of his mouth.

Many a Palace employee had been glad when he emerged from his accident half the man he used to be. If their hope had been that he might not emerge at all, it was dashed by his speedy dispatch to Germany for medical treatment. In the event, God was thanked for a half-fulfilled hope: Nadir returned in a wheelchair, but his tall body and wide appetites brimmed from the ambulatory device.

His accident in no way curtailed his lust although it took on such a form that Osama was led to leave his employ.

He had a series of unsuccessful marriages – the women were turned off by his limp rod and his overactive thumb.

He did not want to accept that his medically induced impotence constantly placed him in the embarrassing position of having to pay women to divest themselves of their modesty and butter him up with affirmations of his prowess.

He was bent on going with Osama on his nightly recruiting sorties and insisted that he, rather than the servant assigned to the task, wheel him around the malls and souks they went to. He thought that the young women who looked at him with pity because of his condition were captivated by his good looks, and he flirted with them coarsely and aggressively.

Osama was at the end of his tether: whenever a girl caught his eye, Nadir insisted that Osama hand her his calling card. Some of the girls would take it and then leave it at their table and others would tear the card up right under his eyes, but a few who recognised the name on the card were sufficiently enticed to keep it.

He made Osama wheel him up and down the hallways of the malls in hot pursuit of the young girls he favoured. If his aggressive banter was ineffective, he would resort to tempting them with money; if that did not work, he might threaten to take them by force. This worked with some of the girls who would climb into his car, enveloped in the obscurity of the dark-tinted windows and the partition that secluded the rear passenger compartment from the driver.

As soon as he was transferred to the car from his wheelchair, he would hurl himself on the girl, petting and fondling her with his hands as well as his tongue, oblivious to her screams and cries for help. Generally, the frenzied groping would suffice and there would be no need to bring the girl back to the Palace.

The pleasure he derived from such acts was their performance in public places. After a period of avid and eager interest, he grew bored with the repetitiveness and monotony of such escapades and began to look for a new pleasure to cultivate.

He was well aware of what Osama did when he poached him from the Punisher Squad. Soon afterwards his desires blossomed and grew as twisted as his facial features.

He began to exhibit undisguised effeminate mannerisms. He spent entire days at the hands of Filipino men who smoothed and lightened his complexion, and removed every last trace of hair from his body. His obsession with hairlessness extended to his goatee which, when it was also removed, left his face formless and even more elongated and ugly. Every crevice of his body was exfoliated to loosen dead skin and calluses, and he was slathered with moisturising lotions to soften his skin. He favoured tight-fitting silk clothes, acquired a toupee made of long wavy chestnut-brown hair and began applying light foundation and eye make-up.

The sight of him was enough to turn anyone's stomach, and it was what Osama had to contend with whenever he was summoned to Nadir's bedroom. Recounting what had gone on in there, Osama would gag and curse his very life.

I still had a way to go along King Abdullah Street.

The checkpoint right before the Globe Roundabout slowed the northbound traffic, and as my thoughts darted from the past to the present, I wondered what was in store.

I no longer lived at the villa and had gone back to living in my quarters at the Palace. My aunt's moaning and whining had become intolerable; whenever I threatened her, she played dead. Under her clothes, there was nothing but a disintegrating corpse, a heap of rattling bones and shrivelled skin.

By this time, the Master had moved to the new palace in Sharm Abhar. He would go back and forth between the two palaces as he pleased, maintaining the old routines and refusing to loosen his hold on the old shoe of a servant that I had become. The alertness of the cat toying with its prey still pulsed through him.

He taught me the importance of keeping one's enemies disarmed but within reach, and of smiting them without hesitation, if necessary.

I had no enemy beside my aunt, and I had kept her in her place. She was my incurable disease, the affliction for which I had no treatment. Whenever I used to see her, venom would run through my blood. The only thing we had in common had been my visits to the prison cell I had fashioned for her. It was as if I used to go there to take a reading of my hatred. Whenever I had been to see her, carrying supplies of food and water with me, we were always on the exact same wavelength of unequivocal and reciprocal hatred.

Nadir remained in the old Palace and as a result of his latest perversion, Osama was desperate to get away. He came to see me one evening, undone.

'Tahani is lying there all alone, and she needs me,' he said, dredging up the story I had now heard dozens of times.

Despite my best efforts, he was still almost certain that I was to blame for Tahani's death.

He fell silent and took another swig from the bottle he carried with him at all times. Telling him not to drink was futile and would have been hypocritical in the light of my own unceasing depravity.

His limbs might have grown heavy but Tahani remained buoyant in his imagination. He had taken to collecting and reciting well-known love poetry.

'Do you know of any famous poets who waxed lyrical about their beloved?' Osama asked me. 'I'd like to collect every poem ever written by a bereft lover.'

I was no connoisseur of lovers' deliriums and was not taken in by the fraud that poets and lovers perpetrated with their cleverly crafted words. I had learned early on that the only true possessions are those which are tangible – the things we can hold in our hands. Whatever slips from our grasp is gone for ever.

'That faggot is making my life unbearable.' There were only two things left that mattered to Osama: getting out of the Palace and tending Tahani's grave. 'Why shouldn't I set up camp in those sand dunes and spend my time planting seeds and watering seedlings on my beloved's tomb? Is there any reason why I shouldn't?'

Ever since returning from Salih Khaybari's village, he had been collecting varieties of drought-resistant seeds that could grow into lush plants around Tahani's grave. He had acquired this enthusiasm from Kamal Abu Aydah. After Samira's death, Kamal had gone to her graveside every evening to commune with her and water the trees and plants bordering her tomb. Osama loved the idea of following in the footsteps of that star-crossed lover.

Helping him up, I tried to convince him that he should spend the night at my place and that we could carry on the conversation in the morning. But he staggered to his feet and set off towards the shore. There, he launched into reciting verses he had memorised and slowly sank to the ground. When I went to help him again, he jerked my hand away violently.

'You were the thief,' he yelled. 'You killed Tahani!'

He tottered off towards his quarters, swearing and cursing all of creation.

When I reached the checkpoint at the Globe Roundabout, a soldier waved me on. I was always terrified at checkpoints whenever I was with Maram. I would worry that something would happen, and that the news would reach the Master that I had appropriated the one heart that kept his beating.

I never understood his attachment to Maram; he could have any woman he wanted on the face of the earth and yet he remained true to her.

I had promised myself that I would spend two whole days with her, but his stern manner on the phone had revived my anxieties.

'Tariq! Get over here!' His voice over the cell phone was irate.

How I wished I could elude that summons as easily as I had eluded my mundane existence in the old neighbourhood when I had left everything behind in my rush to get ahead. I was determined not to look back and would not allow my emotions to rule me, or my memory to hold me hostage to the past. Even though Osama stirred up old memories from time to time, I turned the other way and focused on the present. I was bent on obliterating every moment I had spent in the clutches of privation.

310

I was able to shed my past thanks to the Master. Now, I needed to shed him.

Trying to block him out was futile. He had the power to make himself heard and ensure I did his bidding, regardless. Ever since the night that Issa had led me to the Palace, I had been a captive to his every command.

I drove toward the palace in Sharm Abhar, terrified at the thought that he had found out about my relationship with Maram.

22

J UST AS I PULLED up at the gates at Sharm Abhar, the Master
called and told me to turn around and go back to the old
Palace to meet him there.

Deferential words of submission were on my tongue before
he had finished speaking. Expressing irritation or impatience
at his erratic moods was out of the question.

'Hurry up!' he ordered.

My imagination ran wild and I had visions of blood and
gore. I saw my skull cracked open by a hatchet whose
sharp and jagged edges would tear down the entire edifice
of my actions. I became convinced that he had summoned
me either because he had found out about my relationship with Maram, or that he had discovered that Mawdie
had been calling me on a private line. I hoped now that
he was merely lusting for another of my stud performances and the abuse of some new victim, or that he wanted
to hand me a video of my most recent skirmish with my
aunt.

I had never gone back to see Aunt Khayriyyah after fleeing
the villa and going back to my quarters at the Palace. Had she
breathed her last thirsting for a drop of water? I had conveni-
ently forgotten to bring in more supplies in the hope that it

might cut short her remaining time and she would simply die and relieve me.

I returned to the old Palace and parked in the lot reserved for residents. On my way in, I saw Hamdan flanked by two guards and looking awful. As soon as he saw me, he appealed for help.

'What's going on?' I asked as I approached them.

He tried to wriggle free but the guards quickly stopped him. I drew closer and he told me in a jumble of disjointed sentences that Issa had come to the gate and that he had let him in, and that he was not aware Issa was carrying a weapon and that he had attacked the Master.

I hastened into the marble foyer where the Master usually held court.

'Your friend here wanted to mess with me,' he said with a smirk. 'I couldn't think of anyone more qualified than you to mess with him – and please me to boot.'

The sight of Issa lying on the ground surrounded by guards with their boots shoved into his abdomen horrified me.

The Master ordered two guards to pick up Issa and take him to the punishment chamber. 'Now to your final assignment,' he commanded. In an unprecedented gesture, he put his arm around my shoulder and whispered, 'In addition to tarnishing my honour, your friend here tried to kill me.'

He turned and when he saw how many guards surrounded Issa, he told some of them to stand at the door of the dark space.

'Bastards like him can't be trusted, and I'm going to teach him a lesson,' he said, with his arm on my shoulder again. 'When someone trusts you, you don't betray them. You get my drift, don't you?'

313

I feigned ignorance and he lost his temper.

'Listen to me, you son of a bitch,' he warned, his hand dropping from my shoulder. 'When I tell you to do something, you do it. You know the score if you don't – I'll get someone in here who'll do you *and* him.'

He waited for that to sink in and then added, 'You'd better give it your all, or else—' His voice trailed off with the unspoken threat.

I looked around the room I knew so well as if I had never seen it before and a shudder of revulsion ran through me, spreading outwards into a pool of total darkness.

I was completely shattered. It had never crossed my mind that one day Issa and I would confront one another here. We looked each other in the eye, taking in our defeat and our torment. Like water dripping off a block of ice exposed to the heat of a flaming hearth, the briny droplets of our long years together brimmed in our eyes. All the excitement and adventure of our now faraway adolescence coalesced in the memory of that night when Issa came to my rescue and stopped Mustafa Qannas in his tracks, and of that other, even darker night when he had saved me from Salih Khaybari's bellowing from Tahani's window.

Who would shield us from one another now?

Everything was wrong – the place, the person, the timing. No sooner had I begun working on Issa than the evening call to prayer rang out. Its lustrous melody pierced us to the core, the words echoing as our bodies shuddered, convulsing, and we begged each other's mercy and choked back agonised cries to end our mutual suffering.

The evening call to prayer seemed endless, as if the muezzin's appeal to the faithful had gone unheeded. The

314

words of the sacred call reverberated through me but could do little against the age-old darkness that was trapped inside. The doors to my heart had been slammed shut by sin, and the inky pool had grown and widened, enabling my wounded spirit to engage in ever more cruel acts of torture. The process did not stop just because the time was up.

Our wounded spirits carried on with their outpouring of pent-up grief until all our days and nights in Jeddah appeared like a journey through a vale of tears. We were like boats racing towards some nearby harbour only to be blown back out to sea, the shoreline obliterated by a sprawling mass of walls and buildings. Time passed, the call to prayer continued uninterrupted and night fell, gathering up its cloak, not to cover us, but rather to expose us, bound together in our shameful act.

In all such instances, torturer and victim are irresistibly drawn to the edge of the abyss and their individuality is obliterated.

Our agony persisted and the imam's dewy voice went from the call to the prayer itself. But he must have been praying alone since his chanting had grown more melodic; it was as if his voice was trying to hurry along the faithful who had not yet arrived. The recitation amplified our sorrow and our moaning echoed back and forth like a weaver's flying shuttle.

I could hear a verse: 'And to him who fears God, God shall find a suitable outcome, and shall provide for him from where he never imagined.' I wondered if it was directed specifically at me, if the imam was delivering a coded message to me at that very instant.

I was shattered. I could do no more. The Master seemed satisfied with what had already been accomplished.

Gathering up my clothes, I left Issa to collect himself and dry his tears. I was now certain that I could no longer carry on with such terrible misdeeds, but said nothing for fear that my turn would be next.

The Master looked me in the eye and congratulated me on successfully completing the assignment. 'You're as good as you always were,' he exclaimed. 'Maybe I should reconsider that decision to retire you.'

I spat on the ground without him seeing, while he directed a thick wad of spittle at Issa. He brimmed with contempt for him.

'What brought you back here?' the Master barked at Issa.

'I want my wife.'

Flying into a rage, the Master kicked Issa in the face, his shoe smashing into his nose. Blood streamed down his face.

'You will never get to say those words again!' he roared.

He pushed him still naked out of the punishment chamber and towards the Palace gates.

'Many years ago, you were welcomed through these gates,' he said. 'But now your time is up.'

He pulled out a revolver and, without further ado, he pumped two bullets into Issa's naked body: one hit him in the stomach and the fatal shot ripped through his chest and exited through his back. Issa fell to the ground motionless.

'Where is the son of a bitch who let him in here?' he thundered.

Two guards steered a terrified Hamdan before him. His eyes darted from the face contorted with rage to the view of the heavenly gardens he had spent a lifetime dreaming about. He was trying to blurt something out but the Master took the words out of his mouth.

'You will say that this criminal tried to break into the Palace, that he shot you, and that you therefore killed him.'

He was uninterested in whatever Hamdan might have to say, whether by way of explanation or anything else. The Master took aim at Hamdan's shoulder, fired one shot and tossed the revolver on to the ground beside him. 'Do what I say and you might just live to see another day.'

The ambulance took off at breakneck speed with two people inside: one a motionless corpse and the other writhing in pain. Sirens blaring, the ambulance raced down the thoroughfare that separated Paradise from the Firepit. Hamdan seemed indifferent to the lifeless corpse sprawled next to him and only had eyes for the houses and alleyways flashing by. The ambulance flew through the streets as if trying to shake them loose.

It was a night like no other.

After I was done with that abominable task, I had expected the Master to issue some other order. But he kept his distance; his preoccupation had been with Issa, who had slipped from his grasp while I remained under his thumb.

I returned to my quarters inside the Palace, feeling drained. My tragic flaw bore witness to the ruin that my life had become.

Issa was dead.

He had taken his last steps with the Master pushing him towards the Palace gates. He had teetered, unable to decide whether to cover his nakedness from behind or from the front. Head hanging and gaze lowered, Issa could not see how many people were there, only that their boots crowded around him, as he switched his hands back and forth, between his backside and his groin, and tried to feel around for a wall or pillar to lean against.

Issa was utterly broken and unable to look at anyone. I was desperate for our eyes to meet, hoping he would accept the unspoken apology. But his eyes were riveted to the ground, and whenever he looked further afield, it was to follow the guards' motions and mind their boots.

The Master told him to look up at the window facing him but he did not respond. I craned my neck to look in the direction he pointed to and saw Maram, her hair loose about her face, her eyes on the scene unfolding before her.

'Look over there, your lady's at the window!' he taunted him.

Issa made his last stand and refused to do the Master's bidding.

The Master made his final decision and fired the two shots. Everyone recoiled in horror, and even Maram flinched before retreating hastily. He went to his car, turned on the ignition and drove out of the Palace gates as if nothing had happened. For a moment, I was tempted to tell him about my relationship with Maram, and to join Issa by putting an end to the life slowly wasting inside me.

Issa was dead. Would I tell Mawdie? She had been so worried that Issa was losing his mind.

She had scoured Jeddah looking for him in the places I had told her he favoured. She finally had found him squatting in front of the entrance to the Hilton Hotel. He had looked so awful she barely recognised him: he was skin and bones and, of course, naked. Seeing him in such a state had practically obliterated her cherished image of him.

He had disavowed her completely. She had tried to get him to climb into the car. She had told him she would book him a suite in the hotel and then offered to take him home to his mother and Salwa, but he would hear none of it. He began haranguing passers-by claiming that she was trying to seduce him. Worried about attracting attention, Mawdie had slipped a security guard some money to look out for him, and had left, shaken.

He had tried to escape his predicament. He had drowned in his own blood when all he had wanted was to drown in the Master's.

Should I tell Mawdie that Issa was dead?

Going to my room, I felt confused, humiliated, defeated, with only my dark thoughts for company. How to escape from all this? I wondered how I could stem the tide of a tumultuous past that had surged over me and was sweeping me in its wake.

What I wanted was to wipe out this memory of mine and I turned to alcohol for the escape I sought. I drank so much that I finally crawled into oblivion. I paired the alcohol with hashish in an attempt to shut out the people whose voices were ringing in my head. The ones who said I was despicable, the ones who condemned me, the ones who at every turn had nothing to say but 'Grab that thief!' and 'Catch that killer!' and 'That bastard ruined our lives!'.

They swarmed around me like fruit flies. They closed in on me, combing through my life and issuing their condemnations, citing this or that criminal act I had perpetrated, some wrong I had done, ending their litany with a stream of abuse. Cursing, spitting, screaming, raining shoes down on my head, their fingers poking and pulling at me until I was eviscerated, all of them watching and waiting for me to die.

Despite the alcohol and hashish, the desired amnesia did not envelop me. But I finally lost consciousness and passed out. I slept like the dead, and woke up sullied and defiled, ever the thief, killer and bastard.

It felt as if a drill were boring into my skull because my hangover was so bad. I went looking for painkillers one of the Master's cronies had brought back for me from London and in exchange for which I had given him the phone number of one of the Palace girls.

I saw that Mawdie had been calling the private cell phone non-stop and that she had sent me nineteen text messages. I read the last three:

'Issa called. He said a whole lot of things I didn't understand. He said, "See you tonight."'

'I couldn't sleep all night. You're not picking up and I don't know what's happened to Issa. I beg you, answer the phone and tell me what's going on.'

'My mother heard that Issa got into the Palace and that shots were fired. That's all we know. Please let me know everything's OK. God bless.'

The first thing I did was to turn off the cell phone. Finding that this did not ease my mind, I smashed it with a mallet I found in the kitchen. Despite repeated doses, the painkillers had done nothing for my blinding headache. I had to get away from it all. But I wondered where on earth I could go.

★ ★ ★

Maram had been as beautiful as ever as she watched Issa's final moments framed inside the window overlooking the Palace gates. Had she avenged herself?

I was the one who had given him away. Secrets cannot be secure in the hearts of women because their hearts, like their wombs, seek fertilisation to bear fruit. A barren breast is not fitting for a woman since a woman's heart is the source of utterance. The rib in Adam's clay was so embedded with names and stories that it fell to women to transmit human lore and bequeath stories.

That is how I sent Issa to his fate.

He had been in love with Mawdie for years without anyone knowing about it. When Maram told the Master, she had set off his anger. Standing in the window, she had appeared like a marble statue, but after the two shots pierced Issa's body, she abandoned her fossilised stance and exited the stage. As though entranced by the sight of his thrashing limbs, her neck had craned to follow the arc of his fall, and she ignored my repeated attempts to catch her eye.

I did not want to call her. The last time I had spoken to her, I was panic-stricken, worried that the Master had found out about our relationship. She responded to my call, fresh from the scene of her crime, so to speak, and was awaiting the curtain to rise so that she could witness the fall of the protagonists on the stage.

The painkillers eventually had an effect and my hangover subsided. I was haunted by Issa's face, among others. Before passing out drunk, I had had visions of myself apologising to him and sealing the two bullet holes with my fingers as he lay covered in a funeral shroud at my feet. He had not removed his hands from covering his backside when the two bullets had surprised him in his last stand. He had gone to his death, blood gushing down and coagulating in his groin.

He had managed to penetrate my stupor and during my drug-induced sleep had visited me in the guise of the young man I had known in the alleyways of the Firepit. Not one to abide injustice even in death, he had come back to exact punishment, indifferent to the blood gushing from the bullet holes. But I had managed to give him the slip by waking up with a jolt.

Afternoons on the streets of Jeddah drag on like beggars searching for a drop of water to drink, shuffling between cars and buildings, intersections and shops, wending their way through the crowds desperate for people to take pity.

The disaffection that permeated my being led to a stupid and rash decision, like others I had made in similar circumstances. When nothing matters, choices are meaningless.

Getting out of the car and proceeding on foot would have been unwise in the torrid heat. While it did not kill you, the heat did not spare you, either. I parked my car in a lot near Bab Makkah Street and set off on my burning quest.

The gate to the Cemetery of Our Mother Eve was flung wide open and workers inside the grounds were busy digging a grave. A shrouded body had been set down next to the wash-basin area while the relatives were busy supervising the gravediggers. They were digging up a new space after the family had refused to see the deceased buried in a concrete vault and had paid them handsomely to have an individual tomb.

Three funerals had succeeded one another and each had had to wait for the gravediggers to finish with the previous one. The cemetery thronged with mourners eager to be relieved of the burden they carried and see it lowered into the ground so that they could get out of the heat. I wondered how the burning blaze felt from the bottom of a grave.

The trees and shrubs scattered about the graveyard had all turned to thorns and their bleached colours cried out for water. I was tempted to fetch some water from the wash basins at least to moisten their roots. That was the sort of nonsense my mind was occupying itself with as I waited to ask the chief gravedigger my question. He had just finished taking care of three obsequies when I asked him where I might find two particular tombs and proceeded to give him the names of my mother and of my friend.

Despite the solemnity of his vocation, he burst out laughing. He turned and related my question to the others, and all of them fell over laughing.

After I insisted and repeated my question, he turned to me and answered, 'We don't have gravestones around here. We don't know the names of the dead or where they're buried. Our job is to bury bodies, not to remember names and dates. Don't bother us any more, brother – and we won't bother you, either.'

He must have thought I was mad if very generous when I handed him a note of 1,000 riyals. He immediately changed his tune.

'When were they buried?' he asked.

'The man, two days ago. The woman, two years.'

He went through the motions and pretended to look for the burial papers that he now claimed were in the cemetery files. Stored under his cot pillow, this archive yielded the records of two graves, pulled out at random. I knew they would contain no useful information, such as names or numbers, about anyone buried a month ago, let alone two years earlier. But I needed some kind of a platform on which to stand and address these two people as if they were still alive. I played his game.

The gravedigger's choice of a tomb did nothing to improve the charade. He picked an old grave telling me it was Issa's and concocted some implausible story of his burial. I really did not need to hear any of this fabrication, but I listened anyway as he spun his tale that portrayed an angelic Issa, even in death.

Playing into this absurd atmosphere, I cast fervent words on the two graves.

I stood before my mother's presumed grave fleetingly and effortlessly. I could hear her speaking to me with unprecedented severity: 'Go and get your aunt and bring her here right away – before you beat her to it.' Her amputated tongue had apparently regained some of its agility. But she did not apologise for having abandoned me; all she wanted was my aunt because she missed their endless altercations.

The sun's rays can illuminate every dark corner of the world, but not the human heart. The sun bore down on me as I walked around dazed, stumbling through my own inner darkness. I was lost and felt incapacitated. The darkness that had seized hold of me was so profound that I could neither feel nor imagine anyone anywhere willing to reach out to me.

The gravediggers watched me and probably thought I was soft in the head. Before their laughter could reach me, however, another funeral procession came through the cemetery gate and they moved as one to greet a new set of mourners.

Leading the procession, tearful and red-eyed, was Kamal Abu Aydah. I would not have recognised him but for the imperious mole perched on his right eyebrow – it gave him away immediately and was so grand as to be etched in my mind. Time itself could not have worn down the rude growth. His good looks had faded with the years since his youth, as had the twinkle in his eye that would light up whenever he caught glimpses of Samira.

I found myself wondering whether he remembered Samira the way I remembered Tahani. Moreover, did I truly remember Tahani as my beloved or simply as a victim who had left me bloodied and howling at the moon?

I was certain Kamal's feelings for Samira ran deeper because when she died, she still thought the world of him. Tahani, on the other hand, could only have gone to her death despising me. The chronicles of lovers are not recorded in their times. Before the stories can be written or even made known, time must pass. Only then can they be assessed at their true worth.

I was a fraud. An animal that ate its own excrement. Kamal nearly lost his mind the day Samira died and yet not even his hand had touched hers following the declaration of his feelings. They were content to gaze at one another and flutter around the dream of a shared life.

Following her death, his frequent visits to the cemetery had apparently given him the necessary experience to lead funeral processions. He was almost zealous as he guided the mourners to the right location, removed his head covering and rolled up his sleeves to help the pall-bearers lower the shrouded corpse, smoothing the green cover that was stitched with the Muslim profession of faith, or *shahada*, and urging the mourners to watch that the cemetery staff performed the burial rites properly.

I had not seen Kamal again since leaving the neighbourhood. I left my mother's presumed grave and went towards him.

'My sincere condolences, brother,' I said.

He turned to face me and then pulled me to him in a forceful embrace, greeting me warmly. He grinned, apparently delighted at seeing me and momentarily forgetting that he was there to send a man to his grave. 'Tariq,' he said. 'You haven't changed one bit. What are you up to these days?'

'Still in the land of the living.'

He nodded at that. 'My condolences on Issa's passing. His death came as a big shock.'

I did not want to exhume the spectre of Issa that was buried in my heart and so I quickly asked him whom he had come to bury.

'Our brother, Hassan Darbeel,' replied Kamal. 'He died last night.'

Hassan, too, had once worked at the Palace, training the dogs. So Hassan, too, was now dead.

The bodies of the dead may be covered with earth but their stories poke at our memory whenever we have a moment to reflect. We all shrink from death. Tahani went to hers willingly, without asking for her raptor's permission. She chose death over betrayal.

It was thanks to her exemplary courage that Tahani kept the image of womankind branded on to my heart. The women of the Palace were poor replicas of the real thing by comparison. Or maybe they just reflected the vagaries of circumstance that tossed one here and the other there. Samira, too, was an exemplary paramour. I wanted to ask Kamal whether his memory was still suffused with her but that would have violated the sanctity of the dead and I was prevented from speaking out of turn by the press of mourners crowding around him.

Setting out towards the vault ahead of the procession, Kamal invited me to join them in lowering Hassan into his final resting place. 'You know that besides his childhood friends and his dogs, Hassan had no family. Now that you're here, you can share in the divine recompense.'

Hassan had been banished from the Palace in disgrace after a feral dog he had raised without the Master's knowledge attacked a guest and mauled him.

Kamal patted me on the shoulder to signal that I should come along, and I fell into step beside him. As the chant of the mourners' prayers and supplications grew and swelled and their footsteps churned dust up into the air, all I wanted was to run away. Kamal proceeded down the steps, flanked by two gravediggers while the others adroitly guided the body and lowered it into the narrow space.

I left quickly, before he came back up from the vault and before Hassan Darbeel had been covered with dirt. I hurried to the cemetery gate, where packs of dogs howled mournfully. I wanted to believe that they had come from the city to pay their last respects to the man who had devoted his life to them.

Like someone trying to shake off a person on his heels, I wended my way through the maze of the neighbourhood and into the back street where I had left my car. As soon as I turned the key in the ignition, the spectre of my mother rose once again to reiterate her last wish with urgency. 'Go and get your aunt,' she had said.

It was a wise command and one I could not refuse because it had issued from a truly loving heart.

It had been more than two months since I had last brought in groceries and water. I wondered if Aunt Khayriyyah had survived, like a lizard whose constitution is designed to cope with extended periods of scarcity. I did not think it likely because the one thing she could not stand was thirst. Whenever we had water shortages, she would send me out to fetch some, and woe betide me if I came back empty-handed. Aunt Khayriyyah quivered with happiness when she could float little chunks of ice in her glass of mulberry juice or lemonade and suck up the liquid through them, her eyes dancing between the ice and the liquid, as she smacked her lips with pleasure. She always needed to have a glass of water or juice close by, maybe to keep that tongue of hers well lubricated and moist.

I wondered what had become of her old carcass. I would have to come up with a convincing explanation for the death of an old woman alone in a room as squalid as the one I had left her in.

Rushing to the conclusion that she was dead was perhaps an expression of my barely repressed hope for her demise. Neglecting her all this time had been a mistake, but I did not think she could have died. If she had, the foul smell of her decomposing body would have led everyone by the nose, and investigators would have ferreted out the owner of the villa and questioned him about the decomposing corpse inside.

I dreaded going back there. If she was going to attack me again, I would end that life that already hung by a thread. I was not going to let her take me down with her. I would of course be careful and bestow her just deserts with caution.

The villa was in shambles: its gate was flung wide open; the trees in the courtyard had shrivelled up, their roots exposed; the outside lights were smashed; the swimming pool was covered in leaves and slime, and all the fixtures, including the diving board, had been vandalised.

I waded through the desolation and found the front door ajar. I pushed it open and was stunned by the wreckage before me. The villa had been laid to waste and only a few bare light bulbs still burned.

I bounded up the stairs, having armed myself with a metal rod I had picked up from the rubble in the courtyard. Her room was in the same abject state I had left it. I advanced cautiously, tiptoeing between the heaps of detritus, on high alert for a surprise attack.

I shoved aside the mounds of rubbish in search of her. I looked carefully but could find no trace of her or her carcass. I combed the entire house: all the rooms, the bathrooms, the kitchens, as well as the roof and even the courtyard and the pool house. She had vanished into thin air.

I remembered that the last time I had been at the villa, I was unsure as to whether I had locked the door. Clearly I had not and I wondered where she had gone and whether I needed to notify the police. Hesitant to do so, I remembered that there were surveillance cameras everywhere. Had they recorded what happened after I was here last time? How on earth would I raise such a matter with the Master?

Before notifying the police, I thought, I should try and obtain the video. But the Master had to be in a calm mood, and even if he was, I would hardly dare to ask.

★ ★ ★

Hamdan returned to his post as a distinguished security guard, having passed with flying colours the test of protecting the Palace's inviolability.

He was not aware of my role in Issa's demise, whereas I knew what his tongue had done to him.

The judge was lenient and held that he had acted in self-defence as a guard whose duty it was to protect the Palace. A man is duty-bound, he ruled, to defend himself, whether his wealth, his honour, or his blood.

It was Hamdan's injury that had convinced the judge and enabled him to hand down his verdict with a clear conscience. Hamdan did no jail time, spending two months being pampered and coddled at the hospital until the brief court appearance when he was found innocent.

Although he had proof of his innocence through the judgement, Hamdan's heart felt heavy with guilt, especially when he was around someone who had witnessed the scene. He would sidle up to me any time he saw me going through the Palace gates, but I would hurry away before he could delve into what had really taken place.

He would often greet me from a distance and I would pretend not to notice. But he nailed me one night as I stood at the gates supervising the orderly departure of a cavalcade of dignitaries visiting from Washington DC. They were leaving a reception held in their honour by the Master with whom they had close business ties.

As the departing guests thinned out, he abandoned his post and approached me. He mumbled a few words, visibly nervous, as if trying to avoid reminding me of something unpleasant or to shield me from it.

'I expected you to visit me in hospital,' he said. 'But I

figured you were busy, so I didn't hold it against you.' He paused and then added, 'Your brother Ibrahim came three times. He was very kind, and it cheered me up.'

'Ibrahim?' I said with surprise.

'He spoke well of you, every time. When I complained that you hadn't been to see me, he laughed, saying that you always had been a busy man. He said to remind you that it had been seven – or maybe nine – years since you last promised him a visit. I think he said nine.' Hamdan frowned. 'Is it true that you haven't visited him in nine years – or was he joking?'

'None of your business,' I snapped.

Sensing my annoyance and my resistance to being questioned, he abandoned the preliminaries and got to the point. 'Issa was a good man. He didn't deserve that kind of an end, but I couldn't say anything other than what I said.' The words tumbled from his lips as if he were finally unburdening himself of a weight he had been carrying and could not take another step without dropping it to the ground. 'I just want to know – what really happened?'

'You know better than anyone what happened. Didn't you say that you killed him in self-defence?'

He was stunned by my response. He had clearly not expected me to pin Issa's death at his door after witnessing every detail of the scene.

He was about to say something when I cut him off. 'Are you going to stand here chatting all day? Aren't you on duty? Go on, get back to the guardhouse.'

Hamdan returned to his post but his eyes darted towards me repeatedly. My aunt sprang to mind and I wondered whether she had gone back to her house in the neighbourhood. I should have asked him.

23

SOME THINGS ARE INESCAPABLE.

The past is like a dormant volcano. We settle on its slopes, firmly convinced that the lava has cooled and petrified. But before we secure our hold, the volcano erupts and we are swept away, scorched and covered in ash. Every hurt I had ever caused anyone was erupting into flames before my eyes and all the grief of my past was surging into view.

My aunt was like an umbilical cord linking me to the darkness of the primeval womb, a deadly germ wreaking havoc in my lungs. She had completed her inventory of my transgressions and misdeeds. She could shut off my air passages and bring me to dark and silent suffocation, alone without solace or succour. She would not die before doing me in first. Where could she have gone?

It was plausible that the worm might still be wriggling after all this time. More than seventy years had passed since it had begun slithering. Her staying power was extraordinary, like stagnant water that neither evaporates nor is absorbed.

Women are survivors; no matter the loss, they are able to regenerate.

Did I hanker for Maram? It had been three months since our last encounter and in my mind I was the one who had ended the relationship. But she never again asked after me following Issa's death, as if I had been no more than a bothersome button rubbing uncomfortably on the neckline of her blouse. With the button removed, she could breathe more easily and also be more alluring.

She had grown distant after I left the Palace.

One day, out of the blue, the Master had summarily dismissed me.

'Didn't you say you were keen to move on?' he said. 'I don't want to see you around here any more. You remind me of things I'd rather forget. Tomorrow is your last day.'

'But—'

'Don't worry,' he said. 'As long as you mind your step, you'll be fine.'

'I just want to say—'

'We're done. If I need you, I'll find you.'

He left me frozen in place, just as he had the very first time I was ushered into his presence. He walked away with his usual swagger, declining to offer any explanation for his sudden decision and indifferent to my turmoil.

Had he found out about my relationship with Maram or that I had been in touch with Mawdie? Was he worried that I would expose the truth about Issa's killing or did he sense my unwavering hostility and the murderous thoughts I harboured?

I doubted it. Had he sensed the merest wisp of an inkling about any of these, he would have ground me into the dirt, not just thrown me out.

What, then, had happened exactly? I wondered if the decision had been instigated by Maram to pre-empt anything that might threaten her life with the Master. I was already more or less convinced that she had carried on with me simply in order to destroy Issa and, therefore, that I was as expendable as an old shoe that was no longer fit to be worn to a filthy toilet, much less to fancy parties.

My decision to leave her was a considered one but when she responded with indifference, I was stung. I could find no trace of her at the Palace even though I looked for her everywhere. The Master's sudden decision added to the distance between us and compounded my banishment.

Maram was just the same as that old worm I had for an aunt – maybe the same blood ran in their veins. Both of them were devious and underhanded and they dragged people down without the slightest compunction.

My only hope of finding her was to contact her girlfriends whose homes we had used for our trysts. Those women could always be found in a shopping centre, particularly Iceland Mall. I loitered around there, convinced that one of them would help me to track down Maram. The mall thronged with women of every hue, all of whom had some shady story or other.

Could they sense I was on their trail?

I saw a friend of Maram's, a woman called Lama'a, but after that one time I was never able to catch her or any of the others. The day I saw Lama'a she was hanging on the arm of a young stud who looked for all the world as if he were some gold insignia shining alongside the rest of her glittering accessories. He brimmed with health and vitality, and his muscles rippled under his shirt.

She removed her arm from his and he looked around peevishly, maybe for something or someone to shore up his machismo. I went up to Lama'a, raising my hand in greeting.

'Do you know where Maram is?' I asked without preliminaries.

Flustered by my sudden appearance, she reached for the young man's arm.

'Umm,' she faltered, 'who *are* you, mister?'

'Have you forgotten me, Lama'a?'

'Lama'a?' Her voice was shrill. 'No, no, you must be mistaken,' she said. 'I'm Shama'a.' Her laughter was shameless and coarse as she tugged at her boyfriend's arm and moved on. I almost insisted, but looking at the stud with bristling muscles, I thought better of it.

A few young women nearby who had caught the gist of our exchange looked at my frozen countenance with evident scorn. Did I seem that decrepit to them?

I suppose that the sight of an older man feverishly scanning women's faces and looking women over as they congregated in the malls and around the shopfronts was cause enough for ridicule.

Young women evaluated contenders for their affections on the basis of age. Men deemed too old for such inappropriately youthful pleasures as banter and flirtatiousness were simply put in their place with a couple of well-chosen forms of deferential address, such as 'uncle' or 'mister'.

When Lama'a first came to the Palace, she had taken up with a sixty-something man who disguised his advanced age with hair dye, Viagra and frequent medical treatments. Age was no object to her, and she never called him anything but 'dearest' and 'darling'.

But a scornful 'mister' was all she had for me.

Maram had been a luscious sweet that no longer wished to tickle my fancy, but at this point finding my aunt was the greater priority. After leaving the Palace, I had gone back to the villa and lived there holed up like a rat. I was paralysed with fear that my aunt's condition would become public knowledge. I no longer had the Master's impunity to protect me and I was sure the discovery would set me on a downward spiral to perdition.

The Master had told me I would be fine as long as I minded my step. For a moment, I wondered whether he was holding my aunt hostage. But the notion was too preposterous: I was hardly the kind of threat to him that would warrant taking a hostage as a bargaining chip. The jumble of events blurred together in my mind and ended up like a foul-tasting, grit-coloured liquid.

I tried to clear my mind and hang on to just one idea but no sooner had I done that than a myriad of other possibilities bubbled up inside my head.

I needed to find her before she blew up in my face. Her story was grizzly enough to land me in big trouble. If he wanted to, the Master could have me led to the execution block purely on the evidence of what had been recorded in the videos.

I reminded myself to keep my priorities in order. The videos and the Master were irrelevant. My aunt's disappearance disturbed me, and I would have no peace of mind until I found out where she was. Even if it killed me. Or her, for that matter. Where could her tired old feet have carried her?

A visit to Ibrahim had clearly become imperative if I was to get rid of all the static that was buzzing in my head. It was more than likely that she had gone to him.

I rang the doorbell and also knocked for good measure, and a boy of about twelve or a little older opened. His poise and good manners were striking and without first trying to ascertain who I was or the purpose of my visit, he invited me in with the customary words of welcome.

'Are you Ibrahim Fadel's son?' I asked him.

'Yes, that's right. Welcome.'

'Is your father at home?'

'Please come in. Welcome to our home,' he said, adding formally, 'We are blessed by your visit.'

He showed me in and ushered me to the seat that had pride of place in the parlour. He asked after my health and invited me to make myself comfortable. He disappeared inside the house to fetch his father and his little brother joined me.

The boy was the spitting image of my father. He greeted and welcomed me as is proper but with far more reserve than his older sibling, and then sat absolutely still watching me. He scanned my features and my general appearance and when our eyes met, he smiled. It was the exact same smile I had worn at his age.

'What's your name?' I asked him.

'Tariq. Tariq Ibrahim Fadel.'

A chill ran through me and goosebumps covered my skin. His expression betrayed nothing; he did not notice my reaction and just fiddled with the armrest of his chair. Then he turned his attention to rearranging a pile of religious books on the table in front of him.

I looked around at the simple furniture in the room. It was a modest house and somewhat ramshackle with steel girders that protruded from the roof. I had the impression that the structure was just barely standing. But it was a home and it was full of the smell of life.

Voices drifting in from the back of the house sounded

337

loving and sweet. For the boy called Tariq, I was merely a distraction. His features were my father's and his demeanour mine.

'Do you know who I am?' I asked him.

He shook his head indifferently. I had wanted to spark his curiosity, but he was not interested. He continued to examine me as he fiddled with the armrest. Then a precociously good-looking boy came into the room. He looked somehow famil-iar and greeted me bashfully before hopping over to sit beside little Tariq. He melted my heart and I wanted to give him a hug, but he shrank back and just held out his hand silently. I asked Tariq who he was.

'This is Aghyad.'

'Your brother?'

'No, my cousin. My auntie's son.'

So here was another Tariq with a paternal aunt of his own. Who was this sister who had appeared all of a sudden at the end of my life? Life plants the seeds of stories just as it propa-gates the events that move stories along. Was life breeding a new version of the Tariq and Khayriyyah story? Was this a hereditary propagation of the story of an aunt and a child with minor variations?

The boys sat together like two cats eyeing their prey, slowly following my movements and exchanging sly little glances with one another. One of them would get my attention and the other would look over my appearance. The older boy returned and saved me from this monitoring. He carried a tray with coffee and a plate of dates, intoning hospitable words of welcome.

He was meticulous in his presentation of the coffee, as if he were practised in the art of hospitality. He ignored his little

338

brother's antics and contrived to come up with a suitable topic for adult conversation.

'The rains are very late this year.'

'When was the last time it rained in Jeddah?' I asked. 'The rain has gone the way of better days, son.'

My remark flustered him. He said nothing and I continued to be the object of attention in the room. I held their gaze in an attempt to stare them down and slow their overactive imaginations. I looked at them thinking these were the new branches that had sprouted from our common roots. I wondered whether I was sharp enough to tell which of them would be the ill-starred one.

Tariq seemed to me the most likely candidate to replay that story.

I erased the images taking shape in my mind and set them aside as one might put away unsharpened pencils.

Here then were people who were part of my family even though they did not know me nor I them. These were the people whom I was running away from and whose veins pulsed with the same blood as mine, although they did not know it. Did that insolent little wretch, Tariq, know that his impudence was my legacy?

Their eyes on me like wayward flies began to wear me out. When the silence had gone on long enough, I asked the eldest boy what his name was.

'Fadel Ibrahim Fadel, uncle.'

He had used the term 'uncle' deferentially, but I was sorely tempted to confirm my status as his uncle. I wanted to tell him that I truly was his father's brother, and the son of Fadel the elder who had sown his seed in two different wombs.

'Isn't your father at home?'

339

'Yes, yes, he's here,' replied the boy quickly. 'He's just finishing his ablutions. He'll be here any minute now.'

As though prompted, Ibrahim poked his head around the door just then, water still dripping from his face and down his thick beard.

Seeing me, he shouted with astonishment, 'Tariq!'

Little Tariq jumped up, thinking that his father meant him. Ibrahim rushed in and flung his arms around me, squeezing me so tightly that I lost my breath. I was unable to contain myself any longer, and the tears streamed down my face. I sobbed as Ibrahim held me close. He wiped my tears and I dried his.

He waved at me grandly to the boys and said, 'This is your Uncle Tariq – my only, my dearest and most beloved brother!'

As if he felt that the introduction was inadequate, he cried out, 'Kiss his hands! And his feet too!' Fadel bent down to kiss my hand and I picked him up and showered him with kisses of my own.

'This is my eldest, Fadel,' Ibrahim said.

Then Aghyad came forward and accepted my embrace without reticence. 'And this is Aghyad, the son of Mariam, our sister. He's been wanting to meet you for a long time.'

That left the devilish little Tariq who, yet again, did things in his own time. At his father's insistence, he finally followed Aghyad's example.

'This is Tariq. In some ways he's like our father, but in others he's just like you.'

Ibrahim kept his arm around my shoulder and called out, 'Mariam! Come over here, Mariam!'

I could not bear the flood of emotion any longer. Suddenly the branches of the tree had sprouted new shoots – nephews from both a brother and a sister – and here I was having lived my entire life like a severed limb, with nothing to sustain me but my dry and withered feelings.

What would I say to this Mariam now: I am your wayward brother who broke with his family? How was I going to justify my disappearance from before the day she was born?

A little girl, who could not have been more than ten years old, stepped into the room hesitantly and hurried shyly towards me.

'Say hello to your uncle. This is Mariam, the last of my bunch. She looks just like our sister.'

She greeted me, speaking with a pronounced lisp. Her father's eyes glowed with love as she spoke. He pulled me down affectionately to sit by him.

'When all of you left the neighbourhood, I named my children after you – Tariq for you, Fadel for our father and Mariam for our sister – so that I could still feel your presence even though you were all gone.'

After a while, Ibrahim asked, 'Where's Aunt Khayriyyah? Why didn't you bring her with you?'

'She's fine. I wasn't planning on this visit, otherwise I would have brought her along.' It was a stupid thing to say but it silenced Ibrahim.

So my aunt had not returned to her house in the neighbourhood or gone to her other nephew, Ibrahim. The worm was still wriggling around somewhere on the face of this earth. I thought I should cut short my visit as quickly as possible before I got mired in this sludge of emotions that already had me out of my depth. Before I could say anything, however, Aghyad was tugging at my sleeve.

'Are you my mother's brother?' he asked. I nodded but had

no desire to embrace him. 'My mother never told me much about you,' he added.

'That's because she hasn't seen me yet. She doesn't know anything about me.'

'But you're her brother,' said the child, not quite understanding. 'How could she not know anything about you?'

'Well, it happens.'

'Have you been away ever since you were born?'

His probing and unsettling questions silenced me.

They stirred up bitter feelings, reminding me that I was nothing but a transient, a stranger, a wanderer – and that I was lost. The journey had been so long, yet I still had not reached safe harbour. I had dropped anchor in many ports but had only seen land from a distance. When the journey is long, our memory is like a desert island; we no longer recall the people who washed ashore and could not but endure, or die.

'Please tell me,' Aghyad demanded, poking at me.

Would I ever be rid of the pest? For every question I answered, he nailed me with another as if he were trying to establish that I was the only crooked board in the lot. I looked at him closely: the boy was very handsome and he was determined to stick to me. I was not accustomed to being around kids, but I tried to be friendly and placed my hand on his shoulder. He jumped right into my lap and hugged me. The boy should have been named Arghad rather than Aghyad – cuddly rather than delicate.

The flow of questions was unstoppable now.

'Did you just get back from your trip?'

'Sort of.'

'They said grandmother was away with you. I want to see her. Can I see her now?'

The boy's questions were aggravating me. 'Your grand-mother? What grandmother is that?' I asked him.

Ibrahim intervened. 'He means Aunt Khayriyyah. He had been complaining to his mother that he doesn't have any family, so she told him all about everyone in her family and in his father's family. He knows most of them by name now and studies them as if they were one of his school subjects. If there's someone he doesn't know much about because they haven't been around, he fills in the gaps with his imagination.'

Aghyad started tugging at my sleeve again.

'Uncle, can I have a picture of you?'

He had a family photo album which he showed me now. Every picture was identified by type of relationship and there were a few words about his impressions of the person. Aunt Khayriyyah and I were on two facing pages. In the space left blank for our photos were pictures of two cartoon characters. Under them, he had written 'Don't know him' and 'Don't know her'.

I flipped through his album and found his mother's page. But instead of a photo of her, there was a picture of the Lebanese pop star, Haifa Wehbeh. Underneath the photo he had written: 'Heart-throb'.

'You little devil, is this your mother?' I exclaimed with a laugh to take the sting out of my words.

'No, but it wouldn't do to have a real picture of my mother in here.'

Everyone sensed that Aghyad was monopolising the conversation. Tariq's response was to giggle at whatever his cousin said or did. Desperate for the flood of questions to end, I turned to Ibrahim.

'Honestly, I'd like to meet our sister, Mariam. Where is she?'

'She lives with her mother and sometimes comes with Aghyad to visit us. And I take him to see his father, sometimes.'

'Are they divorced?'

'It's a long story. I came to see you some years ago, asking for your help with her situation. But you weren't concerned at the time.'

I tied myself up in knots offering an apology. The excuses were flimsy and unconvincing.

'What's done is done,' Ibrahim said, cutting me off. 'It's over and done with. She is now working and supporting herself, as well as her mother and her son.'

'Does she need any help? I could—' I started to say.

I pulled out my chequebook. Ibrahim placed his hand on mine as he had many years ago when he had uttered the words that had stuck with me since: 'Foul money has a foul smell.'

This time, he said, 'I don't think so. Her work pays well.'

'And what does she do?'

'She manages a women's clothing company. She apparently also got some money from her husband before he went into the hospital. If you saw the state he's in you'd feel sorry for him.'

'Is it serious?'

The evening call to prayer rang out, a harmony of cascading chants from nearby mosques, and it interrupted our conversation. Ibrahim turned to the boys.

'Come on, get ready for prayers,' he instructed.

They said their ablutions were done and that they were ready to go.

344

'Have you done yours or do you need to do them?' Ibrahim asked, turning to me.

'No, no, I've done them.'

My tongue raced ahead of me and even though I said I had done them, the last time I had completed any ablutions was way back in the day of the Qur'an study groups. Ever since I had entered the Palace, I had been in a state of ritual impurity.

Ibrahim told the boys to get going. Fadel and Aghyad jumped to it, but Tariq dawdled again.

'Tell me about Aghyad's father. Does he need treatment abroad? ' I asked Ibrahim. 'I can arrange for his travel.'

'No, no, his disease isn't serious like that,' Ibrahim chuckled, patting my knee. 'He's perfectly healthy. It's just that there were some really bad complications and his case had to go to the governing council. Things will turn out fine, God willing.'

I did not understand how his treatment could be linked to the governing council and I said so. 'What's his sickness got to do with the *diwan*? If he needs treatment abroad, I am more than willing to help.'

'Don't worry about it. I'll tell you the whole story later.' He pulled Mariam off his lap and added, 'We'll finish the conversation when we come back from the mosque.'

'We still have a few minutes – tell me the story.'

He shook his head. 'I'm the imam. I can't be late.'

We stepped out together. He held on to my hand joyfully, sensing maybe that what I wanted was to bolt and disappear into the long, narrow alleyways.

'Don't worry, Tariq. Prayer will ease your mind.'

He must have known that I was impure; he just did not

want to embarrass me when I told him I had already performed my ablutions. He gripped my hand firmly as if he were afraid I might slip from his grasp and vanish again.

We entered the alley leading up to the entrance of the mosque and caught up with Aghyad, who took hold of Ibrahim's other hand.

'We'll go and visit your father today. And we'll take Uncle Tariq with us, all right?'

Ibrahim's strides lengthened and he was literally pulling me along now. We reached the gate and many of the old neighbourhood folk flocked towards us, showering me with greetings and expressing their pleasure at seeing me after such a long absence.

'By God it's been a long time, Tariq,' exclaimed one of my neighbours from the past. We embraced as he added, 'Where have you been all these years? Is this your son?' He bent down to kiss Aghyad.

'No, this is Aghyad, the son of Waleed Khanbashi,' Ibrahim replied on my behalf.

For a second, I thought I had misheard.

It was as if I had been struck by lightning and was rent asunder, splintering and scattering like shrapnel, swallowed up by the earth, hurtling into the chasm, down, down and further down until finally, I hit rock bottom, screaming silently.

It was the same Waleed Khanbashi who had driven us to the receding beaches and charged us half a riyal to use a tatty old towel; the same Waleed who had married Issa's maternal aunt and suckling sister, Salwa, only to cheat on her by marrying ...

My frown turned to horror as I looked at the boy, my nephew.

346

When a building collapses, the roof tiles and the brickwork do not ask who betrayed whom. As soon as the soul rises and departs the body, the dead begin to decompose, and the flesh sets to rotting. The earth opened up and I fell head first, seized with terror.

There was no longer a place for me on this earth.

Ibrahim pulled me along, hurrying into the mosque, and placed me in the first row of worshippers behind him in the *mihrab* – the niche in the wall of a mosque that indicates the direction of the Kaaba. All I wanted to do was run but could no more have done so than scoop up my spilt guts off the floor.

The congregation rose in unison to begin the opening prayer. In the throes of collapse, I looked around desperately for some way out. Ibrahim was already intoning the very first couplet of the prayer cycle – the *takbeer* – signalling to the faithful to adjust themselves and straighten out the prayer lines.

He looked straight at me and smiled. A block of bodies jostled me into position as I continued looking for an escape route. Aghyad, who had ignored the first *takbeer,* was following my turmoil. He flashed me a smile and there, before my very eyes, rose the vision of the bewitchingly beautiful Maram, her nakedness concealed.

Aghyad and I looked into one another's faces as the faithful began their chanting of devotions. Ibrahim intoned the opening chapter of the Qur'an and the mosque echoed with the booming 'Amen' in response. A momentary silence followed as he searched for the Qur'anic verse with which to comfort me and then his voice rose in the air as sweet and melodious as a tinkling waterfall:

347

'Oh my servants who have transgressed against themselves, do not despair of God's mercy. God forgives all sins: He is all-forgiving, compassionate to each.'

This was the exact moment I had hit rock bottom.

As the rubble settled, I looked at all the dust billowing up from within me filling the prayer hall. Smashed into a million shards, my spirit gave up the ghost. I disappeared behind a veil of tears, and with the breach not yet healed, I sobbed as Ibrahim's voice finally vanquished the demons playing havoc with my soul.

The tranquil atmosphere of the prayer hall was broken by my wailing sobs and even some of the worshippers were rattled.

A solitary tear trickled down Aghyad's cheek as the boy looked on, bewildered.

Ibrahim commanded the *rukuu'*, the bowing posture during prayer, but I could not even bend from the waist; when he voiced the *takbeer* signalling the ritual prostration, the sea of worshippers went down as one while I remained erect in the open expanse of the prayer hall.

Aghyad's eyes were glued to me and in them I beheld Maram, like a melting pillar of salt. Tranquillity enveloped the prostrated worshippers.

I was running. My shackles and chains dragging, I wanted to catch up with the procession of people fleeing their destiny, gathered in a wide open arena to meet our fate. Some were proceeding on their way, others lingered: Tahani, Mustafa Qannas, Issa, Mawdie, Joseph Essam, Aunt Khayriyyah, Maram. Behind me was a long line of people – pointlessly hurrying on.

My decision to kill the Master had fully ripened. I had been

348

carrying around images of his dead body in my mind for a long time, summoning up visions of murder while lying in bed, killing him a different way before falling asleep every night.

But how vast the ocean that separates imagination from reality. I closed my eyes.

A NOTE ON THE AUTHOR

Born in Saudi Arabia in 1962, Abdo Khal studied political science and began his career as a preacher before becoming a primary school teacher. He turned to writing as a way of attacking the corruption of the wealthy in the Arab world. *Throwing Sparks* won the International Prize for Arabic Fiction and is his first novel to be published in English.

A NOTE ON THE TYPE

The text of this book is set in Bembo. This type was first used in 1495 by the Venetian printer Aldus Manutius for Cardinal Bembo's *De Aetna*, and was cut for Manutius by Francesco Griffo. It was one of the types used by Claude Garamond (1480–1561) as a model for his Romain de L'Université, and so it was the forerunner of what became standard European type for the following two centuries. Its modern form follows the original types and was designed for Monotype in 1929.